Praise for Gloria Nagy's
Natural Selections

"With searing wit and compassion, Gloria Nagy's Natural Selections taps into the issues of the eighties with fascinating precision. I couldn't put it down."

—Bonnie Straus, *Hour Magazine*

A House in the Hamptons

"More than a summer page turner...Ms. Nagy has slapped her well-heeled characters beyond what they thought they could bear, by making the unexpected manifest."

— *The New York Times*

"Tom Wolff, take note... A staggeringly honest book about a special piece of the American Dream."

— *Playboy magazine*

"Hilariously pierces the Seaside Social Set right through their Patagonias".

— *Los Angeles* magazine

"Gloria Nagy's style is fresh, her pace brisk, her humor delightful."

—Los Angeles Times

"Who says money can't buy happiness?...Spend a few days in A House in the Hamptons."

—*The Cincinnati Enquirer*

"Bubbling with plots and personalities...colorful, thoroughly likeable characters...fast paced and funny."

—Booklist

"Number one on your summer reading list. Honest...teary...hilarious...the thinking person's fun fiction. Gloria Nagy is a comic genius with heart."

—Patricia Auberdene, author of
Megatrends 2000

"Seashore of the Vanities...no beach bag will be complete this summer without a copy."

—Trump magazine

"Fabulous entertainment—and a quintessential summer read... combines a savvy urban sensibility with a sharp, sassy sense of humor to create a superb comedy of manners."

—Kirkus Review

"Amusing, hip, highly readable...keen observation and psychological insight."

— Publisher's Weekly

"A House in the Hamptons is selling faster than NO. 25 sunscreen."

— USA Today

"Quicker than a gelato meltdown, mortality tips a designer hat at the best social gatherings. Temptation arrives wearing knock-you-down perfume and clingy white cashmere...there is a sense of history... mixed with social satire on the east end."

—The New York Times

"Nagy knows people, Nagy knows places, Nagy knows prose...A House in the Hamptons is a tour de force—a 'warts-and-all' portrait that exposes an entire life-style with a perfect blend of insight, sarcasm, and tenderness. Nobody beats Nagy at creating outlandish characters and then making you care about them...[Her] writing is so adept and sensitive, she can take a staggering mix of characters... and humanize them until they seem as comfortable and familiar as the people next door...She can make you laugh and cry, and often on the same page."

—*The Press-Enterprise* (Riverside, CA)

Virgin Kisses

"A stunning accomplishment—funny and sad, erotic and ultimately very moving. Gloria Nagy's dazzling portrait of the sex-obsessed narcissist and his eager victim will make readers tremble with the rage and sadness of recognition."

—Gael Greene

"Virgin Kisses is like a nightmare Woody Allen would have on a very bad night—the humor is quite literally hysterical."

—*Time Out*

"Gloria Nagy's gift is to move you as she elevates the ultimate joke into tragedy, marshaling absurdities for a final triumph."

—*New York Magazine*

"A lacerating, literate, funny, and obscene expose."

—*Vogue*

"Nagy is a tremendous writer who tiptoes along the fragile line between the believable and ridiculous but never makes a false step."

—*The Californian*

The Beauty

"Question: What is enticing, thrilling and can cost you a day or a weekend?

Answer: Gloria Nagy's new novel, The Beauty."

—Norman Lear

"If every good novel is a mystery story, this particular mystery story has lots of other tasty novelistic virtues going for it—a sense of mischief, sharp social observation, doses of complicated wisdom. *The Beauty* will have legions of delighted readers."

—Kurt Andersen,
author of *Turn of the Century*

"Nagy imagines the present as a burning building which her characters must make their way out of. *The Beauty* is a terrific fable about the futility of escape, the inevitability of evil, and the power of redemption."

—John Hockenberry,
author of *A River Out of Eden*

"*The Beauty* starts fast and speeds up. Gloria Nagy is a skilled driver on a very scenic road, and keeps her passenger guessing what's waiting around each new turn. It's well worth the trip."

—Forrest Sawyer, NBC News

PEOPLE DIE IN SUNSHINE

A NOVEL OF MIAMI

by New York Times best-selling author

GLORIA NAGY

Sheer Bliss Communications, LLC

PEOPLE DIE IN SUNSHINE

Author services by David Ivester
Literary Publicist & Marketing Specialist, Author Guide
www.author-guide.com

Publishing services provided by Pedernales Publishing, LLC.
www.pedernalespublishing.com

Library of Congress Control Number: 2020911132

ISBN 978-1-7352439-2-4 Hardcover Edition
ISBN 978-1-7352439-1-7 Paperback Edition
ISBN 978-1-7352439-0-0 Digital Edition

Printed in the United States of America

For: Max, Oliver, Solomon, Little George, Daisy, Abraham, The Dude, Lucky, Isaac and the sole survivor, Jacob

Acknowledgements

My deepest thanks to Jose Ramirez and Barbara Rainess for bringing it to life and restoring my faith in and the joy of creating a work of fiction. Stephane Philippe, without whose enormous skills, enthusiasm, calm and diligence I could never have done it; Louise Armour for that wonderful brain-picking lunch, her passion for everything financial and sage counsel. David Ivester, a warm, wise hand in the tunnel of new publishing. Roger Baumann, for his invaluable insights into old Miami. And Joshua, Ling, Vanessa, Lior, Tony, Farrah, Misha, Ilana, Chaya, Tamara and Ethan my continual sources of insight and inspiration; Lily Perez who fills our hearts and keeps our world in perfect harmony with whatever the universe throws our way and Richard for everything.

"People Die in Sunshine. Sunglasses fall from relaxing noses, under the glare of swimmable pools."
— A poem by Gloria Nagy.

"There are 50,000 young fellows facing the same problem: how to make a fortune and make it fast. You're just one among many. So, think how hard you'll have to try, and what a desperate fight it'll be. You'll all have to eat each other, like spiders in a chamber pot."
— Honore de Balzac/ Pere Goriot

"The sheep will spend its entire life fearing the wolf, only to be eaten by the shepherd."
— Robert Mugabe

CHAPTER 1

Money. Money. Money. Money. Euros. Shekels. Yuan. Swiss francs. Gold. Silver. Bitcoins. Rubles. British Pounds. Bearer Bonds. Cash. Filthy Lucre. Greed is Good. Greed is not good. Money can't buy you love. Really? Money makes the world go round.

Why begin this true story, that you, my reader, may find somewhat hard to believe, with money? Maybe because money, murder and Miami are such a true troika and money is more difficult a subject for most people than sex or any other sources of envy, shame, pride or embarrassment. So, I decided to just get it out there right away.

If I was attempting to tell this twisted tale even five years ago, I would probably have said "difficult" instead of "somewhat hard" to believe, but now it's just about impossible to make anything up more bizarre than our daily news cycles, and that is true even if you don't read the N.Y. Post or subscribe to any one of the endless unorthodox news sites.

This story is worth telling, though I certainly have my own reasons. My name is Edith Weller and I am your narrator, but since I am also a character and thus a suspect, and the end hasn't happened yet, let's just start with the murders.

Sometime before dawn on a very hot early summer day in South Miami, two people were savagely killed in one of the mammoth, lavish—if the idea of a two-mile-or-so stretch of extremely expensive, mostly hideous condominiums packed almost on top of one another, waterfront views being as desirable as they are, can be called lavish—monoliths of what passes for glamour in South Florida. They rise high into the bright blue sky like steel and concrete versions of a glossy ad in a sex toy catalogue, all sorts of odd shapes and jutting out columns and walkways to nowhere, each architect seemingly motivated by the need to one up.

Anyone who cares about such things as urban planning (two words, that seem to not have been translatable into any of the various languages spoken in Miami) have been silenced by the Emperor's New Clothes sensibility of "name value." Porsche, Ralph Lauren, I.M. Pei, Koolhaas, Hadid, Piano, Gehry, Ingels, Herzog and de Meuron even Trump. At least, unlike their lurid vibrating sexual spaceship inspirers, they are, thus far, not pink, purple or have sequins attached.

Outside of the private interior, maximum security steel re-enforced gigantic split penthouse of the owners/developers and residents of Silver Sands, the most prestigious and costly of the entire Sunny Isles condo strip, in a very fresh pool of vomit, lay a completely hysterical young Latin dog walker, named Leena Martinez.

Leena who had arrived as she did every morning at 6:30, riding up in the private elevator, using her eye scan and codes to enter the penthouse, found two sights that led to her collapse.

Within minutes of her arrival; the housekeeper, a serious, no nonsense Russian immigrant named Katya Orlov appeared at exactly 6:45 a.m., as she did every weekday morning to start the coffee and open the two split apartments (this will be explained later).

Seeing young Leena, of whom she was very fond, having no daughter of her own, in such a state and too hysterical to speak and well aware of the fact that Leena worked three jobs to help her family and save for her education, Katya marched first into the inner sanctum of Mr. Frederick Rothenstein, patriarch of a real estate dynasty, massive even in Miami terms. A gentleman in his late seventies, immaculate in everything he did. Except for this morning.

This morning Mr. Rothenstein was most certainly not at his best. He was bound to his favorite Art Deco chair with several of his handmade silk Sulka ties. Protruding from both of what had been his eyes was a pair of extremely high and sharp gold metal Manolo Blahnik Stilettos. In what could only be called overkill, two more, of similar deadly shape and height were jammed into his ears. He was naked. Needless to say, he was also quite dead.

Katya, having lived through some very tough times in her early life and all the travails of immigrants everywhere who have managed to escape and form lives of meaning and purpose in a foreign land did not shock easily, but this sight sent her racing across the internal hallway to the other apartment, the home of Mrs. Frederick Rothenstein, or Coco as she was called, given her obsession with all things Chanel. She was, also, not at her best. Naked, her feet and hands bound to her favorite Le Corbusier chair by some of her Chanel scarves, two enormous Graff diamond earrings protruding from her surgically restructured nostrils with an Hermès gag over her mouth, which would later reveal an impressive emerald and diamond Harry Winston necklace jammed down her throat.

Even an older rather stoic and life toughened lady like Katya could not absorb this doubleheader. She ran screaming back to Leena and called 911, gasping for breath and trying in her usually quite good English, which became almost gibberish under too much stress to describe the scene.

While Katya waited for 911, holding Leena and rocking her like a small child awakened from a nightmare, and praying in her native Ukrainian dialect, one floor down, Ooma Lovee, was leaving her unit/condo #120 called Bismarck after the palm tree, (all units had personal names given to them by Coco Rothenstein to add extra elan and a personal touch), to take her morning stroll with her adored Japanese Chin, Lola. Since Miami has been voted the most "dog friendly" city in the U.S., and because most apartments and condos will not accept any pup who weighs more than twenty-five pounds, the abundance of rare breeds of exotic pooches abound. Lola, who, when wet, looked exactly like a black and white version of E.T., was a bit hyper, most certainly spoiled, but too small to do much damage and was generally well behaved. As Lola approached the elevator bank, however, she went into a frenzy, unlike Ooma Lovee had ever seen; leaping in the air, drooling, barking and spinning in circles, totally panic stricken. The smell of death, for sure.

Ooma Lovee, who is the erstwhile grandmother to me, my fifteen-year-old adopted Chinese daughter, Sunny (more will be revealed) is also the Grande glamour dame of the Silver Sands. No one really knows anything much about her, which is part of the fun (that includes us!). She is an Eastern European woman of immaculate manners, grooming and diction in one of the many languages she seems to speak. At eighty-eight she carries herself like the former dancer she says she was. The wonders of good genes and expert plastic surgery have taken at least a decade off her real age and she wears her very thick, very long platinum hair in one dramatic side braid. She is always (even at 7 a.m.) walking Lola, fully made up, jeweled, and dressed for any occasion from charity Ball to lunch at the neighboring country club, where little Leena worked after she finished her Rothenstein dog walking chores.

Ooma immediately swooped Lola up, and trusting her very keen and well-honed intuition, moved swiftly for my door, several floors below. The higher up you were, the more expensive the unit and fancy the personal moniker. Sunny and I resided on the third floor, fine with me, hating small talk in elevators, especially with the likes of my fellow condo dwellers and really a stair person, twitching limbs of my New York walk-up. My unit was called Sparrow.

By the time Ooma Lovee reached my door, our elitist bunker of quiet and security had been transformed into a scene from any current crime show. Ambulances, paramedics, a sea of pistol drawn policemen in flak vests, SWAT team machos with machine guns or what looked like machine guns, grenade belts, body armor, helmets, and with that deadly serious grim mouth set, a combo of their adrenaline rush, fear, excitement and, just possibly, a kid's desire to shoot something.

Ooma was banging. I was sound asleep. Sunny was awake and got to the door first, yelling for me to get up, which I managed to do, shuffling forth and as quickly as possible, considering I was still half-conscious and not adept at high tech security (or any security for that matter). I punched in the codes and opened the, supposedly, burglar proof door. A voice behind Ooma screamed, "Get inside, lock the door and don't move!"

Um. Okay, officer. I pulled Ooma in and did as I had been told. She was shaking all over, a very unusual sight in a woman whose Royal Wave persona never revealed any sign of agita; though,

I have to admit, even given the unusual nature of our relationship, I didn't really know her very well.

Lola was still spinning around and flipping over and almost frothing at the mouth. "Oh my Gott. Something very, very bad is happening. Edy dear, please give Lola something. Rescue Remedy or a tranquilizer. I think she might have a stroke. Me, too, give me one, too!"

I complied. Now awake enough for my heart to be pounding and my over-active imagination to be conjuring up every recent terrorist act, especially the last three in Florida. This seemed like a one-for-me-too Xanax morning. I dispensed them and went to put on a big pot of coffee, my hand, I noticed, was trembling.

Ooma had moved to the couch, Lola on her lap. Lorraine, our male bull terrier and Lola's best friend, though a more unlikely pair of canine buddies is hard to imagine, had entered (he was also a late sleeper) and laid down at Ooma's fancy designer sneakered feet.

"What in the hell is going on?" Became my first sentence of the day.

"I don't know, Edy. I get to elevator with Lola, she goes into some fit, I think she is going to have stroke at the elevator to the Rothensteins. She just got crazy, she is so sensitive, I think, 'there is something evil up there' something very bad. I don't see a thing, I just grab her and come to you. And then all of a sudden, you see, police, guns, like the old country, like the war. Oh Gott! What do we do?"

Sunny, who is not your average fifteen-year-old, whatever that means, anymore, but who is far more laid back about hysterical people (having been raised by me, for example) and being an avid user of social media and whatever the continual undulating new waves of media freakdom has available, had, of course, the most logical answer. "I'll get my phone and turn on the TV. If the SWAT guys are here, it's got to be on the news."

"Good thinking!" I hugged her on my way to pour coffee, wondering why I didn't think of that. Are the roles already reversing?

So, there we were, our entire little newly formed family, huddled on the couch, tranquilizers inserted in terrified adults and pup, watching what we had thought was our safe and serene little haven turn into something quite different, something no one could have predicted and that would change all of our lives forever.

"This is Heather Grant reporting for Miami 10 News from the entrance of the Silver Sands apartment complex in Sunny Isles, the elite strip of condominiums between Bal Harbour and Aventura in North Miami.

"We're still waiting for the police press representatives to give us the information, but something extremely serious is going on inside this most exclusive of all the Sunny Isles condominiums, which are home or one of many residences of international billionaires, sports and music stars and the 1% of some of the world's largest cities.

"There are ambulances, police cars, armed support vehicles, and, of course, hundreds of curious on-lookers, some clearly on the way to the gym, the beach, morning jog or a walk with their pets. We will stay on the scene until we have all the information we can gather, so stay tuned to Miami's most watched news station."

"Mom, I've got more on my phone, TV news is so retarded. There are bodies in the Rothensteins penthouse. Dead people! Someone up there texted their husband. OMG. Mom, it's all over the internet. It's the Rothensteins. They were murdered!

"How bad is that! I mean right upstairs! I think it's Katya, you know, their Russian housekeeper, who sent it. I bet the police are going to be really pissed. Yep, they must have taken her phone. It's cold. Really, really bent."

"What does it mean, "bent" They were bent?"

"No, Ooma, it's just an expression. Sort of like saying it's sick."

"Evil. It is not 'bent' there is evil here! Lola has powers, she is a channel. She knew. She felt it! Oh my Gott!"

I think this might be the time to properly introduce myself and give you some background on how my kid and I came to be here in the first place.

So, who am I? Edith Weller formerly of Canarsie, Brooklyn, fifty-eight years old, never married. I realize as I write this, that I could bore even myself with my absolutely un-special life story. I am, like my name, on the outside completely ordinary. On the inside I actually think I'm pretty wonderful. I'm not too tall, too short, too fat, too thin. I have regular features, nothing stands out or peculiar, just an average face. I have plain, medium brown hair, thinner now, and touched up, but basically exactly the same style it was when I was a teenager in Brooklyn; parted slightly off center and grazing my neck. I wear solid colored plain comfort clothes most all the time. Being a writer, reporter and columnist, I am not now nor never really was, even in N.Y., when I had a column in a well-known counterculture newspaper, part of the real work world or on display. Fine with me.

If I could be invisible, that would probably be my first choice; free to snoop, eavesdrop, attend things I mostly loathe, like any form of a party or conference and observe without having to make soul draining small talk or participate. I have no special talents besides my opinions and the ability to put them in a form that fellow outsiders seem to find worthy of their time.

I grew up in a brick row house in Canarsie, in a middle-class Brooklyn neighborhood, before it was cool to live there, though Canarsie, even now, would not be on anyone's status radar. Both my parents were (now this is really stimulating) teachers in the

Canarsie public school system! My mother taught Home Economics, a subject, I am assuming that has gone the way of the hoop skirt. My father taught 8th grade math. Shall I bother to mention I am hopeless at both subjects?

Once a week we would go out to our local Italian restaurant for dinner and to a movie. In the summer we would go to the Catskills for a week and pretend to enjoy the freezing lake, mostly not funny comedians, excruciating music and endless group activities. I read a lot.

My parents were absolutely unexceptional in every way including parenthood. They didn't argue and they were nice to me. I can't really remember a word of wisdom, guidance or any sense that they had a clue as to who the hell I was. That made three of us. I don't remember a special event, meal or lively conversation. I never rebelled; against what? I wasn't popular, I was an introvert at a time when the long-ago coined Carl Jung terms, introvert and extrovert were most certainly not in the common lexicon. I was almost eerily self-contained.

I had a few girlfriends, outsiders like myself, who shared the same sarcastic sense of humor as self-protection. No boy noticed me. I had crushes, but even I hardly thought about them, since the chances of actually turning any of them into a real relationship seemed as remote as another galaxy.

I graduated and applied to City College to study journalism and English, the only things I was interested in that seemed remotely feasible and because it was most certainly all we could afford.

And then, came the first curve ball of my still pretty normal, if plodding, young life. On their way to work, not so long before they intended to retire (I was a late life only child, and all grandparents were dead) a very large moving van (some irony there, since up until that morning, movement was not really a factor in our lives) ran a red light and hit my parents old, flimsy car head on. And I was an orphan.

I had no aunts, uncles, cousins, grandparents and my friends had gone off to schools not close by. This was also, I might remind you, long before computers, cell phones or the rest of it and staying in touch with people was a very different deal. Also, I think I was just totally stuporous with shock, loss, terror and grief. They may not have been much, but they were decent people and all I had.

I find that word to be diminished almost out of existence, but it shouldn't be. Decent people are rarer and rarer, no one seems to have the time or energy left after getting through their insanely overburdened days to even think about such things as their character. Or maybe it was always like this. I'm with the Greeks on that one. Character is destiny. Period. (I also tend to be quite opinionated).

So, there I was. Mercifully they each had some life insurance plus the settlement from the moving company and they owned our Row house without a mortgage, or I would have been living over a heating grate in midtown or something.

I think the next few years are sort of a blur. But I did find my "voice" so to speak. To the other City College kids, I was an "heiress" (everything really is relative) and I started to make my presence known in my columns and coverage of campus events. I even wore jeans and tight tee shirts and put a blond streak in my hair and pierced my ears. Practically a vixen.

Whatever it was, the opposite sex started to pay some attention to me. And, of course, I chose instead a professor of short story writing, twice my age and very married (well, if he got hit by a truck, at least I wouldn't have over-invested).

To speed things up here so we can go back to this bizarre journey on which I am your self-appointed guide, I'll skip the next couple of decades. I worked for various newspapers, wrote for anything I could, trotted around, sold the row house and moved into the city, guarding my little nest egg like any sensible motherless bird. I dated--had some extremely unfulfilling affairs, found out I would probably not be able to have children, and just sort of moved on along--all my unhealed wounds throbbing underneath, with no safe place for me to stop and mourn, let alone heal.

And then two things happened. I lost my one and only real job and column when the paper was sold; and I turned forty. Boom. I can't say what happened to me was a nervous breakdown. I like to think of it more as a nervous breakthrough, but it was a very tough couple of years and a long-needed road trip inward with the help of a very good therapist. Despite the unfortunate name of Rod Doran which made him sound like something you'd get at Home Depot if you were remodeling your bathroom; he was the first person I had ever talked to about my parents, let alone about myself! Well, at least I now actually had a self to talk about.

Now, Sunny. It even makes my eyes roll, it's such a cliché. Lonely, middle-aged woman, with not much going for her suddenly feels an urgent desire to have a baby, for all the wrong, selfish reasons (not, however, that there are really many non-selfish reasons to have one, anyway. Certainly, it's not the unborn baby's idea or need, now is it!) The universe swirled and I read a news item about a newborn Chinese girl in some remote province who had been left in a large empty KFC bucket on the steps of a Buddhist monastery. I think it was the KFC bucket visual that decided for me, but I just knew this was my kid and off I went to claim her.

So, there I was, forty-three years old, semi-employed, newly reconstituted, like lemonade or something; add mid-life crisis, unemployment, PTSD, therapy, medication, meditation (at least, I didn't do yoga or read Elizabeth Gilbert) who had rarely been further outside of the New York area than the Catskills, put her on several endless plane flights into the heart of China, add a two-week-old abandoned female child and stir.

This was 2003, when the one child laws were still strictly enforced and female children were routinely thrown off piers or stuffed into dumpsters, so many of them abandoned and unwanted long before the current #MeToo era and this was rural China! Point being, it didn't take much paperwork or convincing to adopt her.

And there we were, orphan to orphan. I named her Sunny because having a really bland, uninteresting name myself, I wanted her to have a name that by just saying it, you felt better and Sunny just seemed right. Also, it's my favorite jazz standard, which happened to be playing in some coffee bar I liked on the very day I was leaving for China.

I can say the journey from the monastery home was STRESSFUL. I hadn't even thought about the fact that I'd never actually held a baby before, let alone fed one, changed a diaper or had any idea how much more difficult such a journey would be with a two-week-old infant who could not be stowed in my carry on or stuffed in my suitcase. Somehow, we made it. When they first handed her to me, she opened her eyes and looked right into mine, really looked and reached one of her tiny little hands up and touched my face and she smiled. Some would call it gas, but I know she knew, and she smiled.

If prospective mothers were given a handbook of the pros and cons, best and worst-case scenarios of what to expect over the course of the rest of their lives, I think that would solve the birth control issues of the world. I adored my little miracle and she was one. That said, I had absolutely no clue how exhausting, scary, overwhelming, expensive and confusing it would be, especially since they do the dangdest thing. Just when you've figured out how to handle one stage, they change! They're always one step ahead and so, it's just about impossible to stay away from the Doubt Demons.

The best decision I made was to avoid all contact with other mothers of infants, especially of adopted foreign infants. I did not have chats in the park, hang around the pre-school (when we survived that far) or see shared motherhood as any more of a bond than liking the same yogurt. I stopped reading all parenting books and nutritional terror material. I did not grind my own baby food or try to turn a three-year-old into a meditating vegan.

Since she was absolutely, totally an American, Lower Chelsea before it was fancy, kid, I did not try to force Chinese classes on her or wax on about her homeland. I told her the truth which she found hilarious and took to regaling her fellow preschoolers and later, elementary schoolers with the tale, adding for impact, that she had kept herself alive by gnawing on the one chicken wing left in the KFC bucket. She was two days old.

Somehow it worked. By the time she was ten, she was one wonderful, honest, clear, funny, brilliant, beautiful (not my genes!) and totally confident and wise human being.

I will share an example of one conversation between us when she was about ten and could see I was getting really nervous, nervous even for me, about how in the hell I was going to give her the education and opportunities she was capable of with all those obstacles like little money or a real possibility of moving or getting her into any of the elitist bastions of what seemed to all aspiring N.Y. parents as the path to their little miracle's chance of success.

Somehow, the solution to this had translated to her into finding me a husband.

"Mom, you should try one of those dating sites. I can take a good picture of you, give you a make-over and photo shop it if you want."

"Gee, thanks for the ego boost. How's this for my profile: "Fifty-three-year-old, half deaf, half blind, half bald, half broke, half-employed recluse complete with ten-year-old Chinese loudmouth kid and transgendered rescue pup, seeks soul mate." I could have to shut it down; the site may actually crash from the responses."

"Why do you do that? You're not any of those things. You're funny and smart and beautiful, just simple and not showy offy."

"Ah, thanks pal, but better I say it then they say it!"

"That's retarded."

"Oh, good. I'll add that."

"Why are you so mean about yourself?"

"I had an indifferent father and I inhaled that self-image."

"Well, I think I'd rather have an indifferent father than no father."

"Oh, pa-leese. You can say that because you never had one, or a mean one, or an abusive one. Look how wonderful you are and more important how wonderful you think you are!"

"Okay, you have a point, but that's because of you and you're not even my real mother."

(Pause for dagger to leave my heart)" I beg your pardon. I'm not your birth mother, a fact I can't help, but I most certainly am your real mother, not to mention your ONLY mother. Blood. Schmud. Love is love and it has nothing much to do with what hole you popped out of. Does it bother you being an only child, is that part of it? There are lots of discarded KFC buckets in Manhattan, we could start a search."

"Yikes! No. Everyone I know with brothers or sisters hates them and then, there's all that random stuff that one of them could come home from school someday and just slaughter all of us. But I do sometimes wish we had a normal family."

"Define normal?"

"A Mom. A Dad. Two kids, grandparents, I'd really like a Granny, some odd ball, eccentric one who drinks too much. That stuff."

"Okay, fair enough. Now name one family you really know like that?"

"Ummm. Hmmm. You set me up! Oh, Walt and Helen across the hall. Robbie and Annie's family."

"That's it? Except Walt used to be Wilma and Robbie has been suspended three times for trying to set fire to Oscar the hamster in the science lab and Annie's Granny has dementia and thinks Annie is her grandfather."

"Okay, let's sort of ecto scratch this entire conversation. In fact, I think I had a really bad idea, considering your self-image, you'd probably choose the biggest dork on the planet or a child molester."

"I appreciate the vote of confidence, but you may be right. Besides, I'm more interested in how we get you into the kind of school you would thrive in and I need your help. You have to tell me what you want, since you're the one on the phone and computer all the time. Is that what kids are talking about? The end of elementary school and what to do!"

"We could move to some deserted island where it isn't an issue and I can self-educate which I basically do anyway."

"Hmmm. Not bad, except there wouldn't be a library or internet, so you might end up as a Coconut husker."

"I don't think you "husk" Coconuts, but I'll Google it."

"Not now. You have managed an entire conversation without picking up your phone. I consider that enormously encouraging. It holds the hope that someday you may see all that stuff as necessary evils, rather than your God of choice. Something like kitchen and bathroom appliances for use when necessary. We don't keep rushing back to re-start the blender after the smoothie is made; just an example."

"Mom don't even go there, it's too embarrassing. You sound like some prehistoric creature."

"Well I'm a lot older than most of your friends' mothers and I see this as a sort of madness, and it affects your entire life view and character."

"Well, you can always stuff me into some giant holiday KFC gift box and ship me back. As long as I have my iPad and phone in there, I'll be fine."

"You forgot the chicken wing, and that was a low blow, but let's just drop this now."

"Okay, but look, Momma (when she felt bad for me, she called me Momma) I don't want to hurt your feelings and I'm sorry for bringing that stuff about a normal family up because the truth is, we're mutts; you, me and Lorraine--that's just the way it is, so we can make a little mongrel family, but I think we know it's all kind of strange and it's not going to be like any of those probably phony normal ones we see on TV and everyone else pretends to be."

"Ah, baby. I wouldn't trade, would you? I like that image."

"Yeah. Me, too. Normal is so over."

Two more introductions to go and then we can move on with the real story. Lorraine. Once I had Sunny and began a new life, aspiring to be part of the more functional world, my very old yearning for a puppy kicked in.

I'd never had one as a kid but now that I worked from home most of the time anyway, well, it sort of emerged. Puppies were everywhere. On the street, in the park, all over TV but Lorraine appeared in almost the canine version of Sunny.

Sunny and I were walking to the little playground park we liked (quiet, no attractions to draw other mothers, but a swing set and sand box.) And as we waited to cross 23rd Street, someone threw something out of the window of a beat up old generic looking car into the street.

I thought it was litter, which really pissed me off and then it moved. There were all sorts of reasons why I should leave it there but clutching Sunny's hand, I dashed and scooped the creature up. I say creature, because, I had never seen anything quite like it before. Was it a premature rabbit, deformed raccoon, what? I wrapped the poor little terrified whatever it was, in my jacket and pumped over to the nearest vet.

After panting out what happened, I handed it over and waited for answers. It was a dog. A breed I'd only seen on Budweiser ads, "It's a Bull Terrier, about six weeks old, not even weaned. One sick son of a bitch did this. It's a male, but it's already been neutered, probably a home job, not very well done. Do you want him?"

Did we want him? I'd never been anything but a professional cynic about all that "universe sending signs, stuff" but between Sunny and this, I mean of all the Gin Joints? This very peculiar creature is tossed out of a car window almost at my feet, just when my 'I want a puppy' light goes on? We did.

Home we went, with me, once again, knowing even less about having a dog then having a baby. Sunny was about five, going on thirty. We examined him. We went online and did all the research we could stand. We went to Petco and bought all required products, except, of course, they did not include the reality of house-breaking a dog from a third-floor walk-up, schlepping a five-year-old up and down at all hours and in all-weather situations.

And then came the naming. "Sunny, what do you want to call him?"

"Lorraine."

"Lorraine!!!!" Lorraine??? (I did repeat it twice). Having not even heard the name except on one of my old jazz cd's "When I kiss my sweet Lorraine."

"Honey, he's a boy and it's a girl's name."

"Actually Mom, he's not a boy. I saw it on a YouTube video. He's gender neutral. They cut off his balls, so he's not really a boy anymore and everyone's trying to be another sex now. Don't be so Twentieth Century! I think Lorraine is a perfect name and no other dog will have it, not like "Buddy" or some trendy, dumb name."

"Okay. I guess he or "it" is so peculiar looking, it's the least he, she, it will have to deal with."

And so, Lorraine it was. We did have hope that as Lorraine grew, he (I will call him that to simplify) might grow into his extremely strange appearance. No one ever tried to pet him. Rude people asked questions one would not ask if you had a funny-looking baby (or maybe they would!).

One horrified man stopped us, pointed at little Lorraine and demanded to know, "What in the hell is that!" Poor Lorraine. But in all fairness, if you've never seen a Bull Terrier (and I do not think Lorraine was one of the breeders evolved Best in Show variety) they really do look as if God dozed off on this one, rather like a bad Leggo construction.

His little slit eyes were so far apart on his head it seemed to us he would hardly be able to see. His entire face was a nose, protruding so far down, that his tiny mouth was almost invisible. IF he had a nose job, you'd have to cut his head off.

The middle of his body looked like one of those blow up balloon dogs they make for kids at clown centric birthday parties. Long, dirt colored and like one big muscle. His tail looked like a pretzel stick and his legs, which were so bowed he almost moved sideways, seemed to have been cut in half or part of another dog, making stairs and getting up on my bed extremely challenging.

When he ate or drank (both activities he was extremely fond of) he had to put his entire head in the bowl, meaning suffocation was a distinct possibility and required him to frequently lift his head out and gasp for air. Was this a good idea, God? It did, however, provide Sunny and I with stomach clutching hysteria, our frequent entertainment of choice. Not very nice, but the sound effects alone, were beyond hilarious. So, there we were, mongrel family complete. Or so we thought, not knowing that good old Universe had one more screw to turn.

And, finally Ooma Lovee. Sunday was always sloth and newspaper day in our apartment, including Lorraine, who had a strange relationship with the *New York Times* Travel section. He would lie down with it in front of him and stare at the cover story for a long time, seemingly fascinated regardless of the subject.

I also had a subscription to the *New York Review of Books*, which I saved for Sunday. I don't know if they still do, but then they had a small "personal" ads section in the back. I'm sure the thinking was, if you placed a personal ad there you were probably not a raving idiot or serial killer, then again Ted Bundy probably read it.

Down in the corner, of the last page, almost invisible, something caught my eye. I think it was the word "Grandmother" reminding me of what Sunny had said about wanting one. It was an ad; unlike anything I'd ever seen. So, I'll just transcribe it.

"I am an elderly but active and healthy European woman of considerable means. I am alone in the world, widowed, childless and with no heirs. I would like, at this last stage of my long life, to be part of a family. I think that, besides economic advantages, I have much to offer as a kind, well-educated and wise role model. I have no one to give to but my precious little dog, Lola.

"I am looking to adopt a family and become their grandmother. My requirements are as follows: They must submit along with a recent photo, all the reasons they would want to have me as their grandmother. They must not have any living grandparents of their own, cats, or serious health issues.

"If you are interested, please send your response to the enclosed P.O. Box. Rest assured, I have extremely competent lawyers advising me and if you cannot withstand an intense background check, do not waste my time. If I respond to your application, I will arrange a meeting at which time you will be able to find out all the same information about me. I am aware that this is a quite unusual ad, but I am quite an unusual person."

I read it. I read it again. I scrolled through an internal loop of thoughts and feelings from snicker, to intense longing, tears, hope, anxiety and then I read it to Sunny and we just sat and stared at one another for quite a long time. Our vibe certainly reached Lorraine, who pulled his considerable nose out of the travel section and waddled over and sat between us, checking us out with those tiny squinty unreadable peepers of his.

"Whadda ya think, kid?"

"Well, she could be a white slaver, some sinister front for a ring of really bad people who would take me away and put me in some drug-induced coma and I'd wake up in a middle Eastern harem/dungeon. Or Hannibal Lector's only child. Or, she could be real. I think we should risk it. After all, she's taking as big a chance as we are! We could be thieving, psycho grifters or worse. I'll get the camera!"

Sunny took a picture of the three of us (I mean if Lorraine was the deal breaker, better we know fast.) And I, not knowing how in the hell to do this, decided to just be as honest and human as I could.

I had some really lovely stationary in a sort of hydrangea blue color that smelled like roses and I took it out of the special place I kept it, not having many opportunities to use it, and sent her as short and clear a description of the three of us without making it sound too sentimental or melodramatic (I mean moving van massacre, KFC baby, ugly mutt tossed from car window) the stuff of bad fiction, for sure. Sunny and I both signed it. Sunny wrote her own paragraph about her longing for a Granny, even including the part about wanting an eccentric one who drank too much! And we mailed it. I did wait until I could get a post office box, just in case Sunny's possible scenarios were true.

We both tried to act as if it was no big deal; probably just a joke, but also, figuring the large pile of responses, if she was for real, it would take her months to get through, even from such a remote placement as the NY *Review of Books!*

But human nature being what it is, the flood gates of longing had been pushed open. I barely made our rent payment, we were applying to middle schools, filling out endless, impossibly soulless applications, both our health insurance and utility bills had almost doubled and New York City, that close to 9/11 was not exactly the place I wanted Sunny and Lorraine to spend the rest of their childhoods.

Three weeks later, an envelope arrived. A very expensive

envelope, totally old school, which included real stamps. "Dear Edy, allow me to formally introduce myself. My name is Ooma Lovee. I am the potential Grandmother who placed the ad. I have enclosed as much background information on myself as I think is required to calm whatever fears you may have about who I am. I am sure our fears are the same.

If you and your lovely daughter and most intriguing canine are still interested and willing to trust me; I will have my attorney arrange for a private plane to bring all of you here to Miami, where I reside most of the year. I have enclosed my attorney's cellphone and other contact information. I received an enormous response because somehow word got out on social media, but yours was the only letter I read. I saw that lovely stationary; my favorite color and scent and I just knew. I do so hope you are willing to take this risk and come to meet me. With much anticipation, Ooma Lovee."

And there we were. I read it to Sunny and we just held one another and sobbed our orphaned little hearts out. Lorraine, too, even though her sob was more like some sort of snort, it was very effective.

The next month was a blur of arranging to take Sunny out of school and all the other things involved, including lots of e-mails with Ooma's lawyers, documents sent, and the rest. And then, the day arrived. Except for China and one impulsive vacation in the Bahamas, I'd never been on a plane, let alone a private jet and Sunny, well, her solo excursion was hardly one she could recall.

The thing about a limo service and a private jet experience, is, rather like Alice down the Rabbit Hole, no going back. I think we grinned so wide our jaws locked. Even Lorraine seemed to be smiling (the unfortunate location of her little mouth, making it rather hard to tell). And since it was still freezing and bleak in NY, Miami appeared before us like the Emerald City. Even the Dildo-scape looked thrilling.

Up we went into the sky via super speed elevator to meet the potential Granny as fairy Godmother. We'd seen pictures of her or the actual person would have been really intimidating. I felt like some derelict dumpster Mom. She towered over us in all her lustrous six feet of what seemed like legs, dressed in flowing, billowing white silk, Satin mules, ropes of pearls--perfect make-up and that Rapunzel hair.

And then, there was her condominium. In one of my survival jobs, I wrote captions for furniture in design catalogues, so I do tend to get rather corny in describing people's stuff. The apartment was vast, with walls of ocean-viewing glass and terraces, but her taste, being completely European and of previous centuries, had absolutely nothing to do with a super-modern, white marble floored mansion in the sky. There were antiques from various periods and styles, enormous Persian and Chinese rugs, couches and chairs, built for people her size (my feet dangled somewhere over the floor) in a pallet of hues ranging from violet to emerald, without stopping at anything in the neutral range. Art covered what walls there were. We were too awe struck to gape or move closer, but they all looked like museum level works, even if still lives, vast canvases of frolicking maidens, ship battles and nativity scenes were not exactly our taste.

Ooma Lovee was flanked by three lawyers, a maid dressed in a real maid uniform complete with starched white apron and head doily, and someone I assumed to be probably a security dude. I did see him sort of chuckle because it was pretty clear we didn't pose much of a threat.

Her enormous what looked like Victorian Era mahogany dining table was filled with exotic pastries, sandwiches, champagne and all kinds of kid friendly snacks carefully arranged in sterling bowls.

And there was a little silver water bowl for Lorraine on the marble floor and all form of dog treats in a crystal jar at the end of the table which said (Dogs) or we probably would have grabbed a few.

My usually extremely gregarious and self-assured ten-year-old held onto my hand as if we were lining up for the Dachau physical. Only Lorraine and Lola who ran for one another like a canine scene from a Hallmark movie, an instant, however unusual, love affair and the best icebreaker since Shackleton entered Antartica. We all laughed so hard even the security guy uncrossed his arms.

I relaxed enough then to see that Ooma Lovee, behind the pomp, and ceremony and glitz and movie star level presentation, was as scared and nervous as we were. So, I just said what felt like the truth.

"Can we all just curl up and eat now! I think we're safe enough!"

Ooma, started to cry and strode across the seemingly vast distance between her column of protectors and us, the three Wizard of Oz characters, threw her very long arms around me and held on tight, and that, more or less, was that.

After a fair amount of champagne, and enough exotic delicacies to last for days; she sent everyone home but her one lawyer, a kindly-looking grey-haired gentleman with a very gentle manner who seemed to be genuinely trying to make this work, rather than doing that paranoid lawyer thing and he presented what she was proposing.

We would have to go through a formal adoption process, but since it was an adult adoption (Sunny was automatically included) and my parents were not living, it was rather straight forward. We would be housed in another unit (Thank God, we'd need roller skates and Lorraine would need a stroller to find our way around something like Ooma's place, not to mention how not US it all was). She had a second condo, much smaller, but with three bedrooms on the third floor, that we would be given to live in at no cost and deeded to me so, no matter what the future held, Sunny and I would not be homeless. After all, we were moving from the only city and abode we knew to a strange place and entirely different lifestyle.

A bank account would be opened in my name and a monthly allowance would be deposited in it, enough to cover all our living expenses and an educational trust (OMG!) would be set up for Sunny, starting with private school beginning in her next term and seeing her all the way through graduate school if she so chose.

In return, she would ask only to be included in some regular way in family events, potluck dinners, movie dates or vacations that she would suggest. And, most important, we would never lie to her about anything, nor would she to us.

This seemed as important a deal breaker to her as it had always been to me (though, on an entirely different scale!) "Put it in writing," Sunny and I said almost in unison.

There were other boiler plate items, lots of scheduling details. She took us (herself) down to what would be our new home (Condo Unit 300/Sparrow) just about perfect for us. We were, by this time, so sensorially and emotionally overloaded (not to mention stuffed with goodies and champagne) I don't know that we were able to even say anything but WOW. Was this conceivably real?

Her nice lawyer insisted that we have our own lawyer and I decided to use my parents old neighbor and friend in the City, because, well, she was the only lawyer I knew, or trusted! We were supposed to go back the same day, but Ooma begged us to stay over and get a feel for this new world. And we did, sleeping in one of her guest rooms, which looked like Marie Antoinette's decorator had been at it and we actually fell asleep, so exhausted and so overwhelmed; sleep, if not a medically induced 24-hour coma, seemed like the only way to settle us down (with a little help from an Ambien, I do admit!)

By the time Sunny's school year ended, everything was completed, we were packed and on our way into what still seemed like a fairy tale. Everything in my naturally wary and catastrophizing prone nature (See PTSD and bad wiring) should have been sending me racing back to my shrink with major anxiety attacks, but some never before experienced state of grace had descended on all of us. Go figure. Also, not that I'm proud of this cynical streak, but, considering where we were when I saw the ad, once white slavery and serial killer had been ruled out, we didn't have a helluva lot to lose!

So, now I will step back and try to be unobtrusive and appear when relevant and then retreat, because there are many parts to this and I am only one of them, and, as I said, the ending still hasn't been written.

CHAPTER 2

Roy Rogers was smiling. His chocolate Lab, Hildy, was smiling. Hildy smiling was no big deal, but Roy was not a smiler. All those years in homicide had shrunk all the smile muscles; giving him what would be called a poker face, despite his unfortunately cheerful name and his long, lean, loopy persona, which included a slight, ironic upturn at the corners of his well-formed mouth and his eyes—heavy lidded, slightly sleepy like his Tallahassee, genteel Southern roots; unreadable except for a certain inner twinkle that seemed to be telling him private jokes about everything.

They were on their early morning run around the Aventura lake near his little condo and he realized he was happy and smiling! This awareness of feelings not much in his conscious daily life experience, almost brought him to a stop, but he kept going, not wanting to break the mood. Happy? Was he happy? Cops generally, especially retired Homicide cops did not really do happy. Hmmmm. Must be the great weather, his new job and having Hildy back with him. No Gift Horse sniffing, not today. This felt too good.

And so, he and Hildy trotted on, finally taking the long swoop back across the Lehman Parkway Bridge to the Silver Sands, so he could clean up, dress up and start his day (Hildy too) as the new Head of Security of the vast Condo and Country Club complex.

This was his first on shore job since leaving the Palace of the Dolphins, the largest, most expensive cruise ship in the world (or so, the brochure said) leaving a long unsolved series of passenger disappearances behind to haunt him daily.

He had been, and still was, the only official on or off board who saw the conspiracy or cared enough (all those years in homicide) and had enough Son of Tallahassee in him, to keep his obsession with the mystery to himself, once it was clear, no one was going to investigate. It was probably the final reason he resigned.

So, there he was, in his fifty's with his Miami-Dade police pension, a fairly large hunk of savings from all the years at sea with no expenses and a considerable salary, and ready for some new challenge. Miami felt good, and he needed to be with his dog; a long-divorced loner who had not had more than port to port romances for years.

This seemed like a dream job. He was in charge of a security team of fifty people between the condos and the country club, and after dealing with all stratas of society from the super Haves to the package tour groups, not to mention the ship's officers, he felt his grasp of human nature probably put him on the level of most working forensic psychiatrists. This job helped scratch his detective itch more than the cruise ship. He read Freud, Jung, Woo Woo, anything dealing with human nature, that was what fascinated him. Who we were, what lies beneath, how to see deception, pathology, sociopaths, narcissists and the like. The key to all human interactions, even in the civilian world and this was Miami, the daily challenges of being a detective here had turned a laconic, Son of the South, into a paranoid SOB. Tallahassee, the State Capital and, far more southern part of Florida, was much closer in distance, mind set and political persuasion to Mobile or Biloxi than Miami Beach; that's why he liked it here--such different packaging than the town he was raised in.

He had come a long way, career wise, because he was very

smart, very funny and had that kind of *golly shucks*, good old boy charm, that disarmed others and armored him.

The job had seemed somewhat like a land version of his Palace job, but with more demanding, wealthier people and from what he could see so far, the richer they were, the greedier and more terrified of losing anything.

The owners, the Rothensteins, were a tad more intrusive than he would have liked, but he thought that would lessen as they started to trust him more.

The biggest challenge (this was only his third month on the job) was getting to know the players, meaning his staff and the service staff of the hotel and country club and figure out the far too complicated security system. His office looked more like something from a CIA bunker than a condo complex.

As he crossed AIA with Hildy panting beside him, he realized it was too hot for the work out he'd given her, and he pulled his water bottle out of his backpack to douse her. When they reached the curb, he put some water in a plastic bowl and drank some as well, realizing that he was still smiling. Life was good, he actually felt excited about the future, not a familiar feeling for him. He wet a face cloth and wiped the sweat off his head, put his ever-present Miami Dolphins cap back on and headed for the Security entrance.

And then, everything changed.

Why his parents had named him Roy Rogers, he actually never asked, since it wasn't until he reached middle school that the "trigger" jokes started, and he looked up his name and watched several old cowboy movies starring his namesake.

The older he got, the fewer jokes he had to deal with, because no one under fifty had ever heard of Roy Rogers, but even so, he'd decided to have everyone at Silver Sands call him Rogers, just in case. So, hearing a loud shout out of "Roy!" from the apocalyptic scene that greeted him at the Silver Sands employee entrance, startled him.

What in the holy hell was going on? The entire building was surrounded by law enforcement of every level and attire. Hummers, black and whites, tension so high Hildy started barking and Hildy never barked. He could feel his pulse rate, which had slowed after the run, whip up and he swallowed hard, gulps of air, familiar to all old cops who had faced into the wind of peril enough times. He knew the voice calling his name. His old Miami-Dade partner, now lieutenant, a job he had longed for, but never was political enough to snatch.

He knew that strut, a small man's swagger, too well. "Roy!" The way he yelled his name, sounded more like a command, like something he would say to Hildy. Now the other reasons he'd decided to retire started re-appearing. Too many little swagger dudes like, Mikey Martinez.

"Mikey? What's happening. No one called me!"

"No time. They said you'd be in any minute. Sorry, we should have given you a heads up. This is some shit storm you've got here!"

The way Mikey said "you've" like this was his fault, set his Tallahassee teeth into lock jaw. No more smiling today, that was certain. He decided to make Mikey work for it, and stayed silent, not asking the next question.

"Your new bosses, the Rothsomethings. They were murdered this morning. The ME hasn't given us a TOD, yet but the dog walker found them at 6:30, this morning. She's a basket case, took her to the ER to calm her down before we can even question her or the housekeeper. How bout you get cleaned up and I'll meet you inside."

How bout you don't order me around dude, he thought, his teeth staying clenched. "Got it. Give me ten minutes."

"What a coincidence, this should be your new gig! Just like old times, huh Roy?"

"Mikey, they all know me just as Rogers now, you know. No more cowboy and trigger jokes."

"Right, Right. They told me, but old habits die hard, Roy old amigo. Whoops, sorry! See ya in ten."

CHAPTER 3

Rich people murdered in Miami. Rich people murdered anywhere. Celebrity suicides and overdoses. David Carradine dressed in women's clothes hanging in a closet in France. Robin Williams, naked and strangled by a belt on his own bedroom doorknob. OJ. Manson. Ted Ammon. Edmond Safra, cowering in fear in a locked bathroom in Monte Carlo in a self-created bunker to protect him from just such a fate. George Getty suicide by self-inserted barbeque fork. Too many OD's to mention, Michael Jackson should suffice. Jeffrey Epstein.

Bigger than life people's hideous endings enthrall; which may not be the most sensitive word, may make one squirm a bit at the truth of it, but they do. All those family murders, plots, suicide among the ordinary folks or in cities that do not inspire us with dreams of romance, success, fame, fortune, all added up together cannot complete with stilettos in the Eyes and Diamonds stuffed in surgically snubbed noses in seventy-five million-dollar penthouses in Florida.

And Miami now, right now, seems to have soared to the top of the sexy city, glamour pile. This former swamp--previously a Spanish bungalow filled laid back place; intermingled with rundown old Deco hotels, so out of fashion that only ancient Jewish left overs on budgets remained, rocking chairs creaking on their hotel porches, staring at Collins Ave through rheumy eyes to the sound of their IV drips and oxygen tanks.

Jackie Mason in his low period appearing nightly in the Kibbutz Room of one such place, where it is unlikely enough people who could still hear his jokes managed to shuffle into the room every night.

And further back there was a Miami no one ever talked about. A restricted Miami, where Jews were not allowed to own homes on the exalted Sunset Islands, 1, 2 and 3 or above 5th street. Today many of the richest Jewish families reside there-- prominent social, business, art and philanthropy leaders. Now for somewhere between ten for a tear down and thirty and up million dollars, you can live on a postage stamp lot with enough "view of the water" space for a good size dog to make a 180; driveways lined with the most expensive cars in the world, security guards, staffs and a chance to rub golf clubs with J. LO and A. Rod, or Madonna or whomever (some of us would probably pay that much not to).

Mt. Sinai Hospital, a beacon of Jewish presence in Miami Beach, was founded under great protests in the 1940's by one of the early Jewish families, who built it because the other hospitals would not treat them. So even the perception of Miami Beach as this land of Shalom and acceptance is based on a lie.

But America is or was still America and they came; everyone began to come. Jews from Russia and Israel and Cuba (Jewbans— Jewish Cubans were the first wave); Hispanics from Argentina, Columbia, Peru, Chile, Non-Jewish Cubanos, forbidden their Catholicism under Castro, Middle Europeans, Snowbirds from Canada, French Snowbirds from Quebec and Ottawa and Montreal, And Russians from everywhere else; the Ukraine, Moscow, Uzbekistan. And Miami affected by all this diverse, somewhat desperate, influx, also attracted the REAL ESTATE DEVELOPERS, the sun and funners from NY, and Chicago. Not so much Boston, or New England, noses too high to see the ethnic-hued water, Palm Beach was their playland).

But it was all still South Florida, the endless stretches of exquisite powder beaches, the mostly magnificent weather, and across the long narrow state, the Gulf side, the Keys with the world's most magical sunsets and so, what next?

Every mistake that most of the European bastions of sea and sun rejected, they embraced. European sensibilities still connected to their humanity enough to want to see the ocean, rich and poor. Cafes, and promenades, line the ocean fronts. Shops and hotels and houses are across the street or up above. Not Miami. Money talks, Bull-shit walks, a wise, if rather blunt someone said. You can now drive the entire length of the strip from Ft. Lauderdale to Joe's Stone Crab House at the opposite end of Miami and almost forget that on one side you have this amazingly pristine and luscious Atlantic coast and right across the way, the Intercoastal, a water highway that can glide you from Key West to Savannah without ever touching land.

Miami today is rather a combo of NYC, LA and a beach resort, the appeal of which is obvious. And there is all that Money. Funny money. Insane money. Laundered money. International, Global, no outsider can begin to understand. Fifty million-dollar condos paid for all in cash. CASH. Lots of them. If you take the same exact condo, and shift it ten miles out of the trendy, statues mad range, you can have it for oh, maybe a million. Not chump change, but within the range of human understanding.

So, who are these people? We all see the pictures: endless supermodels emerging from the surf, Titsicle size beauties, bigger than life. Russian call girls dressed as if the more designer labels they can cram onto their bodies, the higher their street value, or Penthouse of the Faena value or all those places us regular inhabitants know nothing about.

A world with a daily parade of Lamborghinis, Maserati's, stretch Rolls Royce's, blood red Ferraris and custom Porsches.

Some Publix and CVS parking lots have so many of them, it is a daily miracle they are not all smacking into one another trying to maneuver into the ever-diminishing parking spaces.

Jaguars, Mercedes, BMW's don't even rate a second glance.

More and more condos, the old Miami apartment buildings and one-story Fifties modern homes coming down; no place to park, (all that water on either side does limit one's options). Newly rising supermarkets with condominiums built high above the crowded aisles making it possible to have shelter and sustenance without leaving your room. Smart technology providing just about every conceivable thing one needs to survive and thrive and sustain one's lifestyle by speaking into Alexa and waiting for the door buzzer.

Soon we may not even need fingers anymore or the ability to think, write, read for ourselves, or drive. Considering the reckless rudeness of the zoom zoom drivers and the envy and rage of the less fortunate drivers stuck in their sea-air-rusting old heaps, and the traffic, which now equals all the other overdeveloped urban centers, a home above a supermarket is an increasingly attractive option.

There is one very popular health food restaurant near the Silver Sands, that posts a sign offering patrons a ten-percent discount if they arrive by Uber or some other non-parking conveyance, an omen, perhaps of what the future holds. No fear of sinking into the sea, no hurricane seems to have stemmed the sex appeal or real estate development or new arrivals, and with the flood gates of desperate Venezuelans now open, an entire new Latin element is being added to the mix.

Nowhere to go but UP. Spiraling into what's left of the skyline, prices equaling the heights.

Who are these people? These Miamians? We have a pretty clear image of the answer to that question if one says, "New Yorkers" or "Angelinos" or "Bostonians," but there really is no such thing as a "Miamian." Too diverse, too segregated by cultural lines and motives for being here and way too few natives. In that sense, it is what Los Angeles used to be like. And then Las Vegas filled the gap; people either following the opportunity and the vast money-making potentials, or those in search of a fresh start, a second or fifth chance, better jobs or a fantasy.

Now, Miami seems to be the heir apparent. There is much talk locally about "Real Estate Dynasties" as a way of describing its civic leaders. Even the word, "Dynasty" is rather suspect since no one standing in the never varying line up of society page photo ops, in one or another of the Miami mags, really just bloated ad rags, has any extensive dynastic chops, maybe going back to the first wave of Cuban refugees, or early farmers and retirees, but certainly not in the same play pen as Han or Tang or Ming.

These glossy seductive brochures for the wanters, who long for all they entice, touting Breitlings, and mega yachts, Balenciaga, Piaget and Prada and all those zoom zooms and shiny condos.

The condos are interchangeable in everything. All white, endless glass, state of the art kitchens, health clubs, infinity pools, concierge and restaurant service, immense marble baths, giant human aquariums to be filled with Roche Bobois furnishings or any of the various interior and appliance equivalents of Cartier watches, Fendi wallets or Luis Vuitton luggage that pay for their publication.

But they, of course need "filler," pages and pages of pictures of overdone attendees of charity balls and restaurant openings, art gallery events, concerts and museum parties, all the stuff of affluent cities everywhere.

The photographers, having given up any hope of doing anything but cataloguing as many people as possible (nothing like a photo of oneself grinning with all those gleaming veneered dentals and looking rich and popular and part of whatever the scene is, to increase readership.) And the mix is mainly Latin, Jewish and Black sports superstars.

The women, whether thirty or eighty seem to come in two varieties: emaciated or pudgy. Surgical enhancement (also in the glossy ad section) fake hair, sucked in stomachs, arm in arm and mostly linked to their male counterparts. The Latin men, far outclass the white guys in style and macho.

Also, thrown in to add credibility (this is a real magazine, not just a fancy ad money machine) there are always puff pieces on a celebrity who resides here FULL TIME or a visiting supermodel or successful local entrepreneur, usually involved in (what else) real estate, design or the making and selling of unspeakable fake art (discarded water bottles bashed in the corners with dirt inside; enormous stenciled blow-ups of cartoon characters with mystical captions) the list is long. But it is not a society that blends together in any way that creates a single identity, which is part of Miami's allure. Outsiders welcome because there is no real inside.

If New York "dynasties" started with the Robber Barons and oil, steel, shipping, railroads were the ticket and then merged into law firms and Wall Street; and Los Angeles, which calls itself "Hollywood Royalty" pretentious enough, but far more subdued than "Dynasty" and goes back just about eighty years to the beginnings of the movie industry, then Miami elite can really only claim real estate development, and those are the movers and shakers, wanting to be seen always, out and about.

Competition is keen, but all the dead spaces in the city are being re-invented as thriving hubs of living and playing and shopping mini meccas. Brickell, The Design District, Wynwood, the developers scavenge for any usable buildable land the way old bums troll the beaches of every seaside city with their long-handled coin detectors. Cranes and hard hats and traffic jams and earth movers, power saws, noise and cement mixers and lines of the have nots, working the sites, they line up at days end for their rides back to inner Miami; where there are no beaches close by except Haulover with its nude section and rotating group of water pervs masturbating while ogling frolicking hotties and/or children. They do the grueling, thankless work, the invaluable contribution.

Without them, the rest of it would stop. No more glossy mags filled with peacocking developers and their designer laden spouses. Not that this is more true here than in every city in the world, but it feels more intense, crasser, and greedier and harder to define what the goal is beyond MONEY.

CHAPTER 4

Roy Rogers was showered, dressed and at his desk in ten minutes as promised, Hildy collapsed beside him complete with her own staff collar and badge. As usual Mikey Martinez was late, but this was a great relief to Roy, giving him time to find out on his own what had happened. He buzzed his entire security staff, who looked as if they had just spotted a union official on the lawn, clearly more terrified for their job security than a roving condo maniac. He checked all the monitors in their equivalent of a war room. This was one great big pustule of a mess.

He thought he had learned the security system pretty well. Beneath all that "yes, Ma'am" Tallahassee charm, a meticulous mind resided. The condo had state of any art security trained on every conceivable way of entering. In addition (the Rothensteins being old school by age and paranoia) had security guards who checked every floor every hour 24/7, which seemed almost silly, but did bring great psychological comfort to the tenants though considering the enormous monthly maintenance fees, it was probably more hype than actual help.

The elevators were monitored and all the emergency stairs. The only areas without cameras were the actual floors but given the elaborate eye scans and impenetrable doors and terrace windows

(An intruder would practically have to drive a race car at full speed through them to penetrate the glass) it seemed redundant.

Additionally, there were concierges, doormen, parking guys and a front desk security officer on duty 24/7.

None of the videos showed any activity but the dog walker Leena and the maid Katya arriving just before the building opened for the day. They had the codes, etc. only because they were the personal employees of the Rothensteins. No other employees or service providers who counted into the hundreds when the building was almost full of tenants or their families, (trainers, masseuses, hairdressers, nail techs, spiritual advisers, personal shoppers, PA's, IT support, interior "desecrators" as Edy called them, art consultants, chefs and all the rest of the ever growing work force created for the sole purpose of serving the needs of the new era of mega wealth and Wally World level sloth.

Well, Miami traffic probably would make anyone who could do it, do it! No one wanted to go OUT THERE without some special, fun reason (if it wasn't absolutely necessary).

None of them, however, could be admitted before 7 a.m. unless their names and ID's were on the front desk list. Of course, after awhile they were recognized on sight and things do get a bit lazy, especially if the real sympathy and eye winks of the staff are far more with those people than the tenants (human nature being what it is for those who do not have the luxury of never pumping their own gas or waiting in line at the Apple store).

So, what did this indicate to Roy, scratching his still plentiful mop of graying auburn hair under his Silver Sands official hat. The building, he was sure, knowing Mikey, was already in lockdown. The suspect list certainly seemed to narrow down to the occupiers of the Units. There were 120 units in all the sixty-five stories, the third through fifth floors having the least spacious or expensive ones (still well into the millions) and where more of the full-time residents seemed to live.

At the moment, according to the manifest, his second in command, an eager and highly ambitious young former cop, named Pepe Olivera whose English was sometimes tricky, but whose work ethic more than made up for the need to often have him slow down and repeat every word. There were only twenty units occupied. Summer was slow, mainly South Americans escaping their winter or the full-timers.

Because so many of the units were purchased through intermediaries, often under code numbers without any real name being listed (see money talks, bullshit walks) even in the height of the season (November through May) if you happened to pay attention while driving the strip from Golden Beach to around 157th St. heading toward Miami Beach, the number of dark units, unoccupied and rarely used was far larger than the lighted ones. The relief of that information for Roy, was the suspect list did seem far less overwhelming than it could have been and, even after only three months, he was quite aware that the list, just within the Silver Sands, was still significant.

CHAPTER 5

The regal Rothensteins were very well-known, meticulously well-connected to everything powerful in the city, and constantly mentioned, thanks to their zealous, even by Miami standards, PR machine working every worthy cause and "In" event. Coco kept her personal shopper on speed dial, because the very thought of appearing, let alone being photographed, in the same Chanel outfit twice could bring Mrs. Rothenstein to the point of nervous collapse.

In addition to all their real estate holdings, they had endowed and created an art museum filled with their overflow plus the works of either former participants or rejects of various galleries or Art Basel exhibitions. Their name was emblazoned everywhere possible and in ads running for art related celebrity appearances and events in the Miami Herald and all those glossy hotel room Mags.

If all that wasn't enough to keep them busy, they and their two overindulged and neglected children ran the country club and managed the properties. But everything had to pass through Coco and Frederick first. Like any royal family worth it's crown; the kids had the titles and the allowances, but no power. Real power that is, their name brought with it, a certain small-scale power (best restaurant tables, front row seats at sporting events, cutting the line at hot clubs) petty power, but impressive enough to those less privileged. They were on everyone's invite list.

Frederick was, on the surface, the more likable of the two, lacking his wife's shrill narcissism and aggressive demanding hauteur. He was urbane, soft-spoken, elegant and nutty to a fault, but more tasteful than his wife, whose insecurity was red flagged by her label fetish. (Someone in their coterie once hissed behind her CC ensigned back at a party ("I keep wanting to tap her on the shoulder and say, "Coco, we KNOW you're rich, you can risk a few off the rack schmotas now.") Frederick had custom made suits from Milan and London and he always wore a perfectly cut bespoke shirt and tie and handmade shoes, even in Miami in August.

He was, shall we say, refined and always had a smile, a wad of twenties to hand out to every worker he passed in hotels, restaurants or on one of his job sites. He was, however, totally opaque, and as clueless, underneath about anything even approaching reality as his wife. They lived surrounded, like all royalty, by yes men and frightened sycophants, fund-raisers and real estate brokers, and their children, who, if they had learned nothing much else, certainly were masters at how to play their parents. They saved all the vicious private conversations for themselves and their ever-rotating array of therapists. There were all those layers of self-hate and rage and far deeper, the howling infant wounds, the piercing shrieks of small children raised by two people with absolutely no ability to see the needs of anyone but themselves.

The power of their connection from the very beginning of their fifty-year union, was much like royalty, maybe not Queen Victoria and Albert level, but for Jewish Miami, about equal. A merger as much as anything, between two families already on the move. Her family was far wealthier and that most certainly did not go unseen by Frederick. She was wickedly smart, well educated, not a beauty, but one of those self-created women, who with the help of surgery and affluence radiated the illusion of beauty, chic, for sure with the aura of privilege.

She played golf and tennis, spoke passable French and Spanish (showing how connected she was to her help and the wealthy Latin community whose paths she crossed at galas and on Worthy Cause boards). She was also ruthless, shrewd, ambitious, desperately lonely and almost consumed with longing to be SOMEBODY special and, having grown up in finance and real estate, herself, she certainly knew what she wanted to do.

Frederick shared these wants and manically driven longings for money and, more importantly, the power that it brought, but he packaged it discreetly, tucked inside his Brioni slacks out of view, making him, by far the more appealing of the two, a fact never lost on Coco, not even in the very beginning.

She was completely in love with him or the illusion of him, more so, because beneath all the glitter and rigid posturing and control, there was a lost, heartbroken woman, who had lived for almost fifty years knowing she was not loved back. Not that he didn't need her and care for her, they were Siamese level partners, a co-dependent couple who could never have achieved what they had achieved alone or probably with anyone else.

But women, even ice queens like Coco Rothenstein, do not really thrive or open or grow or thaw when they are not well loved, and that was the deeply buried wound that, no one, not even Coco ever got near.

The Silver Sands had been their pinnacle, their Twin Towers if you will. It had no equal yet, though the crown would surely pass soon. They had held the title of the developer's developer in the forty block Sunny Isles Ocean Front strip for almost ten years. The project had actually killed the first architect and could have done the same to the second, leaving him with spiking blood pressure and some form of PTSD that turned him into the still living Banquil's ghost of insomnia for years after the project was completed.

It did, however, as such attention-getting works of architectural wizardry do, make him into a brand name not only in Miami but in the global world of countries visited by the wandering dubious controllers of global wealth from the Baltic, and Mid-East, several of whom also bought units in the Silver Sands.

By the time some snarky and probably envious friend of the Rothensteins daughter, Rebecca Rothenstein Monroe Dubinski, pointed out, after scanning an early draft of a proposed logo design, that SS was also, um, the initials of the Gestapo, it was too late to change it; thus, no ad or piece of stationary of any kind, ever used the initials. Even so, human nature, rivaling Mother Nature in its ability to bring all of the less obvious flaws in the lives, personalities or appearances of the Feet of Clay crowd, their acquaintances used the initials behind the family's back with great glee.

If everything does have a price and our lives on whatever scale of how high, as Trollope called it, "The way We Live Now," tends to balance our aspirations, thwarted dreams and disappointment by where we stand on the regal lineage scale, the prices the Rothensteins and their children paid for the bloated success of the Silver Sands and the private country club located across AIA with its world class thirty-six hole golf course jutting almost into the Intercoastal waterway, were considerable.

Rebecca paid with the loss of her first marriage to Tom Monroe, one of the project architects on their payroll. Her brother, Arnold who was the only observant Jew in the family, kept his marriage (there was all that doctrine and seven children to consider), even if his wife Goldy had retreated into some form of a still alive version of Lot's bride and he had developed a raging form of Crohn's disease which led to the removal of quite a large section of his lower intestine.

As for Frederick and Coco, well, as the oldest story in the world goes, Frederick's (until the Silver Sands project,) discreet liaisons with a rather continuous stream of avaricious young international hotties, finally took over his allegiance to Coco.

It was one thing for her to suspect, but quite another for her suspicions to be overt and then public. Years before #MeToo, the kind of women men like Frederick (and there were many of them) attracted were never above blackmail when the expensive baubles and yachting trysts in Croatia or Mustique dried up.

No one, including themselves were really surprised. Outside of their business interests, after all those decades, they really had nothing in common. Certainly not their children or Arnold's brood, a rable of annoying little Hassidim (Coco could barely look at them, longing for gorgeous little Prada clad munchkins she could show off at her hospital galas and Battered Women luncheons). The very sight of her daughter-in-law, "schlepping around" as Coco put it, in "Those hideous bag lady ensembles with that schmotta on her head" gave her a migraine. Certainly not what she had hoped for and even the word "baby" sent Rebecca racing for the Patron bottle. So, they did not, even in private, really discuss their dismay at their offspring. Far too tricky, a potential hornet's nest of emotional stings and allergic reactions to the truth.

And then there was taste. What, after all, was the point of all that money and that mammoth penthouse, covering the entire top floor, with 360-degree terraces, an infinity pool the size of the condo's main tenant pool and 15,000 square feet of interior space, if you had nothing to put in it!

Their tastes, which were fierce, and obsessive could not have been less in sync. Frederick, like his personality and savoir faire manner, collected stunning pieces from the Deco and Nouveau eras and the poster art and objects that went with it. He had amassed such a vast array, that it not only filled their apartment but an entire warehouse from which he would rotate pieces when he needed a re-charge of his visual joystick.

Coco loathed it all, being as obsessive a collector of anything au courant, trendy and modern as her art and interior advisor could find, anywhere in the world. Even Jeff Koons and Damien

Hirst were too "yesterday" for Coco and there was not a piece of furniture in her "areas" of the penthouse that anyone without a chiropractor or a serious masochistic streak could sit in for more than a quick drink or expresso.

New. New. New. And it was this clash, as much as the very ugly discovery of his South Beach harem, that led to their decision to divide up the penthouse into two separate units.

To the outside world, nothing had changed, they appeared together and with their brood as they always had. They worked in adjoining offices, even though there were more layers between them, but the marriage was as withered as one of their deserted old motels, waiting to be bulldozed and replaced with yet another Rothenstein development.

They even divided their six little monster toy terriers though how they chose, no one knows, since the compulsively barking, shitting, peeing, creatures seemed to be identical. No divorce, no horrific and far too costly asset splitting.

The façade, which had become their inner as well as their public personas remained unchanged. Or so it appeared to their network, and maybe even to them; but the penthouse reeked of sadness, a sort of invisible film of despair seemed to encase the very air. If where we live can stink of all our unfinished human suffering and self-deceptions as well as bounce with the fresh scent of joy and love, that was the shroud over the royal couple's palace, long before it also became a tabloid circus of true horror and public mockery. Nothing is what it seems, a wise man said. Ever.

CHAPTER 6

By the time Mikey Martinez came strutting in, fingers in his pockets, inflated with the gas of his own ego, *Yeah, I know you guys make more money, but we're real cops, dudes and I'm on TV and moving up,* Roy had gathered a dossier of information and was ready for the passive aggressive pissing contest that Mikey lived for.

"Hey, Roy, not bad, man, looks like the Star Ship Enterprise command center, so do I show you mine or do you show me your's first?"

This was perfect for Roy, who had learned long ago, maybe from some Will Rogers quote, that no one ever got into trouble keeping their mouth shut. "You start, Chief, I still don't know anything about what's going on up there."

"You got any decent java in this joint" I'm not totally wired and I need to keep my edge."

"We even have an expresso machine. How about a double macchiato, best Columbian beans and it should do the trick."

"Well, you have changed. I remember when Maxwell House and jelly donuts were too classy for you."

"Still are. This is for you." Roy turned to Pepe, who knew exactly what he was doing and Pepe went to make a triple, hoping Mikey's heart would race and he would lose his cable crime show performance.

"Okay, so, here's what we have. The owners of this joint were found in their adjoining apartments and man, I have never seen anything this expensive in my life (the fact that Roy was not surprised by this information remained hidden behind his perennially placid facial muscles).

"I gotta take you up, so you can see this for yourself, just waiting for the ME to finish up so we can talk to her; but someone was really, really mad at those two! Man what rage. What a fucking scene!

"Tons of fingerprints, probably all from accountable people but nothing on the bodies or murder weapons, if you can call silk scarves, high heels and jewelry murder weapons. And the perp or perps, even drowned all their little ratty dogs in the bathtub! I mean, we're talking blind fury, crazy stuff. They must have really pissed off the wrong dudes.

"Oh, full disclosure, the young woman who found them, Leena Martinez, note last name. She's my sister Bianca's kid. We took her to Mt. Sinai and they've sedated her. We can't interview her until she's over the shock. She has a tough enough life, too much pressure and now this, plus she's lost one of her main gigs. Poor kid will probably have nightmares for decades.

"The other person who came in after Leena is the Russian housekeeper. She's older and not so loco from what she saw, so I've got her up there to question. Damn broad called her husband and that's how it all got leaked to the entire fucking social network universe. But she didn't give him details, so there are things no one knows but the perp.

"We don't know what's missing and we need their kids for that, but not until we interview them and the people who live in the building who work for them full time. A couple of the old guy's lady friends, one Russian, one Latin. Personal Assistants; man, that's the life. Suspects for sure. We need to see wills, all that shit. Nothing seems to be missing, but I don't know how much cash and jewelry they kept there, but serious diamonds and emeralds were used to kill the wife, so, my gut says, this was someone or a couple of someone's who just totally lost their shit and probably didn't plan it out like this. I mean high heels in the guy's eyes and ears? Really? I mean, do you think the dude woke up and thought, Hmm I'm going to get even with those bastards with footwear and jewelry. Too bizarre, even for Miami.

"So, the rest I'll explain better when we go up and I need you to give me entire plans for the building and copies of all the security tapes and whatever else. I also need a list of everyone who comes in and out and all the tenants currently on site. And then we start knocking on doors, man. I hate this shit. I've got a pile on my desk a foot high and all those damn budget cuts, nowhere near enough good detectives to handle a huge profile case like this. Wait until you see the press out front and it's just beginning. I need to maximize this, know what I'm saying? I have an idea, I'll throw off you after we take a look. Okay?"

"Got it. I have everything you just asked for right here, we can go over it all after we go up or now if you want."

Pepe appeared with the special brew. "Hey, muchas gracias my man, I need this." Roy and Pepe watched him inhale the triple as if they were Russian spies serving a nerve agent to any enemy of the state.

"Ah, perfecto, those Columbians may be pussies, but man, they make good coffee. Hold on, that's my ME."

Roy and Pepe were as still as statues, watching the Mikey show. Pepe, who was Columbian, didn't even blink.

"Okay, amigo. We're on our way. She's done. I've got gloves and shit up there for you. The crime scene has already been messed up, but the damn place is so enormous, most of it hasn't even been processed, yet. Let's roll."

"I'd like Pepe to come, too. He's my second and I'll need him on this."

"Sure. No problema, dude."

Roy led Mikey, who seemed to just inflate further from the coffee and conversation, through the command center to the special staff elevator only used by security that had passed rigorous background checks and been vetted by the Rothenstein's own people.

He entered the codes, did the eye scan and up they went, fast and sleek, all the way to the top where mayhem waited. Roy took a very deep breath, trying not to let Mikey see that underneath his cool, he was truly scared. Mikey, coming from the other side of the coin and fueled by caffeine and hubris, was certainly not scared, jealous, however would probably work as his mind set.

Mikey had not exaggerated. This was the first thought Roy Rogers had after his walk through of the crime scene. For a guy who really liked to over-embellish any activity he was involved in from social to criminal, if anything, Mikey had lowballed this one. It almost didn't seem real, more like one of Coco Rothenstein's Art Basel displays.

Despite the number of cops, crime scene photographers, ME staff and CSI people, there was an almost palpably somber quiet in the vast tainted Rothenstein Palace. Everyone was speaking in whispers for some strange reason, almost as if they were paying respects to the royalty desecrated before them. Even Mikey was hushed, whispering his comments to Roy as he led him from one scene to the other and then into Coco's bathroom where all six of the dead dogs were floating.

Somehow, it was the dead pups, more than the grotesquely murdered old people that really tipped it for Roy. Dog lovers are like that. There was something about the killing of the innocent, the relatively helpless nature of pups, who lack the cat's feral nature and are so completely dependent on the kindness of owners or strangers.

Even though the dogs were mocked and disliked by everyone in the building, including himself, it was hardly their fault they had been raised by a couple of idiots. He shuddered and for a moment felt as if he might burst into tears, an event so rare in his adult life, he had to go all the way back to the deaths of his parents to even recall the last time he'd cried. *Jesus Holy Shit*, he whistled through his teeth. So much for the dream job. So much for the happy smiling morning. Now what!

Nowhere in his Head of Security for fancy condo development handbook were there any guidelines for a double murder. All of his still twitching Homicide Detective muscles were kicking in, but he really had no authority or did he?

Mikey seemed to be reading his thoughts. "Whaddit I tell ya? Is this creepy or what? Follow me, I wanna talk to you about something."

Roy nodded and followed him, humbled now and deferring to his old nemesis, his usually effortless cool and confidence evaporating with the horror of what he was seeing.

Mikey led him across the endless hallway of Coco's apartment and into what seemed to be her yoga studio or Zen meditation chamber or whatever the hell the new rich person's fad was. The room was covered in some silk like deep blue fabric, the ceiling filled with little twinkling pinpoint star lights. There were Buddha statues and Third Eye symbols filling the long black marble shelf that ran the entire length of one wall and also held more candle sticks and incense dispensers than a South Beach gift boutique. Yoga mats and several of those crazy exercise balls that looked to Roy like a very good way to break any number of bones, were stored against the walls and Yanni music was playing from some hidden speaker, which in itself, would be enough to make him a little unhinged. *What is the matter with these people?* He thought, having met way too many of them since taking this job. There were two velvet covered chairs shaped rather like toadstools with backs and Mikey pointed to them and they sat down, both chuckling just slightly at the ridiculousness of how out of their element both of them now were.

"Do you believe this bullshit?" Too much moolah, man. Makes them all totally loco."

Roy nodded. "So much for Third Eyes and inner peace. What she needed was a panic room."

"The whole fucking place is a panic room. No way anyone they didn't know got in here. So, Roy. I've been thinking and I have a proposal for you. I already checked with the Chief and he's given the okay."

"I'm all ears." Roy could feel his heart beating faster.

"This is just too much for me and my guys right now. I mean this is going to be a mega media fart fest. I need your help. You were the man at the main Miami office. Only reason you didn't get my job is you weren't enough of a machismo, too much class to grovel the way I did.

"Anyway, water under, you know what I'm saying? We both ended up where we belong, but what I'm asking is, can I count on you to help me with this?

"I want to deputize you, bring you out of retirement, so you can do the interviews here and work with us officially. You have done more of these than I have or all the rest of my guys combined and you know the scene here. It just all is going to take way too much fucking time and resources than we have and it's hurricane season. FUCK. If we hit another Irma, no way we can add all this onto our plates. Even if power goes out or whatever, this building is going to stay lit and you're right here. We can only keep these people under house arrest so to speak for so long and we have to interview everyone and I need someone in charge who can oversee it all. I don't know who you report to, their kids I guess, but they're also suspects, big time. We need the lawyers names, you know the drill. So whadda ya say?"

Roy felt a tingle of excitement and anxiety surge through his solar plexus and shoot up into his head as if he had just been struck by some unseen object. He exhaled one long, deep breath. "Mikey, I'll do whatever you need. There aren't any protocols for this, but I have to clear it with the company, just in case.

"Frankly, I'm not very sure who the hell to go to. The Rothensteins ran a very tight ship and I just dealt with them and their kids. It's only been three months. I guess we have to start there, even if they're suspects, we should probably talk to them first. Whew. I didn't see that coming, but it sure makes sense and frankly, it unties my hands. I am really not certain what the role of security head covers in a situation like this one! It certainly wasn't in my employment agreement!"

Mikey grinned, his very familiar Cheshire cat grin, exposing what always seemed to Roy like three rows of gleaming white teeth. "That's my hombre. Let's go talk to the ME and then we'll go see the family."

CHAPTER 7

To be a Medical Examiner in Miami is rather like running in front of a freight train every day with no end to the on-going body count. An article that appeared in the Miami Herald listing the ten weirdest things to wash up on Florida beaches ranked "severed limbs and dead people" as numbers seven and eight and that was just the water list.

Olivia Tan was their top ME, a former Navy Seal who had the stamina and intelligence, the military steel and moxy to handle whatever Miami could throw at her. Roy had always been almost in awe of her and Mikey saw her as his best kept secret, making him look good more often than he liked to admit.

She was standing on the vast terrace outside of Frederick Rothenstein's crime scene, smoking a cigarette, despite whatever one of the endless "rules" against smoking at crime scenes. Roy, who was now on detective auto pilot noticed that the hand, holding her cigarette was just so slightly trembling. A first, for sure.

"Hey, Madame Nu, you smokin again, must have really gotten to you, babe." Mikey came right up close to her and patted her shoulder, even though they were all now on red alert about any form of physical contact or personal remark to the women they worked with, or any woman at all. They were basically old school guys with no clue what this really meant and worked with women who were more on their page and let anything but an overtly out of bounds move slide on by, or stopped it with a look or a raised hand gesture. Olivia, thinking more like a guy most of the time and not quite getting the #MeToo frenzy since men had always been so terrified of her, she'd never had a problem, in fact, it was usually her aggression or mention of their body parts, that helped get her rather enormous erotic needs met. Anything to take away the daily images of human beings at the lowest end of their humanity and out of luck, from the inside of her head.

She shrugged and turned to face them, puffing away without excuse, a muscular Asian woman with long dyed blond hair and clear caramel colored skin, showing some blending of other races somewhere in her gene pool. She looked rather like a sexy drill sergeant. She shot Mikey a look indicating her barely hidden dislike, but seeing Roy, her usually opaque face broke into a smile, revealing perfect white teeth highlighted by her deep red lipstick. "Hey Roy, wow, what a treat. How ya doing?"

"Well, pretty good, until about an hour ago."

"Good to see you, Roy."

"Roy's the Head of Security for this joint. I've just deputized him not formally yet, but we want him to supervise this mess. Whadda ya got?" Mikey reached into his pocket and pulled out some sort of lotion in a tube and began rubbing it aggressively into the skin on his face and hands, flakes of which flew off onto the terrace.

"Olivia jumped slightly backwards. "Mikey, what the fuck is that! We haven't processed out here, yet. You're messing up my scene. Now I have to bag it. What is it? Psoriasis?"

"Mikey kept rubbing without apology. "I wish. Nah it's this genetic shit, called Ichthyosis, took me years to even pronounce it. I'm sort of like a fucking snake, got this rough scaly skin, have to keep it moist all the time, itches like forgeddaboudit. But I'm lucky, my great aunt had it all over her body, she looked like a fucking serpent. Mine is very mild, but stress flares it up for sure. Sorry, I can bag it for you."

"NO! Don't touch it. I need to separate it out. I've heard about it, had a floater once, when he washed up, we thought it was one of those giant pythons they're bagging all over the Everglades. You are lucky, man. And very lucky to live here. Cold dry climates make it really gross."

"Spare me the visuals, babe. This scene is making me flake. I'll put my gloves back on."

"Good choice, Mikey," she said sarcastically, and took one last long deep hit on her cigarette, making Roy long for one, himself. Nothing, except probably Heroin, eases the fear stuff quite as quickly.

"Shall we get back from gross to horrifying before I need another cig?"

"Yeah, yeah. What ya got?"

"Well, the causes of death are pretty clear. Easier for her, clearly suffocation. For him, I'll know more when I get him on the table and get the stilettos out of the entry points. Clearly, they bashed into his skull like bullets. You know we found no prints, but the DNA stuff will take a while. Could be a hair or drop of sweat or something. Or even something on the dogs. "Doesn't seem well planned, more a total meltdown, and I doubt if anyone in the building could have heard them scream, but the place is full of security cameras, so you might get lucky and actually see it happening. Looks like the T.O.D. for both of them was pretty close together, early this morning. No rigor, yet. No attempt to make this look like a robbery or anything else, so I'd say they just hit and ran, probably knew how to get out without being seen."

"Yeah, Yeah, I dig that. My niece, Leena, the dog walker came at 6:30 and they were already dead, but almost no one can get in before 7 so it looks like someone in the building."

"Good guess. The sooner you can interview her, the better. Your niece? Poor kid!"

"Yeah, she's at Mt. Sinai. So sometime before 6:30? But not long before?"

"Yep. No blood splatter, so that's one less nightmare. I'll call you from the morgue after the autopsies. Has the family been told, yet?"

"We're going there now but, the thing is, they are also major suspects at this point. Kind of tricky. Oh, and you can copy Roy on all this, but, you know, we gotta be really zipped up on this one, the media is going to be all over this like a rash."

Olivia smirked. "Yeah, well, at least I won't have to bag their itchy shit."

Mikey chuckled. Man, low, O, that was low. I shared something girly and you knocked me hard."

"Oh, so that's what you think we 'girls' do, share our personal hygiene issues as a bonding muppety me thing. More likely to talk about where to get the best tequila shots and buffalo wings and where the hot guys play pool." But hey, why ruin a great macho patronizing op. Right Roy?"

Roy snapped back from where his mind had wandered, realizing she had put him in a very compromised position with his erstwhile new boss.

"Oh now, must I take the Fifth, so soon. I'm here to help with anything, we'll seal this place up as soon as you give the word. Good to see you Ms. Tan. Always interesting."

She winked at him and gave him a quick appraisal--the sort that men are arrested for doing in reverse. No rules really for any of this new stuff, except, Roy thought, we're all turning into tight ass robots around one another and he really missed hugs and friendly light naughty banter. *Welcome to the new world whatever that means*, he thought, waving at her and once again, following Mikey through the labyrinth, past many former colleagues, and out the front entrance to begin the real detective work. Strangely enough, he found himself almost smiling again.

Roy was now in the lead, taking Mikey down one flight to the Rothenstein's daughter Rebecca's unit, aptly named Peacock/Unit 201.

Mikey reached for the buzzer, but Roy put out his hand to stop him.

"Let me prepare you because she is, well, in Tallahassee we'd call her a "Scary Mary." Or maybe I just call her that. First, she's well, you'll see, sort of challenging to behold and one burger short of a barbeque. Gotta be very cool and not express any mirth or sarcasm. Got it? They blocked out all TV and internet service so she may not even know what's happened, but I can guarantee she's gonna be pretty pissy about the confinement, and she has dogs, actually almost everyone in the building does and since they haven't been out, not a great mood enhancer."

"Got it. I know the type."

Roy chuckled, his good old boy mouth-not-moving chuckle. "Trust me, she's a whole new deal."

Mikey pushed the buzzer. And they waited. And they waited. They could hear, even through the seriously sound-proofed doors, someone screaming at someone, who, because they didn't scream back, they assumed was an employee.

Then the sound of clicking heels, an eye in the security peep hole and then a shot of themselves reflecting in the security camera. "What the hell do you want?"

She sounded so angry, they both, stepped back, an auto reflex reaction. Even after all these years of dealing with very irate, aggressive, rude, panicky people, Roy never really got used to how much more unnerving female rage was than any stuff, even a Crystal Meth crazed giant guy lunging at him. When women got mad, man, they scared the Tallahassee turds out of him.

"Mrs. Dubinski, this is Rogers, Head of Security and I have

Lieutenant Martinez Chief Detective of this district and we are here on urgent police business, so please, open the door, ma'am."

Considering how aggressive she sounded, she opened the door quickly without even asking for some form of ID. She did know him, but even so, giving people a hard time was her favorite occupation.

The vast, heavy Steel designer door flew open revealing a woman, as advertised by Roy, but up close and without warning, completely shocked both of them, who, once more jumped just slightly backward.

Rebecca Rothenstein Monroe Dubinski looked to both of them like some animated weezened Barbie Doll brought to life by the miracles of virtual technology. She was very short, probably under five feet but teetering on top of a pair of shoes, they couldn't help noting, closely resembling the footwear sticking out of her father's head. She was as emaciated as a concentration camp survivor, if such a person had had the benefits of breast augmentation surgery and tanning beds.

She was clad in skintight jeans with various tears in appropriately salacious places. Each tear, representing an extra couple hundred bucks, or so, Leena had once explained to Mikey who was totally speechless that anyone not in a refugee camp would choose to wear clothes with rips and tears in them, even if they were free.

Covering her rather disproportionate bosoms, so large in fact, considering her minute, boney body and the height of her heels, it made Roy think that if she leaned forward she would topple over, was a top clearly expensive and cut in a style called "Baby Doll" a look they had seen young women in South Beach wearing. Even on them it was not a great choice, being sleeveless and almost like something a pregnant woman would wear, but on a clearly not young woman whose arms, though almost fleshless--had the unfortunate but inevitable fate of aging female arms everywhere--

the outer skin hanging over the gym tightened muscles and all the veins, having nowhere to hide, bulging out from pit to pinkie.

Her face, which was caked with some sort of orange pancake make-up and featured very long false eyelashes and brows and the lips of a tribal concubine, had been altered to the point of barely looking human.

Her hair, which appeared to be a wig, reached down to her waist and hung in stick straight columns with Cleopatra bangs. The total effect dangled (for the observer) on the fine ledge between horror and hilarity and it took all their years of poker face training to display neither reaction.

"What the hell is going on here, Rogers? They cut off my internet. Call Atlantic Broadband! My dogs are going crazy, they need their park time. We're under house arrest. My maid can't get in and I have a dinner party tonight and all the food is going to rot in her car! This better be good or my parents are going to fire your stupid ass."

"May we come in, Mrs. Dubinski, I'm afraid we have some extremely bad news."

She might have tried to blink, but what had once been her eyelids did not seem to exist, so the effect was rather like watching two black butterflies flinch, the upper and lower fake lashes trying to meet but failing.

"Whatever," she said, with just a touch less hostility, hobbling aside so they could maneuver past her and what appeared to be a litter of dogs of various breeds or mixtures. She saw them look down trying not to step on them.

"They're rescues. I rescue them. I have twelve here now and they have got to go out!"

"Very sorry for the inconvenience and the secrecy. Why don't we sit down somewhere and we'll explain." Roy was calm as a movie cop.

"Fine" She huffed, in that rather bratty tone Roy thought

was usually the domain of fictitious high school girls on TV sitcoms.

She wobbled in front of them, her legs so thin Roy feared they would just snap in half from the weight of her boobs and shoes. "Sit" she said, as if talking to the dogs and gesturing to a very long, tan leather covered sofa that Mikey thought probably cost as much as he made in two months. They obeyed, but without doleful eyes, tongues hanging, or waiting for a treat.

Mikey let Roy take the lead, having worked together for years, they still had an almost telepathic shorthand about who was best to handle potentially volatile situations and given the lady and the news they were about to deliver, this would rate a ten on their scale. Also, Roy was far less excitable than Mikey and better suited to keep his cool with this clearly unusual female.

"Mrs. Dubinski, is your husband here? I think you might want to have someone with you."

"What the hell does that mean? I'm a big girl. He's the baby. Just tell me what the fuck is happening!"

"Well, ma'am I deeply regret having to inform you that early this morning your parents were murdered in their penthouse and that is why we had to lock down the building, since it is most likely the suspect or suspects are on the premises."

Whatever reaction Mikey and Roy might have anticipated, hysterical laughter would not have been it.

Rebecca Rothenstein Monroe Dubinski, shrieked with hand-slapping extremely loud deep-throated laughter, bordering on hysterics, piercing enough to bring her unwanted husband running into the room and sending the kennel full of unfortunate pooches racing for cover as far from their benefactress as possible.

Because of the amount of surgical renovation of his wife's face, when her mouth was open to allow breathing while she continued to guffaw, her face took on the characteristics usually associated with Death Skulls or the Munch Scream painting. Tears slid from her wide-open eyelids and she bounced up and down, banging her stilettos into the marble floor and clapping her hands together.

Mikey and Roy were so unnerved, they instinctively moved closer to one another. Roy fleetingly thought of clutching Mikey's hand. They remained silent, not, having any clue what to do or say, unless she started to hyperventilate and needed resuscitation.

Sergi Dubinski was most certainly her partner in narcissistic body dysmorphia. He was clad in lycra biking shorts, so tight his genitals seemed to be desperately trying to escape. His clearly over-exercised upper body, a mass of rippling muscles, indicating not only endless gym hours but most likely the addition of quasi-legal supplementation. To maximize the effect, he was wearing an equally skin-tight Wife-Beater's tank top.

His leg muscles were so overdeveloped they seemed like his genitals, to be on the verge of bursting through his skin. He was, like his wife, tan from tip to toe, his head shaved in the way of all the Russian men who swaggered around the Sunny Isles CVS shopping mall, drinking endless cups of coffee arguing in Russian and smoking for hours on end.

"What is happening here? What are you doing to my wife? Baby, what is it? What's so funny?"

"Mikey and Roy stood and held out their hands, which he shook without ever taking his steely blue eyes off of his wife. "Yes, yes, Rogers, I know you. What!!!!"

His appearance seemed to have the desired (at least by the cops) effect of snapping Rebecca Dubinski back into some form of reality. Rage and large, gasping sobs now replaced the hysterics, which was actually a relief. Her Rambo padded over, his flip flops snapping as he moved quickly and with all that downward weight hitting the floor. "What did you do to her?"

"Mr. Dubinski, we have just informed your wife that her parents Frederick and Coco Rothenstein where found murdered in their apartment early this morning."

They watched for his reaction, since now, all bets were off about them as suspects or, for Roy, the wack jobs he was going to be working for.

Sergi Dubinski, reacted in the way that a male--raised in the Soviet Union-- who clearly had seen and lived through many sketchy and dangerous situations; a survivor who had hit the honey pot and had a lot at stake and who instinctively knew "suspect" was a viable option.

He encircled his wife which was not difficult to do, with his massive arms and remained eerily calm. "This is not possible. Not possible. My babushka, I am here, I am here. Shhhh. Shhhh. Take some breaths, darling, we must stay calm. We must listen to the police." He turned his unreadable eyes on Roy. "May I get her some medication. Her nerves are not good. This is too much for her. She has prescription. It is required for her to function in stress situations."

Mikey took this one. "Absolutely. Very good idea, because we must question both of you and there is no time to waste."

"Baby, baby, I am getting your medication. Keep breathing. I will be right back. Shhhh. Shhhh, now. It will be alright."

Rebecca had calmed down enough to return to somewhat bearable sobbing and rocking back and forth. Rogers handed her a box of Kleenex that was on the enormous glass and marble coffee table in front of them.

She grabbed them, dabbing at her bat-like lashes, still aware of not wanting to disturb her make-up. "OH my God. My mommy, my mommy. I can't live without my mommy!!!"

They were silent, waiting for her Russian Bear to flop back in with her medication. "Here, my Blini, this will help. And close your eyes and remember your mindfulness prayer."

Somehow the woo woo stuff coming out of the not so incredible Hulk seemed completely ludicrous to both of them; his bride who, seemed familiar with the need to explain exactly who he was and what he did in their empire, offered a very pulled together bio on her husband.

"Sergi was Mr. Ukraine, he was their Schwarzenegger and he runs all the personal training activities and supervises my parent's fitness program. He's invaluable to the Country Club. Oh God, Mommy!!! I'm going to faint." She lowered her head, letting her quite heavy looking hair arrangement slip slightly forward.

"No, no, put your head back, babushka, and trust me. I am going to put my fingers on that spot on your neck, remember. Don't be afraid, it will bring you back. One, two, three, now!"

She obeyed and the color under the layers of make-up returned to her face. Her wig was a little askew and she quickly re-set it. Roy had a momentary urge to whisper to Mikey that this was such a show, they should have brought popcorn.

Roy leaned forward, "I know how terrible this news is, but I'm afraid we must ask some questions now. We have to cover all the tenants in residence before we can let anyone leave and I know you are all anxious to do that."

Smells he was all too familiar with started wafting across the vast living room. "Sergi, put them on the terrace and have Bianca clean this mess up, now!"

Sergi stood, his heavy feet moving with just the slightest bit of the irritation that comes up immediately when any man, even the far less macho versions, is ordered about by a woman in the presence of other men. Those, of course, thought Roy, who are singing for their caviar suppers, are veterans at not showing it. He strode, shoulders rigid as if on his way to a weight-lifting competition.

Roy cleared his throat, in serious need of some water but certainly not feeling safe to ask. "Mrs. Dubinski. I wish we had more information for you right now and there are many aspects of the crime scene that we cannot discuss as you must understand; but I can say it was brutal and clearly an act of personal rage.

"It would be very helpful if you could tell us when you last saw your parents, if they expressed any anxiety or concern for their safety or mentioned anyone coming to see them. Any disgruntled employee, any fights with family members or even the smallest detail that might have seemed unimportant at the time."

"Oh God, this can't be happening! I had dinner with her! She was fine! Oh, Oh, the puppies, where are the puppies?"

Roy let Mikey take this one. "I'm afraid they are all deceased as well."

They braced for another wave of hysteria, but once again, since human nature rather like Mother Nature is crammed with curve balls, she surprised them. She just smirked. "Well, no great loss. A bunch of ratty little beasts and I'd have to take care of them."

The two, already exhausted former partners, let out a small silent sigh of relief.

They were all quiet, watching as her medication seemed to be kicking in. They could hear Sergi yelling at the maid in Spanish with a heavy Russian accent. Mikey rolled his eyes. Sergi, and a clearly long-suffering Bianca appeared together, and he left her with her cleaning cart and padded back over to his wife.

"They killed the dogs, too." She said and they exchanged what looked like another smirk.

Roy sat forward, hands clasped in what he hoped was a benign posture. "Mrs. Dubinski, was there anyone else present at your dinner last night?"

She was not only relaxed now, in comparison to her previous state of mind, but seemed to be enjoying the attention. "Let me think. My brother Arnold came by for a drink but didn't stay for dinner. He and his wife are nutso fanatic Jews and won't eat any of our food and he had to leave by sundown. And Daddy came in to say hello and ask Mommy a couple of business questions, but he only stayed a few minutes, I don't think he even sat down. "They are not on the best of terms at the moment. So, it was just a Girls

Night. We try to have them at least once a week. So fun. We drink champagne and dish all our friends and talk about everything. "She's my best friend in the entire universe. OH my God! My mommy is dead!"

She reached for more Kleenex and the sobbing resumed. Quite a normal reaction, Roy thought, and he was quiet, following her lead. This time she pulled herself together quickly and Roy wanted to know what exactly she had taken, just in case he was ever in any true shit storm situation.

"I know how hard this is, Mrs. Dubinski, but I also know how much you clearly loved your mother and we urgently need your help to find this maniac." He had chosen his words carefully, beginning now to have some better sense of her soft spots and feeling valuable and heard were clearly two long buried but palpable longings. She perked up as he talked, confirming his hunch.

"Yes, yes. I'm trying to remember any detail. She was in good spirits, planning a benefit for one of her charities, Divine Doggies, the rescue where my rescues came from. We care for them until we can find homes. And she showed me her latest Chanel handbag, gorgeous! We drank quite a lot of champagne, she was a bit tipsy, seeing my father always triggers her a little. She told me he was fucking (that was what she said!) both his assistants, though she had no idea how since his pecker was kaput and we laughed and shared some private talk but that has nothing to do with this."

Roy was trying not to show impatience but needed to re-direct her monologue. "So, you saw no tension, she made no mention of any problems with anyone in the building, an employee or staff?"

This brought what would have been a smile on an unaltered face and a snort-like laugh. "Hello! Are you kidding me! We run a multi-billion-dollar empire, we all deal with every kind of liar, dead-beat, incompetent fool Miami has to serve up! We're always in some pissy place about numerous people. We vent and fume all the time! I couldn't even make a list! Right Sergi?"

He nodded his massive head, his neck obscured by muscle, which Roy noted, not having thought of the neck as a muscle site before. "Completely, every day is full of such crap. It's just part of doing business. You wouldn't believe what goes on at the Fitness Center. Dumbniks, falling off the machines and suing, when it's their fault or they are stoned and shouldn't be using the equipment. Sex going on in the locker rooms. Gay stuff all the time. Crazy chicks off their meds, screaming and crying because they do the weigh in and they gain a pound. You name it, we see it."

Roy and Mikey recorded this comment, since Sergei clearly exempted his wife from the "crazy chicks' department, though all evidence to the contrary sat across from them.

Roy nodded hoping to convey empathy. "Well, I certainly understand, I deal with a fair share of it myself, but if you both could try and dig a little deeper into your memories of recent encounters and relationships and make up a list for us, it would be very helpful. Now, I think we need to get a statement from Bianca. Mikey, you wanna do that. My Spanish is not going to cut it and I'll go see the son. I believe his unit is on this floor."

"Across the hall. 203, Shalom it's called. Drove Mommy crazy! So, what about my food and the dogs?"

"I think we can handle that for you. I'll have a couple of my security team go out and find your housekeeper and we'll store the food in our refrigerators and then they can take the dogs out for you, but I'm afraid you'll have to cancel your party. The building is still a crime scene. Sorry about that, but your parent's condo is so enormous, they will be processing up there for hours. Besides, we need to interview everyone and control the traffic."

Rebecca now seemed to be exhibiting the second wave of the medication's effects. Her head dropped forward and she snapped herself awake. "Good, good. Sergi I need to sleep! And maybe a shot of Patron. My poor Mommy!!!"

"Yes, Yes, my Beauty." With this he picked her up as if lifting a four-year-old and carried her off into the hidden private wing.

They weren't really through, but they both realized that was about all they would get for now. Mikey moved toward Bianca, who had finished her onerous duty and seemed both relieved at their departure and frightened. Mikey suggested in Spanish that they go into the kitchen. She enthusiastically agreed.

Before Roy could make his way around the enormous clusters of furniture and toward the door, Sergi re-appeared, clearly eager to ask him something he didn't want his wife to hear.

"Rogers, I don't want to upset my wife any more than she can handle, but is it your thought that whoever did this, may be after her and her brother, too? There are many enemies, much jealousy. Can you put extra protection on them and our families?"

"Good question Mr. Dubinski. Frankly we've just begun to deal with this and we haven't even gotten the ME's report and no autopsies have been done. That's also why any list of possible suspects you can give us will really help. As for extra security, you will certainly have that, but once we re-open the building, you will still have to use good judgement about where you go and who you see. Do you have a concealed weapons permit, sir?"

Sergi laughed, showing a large mouth with several missing back teeth, clearly a left over from his less affluent past. "Are you joking, man. Everyone in Miami has a gun! Everyone in Florida, probably!" And I can handle just about any asshole who would try anything hand to hand."

Roy chucked without smiling. "Of that, I have no doubt. We'll be back after we do some more interviews. I still can't return your cell service. But you have the internal beeper codes, so you can always reach me."

"When can you tell us how they were killed. That would help me know what to expect, just in case."

"Probably not until we find the perps. It was very specific and unless social media gets a leak from one of our guys or the ladies who discovered the bodies, which, may well be the case, we do try and withhold anything only the killer would know."

"Yes. Yes. I watch Law and Order re-runs. I get it." Per-c-ba. That's Russian for thank you."

"You're most welcome, and that's English for just doing our job!"

Roy maneuvered to the door, with Sergi following to punch in the codes necessary to exit.

When the giant fireproof steel door closed silently behind him, he let out the longest, deepest breath of the entire morning and checked his watch. It was only 8:30 and it already felt like the longest day of his life. He crossed the long vast hallway to Arnold Rothenstein's condo and pushed the buzzer.

The sound of people talking loudly, but not fighting, children crying and whining, a man, probably Arnold talking loudly in Hebrew. He waited, not wanting to buzz again unless it was necessary, having no idea what to expect.

He really didn't deal much with Arnold, who was more of the numbers guy, not very gregarious or having his sister's need to flaunt his position or persona. In fact, Roy had never really understood why he was in this business anyway and not living in Brooklyn or in the wealthy Hassidic area of Miami, the only stretch of the beach that was dark and without decorations during the Christmas holidays.

The door opened without any precautions and Arnold Rothenstein clad in his usual black suit with prayer shawl and Yarmulke, quietly motioned for him to come in. "Please, I've been expecting you, though we have been told nothing and we are leaving for our other home by the synagogue as soon as your people are finished with us."

"I apologize for the delay, Mr. Rothenstein, I was with your sister. Is there a private place I can talk to you and your wife? Better the children don't hear this from me."

Arnold's pais locks and beard made it harder to read his reactions, but his eyebrows moved upwards in the only visible indication of surprise or anticipation of bad news. "Yes, yes of course. I'll go get her, go down the hall, please turn to the left, it's my study, very quiet and private."

Roy made his way across the equally enormous condo, but it was as different from that of his sister or parents as he was, filled with oversize couches and chairs covered in plush somber velvet fabric. The floors were all carpeted, a truly odd sight in Miami, no matter how humble the abode. The carpet however, was a richly dense dark red and clearly expensive. The feeling of the entire space was more like being in a condo yeshiva than a home but given the number of children running around all over, the human equivalent, of his sister's dogs, it was probably a very good choice.

The study looked like a smaller version of the living room. The walls covered in heavy gold and green fabric and holding dozens of family photos and religious, probably very rare documents, all encased in expensive wood or gold frames.

His desk was a massive piece of intricate wood carving, which Roy thought must be an antique, something one of the British Kings would have sat behind, someone like Henry the VIII. There were chairs and a sofa across from the desk and Roy, not being sure where to put himself, decided to stand and wait for his hosts.

They appeared as quietly as his sister had appeared loudly. His wife was dressed the way all the Hassidic women he saw at the Hebrew end of the same shopping strip mall where the Russians gathered. Her clothes looked homemade, she wore no make-up or adornments of any kind and her hair was covered with a scarf, quite unlike the silky, expensive ones that tied her in-laws into their death chairs just a couple of stories overhead.

"This is my wife Goldy, I don't believe you have met her. She must be properly introduced to any male not related to her. Goldy this is Rogers, our Head of Security."

Goldy Rothenstein, bowed her head and Roy thought for a moment she was going to curtsey, but she simply acknowledged the introduction and waited for Arnold to tell her where to sit.

"Please, Rogers, let's sit on the sofa and chairs. The desk is too formal, though we still have no idea why all of this secrecy and panic is going on. My children can't go to school and all communications have been blocked. We are quite distressed."

"I apologize, Mr. Rothenstein. We have all had to rally our forces very quickly for the safety of the residents and I must inform you that this building is a crime scene." Roy paused, looking for possible reactions that would indicate how they would take what he had to dump on their humble laps.

"We are in this situation because, it is my very sad duty to inform you that your parents, Frederick and Coco Rothenstein were found murdered in their joint apartments early this morning and since we have no suspect or anyone in custody, we must take every precaution."

Goldy Rothenstein gasped and covered her face with her hands, praying in Hebrew, and rocking back and forth.

Arnold's response, however, was far more interesting. He blinked rapidly, indicating he might have a nervous twitch of some variety, since the muscles on the left side of his face, contracted several times, making his beard jump up and down, rather like a clip from an old Marx Brothers movie. He shook his head rather sharply from side to side, over and over again, sighing deeply.

Before Roy could proceed, he jumped up and began pacing back and forth across his office, his hands shoved deeply into his ill-fitting suit pockets, and seeming to lose awareness of Roy's scrutiny. "God's will," he hissed. "God's vengeance for their sins," he chanted under his breath, nodding and pacing faster and faster.

He never looked at his wife, offered any comfort to her or

seemed aware of the possibility that his words might convey any possibility of motive to the police presence in the room. "Vengeance. I warned him. I warned them both!"

Roy was as silent as one of the sea rocks that littered the beaches after a storm.

CHAPTER 8

Oma Lovee sighed and put one of Sunny's tee shirts over her eyes. The tension and the fear were taking their toll and lying in a quiet, dark room with Lola beside her was her stress relief of choice. She liked to lie down in Sunny's room rather than the guest room. It smelled of her, fresh and slightly floral and young.

Sunny liked her to do it, too. She smiled and tried to relax her shoulder muscles and jaw, breathing deeply and stroking Lola's bony little back. She almost laughed at the irony, that after five husbands and countless lovers, she felt far more comfort stroking the back of a strange little puppy than she ever had with any of the men.

Tears sprang from the sides of her closed eyes. The daily fear was back, in spite of her exhaustion and the medication. "*Will I ever live one day without this terror?*" "*Rather doubtful, my dear, since you've fought it every day for seventy-five of your eighty-eight years.*"

Just saying her age, was enough of a trigger. First thought every single morning, no matter how well or poorly she slept, with or without astonishing dreams. *Eighty-eight. I'm eighty-eight. Oh Gott, how is that possible!* No matter how strong and healthy she might be or appear to be, there was no escaping reality. No one younger, even by just a mere decade, could understand the staggering vulnerability of that reality.

Eighty-eight! Sometimes it completely escaped her, and she would forget the fact. *How old am I?* Her heart would pound. *Thirty-eight? Fifty? Wait. Wait. I'm eighty-eight!* Sometimes it felt like swimming in a huge murky pool where she could not see the edges or the way to shore, blurred by the cavernous uncertainty of where she was, and how and when she would find safety. Death, was probably that safety. She shuddered.

The entire world around her saw her as this almost mythical figure, calm and regal and seamless outside and inside. What a laugh. Her exterior was and always had been her shield, almost her burka, really, where she hid from the truth of her fragility.

The clothes, the make-up all that ridiculous surgery. The false braid that she never took off. Of course, being so tall and having all that ballet training, gave her a better foundation for her façade, but it was also, like all masks, all personas, a trap.

No one, except Edy and Sunny, if she would let them, which she was almost at the point of trusting them enough to do, wanted to see anything else. She had locked her humanity inside her armor, and it had set the stage for her eternal loneliness and isolation. The role became the haven and hiding place and no one was the least bit interested in anything else she had to offer besides her parties and her money and the myths of her mysterious past.

At least that was basically true. Not that she tried to hide it. No one ever asked her, even about where she was from. She snickered. People. Sunny and Edy had made up a word for most of their fellow condo dwellers and the hordes who arrived daily to tend to them. "Rupids." Rude and stupid. Manners seemed to have been lost somewhere around the time the Balloon Broke. No, she always got that wrong. The Bubble Burst, that was it. She smiled. The first time she said that, Sunny and Edy went from mystified to raucous mirth in an instant. Somewhere in the last ten years people just lost some vital part of their humanity, not to mention any conceivable interest in anyone but themselves and the lying as a lifestyle consumed them.

She pulled the blanket up over her shoulders, a chill coming from somewhere deeper than too much AC, from her heartbreak spasmed though her.

Sometimes now, she forgot that part of her journey, old age did that; crowding, it was called–too much new information coming in and pushing the overflow out. More and more in the last five years from somewhere deep inside her daily terror the idea to place that grandmother equivalent of a Lonely Hearts ad had come to her, in a dream, no less. A grand Guignol level dream about loss.

All through the night she was running down a long dark road, barefoot, without make-up or clothes or her braid; her long arms frantically reaching for something, someone and she was sobbing, screaming for help, for love, for comfort. She woke up screaming and crying with her arms stretched above her head, gasping for breath and convinced she was dying. But she didn't die, she had some sort of spiritual brain flare and the idea of the ad, just appeared.

She took a long, deep breath and felt her shoulders relax. The powers of her gratitude to God, the universe, whatever, and to herself for trusting this incredible, terrible, dream and the gift it held.

Edy and Sunny and Lorraine. Gott! What should she be like now without them? The miracle of it. They could have been Rupids or worse! Instead, they were the two most wonderful people she had ever known, and heaven knows, she had known her share! They did help the fear, when she surrendered to the gift they were. But all of those years before, shadowed the joy, made it so very hard for her to trust any gift, even the ones she had fought for and given to herself.

It was about time for her to tell them her history. She knew how much they wanted to know and to be closer to her in that way, to share it and to hold it after she was gone. She had never done that with anyone. Her husbands could have cared less, well, except for Claude, her love, her only love, blown apart in Mr. Hitler's Hell leaving her orphaned again, wandering about away from Ljubljana, her family hone, alone with the two gifts she had been endowed with, beauty and common sense. Nothing common about it, she now believed. It was a kind of brilliance because it was so rare and so vital to all immigrants, outcasts, world weary wanderers who have suffered too much, seen too much and lost too much. It was a deep inner homelessness, that no matter how they adapted, how many languages they learned, how successful their lives might become, they knew, it was all one enormous façade.

And what better place for such wounded warriors than Miami, a land of flash, transients, a water world of evolved sea creatures washing ashore from all over the planet like beached mammals thrashing toward safety. Survival. Not room for any of them for most of their lives from then on beyond survival. Figuring out how this dry strange land worked and finding their way to survive.

Well, she had certainly done that, and now, it all seemed rather ridiculous. All the energy, the enormous compromises of her integrity and self-worth (rich men wanted her, or the surface of her. She used what she had and she chose well). For what? To end up eighty-eight and terrified! As terrified as when the Nazis came and took her parents and she ran, ran on her already long, strong legs, ran for her life, which was now almost over.

And now, this. In Miami! Two elderly rich people, who could be her, murdered almost beside her and a new kind of war that was going on everywhere, was closing in on her again. Was it a hate crime? Anti-Semitism?

No one knew her mother was Jewish. She had spent her entire life, from that horrible morning in her peaceful, beautiful little Slovenian town, seventy-five years ago, lying about it. The fear that there would be another pogrom, anywhere, anytime haunted her every day and often endless nights. No one, not even Edy and Sunny knew. Not, yet. But soon.

This terrible thing going on upstairs from them, this would give her the courage to let them in closer. The only way out of fear is marching right into it. She knew this, had lived it, but now it was time to fling herself through and take a bigger risk. Maybe the biggest one she had ever taken. "After all, Ooma dear," she said out loud to herself, "if not now, when???"

She sat up, carefully folding Sunny's Yankees t-shirt, and re-made her bed. One last thought almost doubling her over onto the bed, again. What if she was next?

She stopped at the door, hearing a man's voice coming from the living room. It must be the police. She hesitated, smoothing her hair and adjusting her outer being, adjusting her mask and slipping back into her shoes. There was a mirror on the wall by the door and she glanced at it, the light being dim enough for the risk of facing herself close up and not at her best. Such ridiculous vanity! No one looked at old women, including her!

Sunny had posted all sorts of clippings and saying on the mirror and Ooma scanned them, trying to better understand the way the mind of a fifteen-year-old in the crazy world of the 21st century teenagers worked, to know Sunny better.

Teenagers were so opaque, even one as seemingly transparent as Sunny. Sunny must want her to, or she would never agree to let her nap on her bed in a private sanctum, where God only knew what she did, or said to her online friends and real friends.

Three post-its caught her eye. The first was torn from a newspaper and attached to a "talk to Mom" post-it. "Dutch OK 3rd gender." "*A court in the Netherlands said Monday that lawmakers should recognize a neutral third gender in a groundbreaking ruling for a person who does not identify as male or female.*"

What in Gott's name was she thinking about? The second was written by Sunny and sounded so much like something her mother would write, she laughed out loud. "I think all tourists should have "Shorts Police" on duty at airports, main tourist attractions, train stations, places like the Eiffel Tower and give out tickets with fines to everyone who should not be allowed to wear shorts in public. So gross!"

And the third, which seemed completely out of character for a young almost woman who seemed completely confident and at ease with herself, at least for a teenage girl in Miami! "Above all else, never think you're not good enough." Anthony Trollope. Ooma felt tears welling building and pressing forward from somewhere hidden from herself. Tears so old, they dried before she could even release them. She opened the door, feeling as if she had learned a great deal about her granddaughter and herself.

Rogers, the head of Security, who she only knew from seeing him around the building, was standing in the foyer, looking rather uncomfortable and a bit sheepish, which Ooma found endearing. She liked the way he looked. And if she remembered correctly, he had a beautiful big brown Labrador, another plus.

Edy, who seemed somewhat unsettled by his arrival, turned quickly to introduce them. "Ooma this is Mr. Rogers, he's Head of Security and he's here to ask us all some questions. Mr. Rogers, this is Ooma Lovee, our um, grandmother, well Sunny's grandmother and my, adopted mother. And that's Lola and you've met Lorraine and Sunny, so, now that's over. Would you like some coffee?"

"I would love some, Ma'am. thank you."

"Um, we have swill and designer. Your choice."

Rogers looked at her as if he'd just discovered a gold nugget in a gravel pit. "Well, well, that's a first. I'm a swill man, never seem to have a choice, anymore."

"Our kind of guy, ladies. I still use my old percolator, and I think it's feelings are hurt by calling it swill, it really makes the best coffee, period!"

"I haven't had a good cup of perc since I left Tallahassee."

"Great. Black or milk? Sugar or?"

"Milk and lots of sugar, how's that for UnPC."

"Perfect. Please sit down. I'll only be a minute. Oh, can you sit down on duty? Never sure what the protocol is. And I watch every true crime show ever made."

Rogers chuckled. Highly unusual event during an interview such as this. "Well, I'm not exactly sure since it isn't in the training manuals for Head of Security, but I've been deputized to conduct these interviews. I was a Miami-Dade homicide detective for many years and the protocol always seemed to be more gut than fact. Never sit with a suspect or in a potentially threatening situation, but from my intuition about those present, I think I'm at little risk."

They all laughed and Edy motioned him over to the couches. Ooma led the way. "Edy dear, may I have a glass of water, please."

"No."

Rogers was startled, not knowing what to make of this, until Ooma and Edy laughed. Who the hell were these refreshing people? After Mikey and the Rothenstein offspring, this was completely unexpected. He didn't even really know why he had decided to go down and work his way back up, but he'd been told that Mrs. Lovee and her dog had been by the elevator and had panicked about something and that she had come here, so he just went with his gut, also any distance between him and THEM, on the Royalty Floor, felt like a reprieve.

He sat, his long legs and Ooma Lovee's long legs, filling the distance between the coffee table and the couches. Edy came back empty-handed and they all turned to look at her, even the dogs.

"Look, I know this isn't a social call, but I think we'll all be more relaxed and can talk better sitting around our kitchen table. Frankly, I'm only really comfortable schmoozing around a table that is close to food. So, let's do that. Okay?"

Roger grinned. Wide. Rogers hadn't grinned like that in years.

"Yes, ma'am." And he stood up and helped Ooma Lovee up and they all trotted over to the table, which was set up with swill, water, cookies and donuts.

Edy poured and they all sat down. Sunny was scoping him and his mother out following some kind of inner kid beam and both dogs were hovering around Rogers feet.

"Are they bothering you?" Edy seemed nervous and a little frazzled not unusual for her, but Sunny thought it was about this guy being there.

"Not at all. I love it. They smell my dog, it's not my charm."

They all laughed, and Rogers took a big slug of the best coffee he'd had in years. Edy, instinctively held up the plate of donuts. Glazed. Hot damn-it. His long-lost favorites. They all waited, eyes on him, not sure who should begin whatever this was. Were they, in fact suspects? Must be. Edy found this to be hilarious. And rather exciting.

"Well now, this is so unexpected after the morning I've had, I only wish it wasn't going to have to get serious now and I don't know if you have any idea what is going......"

Sunny interrupted. "Sorry to interrupt, but we do know. I got it off the internet before they shut everything down, but, you know, there are ways of bypassing stuff and it was on TV before they blacked us out. We haven't told anyone else, though. Honest."

"Well, young lady, Sunny, I appreciate the information, so we'll skip that part, and just move on to anything, however seemingly unrelated you might know about possible motives, gossip, anything at this point would be helpful. I think I'd like to start with Mrs. Lovee who I believe had some sort of incident outside the Rothenstein's elevator this morning. Please try to remember any detail, however small."

Ooma sighed, all encounters with police held horrible memories for her and she had to remind herself this was Miami, not Czechoslovakia and she had nothing to hide.

Rogers sat up straighter as if preparing to move into interview mode and they all seemed to sense this, and sat up as well, even the dogs. "So, Mrs. Lovee, if I can start with you. Can you tell me about this morning?"

He could see the fear in her eyes, and her mouth tighten. This made no sense to him, but he made a mental note of it.

"Really, Mr. Rogers, I do not have much to tell you. I always take Lola out very early for a walk and I live on the same floor as the Rothenstein children and the entrance to their private elevator is at the end of our hall, next to the resident's elevator. Lola always runs ahead, she loves her morning outing, but this morning when she reached the end of the hall in front of their elevator, she became very agitated, almost hysterical. She was flipping upside down and barking and panting, almost frothing at the mouth. Her eyes were bulging out and then she was howling! Japanese Chins are very highly strung, but she has never behaved like this. At first, I thought she was having a stroke or a seizure, but the moment I picked her up and headed for the other elevator she started to calm down.

"I was operating completely on instinct. I think, well, from the war, I have old instincts about danger, and I know that may sound very silly, but it is how many of us survived and I just ran to Edy, away from something that felt like evil.

"And, it turns out, I was right. And that is all I know. I saw nothing, or no one. No sounds or anything unusual. And Edy and Sunny were still in bed and we've all been sequestered here ever since. I wish I could be more helpful."

"Well, you never know what turns out to be helpful. Dogs have very keen smellers, we all know that. Lola may have smelled death or even a fragrance or other fluids. Did you know the Rothensteins well?"

Ooma laughed, a dry, mirthless laugh. "I don't think people like the Rothensteins know themselves, *knew* themselves very well, so how anyone could else. I certainly observed them and understood their insecurity and ambition and such.

"That kind of maniacal drive for more and more, relentless questing, and they were not nice, they treated the people who served them very harshly and I cannot abhor that or their values, which may sound strange considering I live here, too, but well, that's not part of this investigation."

"Got it. This is very helpful, and I don't want to tire you, but I would like to ask you some more questions a bit later, if that's alright?"

"Certainly. This is, obviously very upsetting and I do feel rather tired, but I'll try my best."

"I appreciate it, ma'am. I'm coming into this pretty mystified myself, so I haven't had much time to prepare. Mrs. Weller, can I ask you next. I know you didn't see anything, but any insight into the family would be very useful."

"It's Edy and it's Ms. and I'm not sure you really want me to start blabbing about Bride of Rothenstein and, I guess you've interviewed Rebecca, the anorexic midget spawn and Sergi, the Soviet steroid stud."

Rogers wiped almost spurted coffee on his chin, "Bride of Rothenstein? Now, Ms. Edy that is funny. Never apologize for being funny. Ever. Or honest."

"Mom!" He's going to think you did it!"

"Hello? If I did it would I be dumb enough to call them that? Mr. Rogers, you're the expert!"

Rogers was enjoying this far more than he should be, "Well, now that could be true or you could be using reverse psychology, if you were diabolically cunning, trying to throw me off by saying something that would elicit that response."

Sunny clapped her hands. "Wow, you've met your match!"

Edy could feel the heat of embarrassment rising into her head, a very unusual feeling for her. "Look, I am what you might call a contrarian, I've always thought all that stuff about not speaking ill of the dead was ridiculous. I mean, better when they can't hear it! They were awful people, who did some good stuff, philanthropy-wise, but I always think people who are that rich and sort of do it for personal puffing up and dressing up and strutting around all those horrific galas and becoming local celebrities, not necessarily out of really caring about good causes and the daughter, is a mean, scary chick. So there. But, I'm one of a very large cast of on-lookers who feel the same way and I have no motive, none of us do, but I probably should just tuck in and be quiet-add a little "Go with God tag line, but God would have changed all the locks by now."

"Sunny, your Mom is something. You're a lucky young lady."

It was Sunny's turn to blush. "Yah, I know and I'm her kid for sure, but I don't want our big mouths to get us into trouble. We're weird enough to the other inhabitants."

"Well, I'm just starting my interviews, but I can pretty much assure you, that is not going to be the fact. Probably very much the opposite."

Edy was staring at him as if she had never seen a man before. She had almost disconnected with the fact that she was being seen and others were present. Sunny, was on it, instantly. "Mom, Mom! What is wrong with you? You're out of it!"

Edy snapped back into an appropriate social posture. "Oh boy, sorry, I didn't mean to stare, it's a writer's blindness, sometimes my head just goes into musing mode. I was just thinking about Rebecca Rothenstein and her brother and what this all means. Rebecca is one of those consuming narcissists, histrionic personality disorder or something? What's that great quote, 'she has to be the bride at every wedding and the corpse at every funeral.' And that thug she's married to, he treats her like she was the Princess and the Pea, which is how her parents treated her. I guess I'm sort of ruling them out, well maybe not Sergi, I mean, he has a pretty strange deal and no power or money of his own, but she, no way. She and her mother were like Hagar and her bastard, inseparable.

"And Arnold and Goldy, well, I barely knew them, but I mean, they are really religious, always quoting from the Torah and well, all those commandments, or as Sunny calls them "suggestions." I hope you're not religious! Anyway, he would never break the biggies like, "Thou Shall Not Kill" and "Honor Thy Father and Thy Mother, just no way." Also, from what we do know, the parents had already given them huge trust funds plus enormous salaries, and careers and those condos, what would be the motive? Now, on this floor there are people who work for them and get to live in one of the units, I'm pretty sure rent-free and they are quite a trio. I think they could be of interest. I know I'm doing a half-ass version of profiling here, sorry, it is really fascinating. Human nature is my passion, so sorry if I'm over-stepping!"

"Not at all, this is just about what has been going through my mind. Maybe I should deputize you!"

Their eyes met and Sunny and Ooma both noted it.

The awkward moment was saved by Roger's beeper. "Please excuse me, ladies, I've gotta take this." He got up from the table and moved into the entrance hall. It was Mikey.

"Hey Roy, my man, how's it shakin?"

"Very early, but very interesting. I'm with Mrs. Lovee and her adopted daughter and granddaughter. She's the lady whose dog flipped out at the elevator and I interviewed the son and his wife. Quite a family."

"I don't envy you. Anyway, I wanted to check in and let you know I've talked to the hospital and my niece is alert enough for you to talk to her and the maid is still here, I'd talk to her first and then maybe take a break and get over to the hospital and interview Leena while she's calm and before they have to give her more meds."

"Okay, I do need a little more time in here and then I'll go see the housekeeper. Is she still down there with my guys?"

"Yeah. Pretty chatty, clearly still strung out, but we're learning a lot about their routine, friends, habits, what a family! Like some demented reality show."

"I can't wait. See you later. Where are you?"

"I'm at the morgue with the ME. Wanna trade?"

"Naw. I'll take the talking, blood flowing gang, for now."

Rogers clicked off and turned to see all eyes, canine and human glued to him.

Edy poured more coffee, not quite understanding what was happening to her. Any updates you can tell us about?"

Rogers sighed and lowered his long limbs back into the comfort around him. Man, he'd love another donut, but his belly would rebel later. "Well, I have to go interview their housekeeper and Leena, the dog walker, anything you ladies know about them would be helpful."

Ooma took a sip of water. "I don't really know the housekeeper, she's Ukrainian, I believe and she's very professional, always on time, I see her come in and so is the young girl, the dog walker. Sometimes she walks Rebecca's dogs too and I've talked to her about walking Lola for me. When it's too hot, it is hard for me to do it and my housekeeper has too much to do. I've never heard either of them say anything personal or disrespectful about anyone in the family, too smart for that. Leena is a lovely young lady, very focused and hard-working and I don't think she has an easy time. Too much responsibility for someone so young. I know the Rothensteins trusted them, they had access that very few people had."

Edy nodded. "Lorraine hated those dogs, so if we were all out for a walk, I had to hold him very tightly, but everyone did except Leena, she just seemed to love them, or at least feel sorry for them. I'd see her trying to train them, but that was pretty hopeless. What about you. Sunny, do you know anything about them?"

Sunny made a face, as if trying to conjure up some interesting tidbit to add. "Nope. I've said hi to Leena. She went to my high school, she's older, maybe eighteen. I was a freshman when she was a senior. I know her dad disappeared long ago, and her mom is very sick and there are issues with her brother, maybe drugs or maybe he's got some health stuff so she sort of carries the load, but I don't really know her at all. She always seems really serious and sweet and she works really hard. You know, Mr. Rogers, I keep thinking you should talk to my friend Oscar, he knows everything that goes on here."

Rogers put down his coffee, feeling that extra surge of adrenaline that said, "Enough caffeine." "Oscar? You mean my deputy Pepe's son Oscar?"

"Yep."

"He's thirteen years old!"

"And he's a genius. He's in my high school and he's my best friend. His mother is Olivia Tan, the Medical Examiner. They're divorced but his dad really raises him, and he hangs out here all the time. He's a total computer geek. Unbelievable and because of his mom, he's really into all kinds of forensic stuff, too, and he helps your guys with the security system and the computers. He's really cool. And he knows the camera system, too. I don't know, just a thought. Also, would it be alright if he came up here? He's helping me set up some new software."

"Sure. But not until we can turn your techno stuff back on."

Sunny rolled her eyes. "Mr. Rogers trust me, Oscar can hack into the CIA probably. I'm sure he knows everything about what's going on here. Worth a shot, right?"

Rogers laughed. "Well, Sunny, it most certainly is. And I'm coming back to finish this as soon as I talk to the housekeeper and before I talk to anyone else."

Edy got up to see him out. "Do you eat grilled cheese sandwiches or are you a vegan or something? If you come back in a couple of hours, I'll have lunch on. I happen to make a killer grilled cheese." She heard herself say this and could barely believe these words were coming out of her very own mouth; without looking she knew Sunny and Ooma were exchanging puzzled glances.

"I will do my best, since that's my favorite sandwich and I thank you for turning a very unpleasant morning into a treat." Edy entered the codes and opened the door and as he left, he turned and smiled at her and she knew something that had never happened to her before in her fifty-eight years had happened. She had fallen in love.

Rogers checked his watch after the door closed behind, leaving him feeling as if his innards had just been run through a spin cycle. Damn, it was already after ten and he hadn't made a dent, but then again, maybe he'd found out a lot more useful info that he could absorb. He licked his bottom lip and could taste the donut glaze and the coffee he'd almost spit all over the table. *Bride of Rothenstein.*

He whistled through the small gap in his front teeth, pushed the codes and took out his security elevator key card, feeling sort of light-headed, his heart was beating too fast. Perc coffee could do that, but it was something else; he felt as if a power surge, some sort of electrical current of strange, intense emotion was snapping through him. He'd never felt anything even remotely like it. What in the grits and gravy had happened in there? He tried to take a deep breath and couldn't. But he knew, the way you just know, he heard a lyric in his head, "Bewitched, bothered and bewildered..." it was her. Edy. Edy. He was done. She had him. And it was mutual. He just knew it. What a thing!

He shook his head, snapping himself out of this bizarre emotional trap door and tried to re-focus on the next step. He looked at his list. Katya and then the hospital and then, the rest of the list. Oh, Oscar. Definitely, if it was okay with Pepe. Who would have thought that Dr. Tan, the toughie, brilliant ME had been married to Pepe! He certainly was manly enough, but such a low key, gentle guy, really. Well, that was probably the attraction. The elevator opened and he was back on his turf. Pepe saw him and came over.

"She's in your office. Very nervous and she really wants to go home. Likes to talk, though, no problem there, but you have to keep her on subject, or she'll wander off onto random topics."

"Got it. I know her a bit. Even quiet ladies tend to get pretty chatty when they're excited and scared. And you never know what's going to be important. Oh, I've been told I should talk to Oscar, seems he has a rather major rep as the kid genius on site. Is that okay with you and his mother? Just found out it's Dr. Tan. Would have been helpful to know that!"

"I never had the chance and before today it hardly seemed important!"

"Yeah, sorry. Who could have dreamed up this cattle drive!"

He poured a couple of glasses of water and headed for his office.

Rogers handed the agitated housekeeper a glass and motioned for her to sit down. "My name is Rogers, Mrs. Orlov very sorry to keep you waiting so long. I know you must be exhausted, and I'll try to finish this up as quickly as possible, but since there were no witnesses, you and Miss Martinez are very important to the investigation and we must take our time and get this right."

He watched her reaction, seeing her perk up. Women like Katya, who served people like the Rothensteins were not used to being treated as equals or, sometimes even as people. She was a veteran of this behavior and all those refugee years, moving from Ukraine, to Germany, to England and then here. She sat up straighter, being addressed with dignity, was clearly unique and calming to her. She sipped the water and waited for him to guide her.

"Please, Ma'am just feel free to start anywhere and try to remember any detail and also, I'm interested in any information about the Rothensteins. You have nothing to fear now, they are no longer your employers."

"This is true, but their children, they are the bosses now, so please, can you promise me, whatever I say, they will not know about it?"

"You have my word."

Katya sighed, his reassurance opening the damn of years of pent up resentments and opinions. "So, I will tell you the truth. I did not like these people. "I work for both of them for many years and they paid me good, I had benefits, I cannot complain about that, even if I did not ever get a bonus or raise or Xmas present or day off for special events, not even when my mother was dying and then my brother.

"It was a good job. They were both, when they were together, very particular. They never used the same towel twice. And their sheets had to be changed every day! But they had a laundress to do that, it would have been impossible for me. And Mrs. Rothenstein, she bought very expensive clothes, and everything had to be perfect all the time. Her closets are bigger than my house! But, that is how rich people are and I am used to it. They need us and we need them. Sooo," she sighed and took another sip of water.

"They trusted me and when they separated, they fought over me! So, I was split in two, but that was actually easier. Mr. Rothenstein was nice to me, would even give me little gifts, chocolates or some lovely vodka, he knew I liked it, that never happened when they were together.

"He was also immaculate about his clothes and he bathed at least twice, sometimes three times a day, but part of that was, I must be truthful, because of the women. His "assistants," she stopped and laughed at herself, "one is Russian, so I know the type. Big joke they make behind his back. But, he was an old man and he needed the help to have the sex. I never see this, but I did the cleaning, so you can understand."

"And they had so many antiques and Mr. Rothenstein was crazy for each piece of furniture. I always was afraid I would damage something or break something.

"Mrs. Rothenstein, she was not so nice to me. Very rude, she thought I was just a servant, and she had different personalities depending on how important she thought a person was, she wasn't mean, just, how you would say, cold, not friendly. And her apartment had with all this crazy stuff. I could never understand any of it. I had to clean the art and she was very fussy, but the things, you couldn't tell if they were junk or what. Silly, stupid things--old furniture stacked up with plastic boxes under it. Mounds of dirt, with buckets and old tools on the floor, pieces of wood with big nails and paint splattered all over it, ugly paintings, some were just blank, I could do it, my grandchildren could do it; one was just a piece of canvas painted gray!

"One 'sculpture,' she called it, was a false leg with a pink sock and tennis shoe and part of some animal attached to it, and when they would be delivered, like after Art Basel, the artists would come and I and the chef, we would have to make a very fancy dinner and no one could leave until very late. The poor chef and the laundress, if Mrs. Rothenstein was eating alone, they had to serve her and then sit and wait in the kitchen until she was finished and then clear her one plate and martini glass. She would never lift even a plate herself!

"And she would not talk directly to any of us. Her assistant was also an executive for their company and we reported to her. You must talk with her; she is from Cuba, I believe, and she also works for the children at times. So many people come and go, but she has been here many years.

"They had people spying on us, we knew, so we never spoke bad about them, except in our homes. They were very powerful and if we were fired, they could make it quite difficult to find another job. We were afraid.

"Not like Ukraine, but still, not very safe. If I told you how much she paid for some of that "art" you would not believe me! We could save an entire village in my country for one of those ugly things."

"I've seen the apartment. Never saw anything quite like it before, I admit. Must have been hard to dust it all or whatever and not start laughing."

Katya smiled for the first time revealing two missing teeth on the upper front sides of her mouth. Rogers felt sad for her. So many people he worked with went back to Brazil, or Columbia or Budapest or Dominican Republic, to get their teeth fixed because no one could afford Miami dental prices.

"Yes, it was, I waited until I was home and then I could tell my stories to my children and my husband and sisters."

"Now, that was very helpful, I appreciate it. I know it's still quite fresh, but I need you to walk me through exactly what you remember about this morning. It's very important and at some point, I'm going to need you and Leena to go back up there with me and walk us through, but not today."

"If we must. I never want to go there again, but Mrs. Dubinski has already asked if I would stay and help them. I believe they are going to have to sell everything, but I don't know any more. I told her I didn't think I could, but I don't want to be fired. I have no other job now."

"So, this morning you arrived at exactly 6:45 and what did you see?"

"I heard Leena, before I saw anything. I heard her crying and screaming, and I run inside, and I see her on the floor, she had been sick, and she was hysterical.

"She tell me, Don't look. Don't look! Such a sweet girl, trying to protect me, but I am strong and of course, I didn't know they were dead. I thought someone might need help. So, I run to Mr. Rothenstein first, and you know, I saw him and it was horrible. I knew he was gone, so I ran the other way and found her and then I panicked, maybe the maniac was still there. I want to get us out quickly! I call police and then I helped Leena up and we ran. Out, out of that horrible place. And that is all I can tell you."

"Did anything look out of order? Missing?"

"I cannot say, because it was all like a blur; not that I noticed quickly. But they had so many things and I did not go into Mrs. Rothenstein's dressing rooms where she kept her jewels and things. I don't know. I think they had big safes but hidden and she always had a great deal of money in the apartment. I would see big piles lying around and I told her that was not smart, and she would leave very expensive jewelry just out on her dressing table and I told her about that, well I told her assistant. I was not supposed to speak to her directly, but her assistant would just sigh and say, Mrs. Rothenstein told her, it's all insured, if someone takes anything, they will go to jail and I'll just get some more." She shook her head and put down her water.

"You know, Mr. Rogers, this part of Miami, Sunny Isles, they call it Little Moscow. I read that there are more than sixty Russian residents with Russian passports who have bought hundreds of millions of dollars of real estate here, many of them Russian government officials, many Ukrainians too, some have been charged with the money laundering of and receiving stolen property, many are linked to the Russian Mafia and then there are the Panamanians and Columbians and Brazilians, some big drug people. Miami is full of these people and there are all kinds of things that go on.

"I don't know about who owns these apartments. But, it could be part of some scheme. So much money is here! I will say, I never saw such people with the Rothensteins, except they went to so many big parties and everyone is mixed up together, no one is exactly who they seem to be, I think. I don't know but I saw enough of this in my own country. But, please, do not make me talk more about this. I am afraid someone will find out my name and think I said something! Please!"

"I promise. And I will have an officer escort you home and I'm going to try and have some security assigned to you and Ms. Martinez for a while, until we know what we're dealing with here."

Roger stood up, releasing her from the tension of her truth.

"Thank you, sir. I wish I knew more. This is very terrible. I just want to take a bath and wash all this ugliness off of me."

"He shook her hand, which was warm and soft in spite of all the years of working with them, and he gently guided her to the door.

CHAPTER 9

After Rogers left, I knew I needed to have some alone time, to try and get a hold of what felt like stepping on a live wire, not that I really know what that would feel like or even exactly what it means. I turned around to face two human sets and two canine sets of eyes all evaluating me as If I had suddenly developed some bizarre physical change, a limp, a twitch, a nosebleed. I knew they knew! Worse, no one said anything. I was not going to fill this in and proceeded in silence to clear the table and get ready to make lunch.

"Edy darling, do you think it would be alright for me to call Maria and see if they will let her come down and help us clean up and make up the guest room? If you don't mind, I think I'd like to stay here tonight. I'm a bit afraid to go back up and be there alone."

This was a welcome reprieve. "Mind? This is your apartment!" Of course, you can, and if Maria can come that might be very comforting for her, too. They don't seem to know about her, but she doesn't know anything, does she?"

"No, no. I don't think she has ever even met the Rothensteins, though Rebecca yelled at her once for letting Lola off her leash in the hallway. Her English is very poor, so she tries to keep to herself as much as possible."

"Sounds like a good idea even if it's our first language! I, um,

I think I'm going to take a shower and freshen up before I make lunch. Sunny, can you please finish clearing up the coffee stuff."

Sunny was focusing all her attention on me, and I knew she saw right through my attempt at evasion. "No problem, mom. I specialize in "swill" clean-ups."

"Very funny. And if you could get the cheese and stuff out for the sandwiches, that would be great."

"Sure. Maybe Oscar can come up, too. Your new 'friend' might be able to talk to him here and he loves our grilled cheese. And since when do you freshen up before lunch?"

"When a double murder gets me out of bed at practically dawn and I haven't even brushed my teeth! Not that I should have to justify a shower and would you both stop staring at me!"

They responded at once, which only confirmed my observations. I practically bolted into the only safe zone I have ever had, my own room. And then, I went onto auto pilot performing a series of out of character activities. I showered, washed my hair, normal, but then I lathered myself with lotions shaved my legs and under arms, put tanning cream on white neglected limbs; blow dried my hair and attempted to use a long-discarded curling tool. And then (this would be the confirmation of my state of mind), I opened the drawer stuffed with makeup and beauty aids that Ooma was always dumping on me, not very subtle hints in her on-going efforts to glam me up and applied make-up as best I could. I pulled out my long dormant pair of Spanx leggings and struggled into them, adding a form fitting, as it were, black tee shirt and sandals with just enough of a platform to escape total slipper mode and took several long deep breaths as song lyrics pounded in my head. "I took one look at you, that's all I meant to do and then my heart stood still." Oh brother! What I couldn't know then, of course was that he was doing the exact same thing, not the make-up and Spanx part, just the songs. A knock at my door. I jumped as if the still unknown maniac was about to shove footwear into my eyeballs. (Yes, I do have all that information and since you do, too, my reader, I can share).

"Yes. Just a minute. Who is it?"

"Who is it? Mom? Really?"

Sunny opened the door and marched right in and I thought how unequal our relationship was, If I barged into her room without waiting for permission to enter, she'd be irate. Whatever it is that teenage girls do in there, I never did, but then, I don't remember my mother ever entering my room much, anyway.

"What is it?"

Sunny was looking at me as if I'd just undergone some intense surgical renovation. "What?"

"Holy shit. Mom. You're wearing make-up and your hair is curled. We're right. You like him! OMG, Mom! This is too hilarious! I thought you were gender neutral. I even clipped an article about it, because I was thinking of doing it, too. Third gender so no one would bother me, and I wouldn't have to deal with all that boy and love and sex stuff, since you never have."

Now, this got my attention away from "beware my foolish heart" to the reality before me, and what was at stake here.

"Oh, baby, really? That makes me so sad. Come sit down here for a minute. God, how selfish; I never thought you'd think of me like that, but I, the world's changed so much. Believe me, I never intended to end up as a third gender, unisex what do you call yourself? Is there a name? Third gender is far too impersonal; that door never opened, honey. I didn't have room with all the scrambling and loss and just trying to put a life together and then, well you and Lorraine, sort of filled so many needs, I just let go of all that other stuff, not even in my dreams!

"Wow! I can see how it must have seemed to you, you have absolutely no role model for a man/woman, relationship! So, I guess seeing me, sort of fluttering around, must really feel scary or what? Believe me, I share your shock! But pa-leeze don't let my fear or avoidance or whatever it is influence your life!

"You're a teenage girl and you're beautiful and sexy even if you don't want to be. I think you're just afraid of it all. Turning into a woman, is very challenging and boys are totally nerve-racking, even I remember that.

"I guess I had such nerdy, low self-esteem I didn't believe it was even possible for any one of them who wasn't completely revolting to be interested in me, so I just sort of turned off. But, well, don't roll your eyes, but before you entered my life, I did have affairs and romances, just none of them ever went anywhere, for various reasons. I don't know, this man came into the room and the lights went on. Is that too much to tell you?"

"No, Mom! What a relief! I didn't really want to be gender neutral, I don't like the clothes and there is this one boy. No, never mind, not going there. But, it would be so much easier to just not deal with any of it, like you've done."

"Oh baby, there is no easier, you pay for everything. Now I feel bad about Lorraine. Maybe he really wants to be a boy dog!"

"Mom, he's fine. I don't think he knows it's a girl's name. He's smart, but, he's a dog!"

"Okay, that may be a little out there. I'm sort of dangling somewhere in outer space right now, so please don't make a big deal out of my fixing up! Ooma is going to be all over it and now I'm just completely self-conscious and embarrassed and I'm going to make lunch."

"Good idea. Rogers called. He's going to come back after he visits Leena at the hospital and it's okay for Maria to come down and Oscar to come up. So, it's almost like a little party."

"Now I'm really nervous!"

"It's cool. I'll help."

Sunny came over and let me hug her and kissed me and I held her tight and inhaled all of her sweet smells and warmth and the miracle of her. "I love you so and I'm sorry I couldn't have given you a more normal family. I know you wanted one."

"Mom, we've been there. I'm so over all that."

But I could tell in the way she strutted out of the room, that she had let go of a burden she'd been carrying. And I couldn't help but wonder, if this, whatever it was got something unstuck. "*Blue Moon, you saw me standing alone.*" Oh boy, whatever was going to happen next, I was now completely off my self-protective or stunted grid.

CHAPTER 10

When Rogers pulled up at the hospital, Mikey was there and so was, what seemed like, the entire Miami press corps. By now reporters from all over the country were arriving. This was going to be one of those news cycle filling murders that keep journalists busy for months.

Mikey was being interviewed, practically levitating with his ego feed. How in the hell they all knew about Leena and were on the scene was a clear indication that there was no way to keep anything private in this investigation, or maybe any investigation, anymore. He parked and made his way right past Mikey and into the lobby, which was guarded by enough uniforms to keep even the most aggressive reporters outside.

Mikey did not acknowledge him, he knew him better and also, he certainly wasn't interested in sharing the spotlight.

He waited inside, trying to get some new info from Mikey's deputy. The ME was still working on the bodies, but Leena was awake and had no idea of the media presence or how important she was to their investigation.

Rogers didn't know what Mikey had told her, but he hoped he'd been smart enough to talk to her like an uncle and not do the interview. He saw Mikey do his little sign off wave and enter the lobby, chest pumped outward like a small Hispanic rooster.

"Hey, Roy! Great timing. Can you believe that shit? They all know everything! No way to even plug these leaks, way too high profile and bizarre. I gotta get back to the morgue. The Doc just called, I think she's done so meet me there when you're through. My niece is a trooper and I told her you were simpatico. I think she wants to talk, now. Too much to keep inside. My associate will take you up. See ya later."

Rogers followed the detective, who seemed fairly disgruntled at Mikey's hogging all the credit and attention when most of them knew they would do all the work and provide the brain power.

The detective turned to leave Rogers at the guarded door to Leena Martinez's room, without shaking hands. Rogers knew this was someone who might well be easier to work with than Mikey, so he reached his hand out, and stopped him.

"Sorry, I don't even know your name, detective. I left before you moved up. I guess we're both sort of thrown into the fray here."

The detective, who looked like just about every career cop over forty Rogers had ever met, proving once again that all the clichés we see in the movies or on TV, are true, studied him with wary, tired eyes and held out his hand. "Yeah, I think so. Phil Mooney. Heard a lot about you, sort of a legendary fella. Nice to meet you. Sorry for the attitude. It's been quite a morning."

"Yeah, I get it. Nice to meet you, too Phil. I'll be in touch."

The big, out of shape figure in the brown suit only a cop would dare wear in a city like Miami, gave him a quick salute and lumbered off and Rogers went in to see the main observer of the minor massacre.

Rogers approached the bed in the cool, dark room, as quietly as he could. Her eyes were closed, her face framed by a mass of thick black curls, her clear light skin, revealing no trace of her Hispanic heritage was moist and almost transparent.

He stood beside the railing for a moment trying to check for anything unusual. She had been examined already and any samples under her nails or blood spatter, had been taken. No guns used, so no powder residue, not that she was a suspect, but they had to check everyone for anything. She looked, he thought, like a wax figure of a sleeping Madonna one might see in a local church. He waited, trying to get a feel for where to start and then she opened her eyes wide and startled and he instinctively moved slightly back.

Her eyes were very large and dark with almost back lit white corneas and she blinked several times as if trying to bring him into focus.

She spoke first, which he found to be a relief. "You're Mr. Rogers. My uncle told me you were coming, and I've seen you around the building."

"Yes, miss. Sorry I haven't had the pleasure of meeting you properly and I know this is not a great time, but I'm sure Mikey told you, I have to ask you for all the information you can remember about this morning and anything else you can tell me."

"She nodded, tears sliding down her cheeks. Everything about her, the loveliness of her face, the symmetry of her features, the biblical hair, should have made her beautiful, but Rogers couldn't help thinking, somehow, she wasn't quite beautiful.

Why this bothered him, he couldn't say, except it didn't make sense; certainly pretty, but something was missing. Maybe emanating from inside, the years of stuffing and having to be so mature and never really having a childhood, or so it seemed from what he'd heard, but it had altered her right to her beauty.

He had seen this before in both men and women, once that missing link inside them was opened, shooting up into consciousness, the unburdening that truth brought, an almost magical transformation could take place physically, releasing their true and full beauty, even in people not nearly as lovely as Leena Martinez.

He cleared his throat, wishing he had brought some water with him and she seemed to note this, an instinct to help, to put the needs of others first, that he'd observed in nearly everyone he'd ever met on cases or in his personal life, who had either by nature or lack of nurture, the compulsion to put everyone else's needs first. A constant hyper vigilance that bound their fears, their anxiety of somehow not giving enough, and thus, not being valued enough.

"There's a pitcher of water by the sink and some glasses if you're thirsty."

Wow. World class co-dependent personality type for sure. Perfect for someone who would be loving to animals and be able to handle high maintenance people like the Rothensteins and offspring.

"Thank you, Miss Martinez, you must be a mind-reader as well as a dog walker. A lot of talking and it's either too humid and hot outside or too dry and cold inside."

He reached the sink in a few long strides and poured a glass of hopefully, uncontaminated water. "May I bring you one as well?"

She shook her head slightly and didn't answer.

Rogers found this rather interesting. Clearly, she felt it unnecessary with him to over-do the pleasing posture, not that she would have any idea that was part of what motivated her selflessness. Boy, he was really into this amateur psych evaluation, but he'd done so many of these interviews and read so much and sometimes he just knew.

This also gave him a better idea of how to interview her.

"There's a chair over there, Mr. Rogers, please sit down."

His point was being proved. "Thank you, I think I will. Very kind of you."

A slight pink rose in her cheeks. "You're welcome."

She was quiet again, waiting for him to begin. Reverential, to his rank and age.

There was nothing of the usual teenage girl about her. No attitude, hostility or patronizing, inner eye rolling about how much more they knew about everything than any older people, parents, teachers, cops, the world. Old school, all the way, was her deal.

Probably the kid who teachers loved, and the other kids made fun of until they needed her for something, which she would always provide. He felt sad for her, but he also knew that like her, had little volcanic embers sparking inside them and either they spent their entire lives dousing it or, one way or another, they got strong enough and mad enough to free themselves of the terrible pleasure of being "perfect" and selfless and robotic about their own dependency needs. He took a long gulp of water, wondering how much of what he was thinking was his own projection from his own youth and the prices he had paid.

"How about we just start with a little personal history. Your age, where you live, how long you've worked there, school, whatever else led you to the Rothensteins and where else you are currently working and for who."

She smiled a soft, gentle smile revealing perfect teeth, not yet in need of cheap foreign dental work.

"No offense, Mr. Rogers, but I'm not very interesting and I don't really like to talk about myself, it's sort of rude, you know? No one ever asks me, so, I don't even know if I can tell you much. My uncle has probably told you most of it."

"I understand, but please try and I am interested, and it may be very helpful in solving this crazy case, so it would mean a lot to me, if you could try." He knew this was the best approach with her, but he felt guilty at the manipulation of it, usually he wasn't interrogating delicate and decent young women.

"I do want to help! It's just so horrible! I'm eighteen and I have always worked Mr. Rogers. My mother is an invalid and my brother is, well, it's very private, please, we don't talk about it; he's bi-polar and he's also had lots of medical and substance issues. My father, I never really knew. I mean he's my uncle's brother, but he left when I was tiny, and my mother just couldn't cope. My grandmother took care of us, but she was old, she died. So, I've always just gone to school and worked part-time. I love animals and someday, if I can save enough money, I'd like to be a vet, but that may be impossible. And now..."

Before Rogers could offer any words of empathy, Leena started to cry, hard now, putting her hands over her face, her long, well-shaped fingers that showed no evidence of years of dog walking and hard work, covering her. "I'm so frightened. I need someone to go and check on my mother, she can't be alone, she needs her medicine and she has to know where I am and my brother can't deal with this and if he skips his meds, he gets crazy. Please, please I have to go home! And I can't lose my other jobs with the Rothensteins! I work at their country club as a bar back and pool attendant. I can't just not show up! They have such a waiting list and none of us are on full-time salaries, they don't do that, so they don't have to give benefits, you know, and I have to work!

"Please can someone talk to them. I asked my uncle, but he doesn't know them, and I don't know who to talk to. Mrs. Dubinski, we can't talk to her and there's a new manager at the club. I'm nothing to any of them, only to the Rothensteins, because of their dogs, but they're, they're Oh my God, it was so horrible. Poor Katya, she had to help me. I need to go home!"

Rogers pushed the buzzer by the bed hoping the nurse could

give her something to calm her down. He wanted nothing more than to put his arms around her and comfort her the way a father, if she had one worth shit would, but he knew that was impossible.

The nurse came in, far more quickly than he would have expected and he got up and went over to her. "She's pretty upset, and I need her to be calm enough to interview her, so we can let her go home. Can she have something?"

The nurse, who seemed motherly and not one of the bitchy power mad varieties that also filled the profession. "Absolutely. I was going to bring something, anyway. Her doctor left orders and it's been much longer but she was asleep, so I let her rest."

"Thanks."

"I have it here, I can give it to her right now."

They both walked back to the bed. Leena was still agitated, though she'd stopped crying and was watching them.

"I can't go back to sleep, please don't give me anything to make me sleep. I have to go home!"

Rogers knew it was time to shift gears just a little, from neutral to drive at least. "Leena, this will just calm you down, it won't put you to sleep, and it's important, because if you're too emotional, you won't be able to think clearly and the sooner we get through this, the sooner you can be discharged and I will escort you home, personally. There is a caregiver and an officer at your house, I thought Mikey would have told you that, so you don't have to worry. Your family is okay. But now, I need you to take the medication and drink some water and then I'll try and lead you through this as quickly as I can. Okay. Deal?"

She looked at him all the tears leaving no mark on her Madonna face. He wondered If she had any idea how pretty she was. Somehow, he didn't think so.

Leena Martinez nodded, calming down, well before the medicine had kicked in, proof of how powerful the presence of a trustworthy person is in any stressful situation.

And Rogers had learned, no matter how many "sensitivity training" courses the department might offer or require, it was really sort of intuitive responding, and the more aware the subject, the less likely they would be fooled by disingenuous "trust me" dialogue. Clearly, she trusted him enough. And this was a kid who probably knew the difference.

"Okay. Sorry, I'm so messed up right now. I do want to help."

"You're not gonna apologize for being human and having had a deeply traumatic shock, now are you?" He studied her to see how she reacted to what he'd said, her beautiful eyes blinking as if trying to clear her mind of any expected response, his validation of her experience, clearly an unusual occurrence for her.

"I guess. But, I'm not usually so blubbery in a crisis."

"Well, I think this was a little more than that, but let's get started so we can get you out of here. Let's start with your arrival this morning and try and tell me every single thing you remember and also anything different from your daily routine, and how they lived, the dogs, anything."

"OH My God, they drowned the puppies! I'd blocked that out!!! Oh, my poor little babies!"

"Leena, please, try to tell me in order, okay?"

"Yes, yes. I understand. Well, I arrived at 6:30 like I do every day, even on the weekends. I have all the codes. They trusted me and most of the other dog walkers and trainers quit or gave up, so I guess I was important to them in that way.

"I was always very quiet, because they were usually still asleep, or in their rooms anyway and I was told never to disturb them directly, to call Carmen, that's their business manager, if there was a problem. They usually never talked to the employees directly, well Mr. Rothenstein did once they separated, but even Mrs. Rothenstein, because it was their puppies, she would talk to me if she was up when I was there.

"I remember it was so silent, it felt weird, and the emergency lights that were always on all night were off. They turned off automatically at 7. I checked my watch and it was 6:30 and something just felt off.

"I always went into Mr. Rothenstein's side of the penthouse first, his three were always more active, they were different ages and they had collars with their names, they all looked so much alike, but I knew the difference. I don't want to sound conceited, but I think I was the only person they liked.

"They never barked at me and they wagged their little snubbed tails and got very excited when I put on their leashes. I would tell them to sit and they would! Then I would run over to Mrs. Rothensteins and get her three together. This was harder. They often had accidents and were more hyper and unruly and their leashes and things were very fancy and hard to put on them. But I had gotten it down to a sort of system and they knew I had treats waiting if they behaved.

"I grabbed the poop bags and then we all ran back, and I got their siblings and we went down the private elevator and out to the dog run and the lawns and the beach, when we could.

"No other dogs were allowed on the beach, except certain parts at certain times, but, of course, theirs were and Mrs. Dubinski's rescue dogs. They loved their time, but six dogs are very hard to handle, even tiny ones. And I had to be absolutely sure they left no trace of anything and then I'd pump them around, being careful they didn't overheat and then we'd go back up and I'd give them their treats, feed them, clean them and spray them with fragrance and take them back to their rooms. Mr. Rothenstein was meticulous, sort of a neat freak and he wanted them in their room, which was like a doggy day care, and they were usually pretty tired and calm after their meal and run, so it didn't take long. I'd replace the leashes and everything exactly how it was, fill their water bowls and tiptoe out."

"What about her dogs, while you did this?"

"Oh, sorry. I had to put her dogs in their room first, run over, and take care of his and then go back and do the same for hers but they had different food and special supplements, so it took longer and she wanted them in her bedroom when I was done, so I'd tiptoe across the apartment. It's really big, I guess you know that and I'd punch in her code and open the door and they would run in. She didn't care if they peed or pooped anywhere; poor Katya cleaned it all up, but I hated it, really bad to let them get away with that, so I did try and never bring them back until they'd done their business. I never went in her room, but Katya told me. And then I had to race to get over to their country club and go to work there."

"So, you were only there in the early mornings?"

"Oh, no. I went back at my lunch break and then after work, before I went to night school."

"Seven days a week?"

"Usually. Once in a while if my Mom was really sick or my brother had to be taken to the hospital, they would have Mrs. Dubinksi's lady come or one of their staff, but they really only wanted me to do it."

"I see. Well, you were there quite a bit. What did you observe, anyone suspicious, any fights or family incidents or strange visitors, anything at all out of the ordinary?"

Leena Martinez seemed to pause, as if fighting the fear and the medication, and choosing her words very carefully.

"Look, Mr. Rogers, I really want to help, but you have to understand, I still work for them, at least I hope I do! And if I say things about them, we all signed confidentiality agreements and they are very important, and they own most of the places and know most of the people who might become my clients. I'm hoping to start my own dog services business when I finish this course and my reputation is all I have and their recommendation and Mr. Arnold and Mrs. Dubinski really control that part of the business anyway and they, well, she especially is very hard to please and she fires people for nothing; for dropping a glass or bringing in a Starbuck's coffee container during the High Holy days, everyone is afraid of her. So, I'm scared it will come out that I spoke about them in any way! I guess I'm a coward."

"No, no, I really understand. Katya feels the same anxiety and I can only promise you, no one will ever know anything you tell us, but without your insights a very sick murderer will still be roaming around and may very well keep killing and if we can't solve this fast, it's unlikely we'll find him or them."

This made her sit up straighter. "I never thought of that! Katya did, she practically carried me out of there, she kept whispering, 'they may still be here, we have to go.' Do you think the killer was still there? Did he or they see us?"

"No, no. You can relax about that. And when we have the TOD, we'll be sure, but it seems there was no one there but you and then Katya until the police got there."

"That's very good to hear. What is TOD?"

"Time of Death, very important in murder cases."

"I see. She paused, clearly more relaxed, but her eyes were still darting as if looking for a way out.

"Now, Leena, I need you to tell me exactly as clearly as you can about this morning. You came in and what happened next?"

"Oh God! I saw him! It was horrible! I ran across to Mrs. Rothenstein and then I ran for the puppies to save them and, and they were just floating and then I just got sick and I was so terrified I couldn't move! It was like one of those nightmares when you try to run, to escape and you can't move! The rest is just a blur. I'm sorry!

"I don't know what else I can tell you. No one liked them, some were jealous, of course, he was a gentleman, but he was, rather creepy. All those young women in and out and sort of, well, affected? You know. He had almost a British kind of accent and he was from Brooklyn or something and very vain, but he was kind to me, asked about my family.

"Mrs. Rothenstein, well, no one liked her except her daughter, who adored her. They were always together. I kind of envied that, because my mother just isn't well enough to do things with me or even talk to me that much.

"Anyway, she was always running off to some event or party and getting fixed up, people coming in all the time to massage her, and do her hair and make-up and bring her new clothes to try, personal shoppers I think they're called and her charity board ladies, lots of people in and out. But, I was told to stay out of the way and keep the dogs away because they were so wild. She paused and laughed.

"I know it's bad to laugh now, with this tragedy, but she had a special spa team who came and gave the dogs massages and acupuncture and aromatherapy treatments. It cost a fortune and it was totally insane! I think the people were complete frauds. They would close the door to their room and turn off the lights and burn incense candles, but the dogs would bark and pee on them and I overhead them cursing at them and I think one of them kicked little Tilly, not that she probably didn't deserve it. I could have paid for a year's supply of my brother's medication for what she spent on them every week. But she never walked them or feed them. Ever! I can't say anymore. Please don't make me."

"I think this is enough for now unless there's anything else you can remember about this morning or any unusual events in the past few days?"

He could see her struggling with this question, wanting to tell him something and not sure if it was really safe to trust him.

"Well, there were a couple of things, but I was the only person there, so the family will know it was me who told you!"

"Leena, I promise, we know how to deal with that and besides, they want to find out who did this as much as we do, you don't suspect them, do you?"

She gasped and seemed to struggle to get her breath, "Oh no, no! they are not very good people in many ways, but not like that. Never! They loved them! It was the kind of bond I think families like that have to have because they are the only ones they can really trust, you know?

"Everyone wants something! Whatever issues they had, they were a closed circle, which is why, I think when Mr. Rothenstein wanted to separate and all those women and everything, it was very difficult for her. She was not a warm person, but I think it was because she was so hurt inside, maybe for a very long time and they weren't bad to their children! They had that sense of family being the most important thing, even if they aren't religious like Mr. Arnold. No! Never. There was the world and then there was their family. And they would never do anything like that! I will be haunted for my whole life by what I saw there. They had everything and look what happened. So, I'm trying to be more positive about my life. I only work for wealthy people, we all do, and none of it seems to make them very happy, not that being poor does, either."

"I know you're very tired, Ms. Martinez, but please do try and answer my question."

"I will, but I am worried, because you know.... Mr. Rothenstein had someone in his office when I went to get the dogs for their mid-day walk. It was a woman, I didn't really recognize the voice, but the door was closed and the dogs were barking, so it could have been one of his girlfriends or his assistants, who, I don't know this, but the gossip was they were also his girlfriends. They were yelling at one another, something about 'promises' and money. They were both very angry. I didn't see either of them. I was embarrassed and I waited in the dog's room until I heard her leave and then I grabbed their leashes and rushed out. He didn't see me, and I don't know if he even knew I was in there.

"And Mrs. Rothenstein and Mr. Rothenstein had a big fight last week about some woman, I think and that he wanted to sell or something and she threatened him, kind of sounded like blackmail; he would give her something or she would tell something. I think he wanted to leave, marry someone or maybe just be really free. I heard him say "Sell everything!" And that made her very upset. Crazy mad. And after, her art person, her friend who lives down stairs, he came up to comfort her. I was with the dogs and it was after their nighttime walk. I think she was drinking a lot, I don't think she was even aware of me being in there. I never heard anything like that before, but, you know, it's life; very complicated, all families are so crazy, loco, we call it, you know. Every family has troubles, Mr. Rogers and they don't murder one another, well they do, but not so often."

Rogers chuckled. Quite a clear-headed young woman, growing up way too fast, but that seemed to be an epidemic now, thanks to social media and, all those extra expectations their parents put on them. Every one of them, rich or poor, was supposed to be special and make a fortune before they were twenty-five. Even if it was only for being a savant video game player, super surfer or having a huge butt. No one could get old and no one could be ordinary. All evidence to the contrary.

"Miss Martinez, you are a very special young woman and I know this was frightening for you, I promise we will do everything we can to protect you and your privacy, but this has been really helpful and please if you think of anything, anything, anything at all you can call me 24/7.

"We have a police escort to take you out the service entrance because there is media all over and I don't want them to get anywhere near you. If the leaks have gotten out and there are reporters at your home, the police will keep them away and when you return to work (and you will), Mrs. Dubinski keeps asking about you and wants your help, so please don't worry about your job. But if the reporters start hounding you, do not and I repeat that, do not say one word to any of them. They will bribe you and it will be tempting, but it is Devil's candy. Please, not until we figure this out. Do I have your word?"

"You do, sir. I promise. I just want to go home."

"Ah, don't we all! When you're ready, I'll be back to take you home."

Rogers stood up, feeling a spasm in his calf where he had clearly been squeezing his muscles--the tension settling wherever there was an opening and he gave her a little salute, which seemed better than a handshake. "Thank you," he said, and he left, her innocence, whatever of it she had left in the very gritty real world she had lived her young life in, moving further away than ever.

CHAPTER 11

The morgue was close to the hospital, so even in mid-morning Miami traffic, Rogers got there quickly, wishing he hadn't promised Leena Martinez to personally escort her home, but then again, maybe she would remember something else or feel safe enough to tell him more.

The house and her mother were as described, the entire place was so run down and neglected and reeking of the despair the "have-nots" in glamour cities like Miami exude. One of hundreds of run-down, mid-twentieth century bungalows with brown lawns and folding drugstore beach chairs on cement patios, overlooking, if they were lucky enough, inflatable rubber pools, only a mile or so from the gilded gateways to the intracoastal or ocean front estates with sleek designer chaises, infinity swimming lagoons and swaying palms.

He left her, knowing it would only work against him to push her anymore and not mentioning the need to take her back to the scene. Not today. She was as relieved to be there as if it was a mansion, turning and hugging him before running in to see how her mother was.

All of this, being back in one of the neighborhoods he knew so well from his cop days, made him twitchy with that sense of helplessness that was part of the reason he'd hung it up to begin with. *When worlds collide*, the thought haunted his drive back to the Silver Sands. He was still processing his morgue visit and Leena's interview when he arrived.

The Miami Morgue was most certainly nothing like Crockett and Tubbs, the Miami Vice version that had first brought Miami Beach into the glitz world's interest. Olivia Tan, however, might well have been cast as the unlikely Doc Hottie, slitting open dead residents with a flick of her well-toned wrist.

Mikey had left before he got there and she was cleaning up, shooting him a "Now, YOU" look.

"Dr. Tan, sorry I was so long, I had to interview the Martinez girl."

"Yeah, Mikey told me. Man, I'm very glad Oscar wasn't anywhere near there.

Rogers nodded. She shook her long straight dyed blonde hair and he wondered why she did that to her beautiful natural color. Everyone wants to be someone else, he thought, wondering if that was true. Maybe it was sort of her way of expressing defiance against all chauvinist or raciest intrusions into her well-defended ego.

"I gotta tell you, Rogers, I've seen a lot of really disgusting shit, but this was a new low. Especially the Mister. Man, that would have caused some serious pain. I've got the shoes and the jewels bagged. Very tempting, I must say. Minimum combo 3 mill. I saw a pair of those shoes somewhere and they were over $1500 dollars and the jewels, even Crazy Rich Asians couldn't afford that bling. Can you make this quick? I really need a smoke."

"Well, I'm sure Mikey can fill me in, but I do like your first-hand info best. Any prints or fluids or?"

She shook her head several times as if trying to figure something out. "Not a thing! Not one single print. The killer was wearing gloves, cotton I think, no sexual evidence on her, some fluids on him, we're running it, but I doubt if it was from the murderer. Could have been his own, lots of porno stuff recorded.

"Anyway, we bagged everything we could, and it will take days to get through it. We need the family to check out the place and see if anything is missing. Lots of prints of course; we're not going to check everything, but you know that world, so many people in and out, no cleaning people in the world can keep hairs and prints off and all those damn dogs, lots of secretions and junk."

"I guess the causes of death are pretty obvious?"

"Well, yes and no. Not sure if he was hit first or tied up first or conscious. Running a tox screen, but this was such an act of someone totally losing their shit. I don't think the kind of planning that would go into drugging them first was possible. Looks like they came out swinging. He has a big hematoma on his temple--hit him hard, and he was old, doesn't take much. So I think he was hit first and then pushed back into the chair, tied up and rock and rolled with the footwear. Looks like eyes first, which I'm sure clocked him out, the ears were overkill. Almost like a message. Really savage. But they took time to put gloves on, so that's driving me a little nuts."

"Now it's gonna drive me there, too. Maybe we should get an Uber. What about the wife?"

Olivia rolled her heavily made up china doll eyes, "Well, this is bad, but this may be my favorite murder weapon of all time. She was clearly conscious, tied up--probably stripped first, but her nightgown was right there, so it wasn't much to do. They had to sort of know her jewelry, though apparently, she kept lots of bling just dumped in a big velvet tray on her dressing table. Talk about arrogant and stupid!

"Not paste stuff either, like a lot of her gang. They spend millions then have it all copied and put in bank vaults, sort of defeats the purpose, I mean, they could just buy the fake stuff and, oh well, not going to waste my cigarette time on that nonsense. Suffocation and I think she had a stroke, but that was caused by the fear, I'm sure. Pretty impressive choices, I must say, and I'm not trying to do your jobs, but, hello! Think it was a statement about rich people! I've bagged the murder weapons. Do you want to see the bodies?"

"Naw, not now. Haven't had lunch, yet. Maybe later."

"Oh, F.Y.I. the son is already carrying on because he's very religious and I have to have a rabbi here for the entire autopsies. Talk about a bureaucratic cluster fuck, but, at least they're letting me do them. The bodies are supposed to be buried asap, but the sister isn't religious and they're at odds already about it. Just a heads up. I told Mikey."

"Good, cause they are not going anywhere, yet and if we all rot in hell, so be it. Thanks Dr. O. By the way, I had no idea you and Pepe were married or Oscar was your kid! He's a great one. I'd like to talk to him, word is he's a genius with all the tech stuff and he's always at the condo."

A quick flicker of darkness crossed her usually inscrutable face; her mask of protection. Rogers thought it covered a still, very deep well.

"Yeah, he's the best, too bad he drew me for a Mom. Pepe is more the Mom and I'm more the disgruntled absent, overworked Dad. But, he gets it, he really is something else." She shook her head again, re-arranging her mask. "So, are we done for now. Nicotine calls and no speeches please!"

"Hey, I'm the freedom guy. I'd legalize everything; drugs, prostitution, Big Macs, none of this other stuff works, you know that. Might as well monitor all the crap that goes on anyway, and slow down some of the violence and mega money flowing in."

"From your mouth, never gonna happen though. I'll call ya when the lab results come in. Give my Oscar a hug for me, will ya?"

"Count on it, thanks, Doc."

"Always a pleasure. Boy, seeing you here makes me realize how much I miss you for obvious reasons!"

He laughed. Her dislike of Mikey Martinez was certainly not

a secret. "Yeah. Life's just one long gear shift. Talk soon." And he went, away from the smell of death, the stench of tragedy and the reminder of how fragile and random survival really was, despite our need to believe we were all exceptions to the fate of those poor souls sealed away in their cool metal drawers.

Rogers could smell the grilled cheese through the steel-reinforced door and his heart did a little skip step. Now that he was back here, so were these completely new sensations. "*I get no kick from champagne*" whew. Even Frank Sinatra was in on it.

The door opened rather quickly considering all the security and Sunny led him in. "Hi, Rogers. We're in one of our crazy conversations. You may just have to zone out for a while, but lunch is just about ready, so come on in."

More lyrics, "*Love is lovelier, the second time you fall, like a friendly home, the second time you call.*" Sunny's welcome made him feel as if they were all old pals, and it was no biggie, him stopping by for lunch. The dogs ran over to greet him. He wondered if it was okay to ask why Lorraine, who they called "he" had a girl's name. Maybe Lola was a boy, too?

Ooma Lovee walked slowly over to greet him. "Very nice to see you again, Mr. Rogers and thank you for letting my housekeeper come down and Oscar's here."

Rogers looked over and saw little Oscar, engrossed in Sunny's new laptop trying to figure something out. And then Edy turned around, holding a giant plate of sizzling sandwiches, flushed from the heat, though, maybe she was sort of blushing too. He grinned at her.

She seemed flustered by this and very self-conscious. "Welcome," she said, realizing he had a little gap between his front teeth. She'd always had a real thing for men with gaps between their front teeth, not that there were many. Maybe it had started with her love for Howdy Doody.

She tried to act nonchalant and normal, though she was rarely, either. "Okay, everybody, while they're hot. Rogers, we have plain grilled cheese or with Prosciutto, and salad and, I guess you can't drink on the job, so lemonade, it's fresh squeezed or?"

"Lemonade, would be great." He realized he was staring at her. "You changed your hair or something?"

Sunny snickered. "You might say that. She actually put on make-up and curled it. I guess murder brings out her inner glamour self."

Edy shot her a look only a mother could give a teenage daughter who was embarrassing her on purpose.

"Well, it works," he said, realizing he shouldn't.

They all sat down busy with the passing around of lunch items, the way families do every day, everywhere. Sunny broke the moment when the space between the busy work of filling plates was over and before eating and talking begins.

"So, Rogers, I think you missed the other bit of excitement going on downstairs. Some perv, snuck into the parking garage and was having sex with the tail pipe of a Range Rover and your guys ran in to stop him and he wouldn't stop!" I don't think they knew whether to just laugh or arrest him, so I guess they did both. He was totally wasted. Even for Miami, that is really twisted."

Rogers laughed. "Well, it's a first for me. I missed that one. I guess the report will call it Auto-Eroticism."

They all laughed, even Oscar who probably had no idea what they were talking about.

Edy laughed a little too loud and Sunny shook her head, which she noted. "I wonder if the car will sue, claiming rape and emotional trauma."

They all laughed again and started to eat.

"Lord, Lordy, Ms. Edy. This is the best grilled cheese I have ever had, and I've had plenty!"

Before Edy could accept her compliment Maria, Ooma Lovee's housekeeper came quickly into the room looking upset.

"Maria, would you like some lunch?"

Maria shook her head. "No, gracias, but there's a problem, Senora Edy in the bano."

"Edy looked surprised. Nothing seemed to ever go wrong here. "Really? What is it?"

"Your, your Yak-uzzi is dirty, sticky."

Edy really blushed now, as if some very personal reference to her bodily or housekeeping skills were being revealed. "My Yak-uzzi?"

"Si. Si. Dirty, sticky. I can't clean it!"

"My Yak-uzzi? What is that? Where is it?

"The bano. Dirty, sticky"

"My bano? I don't know what it is. I don't have a yak-uzzi. What is a Yak-uzzi?" They had all stopped chewing now. All eyes either on Maria or Edy."

"Guest room Yak-u-zzi. Dirty, sticky." Ooma looked shocked, but then she said something to Maria in Spanish, one of her many languages and Maria answered in Spanish and Ooma started to laugh. "Edy dear, it's just her English. She means Jacuzzi. I guess the tub hasn't been used in a while and someone cleaned it with the wrong product. Maria takes her cleaning very seriously. I'll go see."

Sunny was clapping her hands, gleeful at her mother's embarrassment. "Wow, Mom, wouldn't want our guest to think you had a dirty, sticky, yak-uzzi!"

"Sunny, you are on a thin edge and you're too old to be spanked, though I might find other means."

Sunny and Oscar were now giggling and clapping their hands, "Mommy has a dirty, sticky Yakuzzi, feminine hygiene police start your engines."

Edy looked right at Rogers who didn't quite know whether to laugh or reprimand the kids or both. "Mr. Rogers, welcome to my world. I hope we're not freaking you out. This is what passes for mealtime conversation at our house."

Now he laughed. "Well, I must admit, since I eat most every meal with Hildy, my dog, this is very new and refreshing, sort of like being in a sitcom without the cameras rolling."

Sunny was hyper now and enjoying the opportunity to tease her mother in public. "Well, you missed the best part, before you came. They turned our tech stuff back on since everything's leaked anyway and, there was a story about this teenage girl and her boyfriend and they wanted to take her mother's car, but the mother didn't trust the boyfriend and she refused and told him to leave. She thought he was a really bad influence on her daughter, so they tied her (the mother) to a chair, forced her to drink bleach and stabbed her twenty-seven times. Took the car and ran away. Cops just found them."

Edy had found her moment. "For the record, daughter of mine, I can pretty much guarantee if given the choice of being tied to a chair, having your guts burned out with bleach and being stabbed to death OR letting your ingrate teenager and her dead beat boyfriend have the car keys, your mom would have wrapped them in a gift bag, added all her wallet contents and carried them to the door. I wonder why they never offer these parents a choice!"

Rogers grinned again, and that gap, lips slightly glistening with ham and cheese grease, caused Edy a fantasy of lunging across the table and kissing him passionately. The urge was so strong, she began gobbling up all food within reach to avoid making eye or any other type of contact with him, as if he had read her mind. Nothing remotely like this had ever happened to her before. There was no GPS for this stuff, she thought, trying to catch her breath.

After the plates had been cleared and Edy offered a second round of "swill," Rogers, checked his watch and realized he had to move on fast and try to interview as many of the tenants still confined to their units as possible and wishing he had assigned more specific tasks to Pepe. Edy saw him check his watch and let him off the departure hook. "Rogers, we know you have to go, do you need any more info from us about other tenants or can that wait?"

"Hmmm, very good question. Well, I think I've found a major gold mine with you all, but I think it will work best if I talk to the other sus, I mean residents first and then get your input." He looked over at little Oscar, who was small for his age, very unlike either of his parents and hard to see over the large dining table.

"Oscar, everyone thinks I should talk to you, since you seem to know more about how all the tech stuff here works than the experts, not that you wouldn't qualify as an expert."

Oscar gave him a serious acceptance of the compliment. "I get it. Glad to be of help, Sir."

"How about we talk at the end of the day, before your Dad gets ready to take you home?"

"Oh, I think he's planning on both of us staying here in the staff rooms, if that's okay."

"That would be really great, please tell him I'll be back down there as soon as I can, and I'll call him shortly."

Oscar got up and went over to Edy and gave her a hug. "Edy, that simple lunch was really exquisite. Thank you for inviting me."

Rogers met Edy's eyes over Oscar's head and she winked at him. A thirteen-year-old boy who says "exquisite", whoa. Now he understood why they wanted him to talk to Oscar. He'd had little experience with kids, which often made him almost physically ache with longing, but this one seemed like a great place to start. *Exquisite?* Too much.

Edy walked him to the door and it took all his will and he sensed hers, to resist the urge to embrace one another. He extended his hand and she did, too and the connection felt like something too corny for either of them to acknowledge. And neither of them wanted to let go. *"Though not a single word was spoken, I could tell you knew."* Simultaneous song lyrics. Very difficult for two hardened loner realists to admit, even to themselves.

When Edy turned back, all sets of eyes were on her. "What?" she said sounding lamely defensive. She raised her hands to indicate no further discussion allowed and led Lorraine and Lola onto the terrace to pee before they exploded.

Rogers whistled as he made his way across the hall and down to the unit next to the elevator occupied, he'd been told by Mr. Rothenstein's two female assistants and Mrs. Rothenstein's art advisor and interior decorator, taking one long deep breath to prepare for what he was trying not to pre-judge; a room full of Miami madness.

He buzzed and waited. A man's voice, or what sounded like a very affected man's voice answered quickly. "Yes, how may we help you?"

Oh brother. *Keep an open mind, Rogers*, he whispered to himself, already feeling hostile.

"Yes, Mr. (he glanced down at his info sheet) LePorte? I'm Head of Security, Mr. Rogers and I'm here to interview you and Ms. Irina Petrov and Ms. Bianca Sanchez. I believe you are all aware by now of the situation."

He heard the door coding mechanisms performing their security run through and it opened, revealing a mid-aged gay man with what Rogers made a mental note to describe as 'bald with long hair,' the long part, which was bright red and tied back in a pony tail held with a pink hair band. He had a freckled red headed fairness, pale lashes and brows, not so subtly covered with make-up, lip gloss and large round glasses with vivid red frames. And he was wearing a blue velvet smoking jacket and matching scarf, Kermit green leggings and black velvet loafers, with gold designs on the top and, of course, no socks.

Rogers thought he looked rather like some cartoon combo Leprechaun and one of those assholes who strutted around Art Basel events, handing out their cards and oozing failure while lost in the delusive self-image that they were being seen as the exact opposite.

Rogers extended his hand, which Mr. LePorte accepted, offering a damp, limp shake, which Rogers thought made it unlikely he was the killer. Then again, underneath so many unlikely suspects, the bubbling infernos of rage sat simmering until some unbearable trigger of injustice brought it forth and Mr. Artsy and harmless could morph into the Hulk in a nanosecond.

Nothing could be taken at face value, then again, he'd done pretty well in this business by trusting his gut.

Mr. LePorte invited him in. His unit or their shared unit, was on the same scale as Edy's but without her taste and simplicity. Walking into the living area, you could see where Coco Rothenstein had let him have a very free hand. There were so many different textures, fabrics, colors, patterns, bizarrely shaped pieces of furniture that looked as if they were designed by a sadist in search of chairs and couches that would provide bodily injury just by being lowered onto one.

The walls were painted in a variety of colors ranging from blood red to shiny yellow. The "art" hanging on them seemed to have been painted by criminally insane children, who had taken a course in LGBT PC etiquette.

Decapitated men/women/armless huge breasted women with facial hair. Madonnas with shaved heads and no breasts holding large farm animals. And on. Sculptures abounded or Rogers assumed they were sculptures, molded plastic globs, balls of twine wrapped around pieces of rubber or maybe plastic plumbing tubes? He fought the urge to bolt or throw up. *Welcome to Monet's nightmare*, he thought.

Mr. LePorte, oblivious to the lack of enthusiasm in his visitor, began a curate's tour of his collection, including the only normal piece of furniture within view of which Mr. LePorte was especially proud, a 17th century chest he had found at some dusty old atelier in Leon. On and on, and Rogers followed along nodding, he hoped in what seemed to be an approving way while waiting for the entrance of the other residents.

He had the feeling that this was their routine. LePorte did the welcome, the guests were then "shocked and awed" by his taste and décor, they were then led to what seemed to be the only viable place to really sit, an enormous purple silk covered couch with no arms and a mass of embroidered pillows with the faces of old movie stars and cats. Lots of tassels, too.

Rogers thought LePorte could have been committed on the basis of the interiors. On one wall were photos of LePorte at various ages, standing beside important Miamians, being featured in local ad rags and in special prominence a feature on him and his interior design business with unctuous quotes from wealthy clients, most prominently Coco Rothenstein. *Why kill the Golden Goose*, Rogers thought, but then again, the back story can never be discounted.

"Please, Mr. Rogers, make yourself comfortable and I'll fetch the ladies." The "Ladies" seemed to emerge on cue, the way discreet butlers did in old movies when an unseen bell or buzzer was pushed.

Irina Petrov and Bianca Sanchez appeared to Rogers at first take to be both cut from the same Miami Magazine cloth. Sexy, glossy, re-touched versions of their original selves, whoever they may have been; surgically enhanced bosoms, and that South Beach bimbo look, which he couldn't quite understand, but something they did to their lips and eyes and noses that made them all look like they had the same face, regardless of their coloring or nationality or age. A sort of genericizing of their features he had gotten used to in his years in South Florida.

Irina was tall, Bianca was small, both were clad in too short, too tight shiny print dresses, very high heels, resembling the ones protruding from Frederick Rothenstein's eyes, very long straight hair; Irina's platinum Blond and, Bianca's almost ink black as if Frederick had created his fantasy Barbie pair to meet his desire for variety and at the same time, predictability. They seemed nervous but also, cocky, which Rogers knew was a set-up for bad interviews.

Clearly, being who they seemed to be, their first instinct was to flirt with him.

"Good morning ladies, very sorry to intrude like this, but I'm sure you are all aware by now of why I'm here. I'm Mr. Rogers, head of security and I have also been deputized to conduct this investigation. I would like to record these interviews and talk with you individually."

Irina who seemed to be the lead personality, moved toward him, clearly using her wares to gain empathy or a proverbial leg up. "We are very glad to meet you and we, of course, know a bit, only that our beloved employer was murdered and his wife, but that is all we know. I doubt we can be of much help. Maybe Mr. LePorte can, he's up there more than we are. We do most of our work from here, in our little office. Isn't that right, Bianca?"

Bianca seemed more than happy to have Irina speak for her. She flipped her hair back and nodded in agreement. "Yes, yes. We know nothing."

LePorte, Rogers thought, was getting a bit hot probably with good reason. His demeanor and the way he placed his hands high on his hips, and cocked his head back, seemed to Rogers to indicate he was aware they were shifting the blame or whatever, suspicion, maybe to him and lying about their relationships with their "employer," which Rogers would expect. He longed for another cup of coffee.

"Well, I understand your reluctance to be more forthcoming, but the thing is, we have a double homicide here and the three of you have closer access to the victims than almost anyone else, so, I am going to have to take statements and I need you to account for your whereabouts in the last twelve hours so, if there's somewhere quiet we can talk, let's start with you, Ms. Petrov."

Rogers could see LePorte smirk and exhale. Somehow this trio probably operated more like cats in a bag than buddies, with LaPorte's future, probably brighter than that of the ladies, since he worked for Rebecca's mother and would probably still have a job and a very nice place to live.

Bianca looked relieved, he sensed, and Irina looked pissed off but strutted past him, motioning him to follow. "Come, we can talk in our office."

Rogers did as directed, wishing he had a bug in the living room.

The office was small with two matching white, laminated desks, clearly not chosen by LePorte, with computers and all necessary techno gadgets, filing cabinets, printers, hardline and cell phones, beepers and no personal mementos that he could see, which seemed strange to him. Clearly, whatever other services they performed for Frederick Rothenstein, he also expected a day's work for a day's pay. Miami seemed to breed women like this in petri dishes.

Irina Petrov, swayed in her very high heels, her rather over-endowed rear clearly on calculated view for Rogers enjoyment, but just like their boobs, it just made him feel sad for them.

She sat first, at her desk, swiveling her chair around and crossing her long tanning saloned legs, revealing lots of gleamingly cared for skin and motioned for him to sit on the one extra chair across from her.

"So, what would you like to know?" she asked, almost defiantly, as if all those years in Russia, not present in her perfect English, but still lurking beneath with good reason, made all government and police officials objects of fear and contempt.

"Well, Ma'am we have been led to believe and, of course the investigation has just started, but we do have all of both Rothenstein's computers and phones, that you and Ms. Sanchez, were more than just business associates to Mr. Rothenstein and may have access to information that would be very helpful in finding their killer. I can guarantee you we will find out the truth, so it will be far better for all of us, if you just tell me the truth and save everyone some time."

She re-crossed her legs and sighed deeply, her face as blank as a re-touched photo, but her fingers were tapping on the desk indicating far more discomfort than she showed. He could almost hear her brain wheels creaking around trying to decide what to say and just how smart he might be or what exactly did he know (which was almost nothing!) The old cop/perp bluffing game. Her eyes blinked quickly, under what looked to be multiple sets of false lashes, giving them an almost avian appearance. Maybe they would start flapping and she would just fly away. He waited, hoping his demeanor was quietly intimidating. He was pretty good at that one.

She flipped her hair back and sighed. "Okay, so no games. Yes, we both were his lovers." She smirked. "Or whatever you would call it. He was old, he had problems with his apparatus. We had to use all our skills, without going into details, I think you understand. And he liked to watch the two of us. It was all part of the job and it most certainly didn't mean we did not have to work very hard and professionally, too.

"Neither of us are stupid and we know we have a limited shelf life in this town, and we use what we have and look where we live, free! Well, maybe that's a joke. Nothing's free. I'm from Chernobyl, believe me I know all about life. He was very generous, and we had gorgeous clothes, fancy trips, he bought us expensive jewelry and we have Mercedes cars to drive, just leased by the company, but still great.

"We are not bimbos, no matter what you think. We save everything. We get lots of cash bonuses, I am trusting you don't tell these things to the IRS. We think, he might be just getting too old or worse, getting tired of us, so we wanted to make the most of it. So, why would we kill him?" Ridiculous! And Bianca is a very devout Catholic, don't laugh, please! And quite timid, really, she could never harm anyone. And LePorte? Really now! How silly! Plus, Coco adored him, couldn't make any decisions about anything without him and he was her "walker" took her to parties, all the things Frederick didn't do anymore. He had it made."

Rogers watched her and, of course, he had to agree that the motive seemed lacking, unless, he was going to dump her and wanted everything back. Jewelry, car, apartment and she just snapped.

"What about your relationship with Mrs. Rothenstein? That must have been uncomfortable. And they did still work on many parts of the business together?"

For this she uncrossed her legs, stopped tapping her fingers and leaned forward, her batting eyes turned cold behind, what seemed to be bright blue contact lenses.

"She hated us, and we hated her. She was jealous. Very jealous. Not just of us, there were many others in and out, but they didn't have the closeness we did and, of course, no one lived here or traveled with him. I understand this, but I really don't think she ever knew about the other arrangement we had with him. I think she just thought he liked to taunt her by having, young, beautiful women around.

"I'm sure her experience for years was that he was impotent, and maybe she believed he only liked to titillate himself and hurt her by hiring women like us.

"I know they fought about it because we were technically supposed to work for her, too and the children, but he made sure we didn't have to really cross paths, just some accounting and e-mails and they never had our names on it. But the daughter has told us we are fired and to get everything in order, turn over the cars, the keys, all files and we have to move out in two weeks or sooner. We knew that would happen."

Rogers nodded, almost feeling sorry for them. He knew that in the lives of so many of the immigrants he had interviewed and known personally in Florida, how tough things could be, and these girls used what they had and that was survival and not something he judged unless it folded over into evil. He hadn't expected her to be so forthcoming, unless of course, that was dissembled and there was more she was not telling him.

"Did you ever see him with anyone, another woman or business associate or someone special he was dealing with who you thought was dangerous, or had a major beef with him or his wife, some business venture gone wrong or an eviction or foreclosure, something that would trigger such rage?"

Irina Petrov threw back her head, her large pink lips opening wide and laughed loudly. "Are you joking! Every week! This is a very tough business and he and Coco were ruthless. They had many enemies and had caused much distress, foreclosing, calling in loans; all with good reason, but without any compassion or leeway. They always said, "once you blink where money is concerned, you're dead meat. And, you know, they were right. This is not a world for nice people, Mr. Rogers. Before I did this, I was a scentologist, and I was good at it. Not much money, but very pleasant. I may go back to that."

Rogers eyebrows wiggled upward, something he did unconsciously when a subject he had no knowledge of was introduced. "What, may I ask, is a scentologist, exactly?"

She smiled and her face actually humanized. "Sorry, I forgot you're not part of this world we live in. You choose different scents for offices and shops and homes and they provide mood manipulations. Everything from warm cookies, bread, to spring woods or florals, depending on the environment. I happen to have what they call a good nose. Some developers hire us before a condo development, for example, is even under construction, to try and match the correct scent with the space. Different for the spa, then the gym and so on. It's quite an art."

Rogers eyebrows went higher. "Holy Hot sauce, now I have heard everything."

"Oh, maybe not. Bianca was a "wantologist." But she can tell you herself. May I go for now. I have much to do."

Rogers stood up and held out his hand, which she took avoiding stabbing him with her very long spangled fingernails and gave him what he assumed was a seductive appraisal. "A pleasure to meet you, Mr. Rogers and you know how to reach me, for now. I don't know where I'll be living but I'll leave all forwarding information. This is still very hard to accept. I'll send Bianca in."

"Appreciate that. And, I hate to ask, but do you possibly have any coffee around? Been a long morning."

"Absolutely. We have very special Cuban espresso. I'll have Bianca bring you some."

And out she swayed leaving Rogers longing for Edy and her "swill."

While Rogers waited, he tried to scan the room for any signs of anything even remotely clue-like. There was only one picture on the far wall, which was so bizarre he got up and went closer. It was the photo of a woman with what looked to be a leg of panty hose pulled tightly down over her face and some sort of large circular mound of styrofoam-like material sticking straight up from the top of her head. He looked closer, and thought it was certainly a kinky choice in line with the Rothenstein's grotesque endings.

"That's Sarah Luca, isn't it wonderful?" He turned, taken slightly off guard and Bianca Sanchez was wiggling toward him holding his designer coffee.

"I have not a clue who she is or why this is wonderful, but I am open to enlightenment."

She laughed, revealing as he would expect, more perfect white teeth. "Okay, so I don't have to pretend with you. Ridiculous isn't it. She's very sought after in Art Basel kinds of circles. Mrs. Rothenstein is, or was a big collector and Mr. LePorte bought the work for her. She's British and she's having some big museum show soon and so, the art world PR mill is really pushing her. I can't say anything negative about any of it, well to Mr. Rothenstein we could, he hated it all, thought it was what he called, "The Emperor's New Clothes" which I didn't understand, so I looked it up. When they were still together he would get really furious about the prices she paid for it all. I mean, pantyhose covered fluff balls as some kind of female power statement or something. Maybe that should be my next career." But I'm more of pictures of the sky and the water, very down scale, I know."

Rogers was surprised again, once you got through the surface, she seemed to be an okay young woman and without Irina's edgy bitterness.

"Ms. Petrov told me you used to be something called a 'Wantologist'. I have no idea what that is, either."

"Oh, she told you that. Yep. She was doing the Scentology stuff, that's how we met and that's how we first got a job with the Rothensteins. Scents for their developments and Wantology for their key personnel, sort of instead of shrinks, I suppose."

Rogers picked up the coffee and slugged the little cupful down in one gulp. "Thank you for that, I can feel it coursing through. Strong stuff."

"Yes, the Cubans get it right. Shall we sit down?"

She wiggled, which was the only way he could describe her walk, and seemed to him to be the price of wearing shoes that were completely unsuited to her small frame and personality, rather than a seductive ploy. He had a flash of her throwing them in a corner the minute she was off duty. "He followed her over to her desk which also had one extra chair for visitors.

"So, Ms. Sanchez, as part of my on-going social media education, please tell me what, exactly a Wantologist is, now that I've learned about the scent choosing business, I'm intrigued."

"Okay, but you can't make fun of me. Because you are most certainly not the kind of person who would be into this." She paused as if remembering something and trying to decide what to tell him about herself.

"Look, I know how we seem and I'm not proud of what we've been doing or how it must look. I will only say, because I hate "poor little me" stuff, but not all of us are Rebecca Dubinskys and life can get very tough for women like me and Irina, too. We have done what we had to do to survive and to get out of this insanity at some point. We're not call girls! It was only with him and it just sort of evolved. We didn't start out with anything other than PA relationships, I know you haven't asked but I sort of hate you guys to think badly of us, though I know you do, anyway."

Rogers was watching her intently, trying to decide whether to zig, zag, say something reassuring even if it was phony or just be still and listen. The latter seemed like the best choice, so he did nothing but try to convey he wasn't judging, and he was listening.

"Oh so, Wantology. Well, I got turned on to it when I was hostessing in South Beach at one of the big trendy hotels. I mean you see everything imaginable and I was hanging out next to one of the concierges trying to learn because I thought that it would be a dream job and this very upset woman, who was dressed like a runway model, clutching a designer dog in a Chanel doggy carry all, came rushing over and she was really sort of losing it and she said she needed a Wantologist immediately."

He was totally clueless, so he asked if I knew what it was and, strangely enough, I'd just read an article about it, so he turned her over to me and I took her into a private lounge, brought her some champagne and tried to calm her down.

"I have lots of crazy aunts and cousins, so I'm pretty good at calming down semi-hysterical women and she started unloading as if I were her Wantologist.

"She needed a local Wantologist to break up with her scumbag boyfriend. Her words, not mine. I was speechless. Anyway, that was the beginning. I did it for her, and apparently, I was really good at it and she hired me and started recommending me to her friends and they paid me $100 an hour! I can tell you that was a lot more than hostessing!

"I really got into it and I did unbelievable stuff for them. You can hire someone to put flowers on a loved one's grave, Rent-a-Friend, a mommy. You can rent a cat or someone to teach you how to use kitchen utensils, come and stay with you if you're lonely or having a bad patch, or just do Life Coaching stuff, which, frankly, I didn't need a Ph.D., to do, just ask simple, common sense questions like, "what do you want out of your life right now?" stuff like that. Or just basic woo woo advice. "Take ten deep breaths before you call your mother. Talk a walk, take a nap, change your meds. Take a bath and watch a Fred Astaire/Ginger Rogers movie." Really sad how lost all these supposedly accomplished, rich people can get. And I built a network of subs who would do just about anything they needed.

"I even found surrogate Soccer Moms, who would stand in for real moms and take their kids to games, root for them, buy them ice cream, give them condolence hugs. I mean, unbelievable. I guess it started with all these Events and Wedding Planners and then Life Coaches, but the world is just more and more complicated and stressful, and people just get so overwhelmed.

"Anyway, I did really well, but it does finally burn you out. It was 24/7 and it got really depressing, too and I didn't really like most of them; so spoiled and whiny.

"I'm a good Catholic, really, I am, and the way I look and the life I'm living is starting to wear me down, anyway, so I guess with Mr. Rothenstein I sort of both hit the jackpot as far as my skill sets and bottomed out. Does that make sense to you? I know it sounds horrible, but having it end without actually having to quit and risk him black-balling me, or something is a relief. I mean, not how it happened, but now I can get out of Miami and try to do something normal or more normal!"

Rogers leaned forward and smiled at her. "No, Ma'am it doesn't sound horrible at all and I really appreciate your candor. If I can be frank, with both you and Irina, well, looks can be deceiving and I was pre-judging, even though I try very hard not to. And man oh man, I have learned a lot! I toyed with the idea of hiring a dog-walker and now I don't think I would even do that! So, I just have one more question for you at the moment. Did you see or hear anything recently that would make someone appear to be a possible suspect or have a motive for their murders?" Bianca Sanchez, for some reason, didn't seem to see this question coming and she sat up very straight in her chair and her eyes, underneath the heavy make-up flashed, with what Rogers thought was fear.

"Well, there was something."

CHAPTER 12

After Rogers left and Oscar returned to the security offices to "work something out" as he described it, and Maria finished making up the guest room and cleaning the Yak-uzzi, Ooma Lovee decided it was time to share her history with Edy and Sunny. The urgency behind the timing, she couldn't really figure out, except the specter of The End, time running out, triggered by the Rothenstein's horrific deaths, had brought up waves of unfinished guilt, fear and loneliness.

The thought that if she died now, naturally or as the next victim, there would be no trace, no living human being to remember her or learn of anything about their own journeys from her life. She could feel her heart beating faster when she stood up and went into the kitchen space to get them.

"Edy, Sunny, now that it's private and quiet here, I need to talk to both of you, now."

She turned and walked regally back into the wide-open living room and sat down in a large white chair, motioning for them to sit close to her on the matching white couch.

They obeyed without a word, only their exchange of eye contacts and slight shoulder shrugs indicating they were a little worried and surprised by the request. This was not Ooma's style at all.

Lorraine and Lola, sensing something interesting and new was happening, trotted along beside them, and plopped down between the chair and the couch.

Ooma threaded her long, perfectly manicured fingers together sitting slightly forward, her long straight back not bending at all. Slough was not a word in her vocabulary.

"I know with all the stressful events of today, this may not seem like a good time to tell you both the story of my life, but I feel some sort of urgency, to share this with the only two people who I love deeply and who will remember me."

They both started to protest this assessment of her worth, but she raised one strong hand to stop them and shook her head and they stayed silent, their faces, however, revealed their own anxiety. Edy thought, *What the hell? Is she going to un-adopt us? Did we do something wrong?*

"Please, let me just tell this story, I will skip everything non-essential for now, anyway and I don't want you to be nervous, it has nothing to do with my devotion to you, the gift of you. They say you are only as sick as your secrets so I am trying to cure myself of a very sick secret.

"I have never really talked to you about my childhood or even the war. I was born in Ljubljana, Slovenia. It is a lovely small country, pristine and quiet. My parents moved there from Pilsen, Czechoslovakia. All those countries have changed hands so many times and been re-formed. The history is quite unique and very complicated, but if you want to learn more I know you can just Google or whatever it is one does now, you know I don't do any of it.

"When the alarms began, warning us that the Nazis were coming, my parents began to prepare to leave. I didn't know why. They were not in politics, we were just ordinary people. My father was a doctor and my mother stayed at home most of the time and ran the house and cared for me and her garden. Simple. What no one knew or few knew was that she was Jewish."

She paused and tears coursed down her still unlined face. "OH Gott! Why was that so hard to say out loud! I have never told anyone that. She never told me, until the Nazis were coming, because Eastern Europe before Hitler, before any of it, was ravenously anti-Semitic and she was afraid, even there and then.

"I was thirteen years old and hardly understood what it meant, but she told me the day before they marched in. She sat me down and took hold of my shoulders and I was already tall for my age and starting to develop, not quite like a little girl, though I most certainly was one.

"She held me tight, almost hurting me and her eyes were glinting and I was frightened. She said that if the Nazis took them away, 'RUN!' she said to me. I was to go and never look back and I must swear to her, swear on their lives that I would never, for the rest of my life, ever tell anyone I was Jewish. It wasn't safe and she could not face whatever she and my father might have to face if she thought I wasn't safe.

"I was speechless and so frightened. I started to cry and she shook me. She told me I must be brave. She told me where she'd put a satchel with money and jewelry sewn into the clothes and food and the things she thought I would need and an introduction to an uncle of my father's in Pilsen who was not Jewish, but I would have to be alert and if it wasn't safe there to just keep moving toward the free countries, toward England, Switzerland, France (which was still free) or Italy which was closest and still fairly safe and to get to America. But even there, never tell anyone I was Jewish, because she truly believed there would, someday be more pogrums. I didn't even know what she meant, but I swore to her. And then she just held me so tight, I could hardly breathe.

"I finally found my voice and I asked her if she'd put the photos in or any document to prove who I was and she became even more serious. She said, if the Nazis entered the country, she was going to burn my birth certificate and all traces that they had ever had a child, no photos, nothing so I could always say, I had lost everything in the war and I was an orphan.

"This, of course completely overwhelmed me and I could not stop crying and she said, 'Cry now. Cry hard and then you must stop and pull all those feelings down deep inside of yourself' and she gave me a St. Christopher medal from my father's mother and told me to never take it off, but think of it as a Jewish star, in my heart."

"The Nazis came two days later. I will never forget the sound of their rifles banging on the door and she grabbed me, put the backpack on my shoulders, led me out through the basement and said, 'run and don't stop until you are safe, not for anything or anyone. Run with our love to guide you.'

"And I did. The Nazis took them, someone my mother trusted told on them, but no one told about me. No one in our community. So, I felt I owed a sacred debt to all of them. I ran. I never saw my parents again. I never saw my homeland again. Now that it's open and free and I hear it's very lovely, and intact, not destroyed by the bombings or re-built like Dubrovnik, but I just can't even think about it.

"I won't bore you or burden you with all the struggle to get to Pilsen, but I did, and I found my Uncle and they took me in, but they were at risk. Of course, I could never have imagined it wasn't for a little while and then I would go home and be with my parents, again. But then the monster arrived. Heyridick, the Butcher of Czechoslovakia, they called him. I would see him in his big, fancy car, reading the papers when he was being driven to his headquarters. The entire country was terrified of him and I truly believe if he hadn't been assassinated right there in Pilsen, on one of his visits, eventually he would have staged a coup and Hitler would have been killed and he would have become the new Fuhrer.

"If that happened, Germany would most likely have won the war, because he was merciless, a ruthless sociopath, without

Hitler's insanity and weak ego strength and neuroses and far more brilliant. He would never have been so foolish as to invade Russia, he would have turned toward England. All Hitler needed to do was read War and Peace, read about Napoleon's defeat because of his Russian mistake and everything might have been lost."

She paused, and Edy instinctively jumped up and brought her a glass of water, which made her smile. "Thank you, my darling. As always, you just know what to do!"

Edy sat back down and neither of them nor the dogs, moved or said anything.

"When he came back, my uncle told me I should go because they would be checking houses and the neighbors knew I was a refugee, and not their child. I took my backpack and they gave me some more money and food and a knife, just in case! And told me to head for Switzerland. There were no cell phones then, remember, no way for me to even know what that meant, and I didn't speak any language but some French and Slovenian and Czech. I was not quite thirteen, but I looked older. And I ran, my mother's voice always guiding me forward. Trust no one. No one and never tell anyone you're Jewish!

"I'm rather tired, so I will skip over the next few years, let me just say, I grew up very fast and I saw even at thirteen that men found me attractive and that was all I had to use. I met many people, who were kind, and many who were not, but I picked up an English dictionary, I learned to speak, and men began to help me. I never told anyone my age, and when I was fifteen, I met my Claude and we fell in love. He was older, around twenty I believe, and I became a woman with him. He was in the army, Polish Armed Forces. He was killed in an air raid, and I have never loved anyone else, not really. I am not proud of how I used my femininity to survive, but I did. I think my soul was absolutely numb by the end of the war and I made my way to a refugee camp and found my way to England. I went from one older rich Englishman to another. I never took money! I danced, used my childhood ballet training and my energy. I was a showgirl and danced in nightclubs, things like that. I worked in stores and modeled for fashion houses, which, of course, was also how I met so many rich men.

"Europe, after the war was a terrible, desperate and confused place, but there was great spirit, the spirit of survivors, mixed with so much shame and fear and confusion and, of course, opportunism and I had a nose for men who could seize opportunity and I learned a lot from them; about business and parlaying limited means into security. My mother had sewn her jewelry and gold coins and money into my coat and I still do that. If anything happens to me, in my closet, next to the evening dresses, there is a rather plain black dress, with a very full skirt, taffeta, because it is a strong fabric and sewn into the hem, the sleeves, the waist and the neckline there are a lot of gold coins and loose diamonds and cash. Get the dress if I die, make sure no one else has it or gives it away. I will show it to you, just in case. It's very important to me that you and Sunny have all of that and that I am buried in a Jewish cemetery with my birth name. And I have never told anyone else what that is. My name is Hannah Sarah Levy, well that was my mother's maiden name. I changed it to Lovee when I had a new identity papers made. Ooma, was a name I saw on a billboard or something, somewhere, and I just liked the way it sounded. It was simple and strong and yet, not common.

"So, this is a lot to absorb, and I think I need to rest now, it is a great relief to tell you, my precious treasures, miracles really, it was time. When I die, I have left you and Sunny the apartment, which is quite valuable and there is a trust for each of you that should allow you both to live free of any fear and worry, even if you live to be the oldest people in Miami, or wherever you might go. All the rest is going to Jewish refugee causes and the Israeli Defense Fund.

"When I finally got to Florida, which I had always assumed was as free of anti-Semitism as anywhere, Mr. Flagler, of whom you have heard many tales of what he did for the development of Florida, but what they do not put in any of his school or museum brochures or bios, is that he was a raving anti-Semite who would post signs on the front of his hotels that said, "Great views, no Jews." And the new rise in hate crimes against Jews and the vicious attacks on college campuses even in cities like New York, have brought back all my old fears. Hatred towards us will never end and will never be cared about the way it is toward other minorities. If one black teenager is shot by the police, whole communities are marching and protesting, but anti-Semitism was not even listed as a hate crime in Florida, until a couple of years ago. We have always threatened something, maybe because we always survive and we turn whatever they have denied us into a way to triumph over jealousy, fear and evil. I know I sound terribly narrow-minded about this, but at my age, I can at last own my truth out loud, to the two safest people I have known since my parents were lost to me. Actually, I don't think I have really known more than one handful of people who were not anti-Semites, however unaware of it they might be.

"I know you did not expect this, and it is a lot to absorb and you probably have many questions, and now that it is not a secret, we can talk about anything you wish, but right now, I think I need to lay down for a while."

They both leapt up and went to her, holding her close and the dogs did, too, licking her ankles and Edy was convinced they understood if not the words, the power and emotion behind them. Ooma picked Lola up and head held high, even for her, she moved slowly, but steadily to her haven for the night.

When Rogers returned to the living room to interview LePorte (first name still unknown, or maybe like some celebrities, he only used his last name). Rogers made a mental note to check him out, since he strongly suspected LePorte wasn't real, either. Rebecca Dubinski and her husband Sergi were huddling beside him on the purple couch. She had a shot glass filled with something, probably tequila, in front of her and he had one of those designer Cuban coffee cups.

They moved quickly apart when they saw him and Rebecca Dubinski stood up and moved to sit across from her husband. Rogers was so hypnotized by her outfit, he forgot for a moment how to make this new addition work for him and save some precious time. He had never seen anyone in real life, dressed remotely like this. She was wearing a dress, well, he thought it was a dress, very short and shapeless, completely covered in various pastel feathers, with long sleeves, covering all but her fingertips. Her emaciated, but deeply tanned legs were clad in what looked like clear plastic leggings, tucked into very high black clog-like shiny heels. Since they were still not cleared to leave the building or have their party, this was an even more bizarre choice of at home attire.

Sergi, was wearing very tight black pants, something male ballet dancers might leap around in and a matching black tee, highlighting his massive upper body and his other more private parts. And the ubiquitous, among all the Russian men he saw around the Sunny Isles cafes, black sneakers with white soles.

LePorte was clearly making a supreme brown-nosing effort to please his new bosses who could snap their fingers as they had done with Bianca and Irina and let him go.

"Mr. Rogers, I believe you had the pleasure of meeting the Dubinskis, they are here to begin, what will be a very long process of archiving and sorting through their parents' vast collections. We're waiting for Carmen Daniels, the Chief of Staff, who has all the files. I have many, but none of Mr. Rothenstein's.

"Clearly this is all rather too soon for the family to have to deal with this, but your Superior, Mr. Martinez is it chief or lieutenant? We're not sure how to address him? He called and said he will need us to go up to the Rothenstein's apartments, as soon as their men have finished, and start to go through everything, see if valuables are missing, and whatever we might notice. The insurance people are already banging at the door, so to speak and the estate lawyers. No grass growing time, alas."

Rogers had not expected this, certainly without Mikey giving him a heads up, which was pure Mikey, so he took his time, trying to decide where to sit, since the couch was quite low and towering over them, did not seem like a good choice.

There was one chair at the far end of the couch, which looked to be made of rubber, with a fur cushion on it, something at least possibly comfortable and he moved toward it. "LePorte is this furniture or an art piece, wouldn't want to sit on a valuable."

They all looked at him trying to see if he was mocking them, which Rogers sensed and tried to give them one of his most innocent, rube-like expressions.

"No, no, it's a chair, though some people collect them as art pieces. Please, feel free, but gentle."

Rogers lowered his long frame as gracefully as possible, realizing that the fur cushion had a head on it which seemed to hit right about where his rectum was located. Luckily, it didn't seem to itch, but what the hell was it? Hopefully a rabbit, not something endangered or with sharp little teeth still attached.

They were all looking at him. Rebecca downed the shot and LePorte leapt up and brought a bottle of Patron and put it down beside her on the massive plexiglass coffee table.

"Well, I was not prepared to do an interview with all of you, but it may be very helpful. Maybe LePorte you can begin by telling me exactly what your duties were with Mrs. Rothenstein and how long you have been in her employ and living on the premises."

He sighed, and took off his glasses, wiping, what Rogers, assumed were tears, from the corners of his rabbit-like eyes. "Oh, dear, so so, hard to accept, I'll never see my Coco again! She was like the mother or the sister I never had. I adored her. I loved working with her, so brave and creative and fun, right Rebecca?"

Rebecca began to sob again, holding her eyes wide to keep, Rogers thought, her intricate make-up from running. "Oh, my poor mommy, oh Francis, how will we bear this!"

So, he did have a first name, Francis reached across the table and took her tiny, skeletal hand in his. Sergi, wanting to assert his power in the scene, moved across to her and thrust one of his massive arms around her feathery shoulder.

"Your mother was the strongest woman I have ever known, she would want us to be strong for her. We will conquer this."

Rogers was getting restless, between the animal intrusion a little too close to his anus and the emotional segue, which smacked of theater to him. "I'm very sorry to have to ask these difficult questions so soon, but I know you all want to find who did this as soon as possible, and frankly, we don't even know at this point, if any of the family members are targeted, too, so I'm afraid I have to ask you to try and focus for a little while, and help me put these pieces together. So LePorte, can you please answer my question?"

LePorte bristled, clearly resenting Rogers tone. He put his glasses back on, pushing them far back against the bridge of his nose, creating an aviator affect. "Yes, yes of course. Duty calls. Let me think. I do have all of this in the files Carmen is bringing, including my entire employment history with Coco, but we met at the opening of their private museum, about ten years ago. She was working with several designers and art consultants, and her taste was not yet formed. She was searching and I had a book of my projects with me and we started to chat and we just clicked. It was instantaneous, the way those major karmic connections always are. And it just evolved, right Rebecca?"

"Yes. Mommy introduced me to Francis, and we all fell in love and he started advising us, before Silver Sands and she totally trusted him. She came into her own because of Francis and started to trust her own taste, so different from Daddy's and they became best friends, too. I was a little jealous, I think you knew this Francis, she would often spend more time with him or bring him along to Mommy and Me occasions, but we worked through all that and we were like the three Musketeers of the Avant Garde Art scene, weren't we, Sergi?"

Sergi seemed surprised to be addressed and nodded his huge head, making his Adam's apple bounce up and down. "Yes, darling. It was a true bond. It was not my world, but I knew how much it meant to them. Of course, I entered rather late. I only met Rebecca three years ago, so I don't have this history and I have been too busy with the Gym facilities to know much about any of this."

Rogers felt his eyebrows doing their elevation surprise motion. "Oh, I see. I thought you two had been together longer. So, you're almost newlyweds?"

For some unknown reasons, neither LePorte nor Rebecca nor Sergi, seemed to anticipate or like this question...Now, this was interesting. Rogers eyebrows resumed their normal position.

"Yes. Yes, we are, but like old souls, so that is probably why you would think, we are together longer. But I was already working for her parents, I ran the gym at the country club, so we were not strangers, but why does this matter?"

"Yes, why! Rebecca pulled a tissue from inside her feathered arm covering and dabbed at her eyes. "There are certainly more important issues to discuss!"

"Well, Ma'am no disrespect, but right now everything is important and all personal relationships involving your family have to be addressed. I know this is not comfortable, but it is necessary." He was pushing his luck and he knew it, shaking sticks at snakes, was part of the work, especially when it wasn't at all obvious who the snakes were or how many skins they could shed before they reacted.

LePorte responded as Rogers would have expected. "We are

not naïve, Mr. Rogers, but this poor girl (choice of word girl seemed especially unctuous) has suffered a devastating tragedy and being interrogated like this is really inexcusable."

"Mrs. Dubinski, do you find this inexcusable? Or is finding the murderer more important? As I said earlier, I'm trying not to alarm any of you, but we really don't know if we are looking at a serial killer who has an agenda with your family or a far more personal attack, but we must explore all possibilities for your own protection."

"I am her husband. Look at me! Do you not think I can protect my wife?"

"I do not doubt it for a moment. However, if you would like some examples of very well-prepared and super strong men, martial arts experts and professional athletes who have been surprised and murdered, well I can prepare a list." Rogers realized he had taken a wrong turn and was trying to find a trap door or a way to change the direction.

Rebecca re-filled her shot glass and Sergi filled his empty coffee cup with tequila. LePorte was still bristling, far more concerned, Rogers thought, with scoring points with his new boss than being the next victim, even without knowing how they had died. *Motives, Rogers, no one seemed to have any damn motive.*

He decided to stay on Sergi since LePorte would clearly design his responses to please Rebecca, but he made a mental note to do a full background check on Francis LePorte.

"So, Mr. Dubinski, how long have you been employed by the Rothenstein corporation excluding your personal relationship with your bride?"

Sergi downed his tequila shot and glared at Rogers. Ego was now emerging, bursting through the macho body wear, which was usually all the backstory he required. "I work for them for five years before Rebecca and I fall in love. I barely knew her, she did not come to the gym at the club and I had a different life. I was still competing in weightlifting competitions. I was Mr. Miami Beach five years in a row. I was a celebrity in that world and I bring many prominent clients to the club. I had my own base and they were very grateful to have me there. I bring in people and publicity. Miami is a very competitive place for people who want to have perfect bodies and be strong and healthy. I was a symbol. I have a book of all the stories and ads featuring me if you want to see it."

Rebecca leaned over and kissed him, patting his cheek with her feathers.

Chimes rang loudly causing them all to pause.

LePorte jumped up. "That must be Carmen Daniels." He almost ran toward the tension relief, which seemed to calm the others down as well. Carmen Daniels did not so much enter a room as storm it. They all jumped up, the way enlisted men did when a general unexpectedly appears.

Rogers did not even have a file on her, which, given the power of her presence, made no sense at all.

She was a big woman, tall and what in Miami Jewish circles would be called zaftig, not fat, but large. Everything about her was large, feet, hands, head; a handsome head, large features, caramel skin, wide mouth, defined by bright purple lipstick and a mane of flowing steel grey and white hair, giving the impression of a human virago, bursting with frustrated energy and, power. LePorte seemed to literally shrink in her presence and Rebecca looked as if Carmen Daniels might just swoop her up in one large, maroon nailed hand and fling her out the window. Only Sergi seemed undaunted by her.

She completely ignored them and all attempts at staying within the social contract, introductions, hand-shakes, offers of beverages. Rogers realized they were all standing at attention, but her eyes were flashing exclusively at him.

"You must be Rogers. I would like to speak to you alone, right away, in your office downstairs, please."

LePorte managed to find his voice, "Did you bring the files, Carmen. The police need to see them?"

She turned on one of her high heeled rhinestone covered sandals, large maroon toenails practically digging into the floor, her anger was so palpable and flipped her mane at him. "When you asked me that, LePorte, I thought it was a joke. If any of you ever bothered to come downtown to the Rothenstein Headquarters, you would know that I'd have to hire a very large moving van, maybe two to even begin to "bring files" to you. There are floors of files. Floors! So, no, I did not. Now can we go?"

And with this Carmen Daniels turned on her heels, and Rogers followed, slightly shrugging his shoulders and nodding to his three fellow recruits, grateful for the chance to re-think his line of questioning and intrigued by this new potential cauldron of information.

"Thank you all for your time. I will be back later, by then we may be able to go on up to your family's apartment." He followed his commanding officer out and down to his office.

He had not been back there for hours and the entire security facility was a buzz with activity. Reporters were encamped all over the parking lot and being kept at bay, phones were ringing, irate tenants wanting to leave, police in and out. Pepe was on the computer and little Oscar was beside him, aiding his father with some file retrieval. They all looked up at the strange sight, their boss meekly following along behind a very angry-looking woman who was leading him around. He saluted, signaling to his staff that he was aware of how bizarre this must look.

She ignored all present in the same autocratic way she had ignored them all upstairs, turning only to demand, "Where is your office?"

Rogers pointed and let her lead the way, somehow sensing he was in the presence of a very overfilled tidal basin, getting ready to flood its banks and allowing her to let loose was his best choice.

She flung open the door and, then, surprised him by motioning for him to take his command position chair while she stood breathing hard on the other side of his desk.

"I bet you don't even really know who I am, do you? Well, I'm not surprised. They are all scared shitless of me, with good reason and I hardly have anything to do with those idiots, anyway. But now that the sons of bitches are dead, I have nothing to lose, so you, Rogers are going to be the beneficiary of my purge. Don't even think about asking me any bullshit questions. I have a Ph.D. in psychology, and I know the drill, if you want to tape this, fine, I so don't give a flying fuck anymore. Turn your phone on, or whatever the hell you use."

Rogers complied, knowing at some point he would need her written agreement but certainly not now. He was almost afraid to breath in case it slowed her down.

"Okay, just to cover your ass, my name is Carmen Daniels and I have given Mr. Rogers, the head of security at the Silver Sands Condominium permission to record my statement. The date today is August 12th, 2019. I have worked as the CFO and the Chief of Staff for The Rothenstein Corporation, for twelve long, revolting years. I have done my job and worked closely with both Frederick Rothenstein and his wife Coco Rothenstein, since most of the other executives have come and gone.

"I stayed the course out of greed and self-interest. I am a single woman. I am what they call here a Jewban, a Cuban Jew. My parents brought me in on one of the early escapes from the nightmare that Cuba was and still is, and my father, who was a highly respected physician in Havana, slaved away, still does at ninety-two at his cabinet repair shop in Little Havana. I stayed with the Rothensteins because I wanted my own piece of this big fat fucking American Dream and they needed me.

"No one was as smart as I was about how to manage people and money and also, I knew how to handle them and they knew better than to fuck with me, so I was treated well and paid fantastically and I now own several small pieces of property and have enough of a nest egg to not give a shit about this job.

"I most certainly wouldn't stay, anyway. Why? You might be thinking, when those retards, Rebecca and Arnold would be in charge and I could flip them back and forth without breaking a sweat? Because I'm just too angry and I've been too angry for years.

"Power turns people into monsters. They were mainly monsters, but not completely, all that money and attention, ruined what was decent in them. I know you're thinking, well then it ruined you, too, honey, but I was still a peon. I worked my big Jewban ass off all my life.

"You need to come downtown. Your boss, I guess the little Mikey asshole and his guys are crawling all over the place, with lawyers and accountants and what none of you seem to know, is the FEDS have been swarming around us for weeks! Bet Arnold and Rebecca failed to mention that! They have to know! If there are any honest real estate developers in Miami or maybe on the planet, I haven't met one! All those deals, all those "investors." You know about the NY *Times* investigation into the Trump estate? Multiply it to the largest prime number any math genius can find. They are all so much cleverer than the FBI or IRS. I mean, really? Those guys would show up, and the entire maze of paper and computer files was so overwhelming, we would run them in circles, they would shuffle shit around and come up with some conceivably believable number to get them off the hook and make it look like they were doing their jobs, check us off and go have their tuna on rye. No way the government can handle this shit, nor are they very motivated since we're talking about some of both parties' main contributors.

"So, who would take the fall for whatever they find? Not the Rothensteins! They were going to hang me out to dry. I saw it coming, and I made my deal. They don't want me, anyway. It's fucking Miami!!! Do you have any idea, (that's rhetorical Dude, I know you don't!) how many shady real estate deals, laundered money ventures keeps this town in Maseratis? It's a bottomless well, no way to stop it, not that anyone really wants to! I am not going to take the fall for those goniffs. And now they're fucking dead!

"Good luck with solving that as old Sponge Bob would say. The list of possible suspects would fill this room, but I can tell you this. No one of the shady, scary shmuck "investors" or any of the minions that worked for them did this. In their fortress? Are you kidding me? If I'd turned on the news and heard they'd been hit in a drive by shooting or gunned down at one of their pathetic charity balls, then I'd have a list, but at the Silver Sands? No one got in there! No way any of us or even your guys could get in there without their codes and you know I'm right.

"So now, I'm really fucked! I can't even quit because of the cops and the FEDS and the lawyers and they would just subpoena me! If you want to understand them, get your skinny, Tallahassee ass (I do my homework, kiddo) downtown and take a look.

"You're never gonna solve this. Certainly, your boss isn't up to it, cocky little prick, I think I completely messed his macho little pompadour up. And I can just about guarantee you their kids didn't do this. Besides Arnold's religious fanaticism and all that Ten Commandment, Torah crap, he's a putz. And Rebecca? Get real! Frankly, I feel very sorry for her. She's the tragedy in all this.

"They really destroyed her. All that 'mommy' dependency, Coco turned her into a grotesque chia pet and her father treated her like a discarded old lay. He could barely look at her, and that was before she turned into some marginally human being. She was never fuckable to him, which was how he judged women, even daughters. He didn't molest her, not physically, but believe me, he did it mentally.

"Little girls know and then adolescent girls know when their 'daddies' don't really love them or find them appealing. It's so classic, you hardly need a degree in psychology, but since I have one, I probably observed it better.

"If the first man in your life, your father, never makes you feel pretty or special or valuable, you are totally fucked and, look at her! What's left of her. Makes me very sad. Really.

"She's a mean little nut case now, but she wasn't born that way! And her mother enabled it, kept her just where Coco needed her to be.

"Sergi will take what's left of her and dump her hard, just mark my words. He's a total sociopath. They are breeding them now like lab rats. I had a great training analyst and I remember going into see him when I'd been manipulated by a very serious sociopath I was working with and I was crying and yes, I am capable of crying! I asked him, how do you recognize the sociopaths? and he just laughed and he said, 'You can't that's what a sociopath is!' He'll dump her when he has enough. I happen to know he's got several gym bunny babes on the side, I mean look at him! Though I do know all those steroids make their pee pees shrivel or something, not my favorite visual. But none of them would want Coco and Frederick dead!

"Hello! There is no chain of command. There was them, then the clueless kids, who actually think they know enough to run this monster and ME. Trust me, this is not the kind of responsibility they would ever choose, no matter what!

"Okay, I'm done. Needed to vent this poison. I have to get back to the office and try to wrap my head around what to do next. I am not going to fucking jail for these fuckers. Good luck with your murders. If I think of anything or anyone, you will be the first to know. I like you, Rogers and I don't like anyone. You were smart enough to shut up and let me rock and roll all over this. I like that."

And with that, Carmen Daniels turned like any good commanding officer, and marched out of his office.

Calm after the tornado. Rogers took a long whistling breath and the air seemed to get cooler in his office. She had left the door open and he could see his team peering in but no one moved. *Whoa Nelly, talk about a blast of intel!*

Hildy, who had simpler agendas, came trotting in, giving him that liquid big-brown-eyed Lab look that made his hard heart flutter. She cocked her head and came right up to him and pushed against his arm with her nose, her very effective signal that she had had enough and needed to pee. He stood up and grabbed her leash from his desk. As usual her timing was impeccable, she seemed to always sense when they both needed a break; had he eaten? Oh, damn! How could he have forgotten those amazing grilled cheese delights. This made him flash on Edy Weller again and more song lyrics, *"Blue Moon you saw me standing alone" take a walk Rogers.* He checked his pocket for dog treats and Hildy leapt up and down. Unlike his fellow man, dogs didn't need a whole lot of fancy stuff to be happy.

"Come on, my darlin girl, let's get some fresh air." Pepe was waiting outside his office with Oscar. "Who the hell was that? I thought she might beat you to death with her voice!" Pepe laughed and Oscar nodded. "I thought mom was tough! Whew!"

"Very unexpected new addition to the person of interest list and a veritable Gulf Stream of information. I gotta take Hildy out and I need to get my head straight. These interviews are all buzzing in my bean. Anything new I need to know about. I won't be long."

"Well, everything and nothing. The forensics guys are through and Olivia has some news she said. She's here, she took Oscar out to lunch and she waited to talk to you."

Pepe motioned across the room and Olivia Tan strutted over, carrying a clipboard which seemed to be surgically attached to her hands. She was always carrying one. Maybe, Rogers thought, it was like some sort of security blanket for overworked female MEs.

"Hey, glad I caught you. I'm still processing stuff, but I think I found a hair that could be important. I'm running the tests and I'll let you know. "Also," she paused, "I think the TOD may be off. I know it makes no sense, but I have the feeling they were killed closer to when they were found. Hard to be exact, but looks more like around 5:00 a.m. and Oscar says he found something interesting."

Oscar gave Rogers a sideways look, as if not sure if he would be taken seriously.

"Well now, how about you come with me and Hildy on our walk and you can tell me what you found. Thanks, Doc. Let me know the minute you get results on the hair. Let's roll, Oscar."

Oscar grinned, revealing several missing teeth, that vulnerable, delicate stage of development when the kid begins to be replaced by the adolescent, and the inner and outer see saw of the beginning of the end of childhood adds layers of powerful and conflicting emotions and confusion in all interactions between the so-called adults and the still transforming pre-adults.

Rogers was childless and he had little experience with kids except Oscar, who he found, reconnected him to that part of himself and the perch between innocence and the loss of it, a road once crossed that can never be recrossed, though God only knew people never stopped trying.

Oscar knew his way around the Silver Sands better than Rogers, having spent way too many bored kid afternoons, wandering and waiting for one or another of his parents to drive him home or watch him on the beach or take him to dental appointments or enforced play dates or any of the endless kid activities that he was scheduled to engage in whether he wanted to or not. Oscar had finally gotten up the courage to tell his mother, "Mom, I'm an introvert and I will do just as much social interaction as required but no more." Pepe told him that and Rogers probably loved Oscar from that moment. Not your average thirteen-year-old, for sure.

"Mr. Rogers, I know a secret way from the basement out to the beach. The media won't be out there."

"Great, Oscar, let's do it."

Hildy seemed to know the way and Rogers followed both of them. "How does Hildy know this route?" he asked, feeling a bit territorial.

"Oh, I've taken her on a couple of walks with my dad, when you were busy. Is that okay?"

"Absolutely, though it makes me feel like a bad dog parent."

Oscar turned and smiled at him. "Get real. She's a Lab. They like attention from everyone. She loves it and I always bring one of those great treats Leena leaves everywhere."

Rogers reached in his pockets and retrieved one he always had handy. "Yep. I have them, too. So, she brings them down for Hildy?"

"She used to leave them all over for everyone's dogs. A couple of people gave her a really bad time, like she was making them fat or I don't know, she only leaves them for Hildy and the dogs she takes care of now."

Rogers pushed open the heavy reinforced steel exit door, which was not coded from the inside, probably a fire department rule, and they were on the walkway leading down to the pure white sand, raked twice a day and kept immaculately clear of seaweed or anything unsightly not up to Silver Sands level perfection. "You know Hildy isn't supposed to be on the beach here, only the Rothenstein's dogs."

"I know it, but since, well, they're all dead, right? And no one's paying any attention, I think it's okay. I know we shouldn't have brought her here before, but I mean, really. Dogs can't run on a beach, but they can go to restaurants and malls and stuff? Pretty dumb if you ask me."

"I agree. Let's do it."

Hildy was leaping with joy. They headed for the water line, Rogers keeping an eye on the possible intrusion by reporters or beach patrols, though, those guys all worked for him.

"This is great. Look how happy Hildy is! Thanks, Oscar. Sooo, what is it that you've found?"

Oscar turned and looked up at him, suddenly hesitant.

"Okay, I have some stuff that may be helpful, but if I tell you, I have to kill you."

Rogers laughed. Oscar laughed. "Oscar, you are my favorite kid, not that I have much of a list."

"Thanks, I don't get many compliments, so I appreciate it. I do kind of mean it, though. I mean not murder, but I really need you to swear you won't tell anyone what I tell you, I mean that I told you. I don't want to get anyone in trouble and I really don't want my parents to know some of it."

"Unless it endangers your survival, your secrets are safe with me."

"I guess I have to give you some history. I think you know I'm over here a lot, from way before you came and because I'm a kid and I'm pretty quiet, no one pays any attention to me, I'm usually just on a computer and unless one of your guys or my dad needs some help, I mean, no one here is really very good at the tech stuff, but they don't want their bosses to know. No disrespect, but you really suck at it! But you're the boss, so I get it."

Rogers laughed. This kid made parenthood actually seem appealing, though having that level of scrutiny might wear a little thin on a daily basis.

"I never claimed otherwise. Go on."

"Well, kids hear a lot of stuff because they don't think we're paying attention, or understanding grown-up topics or whatever, which is great for us, if we're curious or just nosy and I'm both." "I don't think you know this about me, maybe you found out today, but I'm only thirteen...."

"I thought you were twelve?"

"Um, there are these things called birthdays. I just had one. So, I'm thirteen."

"Okay kid. Elder respect required."

"Sorry, I apologize. I picked that up from hanging around Sunny and Edy so much. They're really funny and sarcastic and it's helped me a lot at school, so I've gotten to be a wise ass."

"Why does it help you at school?"

"Now, I'm really trying not to be sarcastic, I know you really don't know anything about having children, so this will be a little patronizing, but I'm thirteen and I'm a junior in high school! A total freak is what the other kids call me and a lot of them are jealous, too. I have no friends and even if I wanted to, which I don't, I'm too small to be on any teams. Sunny is my only kid friend and Edy and Grandma Ooma are my only grown-up friends and Leena, not close, but she's really nice to me and she understands not having any friends, because she just has to work all the time, which is part of the information I have.

"I know a lot about the security system for the building. I really like all that stuff and I'm just sort of really, really good at figuring it out and helping the guys understand more and fix things. This is the confidential part. Sometimes Leena would ask me to help her out with the Rothenstein's dogs, they were really awful and even though they were hardly more than big rats, they bit and pulled and sometimes she was just so tired, she'd ask me to help her take them out for their afternoon walks.

"So, I'd go up there, of course it was only on the days she knew the Rothensteins wouldn't be home or if they were out of town, sometimes Mrs. Rothenstein would ask her to stay over, so she knew the system pretty well. Also, she's wicked smart and very good with technology and I've taught her a lot. Anyway, I'd go up there and because I'm curious and nosy, I'd look around at the system, pretty cool stuff.

"She'd open the door for me and she never told me anything, but one day I noticed something, a little almost invisible hinge on the wall and I asked her what was in it and she said she had no idea what it was. I really got interested then and I did some research when I got back to the office and I found the schematics and there it was, an override button that de-activated the security system. I never told her, but I think Mr. Rothenstein used it when he had lady friends coming in late at night and didn't want to give them the codes, but also, maybe he just didn't want to have to get out of bed or whatever weirdo stuff he was into and YES, I know about all that, being thirteen and in high school, and having a lot of older cousins and being really good at social media, not that I am on any of it myself. I know about the Dark Web and all that junk, plus my mom is totally paranoid about something kinky happening to me, so she fills my brain with scary predator stories. I really like it, so I'm not complaining."

"So, Oscar, what you're telling is Mr. Rothenstein could have turned off the security system to let someone in, maybe anytime during the night."

"Yeah. I was up there several times, Leena would let me take a swim in their pool. I like to swim. Usually I go to the beach; I have to be watched, but they have a life guard and my dad always checks with him, but that pool is really cool.

"We were very careful, she'd get fired if they found out, but I also snooped around a lot and it was weird that for all the fancy equipment, once you were inside, there was nothing. I mean I'm sure they had safes and things, but there were no cameras in the rooms. I think maybe Mr. Rothenstein didn't want any evidence of his girlfriends and maybe Mrs. Rothenstein had her own secret life, I don't know about that.

"Anyway, Leena started to get nervous about it, she felt bad sneaking around and she really needed the job, so I stopped going up and if she needed help in the afternoon, she'd just call my cell and I'd meet her outside the underground exit we went out and help her walk them. A couple of times she was so tired, she'd fall down in the sand and just cry and I'd try and walk them, but I'm not that strong and six of them was hard, I just felt so bad for her. So, that's what I know and I have your word."

"That you do, Oscar and I thank you. This is beyond helpful. Consider yourself my undercover consultant. Please let me know if anything else occurs to you or if you find any other intel, just remember we can't use any of this officially, not yet, anyway."

"I get it. We better go back. My mom will be turning her high beams on me, for sure."

"Well, for what it's worth, I've got your back and the hell with all those jock jerks at school, believe me, when you're through, you'll never look back and most of them will never move forward. The last laugh well, you'll own it."

Oscar was silent, giving him the same, serious, slightly hesitant newly teenage look again. "Thanks," he said, and they walked back side by side, Hildy between them and either of them saying another word.

On the way back through the basement, Rogers stopped Oscar. "Oscar, I just thought of a couple more questions. First, does your mom know about any part of this? And second, wouldn't it ping on all your security cameras and alarm monitors if anyone up there turned off the alarms?"

"My parents only know that sometimes I helped Leena out walking the dogs. They'd freak if they thought I was up there! And, I have to go back into the system and check. It should signal down here, but it might be set up, so if they wanted no one to know when it was on or off, the override wouldn't sound any alert or maybe, you know, it was really late, maybe no one was checking it that closely. I'll let you know what I can find out. Sometimes it only pings on individual phones, like their phones. Maybe Mr. Rothenstein was the only one who had it, didn't want his family to know, but it's more likely they all have them, because sometimes it's just a drag turning it all on and off and the building is like so safe, I mean it's so overkill."

Rogers chuckled. "Well, interesting word choice, Oscar, given the outcome, maybe not!"

"Okay, so I gave you one. Bad word choice."

Rogers took Hildy off the leash and she sat without being asked and waited for her treat and then, they followed her back to the human kennel.

When they opened the security door to the office, it looked like a surprise party without a happy event. Leena Martinez, Katya Orlov, Arnold and Rebecca Rothenstein Dubinski, Sergi Dubinski and Francis LePorte were sitting in a line, looking as if they were all waiting for root canal surgery or biopsy results. Mikey was pacing around behind them, a double (at least if Pepe had made it) Cuban espresso in his hand.

"I texted you a zillion times, Roy, we're ready to go up."

Rogers avoided the defensive bait. Mikey was so clearly peeing on his territory and putting his "deputy" in his place. Rogers knew any reaction but the old John Wayne/Gary Cooper choice would only make him look weak.

"Oscar, can you watch Hildy? Pepe, I need you to come with us. Put Jose in charge down here."

This was not how Mikey had seen this going and he was thrown off course, downing his caffeine jolt and motioning for Pepe to take them all up the security elevator. "Let's do it." All of the participants stood up and without any signal fell into a pecking order formation. Family in front, then LePorte, then Katya, then Leena. Amazing, Rogers thought, how those class and status messages just translate telepathically.

No one but Mikey spoke on the fast ride up. "I know

everyone will find this very unpleasant, but we are really on the clock here and we need your help. We are looking for anything you might remember or didn't notice this morning and I need the Dubinksis to examine all valuables and see if anything is missing. Also, cash and the safes and that we will do privately. LePorte, you're the art expert, so if you will please concentrate on anything unusual."

LePorte nodded not revealing that he knew nothing about Frederick Rothenstein's collection.

They exited in the same order, the royal family in front. Codes were entered and suddenly they were all inside the lavish crime scene.

The smell of death, of fear, of something in the odor and aura of the enormous spaces, with the open door between the apartments, the wide inner hallway, making the tragedy more palpable. To die like that, after all those decades, a lifetime of marriage, a family broken by the underbelly of the American Dream, without even the final moments of their lives allowing for a chance to bring some mutual comfort or connection, went through all of them like a current of despair.

Katya and Leena burst into tears, followed by Rebecca and LePorte. The cops and the husband stood rigid and controlled, but Rogers felt a shiver of nausea move through him. What a damn waste. He had been at too many crime scenes to count, but there was something unique about this one, it felt like a psyche blackout almost too dark to deal with.

And the silence. Not a natural hush. Afterward Pepe told Rogers it felt as if their ghosts were trying to guide them toward the truth. And even as hardheaded a realist as he was, he couldn't argue with Pepe's observation. He'd felt it, too.

No one, cops included had prepared for the smash of this ugly reality. Pepe instinctively moved toward Leena and Katya and spoke to Leena in Spanish. Sergi was at his best being the strong leaning post for his bride and LePorte, caught somewhere between his highly-strung nature and his desire not to look like a limp little fruiter to these macho men, stifled his sobs and kept his head up.

Rogers was observing reactions as best he could, the detective's paranoid trolling for the subtlest sign that might turn into a clue. He also knew this was Mikey's party and he had to let him call the shots, another reminder of why he'd retired; way too frustrating.

Mikey signaled and motioned for him to move off toward Coco Rothenstein's unit.

"Man, this is some shit show. I can't do Leena, so why don't you start with them and I'll do the missing stuff part and then, maybe you'll join in. This is not my scene and you know this rich asshole gig better than I do. Okay?"

"Sounds good. Should Pepe go with me?"

"Yeah, good idea. I'm worried about my niece. She seemed okay, but she's still pretty shaky. One good thing. The Dubinski bitch wants her to take care of her dogs, so she still has a job here and I think they will reward her well."

"Can't look like a bribe, though. We've got to be very careful about that stuff until we have someone in custody."

"Yeah, yeah, Dude. I get it. I misspoke. Scratch that part and that's not Leena, anyway. Oh, and keep your phone on."

"I didn't get a signal, Mikey. I was waiting to hear from you. No call came through. All these tall buildings, service can be very spotty, and I was on the beach and I have some interesting new intel."

Mikey stopped, turning on one of his built up black heels and gave him a slightly angry look. Or maybe competitive would be a better description, Rogers knew the glare.

"Oh yeah. Fill me in, later."

"Confidential informant, so I can't, yet. But, trust me, it may be very useful."

Now Mikey's eyes were flashing anger. "Sure. Sure. But don't forget who's in charge here, Roy."

"Never forget it, Mikey. Not a chance."

And with that, he turned and walked over to the two sobbing women and signaled Pepe to lead them into Frederick Rothenstein's lair, wishing he had a candy bar and wondering how a dog biscuit might work on his dropping blood sugar.

It was soon clear to Rogers, that his "assignment" of crime scene witnesses was clearly Mikey's way of putting him in his place, a choice Rogers could actually identify with, but he understood pretty quickly that nothing would come of it. Katya and Leena were still emotional, but under control enough to re-describe exactly what they saw (not much). Both had seen the horrifying sights and fled. Neither (or at least so they said) had approached the victims, touched anything, moved anything or would have any idea if something was missing.

Of course, now that Rogers really understood that both women had far more access to both apartments than he had been aware of, it was certainly possible, that cash, especially if the Rothensteins left jewelry and money piled up here and there, or at least, Coco did, could be missing but only Rebecca, most likely, or LePorte might know how much.

Since he had promised Oscar, his questioning of Leena had to be very careful. Katya was acting a little strangely, avoiding eye contact, wringing her hands, and blinking a lot, which he knew could be nerves, the memories of Russian interrogations or lying.

"I only look for a minute, then I run to the other apartment and then I run to help Leena. I only wanted to get out! I was so afraid someone was still there! I clean every day. But I don't see anything. I, I see the you know, from the women. used towels and the sheets and things, every day, but I only put in the laundry room, but Mrs. Diaz does.

"Mrs. Diaz, she would know, if she looked. But she hasn't been here since the day before, so, I don't know. I am sick from this. I want to go home, please!"

Something was off with her, but he knew nothing more would come of keeping her there, so he waited while she gave motherly comfort to Leena and let her leave. Leena was calm now, probably the result of the medication the hospital sent her home with and he decided it was worth a shot to talk to her alone.

"Leena, let's go sit somewhere quiet for a minute, so we can talk without you having to be in this room."

She nodded, sighing with relief. "I've only been in the kitchen and the dog's room and here and Mr. Rothenstein's study, a couple of times, I really don't know the apartment very well."

Rogers could feel his eyebrows raise slightly. "How about the outside by the pool?" He waited for any reaction. She seemed surprised by the suggestion, but not suspicious.

"Sure. It's so pretty out there. I look out, sometime." She led him to the enormous French doors leading out from the Great Room to the vast terrace and they instinctively sat at the giant white marble table facing the ocean.

Rogers could almost connect with how being around all this magical kingdom unreal world these people took for granted could infect anyone susceptible. Why was he so immune to its charm and would not want a life like this if it was handed to him without any required Devil deal? On his part, he didn't even ponder. It actually turned him off. But, he certainly knew how many of the tragedies he had witnessed, crimes of mendacity, greed, envy and the panic associated with losing any of it; divorce plots, child against parent, the threats of having to face the world without all the ballast of this huge seductive floaty under them, would lead to acts of both intricately plotted and impulsive explosions of violence.

Leena blew her nose and smiled at him, her Madonna face, mobile and alive now, radiated the kindness and beauty he had thought she was cut off from. Where to begin, that was always the hardest part and he'd already blown the LePorte/Dubinski interview, so this was important.

"Leena, Oscar told me you bring treats for Hildy and help walk her sometimes. I want to thank you. It's very kind of you."

She exhaled deeply, as if sensing he was a friend, not a cop. "I love Hildy. And Oscar, he helps me out too. No need to thank me, it's my pleasure."

"I know you're probably exhausted and I want to get you out of here and home as soon as possible, but I was hoping there might be something you've remembered or can tell me, more about anyone in and out of there when you've been here, maybe a conversation you overheard, anything to help us. Also, were you ever aware that either of them left money and jewelry laying around?

"I've really been trying to remember Mr. Rogers. I was here every day, so you would think I'd know more, but I usually only stayed in the dog's areas and the Rothensteins had rules about directly talking to them, I mean I had a bit more freedom because of the pups, and since I was the only one who seemed to be able to control them, but they were both really private.

"If they had guests, they closed the doors, I mean to their studies or wherever. They did leave, or Mrs. Rothenstein left money and watches and things lying around, but I would never even think about going near anything! OMG! They've been so good to me and I wasn't raised like that. I mean, I don't even know if she did it to test us! And Katya would never touch anything. Sometimes she would pick things up, jewelry and money and put it in a basket and march into Mrs. R's bedroom with it. She hated that she was careless, I mean, we are working people, so it is totally strange to us to see anyone do that."

Rogers was watching her for signs of dissembling. He saw

none. He waited, sensing she had something more to tell him and hoping it would be a confession of sorts.

"Mr. Rogers, I need to tell you something, but I'm really worried it will get Oscar into trouble."

"It won't, whatever you tell me I will keep between us."

Her lovely, flawless face softened. If confession is good for the soul, her face seemed to offer proof.

"I didn't tell you the truth. I was really burned out, between school and my family and all the jobs and I asked Oscar sometimes to help me walk the dogs, when the Rothenstein's were out, which they were most of the time, but I only asked him to come up here a few times. I knew I'd get fired and he'd get in trouble or maybe, even they would fire his dad or something awful, but I think I was kind of desperate, so I'd let him use their pool, to thank him. It's so hot in the summer and the beach has been closed a lot because of that awful Red Algae, and he really loves to swim, I just couldn't help it.

"I never went in myself, I swear! We were really careful, and we never went into any of the private parts of the apartment, but Oscar's well, he's nosy, so he'd poke around a bit, he was fascinated with the techno stuff, but then I got too nervous he'd get caught and we stopped. It was only for a month or so and not every day or anything. But, I felt I needed to tell you the truth."

"Well, I am very glad you did and your secret is safe. Did you happen to see or hear anything when the two of you were up here alone?"

"I've been trying to remember and the only thing I can think of besides what I told you in the hospital, or I think I did, I was pretty doped up, is the day before they were, you know, Mr. Rothenstein, came home early. I was just getting back from walking the dogs and I was feeding Mrs. Rothenstein's and I heard noises in his apartment and I was a little scared, so I took off my shoes and tip-toed across the hall and he was on the phone in his study, the door between the living room and the study was open and I could see him standing at his desk and he was shouting at someone on the phone, something about his business and the government and I heard him say, 'I'm not going down for this, that's what I pay you bastards for and you will all be very sorry if you cross us.' I'm not exactly sure those were his words, but I think it's pretty close and he slammed the phone down. I ran back and put on my shoes and then I had to go feed his dogs, so I pretended. He was always really calm and polite, and he held himself together, but he was clearly upset, he'd even taken his tie off and thrown it on the floor and he never did anything like that! Then he seemed to forget I was even there and he paced around and called Mrs. Rothenstein on his cell and he said, 'Come home, now.'

"So that was all I heard. I left as soon as I could and I always said goodbye if they were there, but I didn't think I should."

"This is very helpful Leena. By any chance did you hear him say a name?" "No, I could be wrong, but I thought I heard that woman, Ms. Daniels, who runs the company, curse at him, her voice is really loud, so I could hear her, or I think it was her, I can't be sure."

"Leena, thanks for this. I'm giving you my card with my private cell, so if you need me for anything or you think of something else, call me anytime and I'll have an officer take you home now. You're one special young lady."

She blushed and the rose tint moving into her cheeks, almost looked photo shopped. "I feel so much better telling you. I'm sorry. I was scared for Oscar."

"Oscar is cool. Don't even think about it."

"Would you tell him, I'll see him tomorrow? Mrs. Dubinski has hired me to take care of her rescues. She still has four she hasn't placed and she's not in great shape to handle them and Mrs. Lovee asked if I would walk Lola for her, I think this has been very stressful for her and it's really too humid at her age, to be out there with Lola. I have time off from the country club, so it's really helpful for me."

"Well, that's great."

"One thing, I think it will make you laugh. Have you interviewed the Shmumpkins, yet?"

"The Shmumpkins? Nope, I have them on the list and I think I'd remember that name."

Leena laughed. "This isn't very nice, but they have these little bratty trophy sons and all these "experts" in and out, these women, some of them I know from the club or from working with them in the Aventura Mall and now they're experts in teaching clueless parents how to take care of their kids. I mean, they come and teach them "sleep training" and "potty training" and "educate their palates." There are a few other couples like them in the building and they do it too, but they are away for the summer. It's really ridiculous and they brag sometimes about how these parents are afraid of them and try to impress them because they're worried about their friends thinking they're bad mothers; they have all these women on speed dial.

"Anyway, Mrs. Shmumpkin called me today and asked if I had time to help her Dobermans recover from their neuticle surgeries. I had no clue what she was talking about and Dobermans are pretty intense if the owners aren't really good at training them, and since I knew about all the "experts" she has needed to help her train her little ones, I hesitated. But I had to ask her what neuticle surgery is and she got really nasty. 'Well, if you don't even know about it, you're clearly not good enough at what you do for my babies' (she was talking about the dogs, I think, anyway!) She hung up! So, of course I was curious, and I googled it and these crazy people are having artificial testicles implanted in their male dogs who have been neutered so they don't get all neurotic about losing their manhood and have self-esteem and dignity issues! OMG. I want to tell Edy about it. She still does a column for the Miami Herald and I thought she'd have lots of fun with that one. I'm sure Mrs. Shmumpkin will bad mouth me to her friends and they all have dogs, but I don't think I could handle it."

"Leena, I gotta tell you, I am learning more about this job of mine from these interviews than from all my years in Miami Police. Give me a good old-fashioned Drug King, any day!"

"Well, I'm not just blabbing, I know you're trying to eliminate suspects and I think you can sort of skip them. Also, I think their husbands work for the company, maybe lawyers and one is a concierge doctor for the Shmumpkins so probably for all of them, so why would they do something like that? Killing the Golden Goose, isn't that an old saying?"

"I think it's pretty timeless, now go home and get some sleep. And eat something! You have to take care of yourself, Leena."

He was probably overstepping since he barely knew her, but she was one of those women who brought forth the protective instincts, probably in every man she met, even kids like Oscar.

She leaned over and kissed his cheek, her silky curls grazing his neck. "Thank you, Mr. Rogers. I'll try. Glad this was helpful."

Rogers stood up and walked over to the same railing he and Olivia Tan and Mikey had leaned on what seemed like days before, but was only this morning.

The sea was calm, but he could feel some wind kicking up and he prayed they would escape hurricane season this year. Last year had been a total nightmare even without a major high-profile killing. Hurricanes, red tide, shores filling with rotting dead fish covering the Gulf Coast and destroying all tourism, from fancy resorts to mom and pop day fishing charters. So much for life in paradise, though life everywhere seemed increasingly loaded with natural disasters or what the Panhandle store front evangelicals might call the countdown to God's Wrath.

Edy, Sunny and Grandma Ooma were glued to the TV watching an exclusive interview, clearly just taped or maybe even live with Katya Orlov on some new hot and heavy mayhem infusing crime interview show. This was the kind of case that had made TV hosts like Nancy Grace higher than helium.

The tearful housekeeper, looking haggard and slightly tipsy was giving a full account of how the bodies of the Rothensteins looked, in all the gory, grotesque details (some of which, Edy thought, she was probably inventing) since no one had been told how they were killed. They were all mesmerized, horrified and of course, human nature being what it is, fascinated. It was, quite a visual, even as described through the teary, broken English of the Russian maid.

"Holy shit, I wonder if Rogers knows about this?" Edy had not stopped thinking about him for more than the time it had taken her to churn out her new column, since, murders or no murders she had a deadline and couldn't really write about today's horror, yet.

Sunny shot her a "really?" look and flipped her hair, indicating that there were no secrets about this very strange new addition to their lives. "Why don't you call him. Everything's back on now." Sunny and grandma Ooma exchanged what Edy thought were winks, but she might be just a tad paranoid about whatever the hell was happening to her.

"Okay, Good idea. "I'll get his card."

"Mom, I have it in my phone. Here, I'll connect you."

Edy could feel a blush moving up her neck and into her cheeks. She had never, to her memory blushed before. *"I've got you under my skin"* ......oh boy.

He answered on the first ring. "Sunny?"

"Oh, Hi. No, it's Edy, I'm using her phone. This may be lame, I mean you may know all about it, but we're all glued to crime TV watching Katya Orlov give all the grisly details of the Rothenstein's cause of death. I bet they paid her a bundle, but I'm sure it's not what you wanted."

"Damn! Well, now it makes sense. She seemed very evasive and nervous when we did the walk through. No wonder. And thank you. No, we've been interviewing non-stop and we're upstairs with the family looking for anything missing. Mikey is going to freak. No way to really stop it though. And I'm sure the offer was too hard for her to refuse. She had no way of getting any severance or anything. Thanks for the heads up."

"You're very welcome." "*You said you loved me, but were you just being kind. Or am I losing my mind?*" Edy inhaled – maybe she was humming out loud!

They were both silent, one very awkward moment of hesitation, Edy thought it was probably the way someone about to do their first parachute jump felt before leaping out of the plane.

"Um, I don't know when you'll be through for the night, but I have some really good Bourbon, small batch, they call it and I made a sort of Irish stew deal, if you want to come down. I'll be up late. I'm finishing a column and I'm way too wired to sleep, anyway. So..."

"Miss Edy, I will keep that in my head to see me though the rest of the interviews for today. Probably won't be until after 9 or so."

"Perfect. I should be done and have this column filed by then."

"Well, thank you, ma'am. I'll let you know more when I get through up here. What channel is this show on?

"Ten, Miami local channel but it's syndicated everywhere. I think this is a big tsunami of a story, so get your scuba suit ready."

Witchcraft, that crazy witchcraft...when you arise a need in me my heart says yes indeed in me... "See you later," he said and clicked off.

Edy kept her eyes on the phone, not risking the two human and two canine eye sets scrutinizing her.

"She slid the phone along the couch to Sunny. "If you ever want to leave this apartment again you will zip it, kiddo."

Edy jumped up and headed for her little office without giving either of them a chance to reply.

Was this like a date? A Date!!! She hadn't had a date in what? Twenty years. OH ba-rother! She hadn't had sex in that long, either. Well, maybe a couple of times, best forgotten. Talk about rusty. Talk about never really not being rusty. Talk about never, ever having understood love songs, let alone that feeling. How sad, she thought. I've never actually been in love with anyone but a kid, a dog and a Grandma and I'm almost sixty years old. Talk about pathetic!

And he will see it. And I don't even want to hide it, but that's what I feel like, like I've been attacked by love bugs. What the hell is a love bug, anyway? One of those stupid expressions we use all the time and have no clue what they really mean. Gotta look it up. Get a grip Edy Weller, calm yourself or you will not be able to handle this. Breathe. Breathe. Finish your column and think about something else. Maybe a book you'll write about this case. Yes. Think about that. Think about Irish stew, make some garlic bread. Oh, shit! An audience! Sunny and Ooma. Gotta talk to them. Funny, privacy had most certainly not been my issue. Life really does just keep getting more fascinating, never easier, for sure, what a crock that is, all that Golden Years crap, well I'm not there, yet, but close enough to know there is no such thing. Probably invented by some Gong head that couldn't handle the truth. Life just goes faster and contains far more dead ends, trap doors, banana peels and magic, yes, magic too. I may be actually becoming living proof, far better than a stiletto in my eyeball. Edy, stop it. Write something funny.

MIAMI HERALD COLUMN:

For want of a better description, I'm going to call
this my cautionary rant on plastic surgery insanity;
these are all true stories (even if I were a novelist, I
couldn't make this stuff up). I offer four tales from
the dark side.

Recently in the city of Shanghai a contest was
held. The competition was for the title of the Ugliest
Girl in Shanghai (which is, a rather massive place).
There were 50 finalists. Guess what the prize was? A
complete surgical reformation of the winner's being.
Now, try to imagine what must have been, a rather
bizarre mix of emotions.

"Oh boy! I won!!! I won! I'm the absolute ugliest
girl in a city of 24 million people!" "Whoopee." Must
have been quite a family celebration.

China, it seems, is even more obsessed with
physical perfection than America or Brazil or Vene-
zuela (I think those are the other biggest consumers
for surgical reupholstery). In China, height has become so mega an issue that (are you ready?) if you
are a woman under 5ft 1 or a man under 5ft 5 there
are law schools that will not accept your application
nor will the foreign service. In some cities women
who are under 5ft. 3 CAN'T TAKE THE DRIVING
TEST.

Being short, also means, you are far less likely
to find a good job or a husband or wife from a higher
perch (literally and otherwise).

Of course, where there is a problem, there is a
market and the new market, not just in China, by
the way, was first developed in Russia to cure birth

deformities, but now, is being used to make people taller!

To be taller, Chinese men and women are having the Russian procedure that involves (I won't be too graphic, if you want the stomach-turning parts, Google it) basically, sawing your femur bones in half (disconnecting your legs from your feet) inserting various metal rods and posts and screws that run from outside your legs into these contraptions and then, as stretching the inside tissues, and while the bones heal you keep tightening, sort of the 21st century version of the Rack or one of the other ancient torture devices.

Besides the agonizing pain, there is the lying in bed for months at a time, and the enormous expense. One totally demented N.Y. man who was 5ft 6 but felt that inside he was SIX FEET spent a year and $85,000 I believe, to add six inches; never pausing to consider that any woman who would not have loved his 5ft. 6 real self, and would love his 6ft. fake self, was not, probably (this is just a guess) worth going through that for to begin with.

I'm imagining the first naked love scene between this guy and his dream girl.

"Oh, darling, you're so sexy, you're so tall! I hate short men. Hmmm, what are those weird scars and puncture marks all over your shins? War wounds? Did you suffer much?

"I did suffer, but I did it for love. I was short, but I spent a year of agony and had six inches added to my height and then I met you."

Off camera, sound of dream girl, fleeing in repulsion. I think the inches might have served his ultimate purpose better if he'd added them, well you know, elsewhere, but, maybe Randy Newman was right. "Short people got no reason to live."

A Chinese man, no matter how brilliant or handsome, who is under 5 ft. 7 cannot apply for the Diplomatic Corp.

One more thing; when it doesn't work? Well how about never being able to stand up again because your leg bones can't support your weight? There are lots of horrific stories, but that one kind of says it all.

Next, ripped from the pages of my beloved N.Y. Post. There was recently an arrest in one of the five boroughs of N.Y.C. of a quite industrious lady, who figured out that in her Hood the women were craving Beyonce Butts, which seems to be the new site of sexual panting formerly reserved for big fake boobs.

Hmm, she thought, probably while on a trip to Home Depot to do some repair work on her basement. HMMMMMMM. What if I got myself one of those guns that shoot silicone into wall boards and fills in cracks and stuff and shot it into their rears? A Eureka moment for the twerking set. And so, an entrepreneur was born. Without any surgical training, she converted (probably using the same materials) a room in her house and started advertising; far cheaper than liposuction from a real doctor and the word spread faster than a butt on a bar stool, women came.

God only knows what she actually did to them, but the result (hence arrest) resulted in the death of at least one "patient" and numerous blood infections, abscesses and lots of gobs of glue gunk moving around and ending up in very unexpected places, more Gumby than Beyonce. And, it seems she is just one of many of these self-styled cosmetic improvers doing the same dangerous, crazy stuff all over the country. WHAT IS THE MATTER WITH US!

Finally the ultimate madness. In Manhattan there was a former model, fifty-nine years of age. 5ft. 9 inches tall and 130 pounds, which even in anorexic circles would be considered damn thin. She was also, according to her husband, so gorgeous that bands would stop playing when she entered a gala (well, that is fairly nauseating, anyway, but whatever). Even this was not enough glam for our girl, maybe a bit of sag around her middle, only noticeable, I bet, under merciless department store dressing room lights after demonic scrutiny. Sooooo, off she went to (at least) a plastic surgeon to have whatever it was liposunctioned out.

Oh, there was just this one little thing. She had a HEART TRANSPLANT a few years before. She actually did put this information on her pre-op information form, so the doctor knew and she listed all the medications, etc., she probably needed to stay alive. No problema for him. Big problema for her. She died on the table of cardiac arrest. But, man oh man, did she look svelte in that open coffin. He then proceeded to delete the information about her HEART TRANSPLANT. Everyone is blaming him. Except me.

There will always be doctors or housewives with spackle guns preying on our insecurity and low self-esteem, which seems to be increasing in social network day by day.

Teenagers are PHOTOSHOPPING THEIR SELFIES. No one wants to be who they are, nothing is enough, the bar keeps rising and the Facebooking of the universe has turned us into a maddening crowd of increasingly superficial, pathological narcissists.

I read about a new disorder of obsessive "selfie" taking where one teenage boy was taking up to 200 selfies a day, because none of them came out looking the way he wanted to look. We are becoming a race of emotional zombies, feeding on the tissue thin surface of what it means to be a valuable being.

So, what's next? Maybe docs will start flocking to the Netherlands, where the average height is something like 6ft. 2 and convincing them that being too tall is a bad thing and performing leg-shortening surgeries and muffin abs, will start being hot and reverse lipo will be the rage and Home Depot will open a Do-It-Yourself, cosmetic aisle using common every day materials (all sustainable and organic) to enhance yourself without ending up either dead or with lumps of globby stuff sticking out of your ass. One can hope.

If he gets this, if he chuckles that funny little insider chuckle he has, I'll know he really does like me, no place to hide who I am after this. She yawned and stretched and checked her watch. *7, maybe a bath. Hmmm. A shower and a bath in one day. There's a clue the "Ladies in the Living Room" would not miss.*

And then, from some large gaping pit of sadness and loneliness, catching her completely off guard, she burst into choking sobs, which seemed to have no end as they had no beginning; not a thought or a memory, that she could get to without Rod Duran, anyway. How long since she'd had a phone session with him? It had been a long time since she'd cried like this, gasping for breath and covering her face with her hands to muffle the sounds. Comfort was not what she needed, some grief is just too private for comfort, a kind of need to connect to the deepest parts of oneself, she sat with it and cried her loss and fear out.

After the purge, there was peace. She inhaled as deeply as she could, wiped her eyes, blew her nose, pushed send and turned off her computer. What the hell was that about? She knew Duran would say it was "transitional," the grief of change, equally powerful before something possibly wonderful as it is before or during something terrible.

If she had a best friend anymore, that was who she'd call, but she didn't. Maybe that was part of the sadness. Women were supposed to have close friends they could turn to raw and ragged and shredded. What had happened to her? She hadn't even thought about it much since Ooma appeared in their lives. When she moved to Miami, she began to realize that her friendships were mostly what Duran had called "lopsided." She had resisted that idea for a long time, but having this new little family and the relief of the wolf leaving her door, made it easier to accept.

All of her friendships were about what she gave and the needs she met for others. Sometimes, after spending an evening or a lunch with someone she considered a close friend, she realized that in all the years she'd known them, they'd never even asked a question about herself or her life. She knew everything about them, both from listening to their rants, vents, whines the way friends do and paying attention. She never forgot a birthday or a thank you or failed to call or email if they were in crisis or sick or going through any kind of life struggle. She knew the names of their pets, their parents, their siblings, where they grew up, all of it, but she had to accept that they really knew not a damn thing about her. Never asked a question, some of them had never even asked about her work or read anything.

It wasn't just any one of these things, it was the whole idea of what a friend should be; something she'd clearly never understood, her neediness and loneliness were probably too blinding. She gave, they took, appreciatively, she wasn't that masochistic, but when she moved, she waited and she realized that if she didn't make the gesture, send the e-mail, call, she never heard from almost any of them.

She was always priming the pump and then she got really mad and then really scared and then really sad (all good things Duran said) and tried to look straight down deep into that hole inside her she had been trying to fill without any idea that all she was doing was digging it deeper. So, she just let it go.

And her life in this bizarre, foreign new place and dealing with it and Sunny and a new and complex "relative" and trying to still do some decent work, was pretty consuming. Love and friendship kind of got checked off her marketing list of necessities.

Miami was not exactly a great place to make a close female friend; not exactly her kind of people, all done up in clothes she would never be caught dead in, shoes that would lead to an ER visit, false eyelashes, eyebrow tattoos, fake boobs, lips, fat suctioning, all sorts of revolting cosmetic procedures to tighten your vagina (talk about rustolium!) or your ass or inner thighs or any movable part and it never ended. There were twenty-four-year-olds in the building gabbing about Botox for their "forehead wrinkles." "Well if we start now, the muscles will stay relaxed and we'll never have wrinkles." Earth to Miami? Fake tans and fake hair and fake faces and acres of beauty and diet products.

Aging was looked on as some preventable and terrible gross aberration only real for the lower echelons. Rebecca Rothenstein may be the ultimate example of the madness, but every trip to the market or the CVS gave Edy another glimpse of how very foreign a land she was now inhabiting and further closing her off from her own need to be seen, known, loved or to have a real friend.

CHAPTER 13

Rogers stood for a moment holding his phone in his palm as if it held some mystical power. He could feel his pulse, maybe he was just in need of a snack or... "*I stand and I wait for the touch of your hand in the moonlight*" ... whoa Nelly. She felt it, too. What a thing! Mikey was almost running toward him, snapping him back into reality.

"Do you know about the maid on TV describing the crime scene? Fucking unbelievable!"

"I just heard. Have one of the guys record it or something, we've got to get on with this deal. No point in questioning Leena anymore, but I did learn a few new things, I'll save for our de-briefing session and Pepe has a list of all the interviewees. I asked him to talk to a couple of people pretty low on the suspect scale, so he can update us on that, too."

"Good Good. I can still shake loose one more homicide guy, Miami is on a violence cycle or something and some hottie was sunbathing on South Beach and got clocked by a fucking palm tree. The whole tree fell on top of her. Talk about bad vacation vibes! Olivia had to run to do that one and this case just went totally off the fucking charts viral, so I really need your help. I think the brother, Arnold is losing his fucking shit. Check him out. He's wandering around, bowing and praying... Davening they call it, I think sort of the Hassidic equivalent of the Muslim prayer rituals.

"Whatever the fuck it is, he's not in a mosque or a temple, and he's got those leather straps wound around his arm and he's kind of flagellating himself with them, and muttering under his breath, some Hebrew but some English, things like, "Sin, sin, Godless, we will all pay; body desecration, sin against God, Sodom, Whores of Babylon, shit like that. We can't snap him out of it, so I'm just having one of our guys shadow him in case he freaks. Maybe you can question him, but the daughter and her husband are tearing around the mother's apartment, like it's sale day at Macy's. I think she's onto something, but she doesn't like me, I'm on her Latino servant mind set I think, so, go charm her; he doesn't seem to know shit. I don't think the mother would have been into him, either. Not Jewish, and a body building peon. Anyway, get ready for looney tunes time."

Rogers followed him across the enormous, dark empty hallway, still thinking about his phone call, as if it were a lovely little rainbow in the middle of this ugliness.

Rebecca Dubinski had changed out of her feathers and plastic leggings into something, maybe appropriate for Sunny Weller or Leena, who both had more sense than to wear anything like it, some kind of baby doll top, cut very low to show off her puckered, over tanned breasts and jeans so tight and shredded all over, that her skeletal legs looked even more unnerving. Her heels were so high, he thought she might just plunge forward in her agitation (most likely fueled by many more Patron shots and God knew what else, which could work for them unless she just slumped over).

"Mrs. Dubinski, have you found anything missing or out of place?" He was as calm and soft spoken as if she was on the balcony ledge preparing to jump.

"OH My God!!!!! Yes. Yes! My poor mommy! She was so good. So generous to people. I warned her about leaving all that cash around. I mean, I'm her daughter, you know, I do it, too and jewelry, I just forget sometimes, we're just all too trusting, too nice, but this is Miami and you have to have lots of cash handy all the time. Tipping this guy and that delivery person and the car attendants and everyone, repair people here and at the club. If you don't, they don't show up! Everyone here knows that!"

Sergi put one of his huge arms with a hand the size of a boxing glove around her shoulders. "Baby, I think, maybe, you are not understanding that this is the way it is for rich people, not everyone does this. People just see you differently, they expect it."

"Yes, yes! They do! And mommy was out all the time, everywhere and so she always kept lots of cash, in her desk, in the napkin drawer, in the kitchen, on her night table and there was a big...there is a big velvet lined box of jewelry. Not everything was in the safe; she would dump things in there and she was always buying more. It made her feel happy, especially after daddy left, it filled a need, so, there's layers and layers of jewelry. I don't know how much cash she had when she, when it happened, but I know she had Francis go to the bank for her every week and get cash, as much as you can take out under the IRS radar, so I bet she had around, oh, not a huge amount, maybe $50,000 or so on hand all the time. It made her feel safe! Right Francis?!"

Francis who seemed to be in robot mode simply nodded.

Rogers and Mikey avoided eye contact, the reality that to this woman $50,000 petty cash funds lying around your apartment "wasn't much" pinging right into their brain stems.

Rogers cleared his throat, wishing it was bourbon time or at least a glass of water, but not wanting to slow her down.

"Look, look here!" Rebecca Dubinski began pulling out drawers that were filled with cash and then waved her bare crepey arm at them, "follow me!"

They did as told, down another long hallway, past the Moon meditation room with the mushroom chairs, the Yanni music or whatever it was still playing and into Coco Rothenstein's enormous master suite.

Rogers thought it looked like it had been designed by someone like Elon Musk, with the possibility of it separating from the floor and propelling her into outer space. By the huge bed, which was suspended on wires from the ceiling, was an enormous mirrored night stand shaped like a small coffin with talon like claws made from some form of stone as legs.

"See!" Rebecca flung her arm out and pointed to a very large blue velvet lined molded resin bowl filled to the top with jewelry.

"Mommy had no idea how much stuff was in there, but I have a perfect memory for clothes and jewels, and I took photos of it all way before this, and I went through it before you came. There are things missing! All from the bottom, I mean things she hadn't worn or thought about for years. A solid gold cigarette case with an emerald clasp and matching lighter from Paris; she dumped them when she stopped smoking, so that's at least ten years ago! I asked if I could have them, but she wanted me to stop so she said no. She, was always trying to help me! You know. Oh, God, my poor mommy!!!"

Rogers and Mikey exchanged cop eyes and Mikey nodded.

Rogers moved just slightly closer to her as if trying to keep her focused. "I know this is very painful Mrs. Dubinski, but I can't tell you how important this information is to the investigation. We admire your courage and we're very grateful for your help at such a terrible time."

Mikey smiled. He had to admire how Rogers just knew what to say. Maybe all those psych courses he was always taking really helped.

Rebecca Dubinski, visibly relaxed, stood straighter, making her almost at eye level with little Mikey. "Thank you, detective, that means a lot."

Rogers was understanding what Carmen Daniels meant about

the tragedy of this woman. Outside of her mother, and her clearly self-motivated husband, this was a desperately self-loathing and insecure woman who inhaled any offer of praise, without even thinking of the motives behind it.

"So, I also found, there's a very expensive diamond and platinum Patek Philippe watch missing and a pair of Bulgari diamond earrings. They weighed about five carats! She stopped wearing them because they were too heavy and they hurt her ears. I kept telling her to sell them, but she just dumped them in the bowl. I don't even know how I remembered them. She hadn't worn them in years! But they were in there at the bottom. Someone took things they figured she would never miss!!! So, no stranger would know that!!!! OH MY GOD, someone is after us!!!

"And my brother is going crazy. He's furious at me, furious at everyone. It's against his crazy religious faith to do an autopsy even with the rabbi there or to not bury the bodies within twenty-four hours!" He won't take any medication. I think he's going to have a nervous breakdown. And he doesn't know where anything is. He hardly ever came up here. His kids drove my parents crazy. So we mostly saw them at their apartments, or in restaurants."

"Any idea about other valuables?"

"Francis says no art or sculpture, or paintings are missing. I can't tell you about the cash, but it does seem a little light to me. I never went into daddy's things. He was totally private and everything was perfect and locked up except one closet the police have crime taped. I know he has a collection of very expensive watches, but they're in some coded drawer in his closet. It doesn't look like the safes or anything like that has been touched."

"I hate to ask this of you Mrs. Dubinski, but maybe later when you've had some rest, you could make a list of the people who were in and out of your mother's apartment on any kind of regular basis. And also, do you know anything about any override buttons, concealed near the alarm systems so they could be turned off?"

"Of course I know! We all have them, the family, not the other residents. Even in an emergency it would let us out faster. But we all got pretty lazy about setting everything. I mean Sergi is always setting it, because I forget."

"Well, unless you can think of any other missing valuables, I would say, we can wrap this up for tonight, but if you would be so kind as to show us where the override button or switch or whatever is, that would be most helpful."

"Yes. Follow me. I need to check on Arnold. Sergi, will you go first, see if he's able to talk to them or if we should send for Goldy?"

"Of course, darling. I'll meet you by the front door unless I need your help with Arnold."

And with that, they re-traced their route, following behind their tiny Empress more confused than ever.

When they reached the front entrance, Rebecca pushed on an almost invisible little spot on the wall by the lighting system not close to the security controls, making it more impossible to detect and a small latch opened. Inside was a button, as low tech as the other equipment was state of the art. "Here. Simple. Push it and a tiny green light next to it goes on and that means it's connected. Push it again and it turns blue, that means it's off."

Rogers took out his phone and snapped a picture, just in case.

"Is that necessary?" Rebecca clicked her heel down, to express her dislike of this action.

"I'm afraid it is, but it will be held in top security, that I can guarantee."

"Oh sure, Like Katya Orlov! She's done and I will make sure she never works in Miami again, I can promise you that! After all my parents did for her! No loyalty. I even helped her mother immigrate! I don't care how much they paid her, she'll regret it!"

Rogers felt an urge to tell her to zip it, making threats in front of cops was not a great idea, but the moment had passed and before they could move across the hall, Sergi appeared looking as distressed as it was likely possible for him to look.

"Baby, your brother is not okay. Get Goldy up here, but we may need to call 911, or Rogers, can you get the paramedics here? I don't think he can be left here or alone. He needs to go to the hospital for evaluation and sedation. He's acting crazy."

Rebecca trotted toward her father's apartment, Rogers close behind, preparing to catch her if she pitched forward. "Arnold? What's happening here?"

Arnold Rothenstein was running in circles around his father's massive desk tearing at his pais locks and his shirt, having already thrown off his coat and hat.

"They are unburied! They are alone! They are unwashed, they are cutting into them! They will never find resurrection; the Messiah will not save them. This is unholy! Unholy!!!! The Torah is clear. Clear!!! God will strike us all. All!!! We have to get them. We have to put them in plain pine boxes and bury them now! Now! They can't desecrate their bodies. It's a sin. A mortal sin!!!!"

Rogers stepped forward, hoping to reason with him. "Mr. Rothenstein, we have consulted the Rabbi at your synagogue and the medical examiner has talked with him at length. There are exceptions in Jewish law when murder or suicide is involved and he will honor that because of the brutality of the crime and the possibility it was an anti-Semitic hate crime, though we've found no evidence of that except from the internet, the usual haters. So, I hope that brings you some comfort and he is there with the medical examiner."

Arnold Rothenstein was too far gone, Rogers quickly realized, to hear anything but the fanatic's panic, eternal hell and damnation, the same stuff he heard in all those Tallahassee churches and the Mosques he went to scouting for potential threats. "In the name of God," caused more hate, death, violence and war than everything else ever laid on the natural or man-made world.

Rogers always felt if there was a God it was something so powerful and vastly beyond human understanding that if whatever gender-neutral energy force or whatever the blazes God was, would find all of this unbelievably insane. What was that Paul Simon lyric? "God only knows when God makes his plan, what information is available to the mortal man." Well, amen, to that.

While they stood trying to figure out what to do with Mr. Rothenstein, Jr., his wife came running in, minus her head scarf, clearly caught in the midst of some private bathing ritual. "What? Arnold, my God! What is wrong? The sight of his wife appearing without her head covering and in a dressing gown and bare-legged seemed to push him from the edge of flip-out to full blown psychotic break. He picked up a paper weight from his father's desk and ran toward her, aiming it at her uncovered head. "You, too!!! Infidels, whores! Like my parents! Like my sister! Shame! Shame!!!"

Goldy screamed and ducked, covering her head with her pale, polishless fingers, Rogers moved forward, Pepe leapt across the coffee table and they both tackled him just as he was ready to smash the heavy bronze object into his wife's skull.

"Pepe, 911. Now!"

They handcuffed him and he thrashed, still screaming about eternal damnation and calling his wife a whore. Rebecca knelt down almost tipping over and helped Goldy Rothenstein up and led her sister-in-law away from the scene. Rogers could hear her saying to Goldy. "It will be all right. I'll give you something to calm you down and you can go with him, but he needs to go to the hospital, he could hurt you or the children. He's had a breakdown. You know, Goldy, it's not the first time. Remember his colon surgery? He needs help and right now he's dangerous."

"He'll never forgive me. He'll banish me. I'll lose my children!"

"No way! Never gonna happen. You know how much money we've given to that damn temple? I promise that will never happen. Besides, I doubt by the time he's okay, he will even remember it."

Now Goldy Rothenstein stood up straight and looked into what was left of Rebecca Dubinski's real eyelashes. "I know about #MeToo. Maybe I don't want that. I hate my life. There I said it!"

Rebecca hugged her and Rogers could see this was a real first for both of them and after all, who else did they really have who could possibly understand this nightmare. "Come with me. I have tequila and we're going to fix you up. This is a miracle. Mommy is applauding, wherever she is and her soul is just fine."

"I have to go to the children. I don't want to go with him. I can't, I have no help. I'll call someone from the Shul. Thank you, Rebecca. Bless you."

Sergi, Rebecca and Goldy, the new trio, departed. Pepe came over to him, "I should go down and lead the guys up here."

"Good idea, tell them to hurry, he looks like he could stroke out."

LePorte practically flew out the door after them, nodding to the cops and not waiting for even the possibility of a question. Rebecca was his meal ticket and with Rebecca he would stay.

Mikey strutted over to Rogers. "What a fucking horror show. When did you do that research. Is that true?"

"Yeah. Though the autopsy permission I wasn't sure the Rabbi would okay it, but he did, probably because of who they are and how high profile a case this is. The last thing any religious Jews need now anywhere in the world is bad press."

"No shit. Hey, I heard Carmen Daniels stormed in here. Man, that is one super scary chicita."

"I kind of liked her. All that fierce, no bullshit straight at you unfurling. She is really mad."

"Mad enough to murder them?"

"For sure, though never like that. She'd probably beat them to death with her bare hands or shoot the shit out of them. No way she'd do what was done and she certainly wouldn't rummage for obscure jewelry and petty cash, nor would she go off on us that way. Highly unlikely, but certainly worth another interview. Plus she's in the thick stuff with the FBI and the business."

"Yeah, I know she wants to cover that very sexy Jewban ass, which I can't say anymore, but not bad."

"Mikey, she would pick you up in one hand and toss you out like a frisbee on Haulover Beach."

"Ever hear of opposites attract?" Mikey's macho was bruised.

"Yep. But I have no actual proof and well, I just don't think you're her type, but hey, ya never know, go for it."

Since Rogers had never had a conversation with Mikey remotely like this, he had a feeling his own newly forming cupid presence might be at play. He checked his watch. 7:30. He needed to meet with Pepe and Mikey and go over all the interviews and thoughts about suspects. Arnold's rage was certainly a new twist. But he'd never take his mother's jewelry or cash, and he probably wouldn't know a stiletto or a diamond from a rhinestone and why? Not lined up with his sinners must pay tirades.

"Mikey, I'm gonna do one last walk through and I'll close it up. Let's meet with Pepe right after the paramedics come. I'll wait with Rothenstein, can't leave him alone and I just want to wander around here a bit."

"Got it. I called an Uber for Leena, had them meet her around the block and she knows how to get out the beach entrance so the press won't see her."

"Good. Shouldn't be long." He walked Mikey out, both of them trying not to listen to Arnold Rothenstein, screaming and thrashing and damning them all to hell.

CHAPTER 14

Sunny and Oscar, each with an ecstatic pup on a leash; Sunny with Lorraine and Oscar with Lola, were racing down the secret back tunnel to the Beach; free for the first time that day. The resident building bans lifted, interviews over for now, anyway. Grandma Ooma was resting, Edy was taking a bath, and they had an escape op. They were running, the warm breeze in their hair, the ocean glistening and the sun setting, Miami at its most seductive.

"Sunny, look, there's Leena with Mrs. Dubinski's rescues!"

Leena was jogging toward them, trying to keep the four untrained and somewhat ill-matched foursome, all different breeds, ages and sizes from chaos.

They waved and shouted her name and she looked up, breaking into a huge smile, clearly delighted to see friendly faces.

"Sunny embraced her and Oscar followed, doing the same.

"We thought your Uncle Ubered you out of here?"

"Well, almost. I was waiting and Mrs. Dubinski called me, she sounded awful and said there was a crisis with her brother and could I please take the dogs for a walk to settle them down. I just couldn't say no, I'm working for her now, so I bagged the Uber and Sergi brought them down for me and he gave me a hundred-dollar bill! I can make a really nice dinner for my mom and my brother when I get home tonight. And just being on the beach feels so great."

Do you want us to each take one of them? It's too much for you, isn't it? They're pretty wild!"

"I'm really strong, but I've got all those meds still working and I'm pretty tired. Thank you." She handed one off to each of them. Lorraine took an instant hate to his enforced companion, who seemed to be of various heritages, but with the same terrier temperament and Sunny had to stop and calm Lorraine down and trade pups with Oscar. Lorraine approved of her new leash mate and off they went.

They were all full of adrenaline and, yet, there was a shyness that set in and they were quiet for a while, not quite knowing who knew what or what they could ask her or even if they should talk about something completely random.

Oscar, who was usually the quietest broke the silence. "Leena you are really exquisite with these animals. They just love you."

"Thanks, Oscar. I think they know I really care about them, even the smelly mean ones. I hear you walk Hildy sometime. Hildy is the best. I wish I had lots of Hildys to take care of."

Oscar grinned. No secrets around here. "I guess my dad told you. It's cool. Mr. Rogers knows."

Sunny slowed down and shot him a look. "So, when did you talk to Mr. Rogers?"

"Oh, I showed him the secret exit and we took Hildy out. I had some techno stuff to update him on. He made me an unofficial deputy."

The girls giggled. "Go Oscar," Sunny said. "Maybe you'll run for commissioner next."

Leena looked at her. "Sunny, that was mean."

Sunny burst into tears, shocking them all, even herself and they stopped and Leena gave all the dogs a treat to settle them down. "Oh My God, Sunny, I didn't mean to upset you."

"No, no, it was mean. I'm so sorry, Oscar. I don't know what's happening to me today. I think I was jealous. I mean, my Mom is taking a bath! Before dinner even and she already had a shower and she's all weird about Mr. Rogers. I think she has a crush on him. And Grandma Ooma told us a very sad, story today and she's afraid, she's very old and I feel like I could lose them both and be an orphan again and you guys will go off and I'm scared, I think and I do what my Mom does when she's scared. I get snarly."

Leena put her arm around her, but it was too hard to hold the dogs and she had to let go. "I know the feeling. My mom is really sick, I don't have a dad and my brother is a mess, mentally and physically, so I really get it."

Oscar, not wanting to seem better off chimed in. "I get it, too. My parents are divorced and my Mom works all the time and my dad has a girlfriend now, so I'm sort of shuffled around and you know I don't have any friends and being half Chinese and half Hispanic—I'm even more of an outcast. I don't even have a dog."

Sunny stopped crying and stuck out her tongue, trying to lighten and share at the same time. "Well, I guess we're our own little band of misfits then. So we need to be loyal to one another. I've never told anyone this, about Grandma Ooma, some of it's private, but I want you guys to know how she became our Grandmother. She placed an ad in a book review section saying she was lonely and old and had money, but no family and she wanted to adopt a family and be their grandmother. And she chose us!"

Oscar and Leena looked at her as if she had just described seeing a spaceship land on the Silver Sands roof.

"No way," Leena said, "that stuff only happens in the movies, or if some homeless person wins the lottery!"

Oscar rolled his head around. "Totally exquisite! I always wondered about it. I mean she didn't seem like she would be your real grandmother. Wow."

"I know, that's why we never talk about it. But she brought

us down here and it was a really tough time for us, so it was kind of like that, a movie or the lottery only it's true and she's just the most wonderful grandma and person and she's had this amazing life."

They turned back after Sunny's disclosure, clearly a little over their heads and not wanting to ruin this honor of her trusting them. Kids are better at not being afraid of just being quiet, if they don't know what to say. Finally, Oscar spoke, just as they got to the secret passageway.

"There's a Chinese proverb, I think it's really cool. "There are three hundred kinds of silence. I tried to find them all. I couldn't. But I think sometimes being quiet is a way of showing, you know."

Sunny leaned over and kissed his cheek. "Yeah, I do, Oscar. And this has to be our secret, guys, Okay?"

Leena and Oscar nodded and Leena took the other leashes from them and ran ahead. "Gotta get them back and go home. My mom needs her shot. This was mega."

Sunny and Oscar followed and Sunny was a little off center, hoping she hadn't said too much, not that Grandma Ooma had ever told her not to tell anyone, but it was always sort of the unspoken truth between them. Oscar sensed this and put his arm around her, now that they were down to Lorraine and Lola. "It's okay, Sunny. Secrets stuck."

Rogers and Mikey were waiting for Pepe in Rogers' office. Mikey was slumped down in his chair, his face, too exhausted to keep his façade up, making him more likeable. "Man, I would kill for a drink."

"Well, you're in luck. That is one need I can meet and save you from a long trial and unpleasant possible death."

Mikey sat up. "Dude! I'm impressed. I thought having a bottle in a cop's desk drawer was only for DA's on TV."

"That's where I got the idea. I'm a bourbon man. Sorry, no tequila."

"Right now, I'd drink Lavoris. Besides I love bourbon."

Pepe came in, looking equally wrung out. "They're taking him to Aventura Hospital for observation. Goldy Rothenstein couldn't go or wouldn't, oldest kids could probably have watched the younger ones or Mrs. Dubinski could though the idea seemed to freak her out, so they called someone from the temple, I think. They had to restrain him and nuke him. He was frothing like a rabid cat."

"Bourbon?" Rogers poured a third plastic water cup and slid it across his desk.

"Wow. Gracias, boss." They all sipped and were quiet.

"Pepe, are the reporters still all over the place?"

"Yep." And I watched some news on my phone. Unbelievable. They're all famous. And it's tabloid heaven. All of the family dirt, and the #MeToo chicks, yelling about Frederick's harassment and then interviews with all these women, most saying he was a gentleman, generous and never forced anything and treated them well. And they all knew about the FBI investigation. There's no way to keep anything confidential, anymore. We might as well just let them all have full access to everything. It's a complete mess. The only one who hasn't blabbed besides your niece is Carmen Daniels, though they are all over her now. We should give her some security, maybe."

Mikey perked up. "Yeah. I want to interview her again with Rogers. She likes him."

Rogers sipped his bourbon, hoping it wouldn't disappoint Edy Weller that he'd started without her. Hildy trotted in and checked out the scene, deciding to curl up next to Rogers who gave her his, "I know you're vamping because you think I have another treat and you're playing on my guilt and you're absolutely right" look.

When she stared right into his eyes, he always felt more connected than having the same experience with any of the humans in his life, well, until, maybe today, anyway. He reached into his pocket and pulled out one of Leena Martinez's treats and Hildy sat up, knowing without that behavior she'd never get anything.

"So, how do we start this? Mikey clearly had no desire at the moment to show rank. He'd never been good at the lead off, Rogers usually did it for him. It never made much sense to him, given Mikey's need to have the attention and center stage, but he was never really a leader, just a strutter.

Rogers sat up straighter, feeling the warmth of the elixir masking his exhaustion. "Well, this is what I have. I've put a board chart together, trying to make sense of the suspects. Of the fifteen units occupied at the moment. We've interviewed everyone possible. The employees: Irina, Bianca and LePort; Ooma Lovee, the Dubinksi's, their maid, the Rothenstein Jr.s', the Seniors are deceased, Sunny and Edy Weller and Leena, Katya, the Dubinski's maid and Carmen Daniels.

"Pepe, you talked to three more, right?"

"Yep, the Shmumpkins, and two other families, they all frankly seemed pretty much the same. Rich, mid-forties, husbands worked in some capacity connected to the Rothenstein's, like lawyers, accountants, doctors, no red flags and I didn't pick up any agendas. They were all too in awe and into social climbing, supporting all their charities and hoping to be put on the A-list dance cards, you know the drill.

"None of them had ever been in their penthouse, all have kids, little ones, bunch of spoiled brats, they were eating sea urchin rolls and quinoa salads and kale shakes! I can imagine trying to get any of that junk into Oscar and they were all too bored to say hello, please, thank you, ordered the maid around like she was, well, the maid. Hate that stuff. But, frankly, I think all those types are too self-absorbed to murder anyone, more likely to send nasty tweets or black ball their schoolmates from play dates for eating hot dogs or something.

"And two of the other occupied units' residents were away, Summer is like that, you guys know the drill, half ghost town, half South Americans escaping winter, but so many of them have three or four houses all over the world, nothing feels right about them as suspects."

"How about staff?"

"Well, none of their gang of cleaning people, tutors, cooks, masseuses, all of those people were in the building or could have gotten up to the Rothenstein's, but I have a list. It just seems kind of wild goose stuff, frankly."

"I have intel that the Rothensteins all have override buttons so they could turn off the security system, do you guys know this? No one told me?"

Pepe looked stunned. Clearly Oscar had told the truth about not risking Leena's secret and she didn't know about the override, either. "Hell no! So, either of them could have turned it off and let someone in or someone who came there regularly knew about it! Dammit!"

Rogers finished his drink and poured another round for all his eager comrades.

"I'll have the wall board of all of them in the morning. I'm going back to the Weller apartment, they seem to know the players habits better than most, but they aren't into the scene, so they're more honest about it and I think we need to go down to the offices and talk to Daniels again first thing tomorrow. I'm still waiting for Olivia to get all the DNA stuff back, especially this one hair she thinks is different."

Mikey slugged down his shot and stood up. "I gotta go home and take a shower and get all this flaky skin shit off of me. Nerves make it worse. I'm peeling like a fucking python or something; then I'll call Daniels and I probably have to make some sort of bullshit press statement. The PR guys downtown are all over me and the mayor and the commissioner and the chief. So, unless someone more famous croaks soon, this isn't going to die down for a while and we are far away from even a person of interest, really. Fuck!"

Since that just about summed up everyone's sentiment, including Hildy who wanted to eat something more than dog treats and have Roger's attention back.

Rogers sighed, cleaned up the empty cups, and checked his watch. Almost 9. He could call her now. The thought gave him a rush of adrenaline, expectation, excitement, fear, maybe. Hildy trotted behind him and waited while he filled her bowl, which made him realize how hungry he was and, what else? Scared?

When Edy Weller hit the entrance to Mo's Deli, she inhaled the way some women inhale the smell of herbal infusion remedies or designer perfume. The smells were like warm baths of pure joy and the best memories of her early life. What temple was to observant Jews, Mo's was to secular Jews. The essence of identity.

There was no way to fake the smell, though God knew (maybe he actually planned the menus) those of other heritages had tried. This joy was always followed by a deep hole somewhere around her solar plexus of sadness and loss. There were almost none left. Not even Wolfies in South Beach had survived. Uncool, not enough old time Jews to keep it running; even the Carnegie in N.Y. was gone.

So, Mo's seemed to her, one of the last bastions, a haven of warmth, comfort and the food of her heart. Those odors of onions and garlic and potatoes frying, fresh pastrami and corned beef slicing, crusty rye baking, pickles pickling, heaven. Even though the crowd was changing; not that there weren't still the regulars, slightly stooped oldsters with white fringe pushing out of baseball caps and gold chains dangling from synthetic leisure suits; ancient widows in wheelchairs and walkers, patient Black or Hispanic care-givers waiting beside them if the lines were long, but it had become almost a novelty cuisine, young Israelis and Russians, Middle-Easterners (falafel and kabobs were not mainstays of deli fare but had been added to the menu). Young Latinos with tight jeans and fancy footwear; and there were still some of the feisty old Jewish waitresses, a dying breed for sure, filled with chutzpa and energy, calling everyone "darling" and "honey" and "sweetheart" and zipping around, coffee pots glued to their arthritic fingers as if time had stood still.

When Edy had first found Mo's, she cried. Sunny loved it and Grandma Ooma, too European to really understand it, had taken her first big breath and cried, too. If some maniac ever bombed Mo's, there would be as much mourning as if it was the Pittsburgh Synagogue.

And then, of course there was the food. Heavenly, perfect and portion sized for recently released concentration camp victims (there were a few of those always there, too, very old now and very devoted).

Edy was still so high from her Rogers evening, that she had gathered her girls and suggested they go have a lavish breakfast at Mo's. Everyone had slept late, though Ooma had probably not slept at all, and just the idea of this special breakfast cheered them up. Oscar was there, too, having bunked with Sunny since his dad and Rogers were crashing in their offices. Oscar loved Mo's.

Their table was soon stacked with enough food to see them through a panhandle hurricane. Latkes with sour cream, cheese Blintzes, sizzling hot reubens with extra Russian dressing; Nova and huge Bagels, Edy's adored mushroom/barley soup. Crunchy semi dill pickles, coffee and cream sodas. Heaven on a table.

Ooma and Sunny had not said a word to Edy about her "date." She had gathered her nerve and told them she had one, sort of, and if they could eat first and watch movies in Sunny's room she would be very appreciative. They showed not much reaction. Sunny having had her catharsis about it on the beach and Ooma was secretly pleased to see Edy with a glow in her eyes and a quickness in her step.

Ooma might be old and completely through with men; the very thought of one of them even touching her, at this point made her twitch; but for precious Edy, she did secretly hope she would find a good man and know what love could be. Not the kind she had lived with for so many years, but the brief beauty of her only real love, her Claude. So rare to find a man worth what they take from our truth, energy, yearning to be loved in a way rarely possible. Men were weak. Even the weakest woman was stronger because we can't afford the egos—we must face reality sooner or later. Most men make it clear that around every corner is someone younger, prettier, whatever; they never think about themselves like that! Rogers seems to be her Claude. A good man. He sees her worth, her beauty—not showcase, real and it will grow as she ages. Those others fade fast. Me, too but not my Edy.

They had copies of all the papers and there was a TV on at the far end of the room. Every table was talking about the murders and the papers were full of tidbits, speculation, terribly negative gossip about the family, possible motives, including the IRS.

Could it be murder/suicide? They laughed at the idiocy. Hard to tie yourself up and then stuff jewels in your orifices or smash metal heels into your orbs. Some people only seemed upset about the dead dogs and others just unnerved that they were Jews and the image of ruthless, greedy rich Jews would stir up all the increasingly aggressive and vicious resurgence of anti-Semitism everywhere in the world. Sunny overhead one, well-dressed and elegant looking woman say to her husband, "I know this sounds awful, but I don't think I've ever worked with or met anyone not Jewish who wasn't at least benignly anti-Semitic."

Ooma caught her eye, having heard it, too and nodded. Was that true? Was Rogers? She shook the thought away.

"Mom, your new column is in the Herald. You didn't show it to me. OMG, it's hilarious!" Good job."

Edy took a big gulp of coffee to wash down her blintza. "Thanks, honey. I liked that one, too."

Is that real? I mean, there really was an "Ugliest Girl in Shanghai" contest? Totally retarded."

"Could I make that up? Could we make up what's happening in our very own building! Pass the pickles, please." Oscar put two more latkes on his plate and finished off the last of his Reuben.

"Oscar, I can't return you with your stomach the size of a watermelon. Slow down!"

"I can't help it. This food is just too exquisite." They all smiled, adoring him.

"My news apps are totally bent today. A London count blocked some wacko's choice of her daughter's name – Cyanide! She named the kid, Cyanide and her reason, listen to this, "Cyanide is a lovely, pretty name because it helped kill Adolph Hitler."

"Boy you lucked out. That was my second choice."

"Mom, so not funny. Oh! More. Michael Jackson used to apologize to his vegetables before he ate them. I'm so sorry Mr. Carrot."

They all laughed. "Well in that spirit, since he never apologized to a human he well, at least he didn't eat their carrots, but I think we should pause and apologize to the lox and pickles, anyway."

"Mom, you're really bad!"

"Oh, more! It's a new trendo recipe I want you to make if we're not going to be vegans or paleo's. Really gourmet: Sea Urchin with carrot-coffee puree and chrysanthemum petals."

"You made that up."

"Mom if I could make that up, I'd be a famous chef or in a locked ward."

"OMG, Mom, the Post is saying Frederick Rothenstein had whips and chains in his bedroom and a syringe so the women could inject stuff into his pee pee to make it work. How gross!"

Oscar swallowed and took a big slug of cream soda. "Make it work for what?"

Edy laughed. "Oscar, ask your dad in about two years." Her phone rang, which was unusual. She rummaged around in her purse and found it just before it went off. God, she hated the damn things. "Hello?"

"Ms. Edy, it's Rogers."

Edy shot a look at her tablemates to see all eyes glued to her.

"Hi. Good Morning."

"Afraid not. Are you home?"

"Um, no, We're at Mo's eating for twelve."

"I think you should get home and I'm warning you, there's a swarm of reporters, don't even try to get to the garage until you see my guys, I've sent a couple down to help you through."

"Why? What happened?"

"We have another murder. Rebecca Dubinski. Pretty bad. Didn't want you to hear it on the news."

"No way! Okay. Okay. We'll wrap this all up and come back. Jesus H!"

She clicked off and faced the sudden silence, worried, especially about Ooma.

"Edy darling, what is it?"

"Another murder. Rebecca Dubinski. I'll get a check. Start piling up left overs. No free brunch, guys. Let's go."

While Edy and her little band were racing back to the Silver Sands, Rogers, Mikey, Pepe and Olivia Tan and their crew were trying to cover all bases and find the missing link in the chaos. Their only account of what had occurred came from Sergi Dubinski. Rogers was handling that while Mikey stayed with Olivia.

"Mr. Dubinski, let's go somewhere private so we can talk."

Sergi Dubinski nodded and Rogers followed him into a dining room, which was not open to the living room the way the other units were set up. This seemed to be the room that he had decorated, probably the one concession to his manhood Rebecca had sanctioned and Rogers had the feeling, there was another dining area for Rebecca's parties--this seemed like some Russian macho cave deal where he and his cronies could eat huge platters of fatty meats and down vodka by the bottle. It was all done in heavy dark wood with high backed royal blue suede covered chairs and pictures of stag hunts and body building contests, featuring Sergi and framed in gold on the dark wine-colored walls.

Sergi sat down at the head of the table and Rogers sat next to him and took out his phone.

"I do have to record this."

"Yes, yes. I understand."

Rogers was looking for signs, bruises, blood, bite marks, even make-up that might link him in some way.

"Okay, so I am recording this interview with Sergi Dubinski, the husband of the deceased, Rebecca Rothenstein Dubinski at their residence at 10:06 a.m., August 13th, 2019 at the Silver Sands Condominiums in Sunny Isles, Florida. My name is Roy Rogers and I am the head of building security and the deputy assigned to the investigation by Lieutenant Mikey Martinez, Lead Detective on the case. Mr. Dubinski can you please tell me in as much detail as possible the events of this morning concerning the death of your wife."

Sergi put his huge hands over his face and sobbed, and Rogers felt the emotion was genuine. Whatever his motives for the marriage or the nature of their connection, it did seem there was a real bond and he was genuinely distraught.

"I will try. This is very difficult and I'm not proud of this, but I'm Russian and I know better than to lie to the police. So, okay. We came home and my wife helped her sister-in-law...."

"Excuse me, to be clear, you are referring to Goldy Rothenstein?"

"Yes, yes, she helped her pack herself and her children up, gave her some new clothes and cosmetics and things and a lot of cash, and her car keys. Arnold didn't let her drive alone and we saw them off. It was very emotional and my wife was amazing. I'd never seen her step up like that for anyone, only for dogs, I'm sad to say, but she was great. They didn't go until after midnight and Rebecca was pretty upset, and she has bad nerves, doesn't eat, doesn't sleep. I try to help her, but she won't listen. So anyway, she drank too much and took some pills to sleep and brought the dogs into the bedroom. When they are there, I sleep in one of the guest rooms that is also my office. So, once I knew she was asleep, I went to bed, too, but the dogs started barking around 5:00, and I got them before they could wake her up. I didn't know if Leena Martinez was coming or not, so I took them out and fed them and brought them back. It was still very early, before 6 and I was up, so I left a note for Rebecca and a note for Leena if she showed up and I went to the gym to work out and check the schedule. I still had a business to run if the bad press didn't ruin everything we've worked for."

He paused, and did some relaxation stretches and rolled his huge head around.

"Okay, this is the difficult part. There are some instructors and patrons there that I have, um, I have personal relationships with. Casual, just sex, you know? My wife, well, there are issues, but she did not know about this. OH God! She would have flipped out.

"So, one of them, who comes in to work out very early, she came in and we, you know. I have a special staff room, it's just for me and we had sex, and then I left.

"When I got back, the door was open! Rebecca sometimes didn't set the system, but I had when I left, I'm positive, and I knew something was bad, very bad. And I came in fast, ready for anything. I was heading toward the closet where I keep my weapons and I saw her! Christ in Heaven! Her door was open! I was crazed; I ran for the closet and got two guns and went racing around in case the maniac was still there, but no one was there, just my wife, that way you found her. Someone really violated her, hated her. I knew I shouldn't touch her. I knew she was dead, I was in the Russian Army, I know what death looks like, I just called you guys. And waited."

Rogers was aware that the scene which Olivia was processing as they spoke was even more horrifying than the parents. She was naked, and the sight of that emaciated body with huge breasts dangling from a pink rhinestone dog leash tied to a very tall wood and concrete sculpture with a cross beam on the top, her wig ripped off, her make-up removed, in what seemed to be a deliberately brutal demeaning way, false lashes and eyebrows hanging from the sides of her face, garish lipstick smeared all over, a rage so intense it was almost impossible to absorb, even for the cops and Olivia. Like her parents, the manner seemed symbolic and the acts were so personal it seemed unlikely to Rogers and he assumed to Mikey and Olivia, that they were the work of a stranger and most certainly they were all connected.

"Mr. Dubinski, since you have identified the body and we have your statement and an account of your whereabouts; is there anything that we may uncover about your past, an arrest record, whatever that you would like to share with me the easy way?"

Sergi did not seem to expect this question. "Yes, but not from America. I have some incidents in Germany and England before I came here. Nothing serious. A couple of drug things and bar fights; stuff with guys trying to be tough with me, when I was body building, and you know, the enhancement drugs, but not enough to stop my visa application, so it was all years ago. Nothing here. I'm not stupid. I want to be a citizen."

"Well, marrying Miss Rothenstein, probably helped that process."

Sergi smirked, knowing what Rogers was not saying. "Yeah, sure. I get it. But I could have married a dozen chicks. We fell in love. I helped her a lot. She needed me, and yes, I needed her, too. I had nothing and now I have everything, or at least for now. I don't know what her will says or anything. They made me a big shot, gave me some dignity and a life I could have never imagined, so, why would I do this to any of them?"

"Well, good question, Mr. Dubinski. All that comes to mind is the infidelity. If they had found out, the parents or your wife. I think you get my meaning."

"Oh yes. Oh, yes. But they had no idea. I was not stupid. I'm a man. I have big needs. But I was very careful, and I knew Rebecca, if she suspected she would have probably shot me!"

"Well, then. For now. I'll take your word for it."

Sergi Dubinski got up, giving the impression of some huge wrestler claiming his mat victory and led him back, skirting around the crime scene. "Can I get out of here. This is too much, and I need to be back at the gym to deal with the staff and I have to make some calls and arrangements. It doesn't seem real, but I can't look at her like that."

Rogers turned to Olivia, who was taking temperatures and getting her team ready to cut what was left of Rebecca Dubinski down. "Can he go? Have you checked him out, Mikey?"

Mikey nodded. "Yeah, he can go, just don't go far, sir."

"Not a chance," said the widower who headed for the door.

Pepe whispered to Rogers. "What about the dogs?"

"Good point. Mr. Dubinski, the dogs? Can't just leave them here. Is the housekeeper coming or can you call Leena, maybe?"

This was the first break in Dubinski's composure, grief aside. "Fuck the dogs. Tell your guys to call the rescue, they have the name and have them get them. It was all part of her craziness. She never really cared about them, it was some needy, wounded little girl shit. I hated it."

Sergi picked up his gym bag and keys and left. Pepe tapped Rogers on the shoulder. "Before you go to see Carmen Daniels, Mikey told me she's at the country club private dining room, not her office and another thing, my guys just checked the security tapes again and Dubinski lied. His car was taped leaving the garage around 5 A.M., but he left the condo at 1:15 and then came back. So, why lie? If he'd already admitted to having a Horizontal Hora moment at the gym, it would make no difference, in fact it gives him a better alibi?"

"Horizontal Hora? Is that a Brazilian term or is Miami getting into your DNA?"

"My new girlfriend is Israeli, what can I tell you."

"I like it. A new Pepe emerges. As for Sergi, the only reason to lie is if the TOD is way off or if he wants it to look that way. Olivia will know, probably already does."

By the time they got back to her and Mikey, Rebecca Rothenstein Dubinski had been untethered from her noose and was laid out in the morgue bag.

Rogers turned to Mikey, very aware of the chain of command. "So, what do we know?"

Mikey turned to Olivia. "Tell him what you have."

Olivia took her hair out of the surgical cap and shook her blond and black tresses around, releasing some tension. "Well, obviously, I'll know more once I get her on my table and do a tox screen. She was clearly loaded, I could smell it and from her pupils, I'd say some serious meds, but not enough to kill her, though being that skinny, not much reserves. Right now, not on the record, yet, I'd say she was strangled manually before she was strung up. Whoever did it wanted it to look like a crazed suicidal moment or Sergi. No prints on the body, or the noose. Weird. Same as the parents. Gloves for sure. Rage and hate don't fit with taking the time to put gloves on but, who the hell knows, the world is so totally wacked up now. I can tell you this. The woman was in the final stages of functional anorexia; she probably would have had a heart attack pretty soon anyway, and she was a heavy smoker, reeks of it. Also, she'd had so many breast surgeries, implants in and out, butt implants in and out. These broads should have zippers."

Rogers and Pepe tried not to laugh out of respect for the poor dead creature on the floor in front of them. "That's good, Dr. Tan and you can say it, if we said it, we'd be fired. Any TOD idea?"

"Well, she's not in rigor. I'd say around 5 or around 6:00 A.M. could be a little later. Husband said he found her before ten?"

Pepe and Rogers exchanged cop eyes. "Thanks, Doc. Very helpful. Call us when you have more."

"For sure. Just another day in paradise. "Pepe, is Oscar okay here? I haven't even seen him since yesterday."

"He's having a ball. Sunny and he are hanging out. Edy Weller took him to Mo's this morning, so he probably ate the entire menu. Don't worry, I'll have him call you, later. He's been staying with Sunny and I think it's really good for him to have a friend. He's alone too much."

The same dark shadow Rogers had seen before crossed her broad exotic face. The superwoman's burden, he thought.

"Thanks, Pep. Tell him I love him, and I miss him and when this is over, I'm taking him on a special trip."

"He'd love that. Really, though? Don't say it, if you can't really do it."

The shadow turned into anger. "Hey, *Mom*, I know, okay?"

Pepe sighed. "Yeah. Sorry. Out of line."

She pulled her hair back and tied it up in a knot, something Rogers saw women do all the time, tied their long hair up, twisting it around without even using any clips or rubber bands. Women were so damn fascinating.

And holding this thought with memories of what seemed to him to have been the most wonderful evening with a woman he had ever had, he stepped over the tiny, abandoned body of a woman who had everything which clearly was not really enough, and followed Mikey to the door.

Edy Weller was swimming, lengths she called them, not laps, which sounded far too competitive and swim teamish for her. Heaven for her was the almost always deserted Silver Sands pool. Warm and quiet. There was the family pool and then this little adult haven, but almost never used, except by a few macho maniacs who would intrude on her meditative peace and dive and splash and kick. Most obnoxious were the few who insisted on doing the back stroke. I mean really? When you could not see where the other human beings in the water might be; forcing her to keep a vigilant eye and dash and change course to avoid being smashed into. So annoying.

But usually, she was alone, and it was her little bliss spot. Swimming and walking were the only sports she ever really enjoyed. Solitary and non-competitive. She had played tennis for awhile and was actually quite okay or would have been if she kept it up, but she hated the competitive side of her that emerged, which is why she avoided all card games and board games, the need to win made her very jittery, while curling up with a good book or movie or swimming laps or walking on the beach, brought non-competitive peace.

She knew chaos reigned inside with Rebecca's murder. Unbelievable! Ooma and the kids were all completely freaked out and she was really worried about Ooma. First, the possibility that they were after all the residents of the upper floors, and maybe Ooma's fears, especially after her stories of the war and her early years would make her far more sensitive to the darkest possible realities. She had whispered to Edy after her confession, that she wanted her to know she slept with a small pearl handled pistol under her pillow and that if anything happened to her, to take it at once. Knowing that, actually made Edy worry less about her safety.

She stopped swimming and started doing some water aerobics, get her newly awakened heart pumping. She smiled in spite of everything. What a thing! The evening with Roy had been so wonderful. It was as if they had been together for years but with that sort of pitter patty kind of manic energy, new romance brought. They didn't have to say a damn thing about it, either.

They just knew. So they did the life story mambo for awhile and then he asked her some more questions about various tenants. She had called Irina and Lupe, the "Synthetic Sirens" and that made him laugh. She really, really liked to make him laugh and then, somehow she found herself talking about Sunny, in more a general way, but about how she was changing and Edy could feel the moments of judgement, hurtful little pin pricks that went right through her heart and her fear the real tsunami of adopted teenager beginning to question and deal with long ignored abandonment issues, plus the impending departure for college would trigger far more. She had thought a lot about this stuff lately, wondering and wishing she'd had a chance to talk to her own mother about it, even if her mother had no desire to or idea what she needed.

More and more as she watched Sunny morph from tot, to teen she was aware that children can never love us the way we love them and long to be loved by them, totally and unconditionally, ready to kill or die for them, adoring and devoted beyond all else, or at least she was, she thought she was anyway, it was what her heart truth was.

No, their love was always mixed with resentment, anger and unmet needs. They were not even aware of the mammothian cavern being more than any parent can ever meet; longings for the maybe better fit for a mother, the fantasy in Sunny's case of whoever, had left her at that monastery. Mother's love or at least a good mother's love, and she did think she was a pretty good one, well (compared to the likes of the Shmumpkins and all those foolish professional moms, breeding shallow, viciously competitive and codified versions of themselves). Far too many Mommy and Me spa dates and yoga breathing classes, which, she had heard from Rhoda Shmumpkin, did wonders for "their stress levels." Her twins, were what, 7?

All she had ever really wanted was to lavish love on her parents, her child, her dog and needy friends, a compulsive need to give, because that made her happy. Huge unmet needs from her childhood, no doubt, but there were worse neuroses, for damn sure. How would Sunny emerge; would they always be close? Would disappointment appear later to shadow her adoration for this child in some way?

She'd certainly seen it happen. So, with Sunny moving, diving deeper into her own private world, door locked, phone and computer always on, Lorraine had moved even further into her heart and need. Lorraine was never going to want to leave or have secrets or meet a boy. Lorraine wanted her 24/7.

As hard as he now was to lift onto her lap and as uncuddly a creature as he was, his purity still moved her to tears, that ability to just wallow in love, the giving and receiving without fear.

Was it remotely possible that she and Rogers, might have stumbled into the human equivalent? They had not had much time or a lot of privacy but he had taken her into his big strong arms (swoon now Edy like a romance novel, Oy) and he kissed her, kissed her deep, left them both gasping and shaking. It had clearly been quite a long dry spell for him, too, which she found immensely sexy and completely reassuring. No lothario here, though God knows he probably had plenty of opportunities. She stopped running in place and splashed forth, doing the breast stroke like Esther Williams, filled with a very rare, combination of excitement and joy.

"Mom!" Jeez, we didn't know where you were! Don't you know we're all totally bent out. You could be the next victim!"

Edy stopped swimming, startled by the unexpected intrusion in her bliss space. Sunny, Ooma, Lorraine, Lola, Oscar and Rogers were all approaching, throwing her into a highly unique social spasm.

Oh boy, now she would either have to stay in the pool or ascend, very un Esther-like for sure, with all those eyes on her. Rogers! A little foreplay in a softly lit living room was really different than her well stretched old tank suit and body in the fierce light of day. Maybe it would be like Shallow Hal, he would only see her as he fantasized.

She swam to the steps as far away from them as possible and practically vaulted out of the pool into the safety of her oversize beach towel.

"Sorry. I just assumed you'd know this would be where I was. Are the cops and everyone still up there?"

Rogers crossed toward her and helped Ooma Lovee down onto a chaise. Edy could see how pale and shaken she was and she clutched Lola to her breast as if she were a small frightened child with her favorite stuffed animal.

"Yep. It's a real zoo up there. I just wanted to make sure you were okay. We're not shutting everything down this time. Middle of the day, it's just impossible but Olivia is almost ready to bag her. Sorry to be crude, just slipped out, so once she's on the way to the autopsy room, and they've finished processing the scene it should calm down."

Edy slipped into her robe without dropping her towel first; a little moment of female self-consciousness. She saw he had noticed...that little smile a dead giveaway. And she was blushing again! What next? A nose bleed!

Sunny took off her shorts and she and Oscar jumped into the pool. "Wanna play Marco Polo?" Oscar said, splashing her with both hands.

"Oscar, No way. I hate that and I hate being splashed. Please don't act your age, just because we're in the pool! I just want to float around and calm down."

He stopped and she knew his feelings were hurt, being reminded of his age always embarrassed him. "She could feel the guilt she'd felt on the walk with him and Leena. Why was she being mean to him?

"Oscar, I'm sorry, I'm being a punk. I guess knowing there's a dead person we know in there, or another dead person we know, is sort of freaking me out."

Oscar nodded, jumping up and down and looking around for some sort of pool toy, all his adolescent hormonal energy needing more release. Edy started to intercede but stopped herself. Boys were just so different at that age than girls. Boys got hyper and girls got bitchy.

"Hey, Oscar, I can't play now, but I owe you a pool catch as soon as this is all over. Ok? Get your arm ready, I'm pretty good at it." Rogers to the rescue.

Oscar grinned revealing newly installed braces, the metal symbol of the beginning of serious puberty. "Cool!"

Rogers saw a couple of styrofoam noodles behind a chaise and threw them to him, making Edy tear up. Such a simple, thoughtful thing to do. *"Why this feeling, why this glow. Why this thrill when you say, hello"....* Oh boy, back to lyrics we go.

Edy slipped into her pool shoes, wishing she'd worn the ones with a little platform. At least her legs were shaved and she had polish on from the day before. God, she was so totally out of practice for this stuff! She sat down beside Grandma Lovee on the chaise.

"Are you okay? Ooma? I'm worried about you. Maybe we should have your doctor come by and check on you?"

Ooma shook her head and clutched Lola tighter. "No, no. I'm alright, it's just the shock, and the horrible way they found her. I know we're not supposed to know, but everyone does. Poor, poor creature. She was such a ruined soul. It does seem more and more like hate crimes. I told Rogers I really think they need to expand the suspect list. Any of the security or maintenance people could be ultra-rightists, part of some secret group. It's not so hard for any of those fiends to find a way into any building. I don't think they've run background checks very deeply.

"What is that thing, the dark web? Yes. They should check all of them! I heard from the Shmumpkin woman that they were going to let Arnold come home, but now they're afraid he'll completely lose control. They sent the rabbi to the hospital to try and calm him down about the autopsies, but now this!

"He was here yesterday. They let him go home with a nurse and when he saw that Goldie and his children were gone, he went berserk and stormed over to his sister's screaming and cursing her.

"I'm not so sure he isn't fully capable of doing all of this. And he's strong enough and so are his oldest boys. They never say a word and they hide their muscles behind their baggy clothes. But I know from Sergi that they work out like maniacs and they are really strong."

Edy was surprised. No one ever told her anything, she must have an invisible, leave me alone sign attached to her. "But they went with Goldy? I didn't think they believed as fanatically as their father?"

"Oh yes. They didn't go with Goldy, they just helped them out. She didn't want them to know where she was going, because she knew they would tell Arnold. I told Rogers, they should be questioned."

"Well, I think you're right, but for the moment I'm more worried about you and all this stress. Let's go up and pour you a nice glass of chardonnay and run a hot bath and let you have some peace and quiet. Is Maria there? Can she stay with you? Or do you want to come to our place?"

"I think I want to go home. I want my gun, actually I have two of them. I am not being paranoid. I really could be on some list."

"But, no one knows you're Jewish? So why?"

"I don't know. Maybe someone found out or maybe it's just because I live here, and they assume and I'm rich and alone. Oh, Edy, it feels like the war, again!"

"Oh sweetheart, I know, but it isn't, and we will not let anything happen to you."

"But I'm worried for you both, too. Talk to Rogers about a gun. I can give you one of mine. We all thought this building was completely protected, but I know better. Nothing is. Nothing ever is or was really safe."

Edy helped her up, and convinced her to put Lola down, Lola was delighted to run in circles on her lead and pee on the pool grass.

"Kids, out you go. I don't want you down here alone."

"Mom, I'm fifteen!"

"Tell it to the serial killer, I'm sure it will impress the hell out of him or her or them. OUT!"

And the not so merry band of survivors, followed Rogers and the official grown-ups back to the mayhem within.

When Rogers had seen Edy, Sunny and Ooma Lovee back to their condos, he took Oscar by the shoulder and led him to the security elevator. 'So, Oscar, you're still my deputy and I need your help."

Oscar beamed, revealing what seemed to be all of his newly bracketed teeth. "Whatever you need, sir."

Rogers, chuckled. This kid really touched his hard old heart. Well, maybe, given his newly discovered love life, he was just thawing out. "So, here's the thing. Ooma Lovee said something to me about hate crimes and I've been thinking, maybe we're really missing something here, not looking at this from the right angle. If she's right, then we need to go much deeper into the employee pool and how they were vetted. Both the security team here and at the country club and the maintenance crew. I know enough about Miami and human nature in general, not to be aware that underneath any of these people can be a deep well of bigotry and resentment. You know more about all of them than I do and your dad worked security at the country club before he came here, so, I'm gonna go in and talk to him now, but anything you might have overheard, since, kids, you know, they can easily forget you're listening, so anything you might have heard, I'd really like to know."

Oscar looked up at him, clearly seeing this as a serious assignment. "Well, I do know that lots of those guys, and the women, too, talk a lot of trash about each other and people. I mean the whole idea that all these cultures are buddies, what a joke. And, you know, I'm a total misfit, but the Latin groups all stay pretty much together within their own countries for relationships. They all speak Spanish, but they are not close, lots of bad mouthing one another's customs and the Russians, too and then, well, no one likes the Jews. Really twisted. So, a place like this or the country club, well most of the members are Jewish, so the staff talks a lot of bad stuff. I think, mainly, it's jealousy, you know, because those people are mostly really rich and the workers are not. The good guys are respectful and grateful to be in Miami, and have good jobs, you know, but there are always grumblers.

"There is one guy, I can think of; dad used to complain about him, so ask him. I think his first name was Walter, not sure but I don't think he was ethnic. He's a motorcycle dude and he was always on the phone with his "posse" he called them. Totally gross. He hated everyone."

"But how could they get into those condos and past all of us and the systems?"

Oscar gave Rogers a patronizing pat on the back. "Hey, chief, I mean no disrespect, but I can get past all of it! It's all just one big joke to any of us hacker freaks. Trust me, someone with the techno nerd skills can break into any of your systems. "I know I'm just a smart-ass kid, but I think whoever sold the Rothensteins their big bucks systems, is LOL-ing at how dumb they were and how much of what they installed is just for show. I wanted to tell you this before, but well, I didn't think you'd believe me and I didn't want to make your job harder, so I'm really glad you asked me."

Rogers let a huge sigh whistle out from the space between his front teeth that Edy had told him she loved. Looking down at Oscar now, he was glad, maybe for the first time in his life, that he hadn't gotten braces. Sexy, she said it was and adorable. What a thing.

"Oscar, you amaze me. Let's go find your father. This is really helpful and I am mortified at how gullible I've been to even have taken this job without doing my homework."

Oscar patted him again. "Don't sweat it, chief. It's an age thing. No way you guys can understand this stuff. My parents are younger and they are totally lost. I help them out all the time because they have to get better at it or, or you know, someone will take their jobs."

Rogers phone beeped. They were at the elevator and he waited. "Let me get this. It's your Mom."

"Rogers. I'm here with Pepe. I've got some pretty unsettling new info, so get here quick, but for starters, I found something on the insoles of all the victims' feet. Written in marker. "Kill the Kikes." So, hate crime may be what we've missed. Damn it! I'm totally bummed that I spaced it. Too busy working on their upper bodies and blood. Shit. I hate that! Sorry, but I have pictures with me."

"Oh, boy. Talk about timing! We're on our way and I have Oscar, my highly valued deputy."

Oscar was watching him closely. "Am I busted? I was supposed to stay inside."

"Busted, hell no. I may give you a medal. I've got your back, relax, deputy Perez."

Oscar was trying not to show it, but Rogers could tell the kid was feeling pretty good.

Olivia Tan and Pepe Perez were waiting for him in his office. When Olivia saw Oscar her entire being shifted and a large open smile lit up her usually stoic face. He ran into her arms and they hugged tight and Rogers could see tears on her cheeks. Man, people were so fascinating. All those masks and layers.

She looked up at Rogers, back to her usual professional seriousness and she and Pepe moved aside so he could sit behind his desk and they sat across. She patted her knee for Oscar, not quite yet realizing no male kid his age would sit on Mommy's lap maybe even in private but certainly not in front of the guys.

"Okay, Olivia, you go first. I'm sure you've already de-briefed

Mikey and he told you to call me, right? I don't want any toe-stepping getting in the way of this mess."

"Yes, of course and he's already called Carmen Daniels and asked her to pull employee records, anyone who might be involved in some hate group."

"Let me see the pictures." He sighed and leaned forward.

It was easy to see how she had missed them. The ink was faint and the marks were in the hardest part of the feet to see. Someone clearly had to hold the skin taut for her to take the photos.

"Dr. O, give yourself a break. This is pretty subtle stuff. I wonder why? The message is so vicious, you'd think they'd have written it all over the walls in spray paint."

"I know, it just doesn't make any damn sense. Our profilers are stumped. Also, there's something else." She paused taking a long deep breath.

"I don't suppose you'd bend a lot of rules and let me have a few ciggie hits in here."

Oscar answered for them. "mom, no way!"

"Whoops, sorry kiddo! I forgot my promise for a minute. It's been quite a few days. Okay, so another curve ball. We're getting the DNA results in. I had them put everything on speed dial or we'd be waiting for a week. There was DNA on the Louboutin's. Irina's.

"Damndest thing. No other traces on the bodies or jewelry or anything, but definitely she had worn the shoes, so she's more of a suspect now, for sure. But hate crime? I dunno. Seems a stretch, though she could have had help, someone else she was sleeping with, maybe Daniels will find some link. The rest of the results should be coming soon, but these two findings really seemed important.

"Also, tox screen on Rebecca. She was totally wasted, and so skinny, not very hard to subdue or lift. It does look like she was strangled first, but she could have just been choked and unconscious and, like I suspected, her heart was about to give out from the anorexia, anyway."

"Whew. This just gets more and more twisted. Very helpful, good work, Doc. Also, Pepe, the hate crime angle. Ooma Lovee had brought it up to me, again and Oscar said there was one guy on the staff, I think maintenance, but I'm not sure and neither is he, maybe Walter someone? Who might fit a hater profile. Any thoughts?"

"Dios, Mio! Yes! Walter Jenkins I think that's it. And he's part of some secret kind of group. Certainly could be a ultra-right group. Made racist comments about all of us, especially the Jewish guests or residents. And he called all of the Latins, "amigo" never our names. And he's working here now in the boiler room, I think. I never see him, anymore. Oh, man! I'm on it now."

"I'll call Mikey. We may need back up here." Rogers dialed Mikey who answered almost before it rang.

"Mikey, you know about the feet message, well we have a new suspect and we may need back up."

Pepe waved at him. "Rogers, he's off today. We need to send someone to his house if we have a real address."

"Mikey, he's not here, we'll get back to you."

"I'll call Carmen again, she's pulling all the employee files, oh, and she wants us to meet her at the country club for lunch, says it's important. I'll come fetch you and by the time we finish with her, we should be able to haul this bum in."

"Good. If it is him, I don't think he's the only one or what the hell their plan is, but I guarantee if it is a hate crime, they have an agenda and they aren't through."

Rogers hung up, all eyes were on him. Oscar moved in close to him. "Chief, I can probably track him faster, but mom doesn't like me on those sites, so will you ask her?"

Olivia laughed, a first, Rogers thought. "Hello? Mom is standing here, very clever, kid, like how can I say no? Okay. But no lingering and NO porn!"

"Mom, gross. No way. I'm trying to help catch a murderer. Special circumstances!" And he grinned at her, full metal level and Rogers saw the love in her eyes.

"Okay guys, onward we go. I just want to tell Edy to keep them all inside and on lock down until we know more and then I'll go meet Mikey. My phone is on, and I want to know anything."

He stood up and for a moment, he almost thought they would salute him! Quite a team, maybe appropriate for the unreal events starting with that peaceful morning run which now seemed like years ago.

Neither Mikey nor Rogers had ever been inside the Silver Sands Country Club private dining room, which was far out of their comfort zone. Hushed, dark, the walls reflecting the expensive, serious decorum of the highly private part of the club. Even with membership fees of over 200,000 bucks and annual dues higher than most of the people who worked there got paid in a year, everything else was also expensive and this dining room was only by invitation.

The place felt about as much like Miami as the Louvre. High ceilings, carved wooden panel walls. Huge Venetian crystal chandeliers, lush burgundy leather booths and lavish oriental carpets lining the hard wood floors. It was almost Talmudic, Rogers thought, as much a place to contemplate and pray as to eat, kosher of course and very expensive.

Mikey whispered to him, "Leena told me that the drinks by the pool are so expensive that the guests, rich as they all are, sneak white rum and vodka in water bottles and then just order juice and pour the booze in! Management knows they're doing it, but they don't want to upset them, so only the waiters get stiffed. Not much tipping on fucking cranberry juice! There she is."

Carmen Daniels was sitting in the far corner as private as possible, even though the room was almost empty and hushed. More like the reading room at the NY public library than a Miami restaurant.

She waved and they made their way past gleaming silver food carts and the tufted leather bar furniture to her booth. She pointed to the banquette opposite her, clear that she would reign and not to even think about sliding in beside her, not that that would have entered their minds. She had a briefcase on the table, hopefully filled with employee information.

"Sorry we're late Ms. Daniels. All sorts of unexpected developments."

"No problem, it was nice to have some quiet time. She raised one of her long, well developed arms, elegant fingers and nails shining with some kind of gold glittery polish and a young waiter appeared.

She stared at him, pushing her glasses down her nose. "Where's Raul?" It was more a demand than a question.

"This is his day off, Senora Daniels, very sorry. I know he always takes care of you."

"I hope he warned you. Do not try and remember this. Do you have a pad and pen?"

"Yes, Ma'am."

And it's Ms. Daniels. What's your name?"

"Arturo, senora... or Ms. Daniels."

"Okay. First, my guests are on duty so I don't think they're drinking. What would you like?"

They answered almost together. "Coca Cola, lots of ice. Please."

Yes, sirs."

He turned to Carmen who removed her glasses and leaned forward, eyes pinned on the terrified young trainee as if she were a neurosurgeon instructing a resident who knew if an error was made he could not only lose a patient but his career.

"Listen carefully. I want you to bring me the following: two small glasses of ice. Two shot glasses full shots of Avion tequila, two shot glasses of Cointreau, one little pitcher of fresh, and I mean fresh squeezed lime juice and a large crystal goblet. I will assemble my own drinks. I know how they tell the bartenders to short the shots. Comprende?"

"Si, si, Ms. Daniels. Would you like me to repeat the order?"

"I would assume if you are working here you don't need to repeat it, right?"

A light film of moisture appeared on his upper lip, the kind of thing cops notice.

They were mesmerized.

"Mikey whispered to him. "Wow. What cojones."

The waiter trotted off and Carmen sighed. She made no reference to the order, clearly not feeling any explanation was necessary.

She leaned back and pulled a pile of manila folders out of her Prada briefcase.

Not that Rogers would have had a clue, but Mikey knew all this stuff. "Prada, right?"

Rogers figuratively rolled his eyes. If Mikey thought that would impress her, man he needed remedial wooing classes, not that he was an expert. He'd almost fainted getting up the courage to kiss Edy Weller.

Carmen put her glasses back on completely ignoring Mikey's attempt.

"I gotta tell you guys, this was not easy. They have a roster of 500 employees, from busboys to housekeepers and everything in between, so I had my tech guy work with your profiling people and narrow it down and we came up with a pretty disgusting group of about thirty viable perpetrators. All have expressed rather uninhibitedly their disdain for various races, nationalities, political ideologies, etc.

"In reports to their co-workers, many of whom felt targeted or offended, guests who overheard remarks or stuff easily found on-line from numerous porn or fascist organization sites. But that one name, Walter Jenkins, does seem the most viable and he was not very careful about hiding any of it. They found his group, some infantilely revolting bunch called the "Army of the Righteous.""

Arturo returned with a massive tray and Mikey and Rogers stiffened, prepared to do a save if he dropped it out of sheer terror.

He was as slow and careful as if he were a bomb squad expert preparing to dismantle an explosive device. Knees bent as he was trained, he lowered the tray onto the setup station and quickly placed the cokes in front of the two silent men.

Then the show began as he one by one, with explanations, served Carmen Daniels her table full of glasses. All their eyes were glued to this performance with the intensity of viewing the series finale of Game of Thrones. When he was through, he tried to review the order, but she put up one of her shimmering hands to stop him.

"You did good. I'll tell Raul. And I'd like a burger, rare, but when the chef (he knows me) thinks it's ready, tell him to put it back for exactly two seconds. Exactly!"

"Yes, Ma'am." the relief on his face was visible and he dabbed the moisture from his lips and turned to Mikey and Rogers, who only wanted to give the kid the simplest possible addition.

Rogers ordered for both of them. They'd had enough meals together and neither one of them had any desire to start deciphering the enormous menu sealed in a huge embossed leather booklet like some ancient text. "We'll have burgers, too; medium and fries, please. Or whatever comes with them."

Carmen had finished her barista task and took a long slow sip of her special drink.

They waited. She took another long slurp and exhaled loudly. "Ah, man I needed that fucker." She seemed to relax and Rogers knew she was going to lead this band on her terms and they had best just shut up and wait. They were both eyeing her drink with barely disguised longing.

"Guess what I was before I started working for these goniffs? I was an activist. I did psych evaluations for disabled workers. I was a true believer, a fervent, violent activist. Can you tell? I stopped because it was eating me alive, that's what it does to people like me. The rage of injustice, the need to protest, to shout, to march. It's in our genes, a calling if you will. We have no choice, really, like having freckles or being black or transgender or a midget. No fucking choice. And guess what the world would be without activists? A cesspool, not that it isn't anyway, but at least it's a hopeful cesspool!

"Imagine a world without people who are willing to march, to lie down in front of tanks, to sit on filthy sidewalks, not give up a bus seat, not get up from the lunch counter, not parade in a mass of human mayhem or be willing to die if necessary.

"We do it so everyone else can stay home, nice and comfy with their Disneyworld coffee mug and watch us ranting and raving on their Smart TV's.

"And it sucks. All of it, sucks. Because, it's not a pretty group. There are all the fanatics and phonies, celebs with hyper PR people, nut jobs looking for something, anything to fill the huge holes inside themselves.

"I know that's all part of every movement; but change only happens because of us, and the price is fucking high. So, some of us just burn out, flame out, give up, get bitter and sick and disappear. We usually make lousy life partners and parents, too emotional and too obsessed with the injustices of the world to care a whole lot about the feelings of the kid in the crib. Divorces, suicides, despair. Lots of it.

"So, well, shit, that's the whole world, anyway, but activists are leaders of one of those statistics, I just know it. Joan of Fucking

Ark. But the truth is, it often works. It actually works. People standing up, fighting back, speaking out, no matter what the price, what the cost. And if that is who you are, surrendering it comes with a higher price. I did. I sold it out. I couldn't' take anymore. Too angry, too lonely, too exhausted and too poor! Hear that? Too fucking poor!

"So, you know what? Now I'm not poor, because I kept my rage, my proletariat roots and I was smart with what I made, so when the feds swept in, and with all Rothensteins basically fucking done, I'll emerge okay! Patriarch's dead, daughter dead, son in the drool ward, all the vultures are circling and boom!

"In a hail of bullshit, lawsuits, investors no one ever knew they had, huge debts and overdue loans. Boom, down it all goes like the Twin Towers in one fiery heap of toxic garbage. So, I'll go with my security intact and where will I go? Back to the wars. Back to my true calling, but with all the battle scars to guide me.

"I have a big fucking voice and I will use it. I will roar. Maybe I'm a tiny lion, but at least I'll go down fighting for something worth it, to me, at least. So, bring it on, boys. Bring it the fuck on."

Arturo practically tip-toed back and set down their lunches.

"Maybe I'm just rationalizing my cop out or whatever it was, but from where I was standing then in the burning rubble of one or another protests that became totally fucking corrupted by all the asshole fringes and delusive idiot idealists with no fucking clue how the real world works, I was done.

This is why so many of these good causes turn out to sabotage the very people they are supposed to be championing. Occupy Fucking Wall Street. Hello, dumbasses! Who suffered? Not the Wall St. guys. Not the Hedge Fundies, they just helicoptered the fuck out of there and did business from their Hamptons mansions, or mega-yachts or Vail ski lodges or ranches in Montana. NO, it was all the working people, the mom and pop delis and pizza joints that made their living from those shmucks. They lost their businesses!!!! And then, of course, the filth, the rapes, the attacks, the nightcrawlers that infiltrate and multiply like cockroaches in a garbage can.

"Or the French Yellow Vests. Who suffered? They bash all the upscale shops, stop tourism dead, destroy gorgeous sources of revenue and pride like Fouchon and what starts out as a valid protest, who loses? All the fucking working people who no longer have jobs, gas prices or no gas prices!!!! Checks and balances, baby. That's why I put my psych degree in the closet and went back to business school and ended up here. At least these putzes I could see coming.

"So, here's what's going to happen. The Feds and the IRS and God only knows who else are descending, plus all the secret investors' reps, banks, you wouldn't even believe how most of these developers hondle! I know that's not a Latin word, but it works.

"Look around you." Here we are at the famous Silver Sands Country Club, well, this is where the rubber hits the asphalt big time. All the Rothensteins shit was cross collateralized, huge loans to pay for all the renovations and additions and expansion of the golf course, you name it, so guess what they put up? You got it! The Silver Sands! And it's all going to implode like one big fucking fire sale for the bottom feeders. I'm fielding raving lunatic calls from the residents, sitting in their smug overdone condos hearing their purchase prices collapse! And the poor sons of bitches who actually needed mega loans to buy the joints, watch out for foreclosure heaven!

"And what will I be doing? Singing my big fat Jewban ass off. Immunity at least."

Now, only because I like you guys, I'll give you a few freebies. I know this for fact. Frederick was getting ready to dump Irina and Lupe. I was putting their 'You're over' packages together; also Sergi was poking Irina. Big time, maybe even serious. I have some ideas about who did it. Don't think you'd believe me, anyway. First I have to deal with my own survival and try to turn over this huge vat of greed piss to someone!!! Who, you may ask? I haven't a fucking clue!!!! No family member alive or capable. Goldie's oldest sons don't know anything not in the Torah; It's a combo of the Homeowners Association (talk about cats in a bag! I walked out of the first attempt at a meeting!) Screaming, yelling, like some horror movie version of adult remedial behavior classes!

"The vultures will descend, some property management group and, of course the lawyers, but I will be gone before that nightmare. You can relax Rogers, the CPA's and the bean counters will keep the payroll going and pay the bills. I don't envy you the residents, however. Fear of loss of status and net worth, turns just about anyone in this town into a frothing beast, so be prepared. Well boys, that's my two cents worth and lunch is on me and if you're still clueless about the perp or perps in a week, you know where to find me, just in case I'm right. Since I am almost always fucking right even when I don't want to be. Gotta go. Enjoy. And if you want to invest in this piece of bullshit, hey, discount prices coming right up!"

And with that, Carmen Daniels finished her drink, picked up her napkin and her burger in one glossy hand, stood up, rising tall, flicked her silver mane at them and strode out, leaving them speechless in awe and the sudden absence of all energy in the room.

"Mommacita, that woman makes my pecker pump. What an ass and what a mouth."

This time Roy didn't even roll his eyes. He was no longer one to judge the power of unlikely attractions, but her teaser about suspects really had his attention. And now what Lupe Sanchez had told him made sense. She'd heard a man's voice in the hall around 1:00 a.m. the night Rebecca was murdered. Sergi said he'd left at 5. So he lied. Irina was getting dumped for real and they were lovers. Sounds more like a motive, or a copycat or? Nothing felt right. No inner bell ringing. "Ok Mikey, let's eat." In a pinch a full stomach is always a better way to see clearly.

Rogers and Mikey devoured their fancy free burgers in silence, both trying to process Carmen Daniels monologue and figure out what to do next. Arturo reappeared to clear her cocktail emporium. Mikey watched, shaking his head, "Man, she didn't even leave a fucking sip!"

Rogers laughed. "Are you surprised?"

"Naw. Just disappointed. Boy, that took discipline! So what now?"

Rogers looked over at him which felt rather weird, since they were still sitting side by side. "How about you move across from me, this feels a little you know."

Mikey was up and over instantly. "Want some coffee?"

Rogers nodded. Waiting while Mikey ordered for them in Spanish.

"I don't think we get a receipt or anything, right?"

"Nope, this place is all house accounts, but I think we should leave a tip."

"Shit, Rogers, the tip will be more than we ever spend on a full dinner with booze!"

"Doesn't have to be huge, I'm sure she covers that stuff, but it's just polite, I think. The kid almost fainted, he was so nervous."

"Yeah, you're right. I just remembered what Leena told me. Mikey looked tired and underneath, Rogers could see he was off his mark.

"So, Mikey, what now? They clearly haven't found this Jenkins guy yet. We have all these folders, but maybe we should start simple and interview Irina again and the sons, since we know where they are and I doubt if any of them are expecting it. Pepe can start going through her folders so we're not just losing time."

He could see the relief in Mikey's face, not competing, looking for a leaning post, at least for right now.

"Sounds good. Just need a caffeine shot and we're on it."

When they got back to the Silver Sands, the street was still overflowing with media and the curious hordes who seemed to live for such moments of voyeured excitement as if just by being in the swarm, their lives became more exciting.

They pulled into the back employees parking lot and made their way inside before any of the press spotted them.

Pepe was sitting with Oscar, intently scanning computer images of Nazi thugs in wife beater tee shirts and lots of leather. Why leather in Florida still seemed like the look of choice for biker hate groups, always escaped him. Rogers put the pile of files down next to Pepe and explained what Carmen had found while Mikey called Irina's cell and asked her to come down and meet them there.

Rogers looked over at him. "So?"

"She's coming, but she isn't happy about it."

"Good. If she's rattled or pissed, she'll be more talkative."

The elevator from the residences stopped and Irina strode toward them, all six feet of over the top booty and designer hooker garb on display, armored, Rogers thought, defensive gear as self-protection.

"Ms. Petrov so sorry to interrupt your day, I'm sure you have a lot to deal with right now, but we do have a few more questions. Would you like something. Water. Coffee?"

She put her well-developed arms on her wide hips and shifted her weight to one stilettoed leg. "No, I just want to do this and go."

Mikey came up beside her. "Please, then just follow us to Mr. Rogers' office."

They all did some awkward version of a perp walk, into his lair.

Rogers moved behind his desk. Mikey moved to the chair opposite and motioned for Irina to sit beside him.

"I prefer to stand, thank you."

"Suit yourself Ms. Petrov but I must tell you, we are not your adversaries here, we have three murders of people you worked for to solve and we need all the help we can get."

This was clearly the right thing to say and she softened and slid into the chair next to Mikey, who seemed even smaller beside her.

"Okay, how may I help?"

Rogers and Mikey had not worked out any good cop/bad cop scenario, but Mikey nodded at him and he saw this as permission to lead the interview.

"Okay, May I call you Irina?" Rogers was stalling, trying to get some gut message on how to deal with her.

"Sure. Whatever. "She looked down, not making eye contact, which he could read many ways. The Russians were so damn impenetrable, almost as if all those years of dealing with an entirely different system of ploys, restrictions, survival skills, and the need to hustle for everything, had actually become part of their DNA. Tough, Rogers thought, toughened by all those years of fear and want. Of course, America was kind of catching up now, he flashed on interviews with black kids, hauled in for drugs or theft and they did the same thing. That surly, not making eye contact posture, a behavior learned to fend off discovery or, what?

"Okay, Irina. I think you're a pretty smart lady, so I'm not going to pull any punches here. We've got two pieces of verified intel that pulls you further into a possible suspect pool."

Now she looked up, suddenly and reflexively and he saw that she was scared.

"What do you mean? Intel? What is that?"

"Well, first the lab found your DNA on the pairs of stilettos used in Frederick Rothenstein's homicide and second we know that you and Sergi Dubinski were having, probably still are having, an affair and that he was with you on the night his wife was murdered."

Now her eyes were searing into him, and real terror flashed quickly across her highly re-structured face. Rogers was groping, taking a big risk with her, but it seemed to be working. The trouble with interviewing suspects who had lots of cosmetic surgery or whatever the hell they shot into their faces, made it very hard to read their expressions, but the eyes, always the best bet.

"This is nonsense. I think I should have a lawyer."

Uh oh. Maybe he'd pushed too hard. "That's your choice, it may be the simple truth is all you need, but if you are asking for a lawyer, that's not just a rhetorical question, we will just stop now, but we will have to hold you."

"No! wait. Wait. No!"

Tears slid down her high wide cheekbones, leaving mascara streaks on her cheeks. "Please. I cannot be 'held' as you say. You have to understand, how people like me, Russian immigrants, feel about the police or any kind of jail. I'll tell you and I want you to record all of it."

Mikey leaned forward, placing his phone recorder on the desk. "Done."

She sat up very straight and let out a huge sigh, which Rogers thought was relief.

"You know, when I first got to America and to Miami, which was my dream, I had to register with employment agencies and go on job interviews and I practiced my English all the time, day and night, but there was one word, I struggled so hard with and it seemed to be a word I needed in these interviews when asked things about gaps in my work history, education, things I could not prove. Un-fort-u-nate-ly. I could not say it. I would drive to these meetings and practice it out loud over and over. "Well, Sir, un-fort-u-nate-ly I had to leave all of these records in Ukraine." She paused and wiped her tears away, making the mascara streaks widen and giving her face a battered look.

Rogers was moved by her story, and instinctively reached into his desk and handed her a face wipe, one of the ones he used for Hildy, which he chose not to share.

"Thank you," she said, her entire persona changing before them. "I don't know why I thought about that now, maybe to show you how much I would do or would never do to risk being sent back, like breaking any of your laws."

Rogers nodded, not wanting to risk interrupting her for a second.

"Okay. They were my shoes. I mean, I did not know this until right now. He had many women, all sizes and shapes and he kept lots of fancy garments and shoes up there to give or to take back. He has a special closet for them, but it's not locked or anything. He would tell us to go in and choose something if he was pleased with us. I am a big woman, I have large feet, so he let me buy my own Louboutins; I remember not believing I could have any shoes like this. I could pay my rent in Russia for what one of them cost! "When he told me he was getting ready to make some changes well I knew what that meant. We argued and he asked for the shoes back. I was humiliated.

"I left, went down to my condo, and got the other pair, I only had two pairs and I brought them back, took off the ones I was wearing and threw them both on the floor. So, yes, they were mine and they would have my DNA, but I left them there and anyone could have used them. Also, I grow up with KGB mentality, even though they were mostly back in the shadows by the time I was born, but we Russians are clever, could I be so stupid as to incriminate myself in such a clumsy way? Ridiculous!"

Rogers nodded. He believed her. He looked across at Mikey and could see Mikey did, too.

"And Sergi?"

"Yes! We did not plan this. I was using the gym quite a lot because Frederick was so critical about how we looked, and our weight and I think we were drawn to one another because we shared a common heritage, we could speak Russian together, we'd both used our bodies to succeed, though I certainly have more skills and, well, I'm smarter, but that didn't matter. We fell in love. And you can mock this. I know he had many women but look at his wife! And there was no sex with them. She didn't want it and he was afraid he would crush her, she was so frail.

"He was at my condo that night. I snuck him in around 1 or so and he left, to go back and let the dogs out and he called me after on his way to the gym. We did not plot his wife's murder! Neither of us was prepared to do anything so stupid or to even try and live together. We are both survivors! We were so careful and in no hurry. We just knew, we knew, we will be together some day. He did not do this horrible thing. And I did not."

"Do you know anything about what happened between the time he left you and when he went to the gym?"

"What do I know? I know he took the dogs out because he did not know if Leena was coming. He did not go into her bedroom, so even if she was, was, already killed, he didn't see anything. He brought the dogs back and went right to the gym. So, from 1 a.m. or so until the police called him, I don't think he went back there, except at 5 for the dogs."

"I know this is hard, Irina, but is it possible he was using you for an alibi?"

She shrugged her broad shoulders and laughed, a quick, bitter laugh. "Of course, it's possible! I have lived a life where most people are not who they seem to be. Have I been lied to and used by men and women I trusted? Yes. Un-fort-un-at-ely! And I have done it, too. I am not some holier than thou person. So, yes, he could have done that, and he knew I'd taken the shoes back. But I do not believe it. More than anything else, he really did care about her, felt great pity for her and he was very grateful to her and her family and very protective, that was not an act!

"He was like me, very careful with money and he had saved a

234

lot and she gave him a lot and they paid him very well and he had no expenses and he built a very strong reputation, so he knew if the marriage failed, he would still be okay. He didn't have to murder her! So, once again, officers, we are Russians, he wouldn't be so stupid to do it like that. She was so withered and sickly, and she took so many pills and drank so much, all he would have to do is put something extra in her drink or whatever. So, yes he could but no I don't believe it."

Rogers could feel his adrenaline ebbing. Damn. He believed her.

"Mikey, any questions?"

Mikey sat up straighter, not expecting him to ask. He was not prepared and took a wrong turn. "Not for now, but I think we will need to ask for your passport until we have really cleared you and Mr. Dubinski. We need to know you are right here."

Now she was back to her armored fight or flight posture. "Let me tell you, little man, I would die before I would give you my passport. Die! And if I was going to murder anyone it would be to keep my passport! I struggled! You Americans have no idea, no concept of what it was like there! Everything is bribes, games, to get a doctor, to get medicine, my grandmother died because we couldn't pay enough to get her into a hospital or for her medicine. All black market! Nothing has really changed except a lot of very shrewd bad men have gotten rich. It took me ten years and everything I had, everything to get here, to become a citizen. You take all of this for granted. You know nothing! You all whine and complain about everything and you know nothing! Try moving to Moscow, not wanted, not welcome, not speaking a word of Russian! Having no family, no friends and no one wants you there! And then talk to me about giving you my passport. No! Arrest me! No!"

Rogers stood up, Mikey needed a save. "Irina, please, Lieut. Martinez has not been involved in this part of the investigation.

We didn't confer before this interview. Please, calm down. We didn't mean to scare you. No one is arresting you or taking your passport. We're investigating. And we have to look at every clue and possibility and I think you can understand how this all looks from the outside."

Mikey did the second part of the correct. "Yes, sorry. I overshot. It's all good. You did great. We do have to make sure no one leaves town but, we know you won't do that now."

She stood up, back in her Viking persona. "No, I will not go anywhere, but If I am not under arrest, I would like to go back upstairs. I have a lot of packing and sorting to do and I must meet with Ms. Daniels and turn over my files."

Rogers stood and walked over to her, taking her arm and gently leading her out. "We really appreciate your cooperation. We need all the help we can get, so if you remember anything else, no matter how insignificant it may seem, you know where to find me."

She turned and looked at him, eye to eye, since they were the same height. "I doubt it, but I will. I like you."

And shrugging off his arm, she strode out of his office and away from the twitching limb of everything she had escaped to get here.

Mikey and Rogers let out a long, collective sigh.

"Shit." Mikey rubbed his temples with his small, sturdy hands. "No real fucking motives."

Rogers bent down and patted Hildy and slipped a dog treat into her eager mouth. She was always where he turned for brain bursts and centering. "So, let's go talk to the sons and then, back to Dubinski. I have the chart up, if you want to take a look and see if anything jumps out."

"Naw. Let's just do this old school. Guts and eyes. What are the sons names?"

"Gotta look it up." Rogers pulled an already bulging file from his in box and sifted through reams of mostly useless information, but he still believed you never quite knew where a seemingly meaningless clue might appear. "Leor and Avram and they're twins. Eighteen. Certainly capable, but why?"

"Why is no longer the main fucking question. They're religious fanatics. Wages of sin all that shit. All those groups are the same, if you want my humble Catholic opinion. The Catholics are starting to look fucking moderate compared to these wack jobs. Doesn't matter shit if they're Hassidic, Islamic, Evangelicals, Vegans, Animal Ultra-Rightists, Scientologists, they all drink the same fucking Kool-Aid. Organized religion and politics, it's evil twin will tear the entire planet apart, eventually. Fear, hate, the fucking insanity of one way to live. I hate it all. But don't tell my mother. The church is still her passion, but shit, I mean, mass and confession seem pretty lame these days."

Rogers grinned at him. "Well Lieut. Martinez I think that's the first speech I've ever heard you give that wasn't part of a press conference and the only one where you actually expressed a POV. I think I like this, even if you left out the priest, altar boy thing."

Mikey shrugged his shoulders, but Rogers could see he was flattered. "Yeah, add that. I think that Daniels dame, inspired me. Okay, let's do it."

When they reached Arnold Rothenstein's condo, they paused, not having had time to make a plan. Rogers put his hand on his shoulder before Mikey could buzz. "Okay, together first, then maybe separate them, go with your gut about who you want. We have no intel on them, and we're flying pretty blind, here."

Mikey nodded and pushed the buzzer. They waited, there seemed to be some commotion and scrambling around inside and finally someone, who appeared to be from the Temple came into view on the intercom camera.

"Yes."

It was not quite a question.

"Lieut. Martinez and Head of Security Deputy Rogers. We are

here to speak with Avram and Leor Rothenstein. It's a matter of some urgency."

More whispering and scrambling behind the heavy door. "We are in mourning here and trying to prepare for a burial and Shiva. I'm afraid we cannot have outsiders here now."

"We can get a warrant and come back with more outsiders."

"No. No. please wait a moment."

They waited, not speaking, intent on the strange sounds coming from inside. And then, locks turning, the door opened revealing a group of men all looking like a scene from the cocktail hour before the Last Supper and in the center, seated almost like Kings of Judea, the sons and heirs apparent, who seemed extremely nervous as if they had been ambushed rather than anointed.

"Avram and Leor Rothenstein, Lieut. Martinez and Deputy Rogers, I am also Head of Security for your family, I don't believe we've ever met, but we do have some questions for you in private."

The twins were not identical, in fact they looked more like Schwarzenegger and DeVito in that old comedy. Leor, was tall, handsome in spite of the ill-fitting outfit, pais locks, black hat, scraggly beard and stained white shirt. They could see his broad shoulders and biceps through the camouflage. Avram, was short, with eyes too close together and greasy blonde hair and beard, but he also had a body builder's physique under this official disguise.

"Is there somewhere private we can talk?" Rogers asked calmly and they pointed to Arnold's study. Their Hassidic protectors shot daggers at the intruders, but returned to their prayer books, knowing there was not much point in interfering, yet. One of them did call the Head Rabbi, who, Rogers knew, would soon appear.

The twins stood side by side in body builder's stance. Feet spread and arms crossed over their chests as if instinctively assuming the opposite posturing of the weak, victim Hassidic kids who were bullied and pushed around or so the world view seemed to reflect. Leor looked directly into Rogers eyes, indicating they would be the lead voices, which amused Rogers since it seemed to come from some internal triage about who looked more virile. The tall two won.

"You have questions for us?"

"Yep. You two, we regret to say, are the only surviving family members who might shed some new light on the three tragic murders. Of course, since we do not know if this was a hate crime, a vendetta or a serial killer who somehow has access to your security system and personal information, well, you and your brother are both potential victims as well as possible suspects and since your father is incapacitated at the moment, yes, sir, we do have questions."

Leor Rothenstein shifted his weight slightly and his brother followed, no wiggle room between them, Rogers thought. "Okay can we all sit down and try to make this a little more relaxed?"

Leor looked at his brother and Avram nodded. "Sure." He motioned to their father's office sitting area with the oversize maroon velvet covered chairs and they all followed his lead. "For the record, our father is recovering quite well and should be released at any time. They are adjusting his medication. He has had quite a shock and behaved out of character, but he is a devout and honorable man and he is in deep mourning as we all are." Leor motioned for them to sit in the formally arranged grouping of the lush arm chairs. Rogers and Mikey let a moment of silence fill the awkward settling in.

"We honor that and regret having to discuss this now, but I think you understand it is necessary. Can you tell us where you both were during the twenty-four hours leading up to the murder of your grandparents and also the twenty-four hours preceding the murder of your aunt?"

Rogers felt the level of tension in the room shoot up into the very air they were breathing.

"We were together. We were at the temple helping the Rabbi and teaching Torah studies to the Hebrew school class and then we were home. If my mother had not deserted her faith and her family, she and our younger siblings could give us this alibi. I guess. The rabbi and maybe a 100 people can tell you where we were until around 5:30. I believe it was a Friday night, Shabbat, so we would have to be home, our other home, near the shul, by sundown. We came to get the family together and we all left, isn't that right Avram?"

Avram nodded, and leaned forward. "We know you have to do this and we most certainly want you to find who did this blasphemous crime, but it is against all the commandments we live by and unthinkable to suspect us."

This seemed to annoy Mikey, probably linking into his little monologue in Rogers office, Rogers thought and tried to make eye contact with him, knowing they were on rather tricky terrain here, but now it was the little guys who were putting their macho in the ring.

"We are well aware of what your faith says, but frankly, Mr. Rothenstein, we now live in a world where religion can be twisted to justify just about anything, and you certainly are aware of that fact."

Avram stiffened. "Yes, we are aware, but we are not heretics or fanatics, no matter what you may think. We would have had to break our contract with God, it is enough that our mother has done this and we have lost her and our siblings and cannot bury our grandparents or aunt according to the laws of our faith, but to murder them!!!! This is unbearable and unthinkable!"

Mikey sat back and Rogers leaned forward. "We do not have at the moment any way of contacting your mother; I think she is afraid, and, with all due respect, she has reason. Your father came pretty close to a violent, possibly fatal attack on her and I was right there, sir, so at the moment, we do have to consider how strongly your father, whose opinions and beliefs you both seem to share, felt about the life styles of your aunt and grandparents and that kind of simmering resentment can make even the most humble and devout behave in ways not in keeping with their faith. So, we will try and contact your mother, and certainly the temple, but if you have witnesses to your arrival and departure from your other home, that would be extremely helpful."

Leor and Avram stood up, in perfect synchronicity, signaling an end to the interview. "We do have witnesses and we will provide you with all this information. We have only one request from you. Release the bodies at once, before the burials become violations of the sacred texts. The Grand Rabbi has made this highly unusual exception because of the nature of the events, but it cannot go on!"

Rogers and Mikey stood up and Rogers nodded at Mikey; let him have this ball.

"We are in constant contact with the Medical Examiner and I do think her work is almost complete. We are aware of how difficult the circumstances are for you and we will notify you the moment we can release them."

Leor motioned for them to leave the den and they shook hands, the tension still making it hard to get a full breath as they threaded their way out of the almost biblical room and back into the overt hostility of the gathered mourners. Rogers thought if looks could well; the front door loomed ahead and they practically sprinted to the exit and release from the coiling anxiety of the interview. "Shalom, "Mikey said, not even knowing if that was the right thing to say or an insult in this situation.

The door closed on them without a response and they both exhaled loudly.

"Fucking wack jobs, all of them. Priests, too, all of them. What a load of Horse shit!"

Rogers chuckled. Better make sure your phone isn't recording any of this, Mikey, social media will have your ass and your badge."

Rogers shook his head. "Well, hells bells, Mikey, I don't think they did it."

Mikey sighed and did a couple of tension relieving neck rolls. "Yeah. Fuck. Me, neither. But we gotta check it all out."

Rogers pushed the elevator button, entering the codes taking them back to their safe zone. "Let's go see if they have a lead of this Walter Jenkins, since we're just about out of ideas."

"Shit." Mikey said and down they went.

CHAPTER 15

"Miss Edy."

"Mr. Rogers." God, when I say that I have an instant flash on that nerdy kid's show dude with the Perry Como sweater that all children seemed to have been hypnotized by. He gave me the total creepies. I hated when Sunny watched him, never understood that whole deal. She loved him."

"Well, I'm sorry to hear that, try linking me to the other one, Roy Rogers and Dale Evans and all those dopey old westerns. At least it was boots and string ties, not a 'Perry Cosmo sweater' in sight, though you are probably the only woman on earth who would so describe his attire."

"I take that as a huge compliment. Anything new you can talk about?"

"Not right now. In the fray, though we just had a very confounding interview with the two oldest Rothenstein sons. Any info about them that might be useful?"

"Avram and Leor? Useful? Hmmm. Well, they both have their heads so far up their asses they think a hemorrhoid is a new solar system, but other than that, not a clue. Our paths didn't exactly cross much. You're thinking suspects? About as likely as Lorraine and Lola. And only if Arnold was calling the plays. They are totally in thrall of their father. Poor Goldy. I have no idea what they will all try and do to her, but it's like *Escape from Alcatraz*. I wish I knew how to contact her. She's going to need all the friends she can get. What's that noise? Are you laughing or crying?"

"Wadda ya think, little lady. 'Heads up their ass', where do you get this stuff?"

"I have no idea. I was born with a bad brain."

"We should all have been so blessed. Gotta go. We're still interviewing and I do wish I could share all this with you, which I can't, but any more brain bursts, however abhorrent to the seriousness of the situation, please call me. We're really scrambling here."

Edy took a deep breath, still shy about asking. "Any chance you might be available for a drink or something later on?"

"Count on it. I'll try and give you a real time after I know where we are now. Do be careful. And keep Sunny nearby."

"Got it. We're closet cleaning. Anything to distract us. Ooma's resting and calmer now. Do you really think she could be a target?"

"Ah, Miss Edy. Can't really say, but I think caution is highly advisable."

"She has a gun, actually two. She offered me one. Whadda ya think?"

"I think that would be a very good idea. There's a stand your ground law in Florida, so you can shoot anyone who threatens you even if you don't have a permit, but I didn't tell you that."

"Wow. Certainly more cowboy than nerd children's show dude. I like it."

When Rogers and Mikey got back to the security bunker, or what they now felt was a bunker, Carmen Daniels was waiting for them. She had made herself at home in Roger's office and was on his phone. Mikey nudged him, but somehow it didn't cause any surge of territorial instinct or anger.

She motioned to them in a gesture that indicated she knew she shouldn't be sitting there, but pointed to the land line which seemed to figure in her choice.

"Yes, yes, Judge. The lieutenant is right here and I'll put him on, if you can just hold a moment."

Carmen pushed the hold button and waved Mikey over to her. "I found Walter Jenkins, but I think you guys need a search warrant and luckily enough, one of the judges who can issue it fast happens to own a condo here. He and his family are in the Hamptons for the summer, they usually rent it out, but it's empty, anyway, he will issue one right now and scan it back if you can send it to him. We got lucky."

Mikey looked at her with a bit of awe, that seemed to affect her. Rogers almost thought she blushed. "That's amazing. I just need his info and I'll have my office send it right now."

"Done." Carmen pushed the button, and turning on all her hidden charm, extracted what they would have thought impossible, since probable cause did not seem to be involved.

Mikey made his call and then came back over to her. "How in hell did you put that together?"

"Well, I did more research on this guy and Oscar helped and besides a vast array of on-line hate comments about the Rothensteins in particular and what he sweetly calls, "Jew-piss People" are threats, rants disgusting ideas of what to do to "Save Florida' from the mongrel hordes, which is just about all of us. And he has a record for fencing stolen merchandise, so if any of the missing items are at his apartment well, worth a shot. I have no idea how the hell he was hired in the first place, but then, I won't even use an Uber, some random person showing up in their personal car? No thank you."

"We just interviewed Avram and Leor. They're pretty tightly wrapped, I don't know, seems like they have an alibi, but I still think they should be on the list and their father, who clearly has the power over them."

Carmen reached back and scratched her mane, which Mikey found to be extremely erotic. "Hard to say, since my family is so lapsed, religion-wise. To us, life is really just one long Yom Kipper, first you atone and then you eat. But they could have. Smart enough to make it look like a hate crime, which it seems is where you're heading."

Rogers realized no one but them knew about the "Kill the Kikes" on the victims' feet and Olivia was doing a test to see what it was written with.

"We're running out of bases, but we have a lead and what you did was truly helpful."

"Ah, hell. I'm actually having fun, awful as that is to admit. Beats spread sheets and bean counters and the feds, man. Also, I remember this Jenkins shmuck. I had a couple of meetings with the maintenance staff when he was at the country club and he just reeked hate. Cocky and surly. Should have fired him just for the attitude. But the turn-over at all the hotels and clubs is so enormous. Training anyone new is a constant nightmare, so he slipped through a crack and they know they can, which brings me back to my Uber fears. If you go there, take back up with big guns. I mean it. He always bragged about his "heat" he called it. Lots of "heat" which I think is biker skin head speak for weapons. And I doubt he lives alone. Really sketchy neighborhood, too."

Mikey's phone buzzed and broke his moment of total focus on Carmen Daniels.

"The search warrant has been scanned to the judge. Shouldn't be long now."

Carmen got up and did an elaborate royal bow, indicating to

Rogers that she had given up the throne. "Sir, your seat is nice and warm for you."

Rogers grinned and moved around her and she slid down into one of the chairs across from him, none of them quite sure what to do next. She had helped, she had lots of important information and access, but she was also a possible suspect or accomplice or, at least, not one of them. She sat up, sensing this.

"Look boys, I know this is all a little out there, but shit, you gotta trust someone, sometime. Right? Except lawyers and politicians, gotta have some line in the sand.

"Before you came in, I was reading the Miami Herald, and there was yet another article about a boat full of refugees, Cubans still coming or trying to and I was thinking of the Port of Miami and all those cruise ships and any one of us could be standing on the deck with a nice cold glass of champagne waving adios to all reality for a week or whatever and just a mile or two away, there are desperate, homeless, starving, terrified people trying to make it to land in some horrible leaky tub for what might be a chance at a decent life. All over the world, there are cruise ships bobbing around not far from overcrowded rafts and home-made boats, coming from any one of the increasingly endless hell holes, willing to die, to suffer anything to be safe, and I thought, fuck! What do we know about anything. Even murder. What makes people so filled with rage, despair, all of it. Or, of course sometimes they're just evil fuckers. I used to think that narcissists were just stupid sociopaths, now I'm not so quick to categorize. But if this was a psychopath, then I don't envy you, not that I did, anyway. Okay, I'm going back to the paper piles."

Mikey jumped up to walk her out and Rogers stayed seated. "Thank you ma'am, we'll be in touch."

Carmen Daniels gave him a little back wave without turning around and Mikey walked her to the exit, summing up all his macho. "So, how about you let me buy you a drink tonight, just to thank you."

She turned and looked so hard into his eyes, looking down to do it, he almost gasped. "Not if I was dying of thirst in Alligator Alley."

Mikey met her stare. "I know a place that has Patron en Lalique Serie 2 tequila. Only bar in Miami. And fantastic Ropa Vieja."

She never blinked. "8. Text me the address." And she was gone.

Mikey exhaled from somewhere way up at Roger's height. But considering he had already stepped off the high dive, what the fuck. He smiled.

Rogers wasn't quite sure how it had evolved, but he and Mikey were back in lock step, a team, even though he had been added to free Mikey up for other cases. Maybe because Rogers was no longer a threat to his advancement or ego, but the tension between them was just about gone. Mikey wasn't even calling him "Roy" on purpose and they were both, though it certainly had not been spoken about, enjoying working together.

They had put together a backup team, three unmarked SUV's, everyone in protective gear and with big guns, which might turn out to be serious overkill, but then again, Jenkins was most certainly a loose cannon and better to be safe. Miami seemed to figure as ground zero in so many bizarre and deadly incidents. Even that one kid, the eighteen-year-old girl who flew from Miami to Colorado to kill people as an homage to the twentieth anniversary of Columbine, as if there weren't enough schools to shoot up right here.

Miami had become the new symbol of hope, opportunity and

last chances that L.A. and Las Vegas and Arizona had been before. Billionaires, millionaires, middle class retirees who could live their dream; no more grinding job, no more snow shoveling, most of them, retired teachers, mailmen, worker bees, could have a very nice condo, nicer than their mortgaged houses in all those urban sprawling suburbs across the country, with activities, pools, yoga classes, golf, maybe a little boat and as much social interaction as they could stand. They could live like rich people and with good weather most every day of the year. And no state taxes!

Add to that the draw of proximity, however voyeuristic, of the new bragging rights that normal people could live within a few miles of most of the top athletes and celebritoids they read about every day, it was the same ocean, after all.

Miami had become the new American Dream city. When visiting in other countries if Americans were asked where they were from and said New York or Los Angeles, they now got shrugs or blank faces, but say Miami, and boom, eyes lit up, smiles spread. Miami was sexy. Miami was glamorous. Miami was a promise of a better way to live, despite rising tides and rising prices and of course, all the problems attached to any have and have not urban center with good weather attracting throngs of not so good people.

The neighborhoods that housed the lower end of the Sunshine State spectrum, where the ocean or the intercoastal were nowhere to be seen and cement was often the lawn cover, rickety rusting porch furniture occupied by sun stained (no funds for fancy blocks and moisturizers) humans, whose body language, whether elderly or young, reeked of defeat. No way to South Beach for these folks, but, better than a similar fate in Detroit in February.

Apathy is almost contagious, and Mikey and Rogers could feel their energy waning, in spite of the adrenaline rush of what they were facing.

They were silent, moving slowly past the strip malls, credit dentists, liquor stores with faded Budweiser posters and dirty windows, run down old houses converted into fundamentalist churches, and homemade signs promising redemption, cheap eats cafes and an occasional McDonalds or Pizza Hut, cheap gas, not even premium pumps around here. Kids running through dying lawn sprinklers. Emaciated old men in bathing trunks and flip flops riding rickety beach bikes in the searing summer sun.

Rogers thought about what Carmen Daniels had said standing on a cruise ship balcony sipping champagne when just over the horizon, desperate people in homemade boats were fighting for survival. He shuddered, feeling a moment of true gratitude for his many blessings. Mikey seemed to be thinking the same thing.

"Whew. What a fucking downer. Makes Leena's neighborhood look like Fisher Island."

And then, they were there. Rogers pulled over to the curb and the backup team spread out, though in this neighborhood, the sudden presence of several clearly not local vehicles, even unmarked ones, was hardly unobserved.

Rogers pointed to a weed-filled yard, partially hidden by a chain link fence, behind which two extremely aggressive looking Doberman Pinchers were pacing, almost a canine version of the combination of rage and ennui of the human inhabitants.

"Uh oh. We got us a welcoming committee. Do the guys have tranquilizer darts?"

"Natch. Man I'd rather face Jenkins and his pals with AK57's than those beasts."

Rogers chuckled. "Well, this may be your lucky day. Looks like we could get both."

They looked at one another. Memories of many such days connecting them.

"Okay, amigo, let's just get this fucker over with."

While Mikey relayed the dog situation to the back up team,

Rogers waited, using, he hoped, all of his senses to get a grip on what might await them. When Mikey signaled that the backup boys were ready and approaching; Rogers and Mikey moved slowly toward the padlocked gate, both thinking who in the hell padlocks their front gate?

Rogers whispered to Mikey, "Well, why should we be surprised. This is just the poor guy's version of a home security system and probably as effective even without the scary dogs."

Mikey was sweating. Mikey was afraid of dogs, even Hildy. "Shit, they look like they would rip our fucking throats out without even barking first."

They stood in front of the padlock, not having the equipment handy to unlock it and not sure, even with the search warrant, whether they had cause to break it open. Before they could discuss the situation, the front door opened and three big men, all looking like dress extras from some B movie motorcycle gang movie appeared on the steps.

It was clear they had guns somewhere inside their jeans, faded and hanging below their stomachs, all of which looked like they could use some gym time. They were shirtless, covered with tattoos, colored images of swastikas, skulls, coiled fists, snakes, "White America" slogans, crucifixes, and that was just what they could quickly observe. They had baseball caps or bandanas tied around their heads and they all took what cops called "the stance." Legs spread, arms crossed over chests, chins out.

The dogs leapt toward the fence growling and teeth bared now and Rogers thought Mikey might just fall over or have a major panic attack.

"Breathe Mikey. Nothing's going to happen. Head up. You're a cop, remember."

"Yeah. A ready to wet his pants cop, but that's sacred trust."

Rogers tried not to laugh, sensitive to the welcoming committee reading anything but tough police postures.

The biggest of the three, who had a Bandana on his head and a swastika on his chest moved down a step.

"May we help you gentlemen? We're not buying Boy Scout cookies this year."

His buddies chuckled on cue.

Rogers moved slightly closer to the fence. "We have a few questions for Walter Jenkins, is he here or are one of you Mr. Jenkins? Also, we come in peace, so, if you could call off the dogs, that would be most appreciated."

Bandana Man whistled and the dogs stopped and moved back toward their master. Rogers had to admit he was impressed. The thought of training Hildy to do that was not even a fantasy. Of course Labs would probably run up and lick a raving axe wielding fiend, protecting their masters was not one of their character traits. Fine with him. He'd always thought any breed that would scare possible criminals would scare him, too.

"Appreciate that, sir. Are you Mr. Jenkins?"

Bandana man took one more step down toward them. "Nope. He doesn't live here no more. Hasn't for quite some time. Still uses this address for mail and stuff. Sorry."

"Are you the only residents or are there more inside?"

"Nope. Just us, though we have meetings here."

"I see. And does Mr. Jenkins attend these meetings."

"Yep. He's the leader."

"And do you have his current address?"

They all laughed at that, as Rogers assumed they would. He was more likely to get an answer from the snarling watch dogs.

"Well, now, we actually do not have that information. And if we did, you'd have to arrest us because brothers don't snitch on brothers. But Walter wants his privacy and we mainly communicate on-line and by phone."

"I see. Well, we do have a search warrant, which we would not like to use now, so if you might just give us his cellphone it would save all of us an enormous amount of wasted time, energy and your padlock replacement costs."

Bandana Man hadn't expected that, Rogers assumed, probably because the house was filled with guns, contraband, Dark Web materials and narcotics.

"I can do that. But it won't help you much and you didn't get it from me. Are we clear on that."

"Yes, sir." Much obliged."

Bandana Man reached behind him and they all stiffened, just in case something more deadly than a cell phone was wedged into his ass crack.

"Okay, officers. It's 555-124-5930, but he changes it all the time, so good luck. Oh, and he never answers if he don't know you. So have a nice day."

"Thank you for your cooperation and I do hope we won't have to come back."

Mikey waved off the back up team and after entering Jenkins number in his phone they moved slowly back to their car.

When they got inside, Mikey told the back up team to wait for further instructions and to follow them out of the area. They drove around to an empty church parking lot a few blocks and a serious relief of tension away.

"Shit. So I can have our IT guys track the number and maybe get lucky with an address. Any other ideas?"

Rogers exhaled through his tooth gap, perfect for spontaneous whistling occasions. "Oscar. I bet he knows how to trace it to an address. The guy has phone bills."

"Fucking A. Do it!"

It didn't take Oscar more than a few minutes to find an address for Walter Jenkins. So much for any idea of a secret hide-out. "Shit, that kid is unbelievable! He's taught Leena so much; better than one of those bullshit computer schools. This creep is living in a condo in Aventura for Christ sake! Isn't that where you live?"

"Yep. I guess Mr. Jenkins has some additional revenue stream. I think we can send the backup boys home. I'll call the police chief there, better to cooperate and let him send a couple of guys."

"They have their own police dept? No way."

"Absolutely. Almost 40,000 people live there now. They have a school, the fifth largest shopping mall in the country, a branch of Florida International University. A major local hospital, a three-mile walking/jogging paved track overlooking a beautiful lake, the intercoastal, parks, you name it and then all those lake front expensive houses and the endless condos; my daily goal is to find my way to the right building. Everyone thinks it's just part of Miami, but it's like a little island of its own."

"I live so close and I never knew any of that. I never go there, though I know there's lots of good restaurants and shit. It's just too massive and confusing."

"That it is. All those cookie cutter condos, like a city of concrete and stucco Legos, but people love it. And it's a helluva lot cheaper than other parts of Miami. Lots of foreigners and snowbirds. I just got lucky, found a sublet, very nice, and I can see the water, but I never thought I'd live in one of those boxes."

"Not for me, man. I need earth, plants, palm trees. It's my Columbian roots."

"Yeah, I agree, but this job came up so fast and it works for now. But I gotta say, the idea of a Jenkins kind of dude living there is a stretch."

They were moving slowly, the traffic picking up as they headed back down Biscayne Blvd. The main artery from where they were to Aventura; moving past parts of what was left of the old Miami, the Meyer Lansky era Miami, two story motels with kidney shaped pools and broken outdoor furniture, moving down to AIA which ran all the way to the real Miami; the old city where the legendary Fontainebleau and Eden Rock were the star hotels, and Sinatra and The Rat Pack, Judy Garland, all the heavy weight gamblers and gangsters; there were still twitching limbs scattered all over Miami, run down hotels and apartment buildings that would soon disappear to make room for upscale new arrivals, who wanted smart houses and full service condos and interiors by Karl Lagerfeld and Ralph Lauren, not creaky wicker, covered in Hawaiian motif washable fabrics and leatherette kitchen chairs.

Rogers had learned a fair amount about Aventura. "wanna hear some more about this place we're going?"

"Yeah. I feel like a dope, not even knowing they were a separate city!"

"Well, fifty years ago, it was all swamp and marsh land, called Turnberry, like the country club that's still there. So these two very smart fellas, Eddie Lewis and Don Soffer heard about the land from Soffer's father, but they were developers and they had a vision. If you look at photos of what it looked like before, man, you'd never believe it.

There was nothing there! Screw Donald Trump, these guys were the real deal and the family still is. So, even if it's a gigantic soulless little nest of generic confusion and bad architecture and the scourage of all urban planners worth shit, it transformed Miami, can't even imagine the city now, without it. But certainly not a bubba boy kind of address."

They were almost there, crossing Country Club Drive, past the mall and turning into one of the seemingly endless side streets, where vast numbers of identical tower building blocks, housing thousands of people from most of Latin America, Russia, Europe, Canada and all over the USA dwelled either occasionally or permanently.

Mikey let out a long deep breath. "Jesus H. Imagine trying to find your way back here after a few too many shots. How the hell do you live like this?"

Rogers laughed. "Well, after all those years in a little boat cabin, it's almost like a mansion and it's great for Hildy, lots of places to run and play, it's just for now. Sort of an adventure, which fits, since Aventura is Spanish for adventure, but then, you know that."

They pulled into a visitor lot, flashing badges and the parking attendant nodded and pointed to two patrol cars waiting for them.

"Mikey, I don't think we should mention anything about being at his other place. How we found him is not any of his business. Okay?"

"Absolutely. I don't even know if the fucking search warrant is good for a different address. Shit, it could all be thrown out!"

Mikey pulled the warrant out of his pocket and read through it and laughed.

"Well good news. It was all done so fast, they didn't write in the address! We're rocking."

They got out and waved to the officers, who looked very grim, this not being one of their usual assignments.

No swat team, but that just hadn't seemed necessary now.

While Mikey briefed them, Rogers walked around trying to see exactly where Jenkins apartment was. Luckily it was on a low floor, cheaper for sure and easier to access. He could feel that adrenaline surge again.

Mikey called to him.

"Are we ready?"

Rogers walked back over and shook the hands of his about to be fellow partners, the way cops bonded immediately in intense, unstable situations." "Yep. I think you guys should take the stairs and we'll go up the elevator and do the front door approach. Keep your walkies on. This guy is probably armed to the molars, and his buddies may have warned him, but my guess is, no, because they wouldn't want him to know they had anything to do with our finding him. Assume the worst, but I think we have the element of surprise. I doubt he has any idea he's on our radar. Do you have tasers, just in case? By the book, okay?"

The new recruits nodded and they all made their way, pace slower in the humid, mid-day summer heat to the entrance of what might just be the murderer's homestead.

Rogers was a true believer in the "whatever you expect to happen in any situation is rarely what does happen," philosophy and when they rang the bell of Walter Jenkins condo, this possibly cynical but mostly just common-sense wisdom, held. A tall bleached blonde, the product of tanning salons and weight-lifting classes, breast implants and plastic surgery, making it almost impossible to even guess her approximate age, opened the door clad from micro mini shorts to barely nipple covering tee shirt in pink leopard; even her sandals were pink leopard. She was clearly drunk with that gimlet-eyed glazed gaze and she rocked slightly back and forth as if trying to hide the appearance of someone clearly under the influence of at least booze but what might be a vast array of substances.

"Hi, guys! "She slurred as if they were invited guests. "Come on in, I don't want the cats to get out." Rogers felt about cat people the way Mikey felt about dogs, except Mikey was afraid and he was just not into them. He had never trusted cats or cat people. Secretive and hard to ever really know. Also, as far as he could tell, no cat had ever fended off a threat to their owner or seemed to care whether they were there or not.

They had been invited in, and that was a big plus. Inside was what they might have expected. Tacky rental furniture, all rather generic and clearly not a space anyone had put any particular personal care into. It made Rogers sad. Places like this always did, even the fancy upscale versions that all looked like Miami Beach hotel suites. Nothing that showed an actual human being lived there, that home had any meaning. Where had he read that everything around us is a reflection of our inner selves? These vapid, dead spaces seemed to echo that.

"I'm Bambi, and who are you two handsome fellas?"

Stripper they both thought telepathically.

"Ma'am actually this is not a social call. This is Lieut. Martinez and I'm Deputy Rogers, Miami PD and we're here to see Walter Jenkins. Just an interview ma'am. Is he at home?"

Mask dropped, fear mixed with fury filled her entire being. "Fuck! Fuck! Cops!

Walter is going to frigging kill me!" She turned away, wobbling slightly and almost ran to the bedroom, or what seemed to probably be the bedroom.

They waited, hands on holsters and Mikey beeped the back up to be ready for anything.

Whatever "anything was," was not what appeared shortly after Bambi's retreat.

A well-built, immaculately groomed man, somewhere in his mid-forties, though clearly having over tinted his beard and hair in that too black color that only made them look older. He was dressed in crisply pressed chinos and the current fashion statement of perfectly tailored Bespoke Robins Egg Blue shirt, and expensive no sock loafers. He even had one of those shoulder draped cashmere sweaters, usually reserved for Italian strutters having dinner at Joe's Stone Crab. He smiled at them. *Calm as a fucking sea cucumber*, Mikey thought, as they both tried to re-adjust their approach to questioning.

"I'm Walter Jenkins officers and I'm a big fan of law enforcement. How may I help you?"

Rogers and Jenkins were about the same height, and though neither one of them had planned it, their eyes met. His eyes were clear, steady, not blinking or shifting away and he smiled, causing crinkles on the sides and belying the vanity of his dyed hair and hedge quality beard. "Gentlemen?"

He stood his ground, not offering a hand, but not shifting into any hint of guarded, hostile readiness to confront.

Rogers instinctively let Mikey lead this. "Mr. Jenkins, I'm Lieut. Martinez and this is Deputy Rogers, who is also the Head of Security at your place of employment, The Silver Sands condominium. I'm sure you're aware of recent events there and we are following up on every possible lead to these brutal murders."

Nothing in Jenkins face or body language seemed to react to this information. Rogers was trying to do some profiling, but this was one very savvy fella, someone probably used to many such situations and an expert at the art of emotional camouflage, or, the "never let them see you sweat" school of suspect. "Well aware, but they've told us not to come in so, I don't think I can be much help."

Rogers moved slightly closer. "Well, Mr. Jenkins, your name has appeared on several of our on-line sites as the spokesperson for an Ultra-Right group called the Army of the Righteous, which preaches anti-Semitic, anti-minority and anti-immigrant philosophy, pretty aggressive and we have some evidence to indicate these murders might be hate crimes, so we have a warrant to search your premises for any incriminating evidence. And we must ask your whereabouts on the dates of the Rothenstein Senior murders and the subsequent murder of their daughter, Rebecca."

Now Jenkins reacted, not with hostility, he sighed, uncrossed his arms and motioned for the inquisitors to sit down on one of his leatherette matching sofas, with a nonchalant elegance they would have associated with someone entirely different than his profile or the blond in the bedroom.

"Sorry you had to make the trip officers. First, I have alibis for those dates, and time sheets to back me up and I'm sure I'm on the security tapes and I was off the day of the last killing and Bambi can swear to that. We weren't even in Miami.

"I happen to be the Local president of the South Florida

Chapter of the NRA and we had a little get together, being law enforcement, I'm sure you are sympathetic to our cause. As for Hate Crimes, it's still America, right? I have my beliefs, but social media is stacked with daily postings that make my group sound like Eagle Scouts. And that is all we do. It's, frankly, for me, a revenue source. I charge membership fees, product sales, E-books. Frankly, most of what we say I don't even believe, it's a niche. Got it?"

Neither of them quite knew what to do next. There was a moment of silence and they could hear Bambi sobbing in the bedroom.

Rogers spoke, playing for time. "Do you want to go check on her?"

Jenkins laughed, making his eyes crinkle again. "Not necessary, it's the booze and the pills. She's recovering from a family tragedy. She's okay."

"Well, I hate to upset her more, but, we have a search warrant, sir and I'm going to have to ask you to let in our back up officers so we can do a proper search of the premises."

Now Jenkins sat up and the eye crinkles hardened and so did his lips. "This is bullshit. Where's the probable cause?"

"We can't really discuss that, and hopefully it will just be a dead end and we can check you off. But we have our orders. Is there anyone but you and the young lady in the apartment at this time?"

Jenkins stood up and his anger appeared. "Nope. Go to it. I know how you guys operate, it's the entire stupidity of the broken system.

"Mostly wrong but never in doubt. I'll get Bambi and we'll be out on the terrace."

Somehow he made them feel awkward and unsure, Rogers almost admired his ability to flip this, probably why he was the leader of whatever the hell it was he really led.

Jenkins walked to the bedroom with the stride of an athletic man, probably former military, straight and cocky. When he opened the door, Mikey moved forward. "Sir, we must request that you leave the door open now."

Jenkins looked over his shoulder and shook his head as if mocking them.

Rogers went to the front door and waved in the Aventura police, who were ready with gloves and the necessary bag and tag containers, their weapons back in their holsters. The fact that they were all wearing protective vests made them feel self-conscious, almost wimpy, Rogers thought, giving Jenkins the credit for this.

Jenkins reappeared, holding the stumbling Bambi creature under one arm, her face now covered in huge pink sunglasses with a pink leopard broad brimmed hat on her head.

"We'll be on the patio. May I get some water from the kitchen?"

"Rogers answered, moving toward the bedroom. "Not just yet, sorry about that."

They moved out into the sun and he helped her down onto a chaise, taking a seat beside her at the glass covered generic patio table and pulled out his phone. Mikey saw this, and moved quickly toward Rogers. "He's got his phone out there? Should we take it?"

"Absolutely, but be polite."

Mikey almost ran toward the sliding doors while Rogers instructed the other cops on what to look for.

What to look for did not take long. There was an entire closet filled with weapons, guns of all size and magnitude, some clearly not for self-protection or hunting. Large hatchets and butcher level knives. Nothing that looked like bomb materials, probably had such ingredients at the other address.

But it wasn't the weapons that caused Rogers heart to pound. Hidden deep inside an air conditioning vent, was a weatherproof bag, the kind recommended to protect valuables in case of hurricane, fire or flood. He crouched beside it, shined his flashlight and pulled it out. Inside were the items Rebecca had remembered as missing from her Mother's jewelry bowl. A solid gold cigarette case, a pair of five carat diamond earrings and a diamond encrusted Patek Philippe watch.

Rogers felt dizzy. Whatever he had expected to find when they set out this morning, this most certainly was not it.

He stood up too quickly and felt a wave of lightheaded nausea, reminding him he hadn't eaten. He was breathing hard, trying to make the pieces fit.

He put the bag in a larger evidence bag, marked it and continued with the search, but he pretty well knew, this was the motherload and since there were no murder weapons, it was unlikely they would find anything more incriminating. He walked to the door and motioned to one of the local cops.

"Would you take photos of all the weapons and remove them. He probably has permits, but we may be able to get him on at least one weapons charge, and we need to cross check the stash with recent shootings."

"The young cop followed him to the closet and whistled. "Holy shit, never saw anything like this!"

"Yeah, well, welcome to South Florida and don't even go near Tampa or the Panhandle!"

Rogers clutched his treasure bag and marched out to where Mikey was searching in the kitchen. "Nothing here, man, but a lot of cheap booze and potato chips and fucking sour cream, Bambi must be one helluva cook."

"Mikey, I found the missing jewelry Rebecca told us about; hidden in an air conditioning vent." We got him. Let's go do this."

Mikey's mouth dropped, "No fucking way! Too easy!"

"Well, it doesn't prove murder. He is a fence according to his rap sheet. But it's big. Arrest the cocky son of a bitch."

Whether it was fake or real, the tan left Walter Jenkins polished surface when they confronted him. "I know the drill guys, but you're gonna look like damn fools."

"That, Sir, is not our problem. Cuff him Lieut. Martinez."

At this Bambi lost total control of what was left of her dignity and threw herself on top of all of them, screaming and punching and sobbing. "You can't take him. I can't live without him! I can't sleep unless I'm in his arms. He's my savior. Jesus sent him to save me. Let him go!"

Jenkins, who clearly got enormous ego rewards from this performance and what was clearly obvious to everyone but him, that despite his elegant façade, his inner redneck was certainly in charge of his love life.

He pulled her off of them and they wrestled her inside and brought her a large glass of water.

Miss, I think it's important that you calm down and call someone to come help you out. We are going to take Mr. Jenkins to the address on this card and I'm pretty sure he's going to want a lawyer and he'll need you to pull yourself together if you want to help him."

"I need my brother. I want my brother."

"Can we contact him for you?"

"No! He's with Jesus. Five years with Jesus. He Od'ed. Everyone in my family OD's. And my cats. I can't leave my cats!

"Well, ma'am I suggest you make some sort of arrangements because Mr. Jenkins is coming with us."

Jenkins did not resist. He turned to face her and the tone of his voice seemed to calm her. "Babe, you know I love you. Be strong now, you know what to do."

They led him out leaving Bambi, looking more like a disheveled Barbie, fighting to stay upright, cats now swarming around her.

By the time Rogers and Mikey had made it through late afternoon Miami traffic back to Mikey's precinct, Walter Jenkin's lawyer was already waiting. Jenkins was still being booked, so the three of them proceeded to one of the interview rooms.

The lawyer, one of the seemingly endless supply of competing for-the-middle defense attorneys in Miami, who, to Rogers, anyway, all seemed to come from some cloning factory. Middle-aged, nattily attired, with everything a little too shiny, hair, skin, clothing and, without even seeing, he knew he would have a slightly more expensive car than he could afford in the lot.

Mikey did the introductions and the lawyer, one Christopher Tyler, clearly not reflecting the preponderance of Jewish attorneys in South Florida, but otherwise fitting the profile, carefully set down his sleek leather briefcase and they all took seats. Mr. Tyler already knew from a probably semi-incoherent Bambi a bit of information, but no one but Rogers and Mikey knew what the potential charges were.

"So, gentlemen," Tyler began, in an even, well-practiced tone of voice, defense attorney opening posturing, they all seemed to have learned from either one another or years of dealing with the police. "My client should be here any moment, but I want to go on record that I have not even been told if he has been Mirandized or informed of exactly what he is being charged with."

This was Mikey's turf now, and Rogers could lean back and fold into Good Cop mode.

"Mr. Jenkins has been apprised of his rights and we had an official search warrant, probable cause due to his association with a known Ultra-right Hate group, and his current employment for the victims of three possible Hate Crime homicides.

"We went to his place of residence and in our search we

discovered a rather extensive collection of serious weaponry and several pieces of stolen and very expensive jewelry and related items that had been the property of one of the murder victims, so we are looking at motive here, anti-Semitic material was in evidence, he had access to the premises and motive, well double motive. Greed and hate."

It was clear this was far more than Christopher Tyler, who had most likely anticipated the usual drill for a client like Jenkins, fencing or arms sales, maybe minor assault of a minority citizen, but since this was the crime de jour of the city, nothing this major had ever been on his legal dance card.

Rogers watched his face, using what he had learned about facial and eye movements for detecting fear, lying or guilt in lawyers, or suspects. Tyler looked stunned and blinked several times, dead giveaway and cleared his throat.

"I see" he said, clearly not seeing and flipped open his briefcase.

They waited, watching him scramble inside his head for how to proceed. 'You must understand officers, that I have had no time to talk to my client and these charges are outrageous, having known and represented Mr. Jenkins for some time. Are you recording this interview?"

"Shit, yes. Mr. Tyler, sir. We have the evidence with us and we have photographs that were taken by Rebecca Rothenstein, one of the victims, of the objects when they were originally purchased. No wiggle room there."

Before they could proceed, a deputy motioned to them and they saw Walter Jenkins in handcuffs, being led into the room. He had regained his composure, though no crinkly-eyed smile was present and his lawyer leapt up and gave him a good old boy arm butt and one-armed hug. Clearly aware of avoiding any sign of metro-sexual proclivities.

Jenkins sat down next to his lawyer and Mikey, who was really in his element, motioned to the deputy. "Anyone want coffee, water?"

They both declined but Mikey was clearly in need of one of his double Cubans and Rogers got up and whispered in the deputy's ear, his need for a candy bar or something, still feeling slightly spacey and too hungry to fully concentrate.

Now the wrestling match between cops and suspect and lawyers began. Tyler leaned forward and whispered something to Jenkins.

"I want to go on record that I have had no time to confer with my client and we have not been told exactly what the charges against him are."

Mikey smiled. "Well, there have been no charges as yet Mr. Tyler. We had no idea we would find articles stolen from the murder victims hidden in a vent in Mr. Jenkins apartment or an arsenal, we were just following a solid lead, which turned out to be more solid than we could have imagined. Would you like to confer privately with your client while we take a little coffee break?"

"I was just going to request that."

"Great. Mikey stood up and Rogers followed his lead. We'll be close by, so let's do try and speed this up. It's been a long day."

Rogers and Mikey headed for the kitchen where Mikey gulped down his caffeine and Rogers inhaled a slightly soggy ham and cheese sandwich and a Milky Way.

"Whadda ya think?" Mikey asked, checking his watch. His Carmen date very much on his mind.

Rogers was feeling far more focused and that was both the good and bad news.

"Aw, Mikey, mi compadre, I gotta say, I don't see it. I know what his shiny shoes is going to say. He's going to say Mr. Jenkins has the right to his beliefs and yes, he is in possession of stolen items and has been involved in fencing of merchandise in the past, but no convictions because he' is just a middle man, had no idea the items were stolen, admits to selling merchandise on-line, the 21st century fencing for the elite, no sleazy pawn shops or nervous sweating thieves and addicts trying to grab a few quick bucks. I can betcha he'll say Jenkins had no idea the items were stolen, won't cop to who gave them to him, and he's just a smart businessman, trying to make extra income by using his knowledge of fine jewelry and the international auction market, even E-bay and receiving a share of the profits.

"They even have a name for these guys, 'fences fences' or 'referral fences' most of them never actually come in contact with the thieves or just pretend they believe whoever contacts them that they own the merchandise.

I don't think Jenkins had a clue where this stuff came from. It was never in the news. And I'll betcha all the stale donuts in the fridge, that he'll say he's been keeping the items for months, probably even has a paper trail to prove it, trying to find the right buyer, way before the murders and frankly, even Rebecca said, they were on the bottom of the bowl and her mother hadn't used any of them in years, so how in hell would this dude know where to look or how to get in there? And if he was going to go to all that risk, he'd take all the stuff dontcha think?

If he can tell us a name, who he got the stash from, now that is a real lead and we should lean in hard, but he may not even know. These guys work behind layers of paranoia with good reason and the internet makes it all so easy to remain anonymous and fencing is usually an honor among thieves kind of deal, meaning, even if he got the stuff blindly through a middleman and he is at least one of the middlemen, they have reputations and they don't mess around with one another, for obvious reasons, like having the crap kicked out of them and losing their livelihood. Damn, I wish we'd called Olivia and maybe we can find out what the hate scrawls were done with. I have a feeling about that."

"Okay. Fuck! You call her and I'll head back to the Bongo Boys."

CHAPTER 16

Ooma Lovee was pacing back and forth on her long, ocean facing terrace. She couldn't sleep, and didn't feel up to a real walk, fear and exhaustion roiling through her entire being.

Today, she felt every one of her eighty-eight years. She sighed and raised her arms over her head and dropped them, taking a long deep breath and leaned against the railing, the ocean always bringing her a sense of peace and a quick 'snap out of it' about what really mattered in life. *Old age is hourly heartbreak and equal joy.* Where this thought sprang from, surprised even her. Was it true? Certainly the first part was!

She resumed her pacing, a warm breeze kicked up and she closed her eyes for a moment, the joy she'd just described wafting over her in the movement of the fresh ocean air. She must stay alert and think. Think clearly! What was it she still needed to do in case she really was the next victim or her time just ran out. She remembered. Oscar Perez! She wanted to add him to her will; set up a college trust for him. Spending this precious extra time with Edy and Sunny the gift in all this horror which now surrounded them, was having a chance to know Oscar better and she was so moved by him. She pulled her phone from her silk dressing gown pocket and pressed the contact button for her lawyer.

A buzz at her door. She almost dropped the phone, it so startled her, proof of just how delicate her nerves were right now or maybe from now on. Who?

She quickly moved back inside, heart pounding and headed for the front entry where the camera was. Leena Martinez was standing there holding Lola and smiling. My Gott! She had totally forgotten that Leena had taken her for a walk.

She entered the code and the door opened. "Leena dear, so sorry. I completely forgot!"

Leena came in, her beautiful face and lovely skin shiny with the heat and exertion. Ooma felt a stab of longing, something she rarely allowed herself; back to a time when beauty and youth and hope and the possibility of love, prince charming, romance was still a part of her belief in the future.

All of that was long gone. Lost forever.

Really lost after Claude was killed, vanished in the ravages of the war; all that remained was survival. Her most vivid memory the one of her mother sending her off, telling her to run and where to go and to keep the secret of her heritage forever. After Claude, survival meant using the one thing she seemed to have besides a quick mind and a skill at languages. She was not going to be Pavlova, and a dancer's career and her beauty were certainly not a long-term security source. Men. She seemed to know how to attract the ones who would provide for her and so that is what she did.

Love, the idea of love as a reason to marry, seemed like some ridiculous fairy tale. Where had she heard the line, 'from twenty-thirty women need beauty, from thirty-fifty they need a good personality and after fifty they need cash.' Yes! Only she had skipped right to the cash part. So, her only way of forgiving herself for that choice, was to try and leave something of value. Sunny and Edy and little Oscar and Israel. She reached up to her neck and patted her newly purchased Star of David necklace. She had three made. Platinum with little pave diamonds, small and lovely, for herself and Edy and Sunny, which she was going to give them tonight. Redemption.

"Leena dear, come in and get some water. You look so hot."

"Oh, I'm fine, Mrs. Lovee. We had a great walk. Lola was very frisky. Would you like me to give her a bath? She could use it!"

"Oh, Leena that would be wonderful. She hates to be untidy and she hates the dog groomers even more! I think you and I are the only people she can stand to bathe her."

"I love it. She makes me laugh so hard. When she's wet, she really does look like some little alien."

"I have to make a call, so please, you know where her things are."

"Absolutely. It won't take long."

Ooma pushed the contact phone button and waited for her lawyer to answer, which was always very promptly. Her urgency to get all her affairs in order, had increased the number of calls and meetings dramatically in the last months and she was a major client. "Hello? Is this Nathan?" It's Ooma Lovee."

"Yes, Mrs. Lovee, how may I help you today?"

"I want you to make an additional bequest in my will, however it is best to do it, I leave that to you. Probably an irrevocable trust. Is that what we did for Sunny and Edy?"

"Well, a version of it, more complicated because of the real estate and personal items."

"Well, I want to set up an educational Trust for little Oscar Perez with enough money in it to put him through a full undergraduate and graduate program and provide for proper living expenses and needs. He's the son of one of the security people here and his mother is the Medical Examiner. Lovely people, but he's a genius and they are not wealthy and they're divorced and I would name you as executor to oversee it. I need to know what your fees would be, if there is a standard and that it would begin when he finishes high school, which will be very young. Possibly at fourteen or fifteen. Can you set this up very quickly?"

"Absolutely. I will do it as soon as we finish this call."

"Will you arrange for it to be brought here with a notary so I can finalize it and have it in effect by tomorrow?"

"I think I can. I'll be back to you shortly. And Mrs. Lovee. I truly admire you. It's a very kind thing to do for the boy."

"It's the least. I'll wait to hear. Thank you, Nathan."

Ooma ended the call and went back out onto the terrace. She felt a release of tension and fear. Something was propelling her, certainly fear of death, fear of dying without having made what, were to her, necessary amends for her using herself and manipulating all those men, even though, they had most certainly been willing and using her as well.

But there was more, these murders had unleashed bigger demons. The clock inside her awareness of how little time she had left, at best, was ticking very loudly and she was not sure why, but she did trust the power of it. Urgency to set things in order was propelling her every act.

"Dr. O, Rogers here. Any more tox results, yet?"

"I was just going to call you. The Foot messages were done with eyeliner pencil. Drugstore level stuff, not fancy, could be Maybelline or a generic. Damndest thing! Waterproof, only reason it didn't just dissolve."

"Holy Hell! Eyeliner pencil!!!!"

"Uh Huh and I'd say, conservatively, narrows suspects down to at least a couple hundred thousand plus all the drag queens, transgenders, men who use it to glam up a bit. I will say, it feels to me more like some panicked impulse, not a big deal statement hate crime."

"Yep. Even Mr. LePorte wears eye makeup. Mikey is gonna hate this. He's in with Jenkins now. Anything else?"

"Well, besides the entire Hassidic community threatening me with eternal damnation. I've had a Rabbi present for all the autopsies. Can't wait to get them buried. They have to be washed by same sex, dressed in a purification shroud "tachrichim" it's called. Plain pine boxes. No flowers. Funny all the rituals are so much like the Muslims. Crazy all the hate between them. I think I can release the bodies. I'm finishing up the last few tox screens. The hair and a couple of loose ends. I'll be back soon."

"Thanks, Doc. Let Mikey know about transporting the bodies, the cops can take all that heat."

"Ya think?"

Rogers hung up. Something about all of this was just too unsettling. *Think, buddy. You're missing something that's right in front of you.*

When he got back to the interview room, things had gone just about how he'd told Mikey they would and Mikey's frustration was showing.

"So, what we've got here, Rogers, is the old Mexican stand-off, but since I'm Cuban and our suspect here hates all of us, maybe we should call it something else."

The Lawyer sat forward, gearing up now that he'd figured out how to play this.

"Okay, so this is what you have and it isn't going to hold much water, so to speak. My client admits to owning numerous weapons, all of which were legally purchased, which he can prove if necessary. He admits to having the valuables, but he had no idea they were stolen and most certainly not who they belonged to. So, really all you've got is a misdemeanor possession of stolen goods charge."

"Well, first, Mr. Tyler, I eagerly await seeing the paperwork on all the weapons and second, the paper trail on when Mr. Jenkins acquired the stolen items or he stays with us for a while, since at the moment, he is our one serious suspect. Now, if Mr. Jenkins can tell us who he received the merchandise from, we might be able to re-consider his situation."

"I fucking told you Beaner Boy. I never met the dude. That's totally 20th century shit. I got a text, asking me to call a number. Clearly a burner phone and some guy, sounded young, no accent, said he had some very special items, not stolen, part of his mother's estate and he wanted to sell them privately, no IRS or probate, I suppose and he'd heard I was reliable and honest, which I am. We discussed my commission and I told him I needed to see the stuff before I could advise him, but it sounded like maybe an overseas buyer and we arranged for him to leave the merchandise in a locker at the Fort Lauderdale Greyhound bus station and he'd mail me the key, which he did. Insured. Priority mail and no, I didn't keep the envelope. I never saw him. Voice was kind of squeaky and nervous and high, I hid the stuff because I don't have a safe and it's Miami!

"Is this too fast for you? All you soft living, liberal jerkoffs, cops included. I live in the real world, boy. I didn't do anything illegal. This is bullshit and I did make up an invoice with the date and what the merchandise was and the appraisals I got, all of which were months before the Jew-pissers got killed. And I can prove that!"

Rogers could see Mikey taking big breaths, trying to keep his cool.

"Well, then, since you don't have anything helpful to trade at the moment, I think we will just provide you with a nice general population suite, full of all sorts of mongrels, while Mr. Tyler finds us whatever paperwork you actually have to prove your story, maybe the Tooth Fairy or the Easter Bunny will come forward with a name."

Tyler leaned over and whispered something to Jenkins. "I'm going to bring you the requested documents and the key and then, I think you had best release my client unless the Miami PD wants a harassment suit filed."

Mikey and Rogers both laughed. Mikey crossed his arms over his barrel chest and leaned back, feeling re-centered. "Oh man, white Boy, we're shaking in our wing tips. You go on and do that. We'll make him real comfortable with some of his favorite minorities."

Mikey motioned to the deputies waiting outside the door and they entered and waited for Jenkins to stand up.

"Take him to holding and keep an eye on him. Those guys can smell Redneck and we wouldn't want anything to happen to him while he's our guest."

Tyler jumped up. "Is that a threat, officer?"

"Threat? Quite the opposite. Now you hurry back and we'll look forward to re-negotiating Mr. Jenkins' status."

When they had all gone Mikey sagged back in his seat and Rogers massaged his temples, feeling the strain of the day and the nagging anxiety of something he felt so close to seeing, but just could not find the clearing in his blind spot.

"Dr. O called. Ready? The hate messages were done with something like Maybelline Eyeliner pencil. Damned depressing."

"You're fucking kidding me? We'd have to get warrants for half of South Florida!

"Well, at least we can try and just look at most possible suspects. Who would have one on them, Maybe DNA if we can find it. So, there's Lupe, Irina, Ooma, Edy, Sunny, Olga, Leena, Rhoda Shmumpkin, LePorte, Sergi could have one from Rebecca, though it seems way too low end for her.

"Dr. O still is waiting for Tox screen on the hair and she said a couple of other pieces. Seems more and more like the message was an impulsive attempt to shift motive, too sloppy and vague for a mega Hate Crime. I just don't see this bastard for it, though if we can follow the stolen goods trail, that makes this all worth it. I'm heading back to the condos. I wanna talk to Oscar and Pepe. I keep feeling I'm missing something right in front of me."

"Shit. Me, too. I'd love to get this prick on something big, but I think you're right. Though a few hours in general lock up, may be worth the entire fucked up day!"

Mikey almost jumped up and checked his watch.

"I gotta go."

"Now?"

"Yah. I have plans."

Rogers smiled, revealing his gap. "Plans, like in a date?"

"Yea. Hard to fucking believe, I know."

"So??? I'm assuming it isn't Bambi, so who in the hell did you have time to hook up with? Rogers stopped, one look at Mikey and he knew.

"Oh my man. Wonders never cease. You ballsey SOB. Daniels! What did you do. Hypnotize her?"

"How about $6,000 a bottle tequila."

Rogers clapped his hands and laughed loudly, realizing how great a feeling it was.

"Well, there goes your pension! I'm on all night. Go get her, hombre! I want pictures!"

Mikey pulled his comb from his suit pocket and smoothed down his hair. You're under oath, pal. Not a word. And no pictures."

Sacred trust. But the visual is pretty impressive."

Mikey practically ran around his desk and out the door, leaving Rogers laughing harder only with images of Edy Weller replacing Mikey and Carmen. Two such unlikely couples only proved the amazing endless possibilities life still had to offer.

Edy Weller lay back in her tub, letting the bubbly warmth cover her like a big watery blanket. Another bath! Well, he was coming for a drink, so just in case. Oh brother, how lame that sounded. She looked over at the clock on her sink. 7:30. Sunny and Oscar should be back by now. Anxiety flooded her. They had pleaded with her to let them take Lorraine for a walk, but nothing felt safe and they'd been gone almost an hour. So hard to say no and they knew it. And Lorraine could vamp it up too lying there looking like a bratwurst with nostrils, while Sunny did the manipulating. She shuddered, a montage of possible horrible scenarios flying across her inner eye. Motherhood has no pause button, no replay.

What a laugh to have thought the older Sunny got, the less fear she would have for her safety! Or that Sunny's needs would get simpler and there they are all the time, kids and canines dripping with needs you can't begin to decipher, while frantically moping up the psychic wetness. Not least of all because we're still soggy with our own unowned and unmet needs and if we never, or, come on Edy, cop to it, if I never had mine met it's almost impossible to understand the needs of these damp little creatures who are not us at all; so easy to project what we needed onto them.

So, the daily struggle of what to tell them or not tell them, to pay attention to, but not get too crazed about every little twitch. What the truth really is and why it's so damn hard to tell it to ourselves, which precedes telling it to them. Why is it so scary to accept life, reality as it is? I don't want to scare her and Oscar too much, but isn't that better than downplaying real danger and having something happen to them? Of course something can happen to them anyway!

Oy. Optimism just might be too overrated. What was that

horrifying piece she'd just read, a column possibility about a young photographer on assignment somewhere terrible, who'd stepped on a land mine, sees his arm and both legs scattered in the trees and bushes and thinks, "Ok. I still have my right arm and my eyes. I can work." Too much optimism, or, maybe he was in shock but clearly not Jewish! OMG. Well, they certainly weren't in Afghanistan, but there was still a murderer targeting rich Jewish people right there in her fancy, safe little world.

I need to get out of this tub and call Sunny. I want her here and I'm going to get out that gun Ooma gave me. Rogers can teach me. All those Lifetime for Women movies may come in handy after all.

She climbed out of the comforting water womb and wrapped herself in a towel. Part of her inner legacy from the horror of her parents' deaths, was the stripping away of the film of illusion that we have any protection, ever against life, all of it. She had lived with that anxiety daily since they were killed, but it was popping back up now, like some sort of perverse crocus not marking the coming of spring, but the possible end of the last five years of illusion of safety.

CHAPTER 17

By the time Mikey and Carmen had worked their way through half a bottle of the tequila and two platters of Ropa Vieja, it was clear they were both having a very good time. Mikey was sipping, now, knowing well enough the risks of one shot too many considering what the next several days had in store for him. Carmen, however, who seemed immune to the effects of the nectar, except that she had actually smiled at him and laughed at least twice, downed her next shot in one gulp and then sat back and ran her long fingers through her silver mane.

"Oh boy, Martinez, it's almost pathetic to think of how long it's been since I've had a night like this. Thanks. And I want to split this with you. Way out of your pay grade, I know."

"Call me Mikey."

"Naw. Mikey's the name of some four-year-old riding around his driveway on a three-wheeler. You're way past Mikey stage."

Mikey felt as if he might start sobbing. Something about the way she'd said it, made him realize that in that eternal nickname, was the way, the discounting way he always felt treated. Wow. Double wow. She was right. It had probably always compromised his authority and dignity, and he'd inhaled it, himself.

She noticed his reaction, her therapist training still tuned to such subtleties. "Did I offend you?"

"No. No, you just gave me a gift. And I owe you the truth about the tequila. The bar owner is my second cousin and I never pay here. Besides, it's part of, you know how it works. Believe me, he doesn't pay retail or wholesale for the good stuff, either. So don't worry about my debt load. I just wanted you to say yes."

She laughed out loud this time and then, hesitating only a moment, the way decisive people do, he could see she was making a decision to tell him something truthful back.

"Okay, Martinez. I'm going to share some stuff with you that may be helpful with this Rothenstein mess. Do you know what the Cross Border Rules are?

Mikey shook his head, not wanting to stop her flow for a minute.

"After 9/11 the feds realized that the flow of laundered money was totally out of control and they instituted all kinds of updated safeguards to prevent foreign investors, drug dealers and terrorists from outsmarting the existing restrictions, which had been in place and updated starting with the Bank Secrecy Act in 1970.

"So anything that was going through a bank, wire transfers, stocks and bonds, treasury notes, those kinds of money transfers, were outed, so to speak, but, in the wonderful way the government always misses the bull's eye, well real estate slipped through one great big fucking crack in their smug macho enforcement swagger.

"The unsolvable problem in all this, is these guys, the terrorists, the drug lords, the hedge funders, the international racketeers from every sink hole on the planet are always one step ahead, thus look around South Florida, as a prime example. Boom. Development insanity. So, the Rothensteins were up to their eyeballs in this, taking money from all kinds of investors, 'don't ask, don't tell' the real estate version. And everything was cross-collateralized and if you don't know what that is, I'll save it for later or fucking Google it, let's just say House of Cards comes to mind, forgive these clichés, but that amazing tequila makes me a little fuzzy on the details.

"What is important is there are all these watchdog commissions now. RICO, FINRA, IRTPA, to name a few, plus an escalating array of electronic monitoring rules, and on and on. But it didn't blip on the developer's screens, really, because all these gonifs are just too ballsy and too clever and the money is laundered like some fancy French dry cleaners.

"So, when the King and Queen were murdered, I saw what was going to happen. I knew way too much to be left alive by the shady shmucks that were on the verge of descending, or their legal teams and front men were and they would all want me to turn over what I had and then they would make me disappear. I'm pretty steely, but Martinez, I totally freaked out. I had to make a very fast decision and I told you guys some of this when I first talked to you. I knew if I went to the IRS, The FBI and even the fucking CIA immediately, and the really scary dudes knew there was no point in offing me because I'd already screamed my big Jewban head off and I had a chance. And that is what I did and am doing. Scary shit, I gotta tell you.

"But, I made a good deal, no charges and I will have protection to get me out of here and re-located. Also, I went to see Arnold Rothenstein and it's amazing the way a significant amount of medication and the reality that he and, I guess, his sons had better get their shit together fast or their empire was going down and a lot of very scary and very angry Big Boys were going to come after their properties. So, he's back, and he's supervising the burials and the Shiva, or Shivas. The Hassidim do one for seven days after the funeral and then Shloshim, which is until the 30th day after the funeral; but for parents, formal mourning lasts a year, though don't ask me what the hell that entails.

"So, Arnold and sons and their temple family will be very much present and that takes the heat off me, too. Not that he knows much, though he may know a helluva lot more than I think he does, or I do, hard to tell with a family business like that. Sort of like the Madoff shit, everything is secretive and cordoned off; I may think I was really in the know and I was just a fall guy. Actually, I really didn't know most of this underbelly until the axe fell, but I knew where to look.

"As soon as the Feds say I'm free, and I'm close, I'm going on one helluva long overdue vacation and they are telling me, wherever it is, I'll have protection until this is over if I need it. So, Martinez, I hate to admit it, but tonight was the first ray of Agave infused pleasure I've had since, well, way before this started; it's been a pretty fucked up few years."

Mikey finished his shot. "Jesus, Carmen, what a load to carry around. I'm honored and anything I can do at this end, you got it." He fought the urge to reach across and take her hand, still feeling her resistance to anything vulnerable and not wanting to risk it. She poured two more shots and they were quiet.

"They have a fantastic Cuban Creme Brulee."

"Love it!"

"He smiled at her. "I think you know you sort of just fucking blow my mind."

"Yeah. You are not exactly a stoic personality."

"A question, but I guess, you've really answered it. Do you think we can rule out any of these investors? Seems like it wouldn't be in any of their best interests to break up that little Billions Bash."

"No chance. It was too personal and risky and besides most of these transactions are laundered and sent electronically with crypto currency or through any cracks in the Feds set up, not sure most of them even knew exactly who or even where the investments were, so many layers to protect them, but believe me, they knew every fucking cent they were making or losing."

Mikey motioned to his cousin who knew what he wanted for dessert, he was about to ask her who she thought might be a person of interest at this stage when his phone rang.

"Sorry. I gotta take this. It's the ME and we're waiting for some tox results. Olivia? What ya got?"

"Well, Lieut. It's a little tricky and I'd rather tell you in person. Can you come in?

"Right now?"

"I know it's late. It can wait until morning, but first light. Very strange combo of results."

"Too strange to just tell me?"

"I think so. It's rather personal."

"Personal? Jesus. I might as well come in, I won't sleep worth shit now, anyway, but you're ruining a perfect evening."

"Awww, such a pity, to those of us who never have them. Expect no sympathy."

"I'll be there in half an hour."

The dessert arrived and Mikey ordered his usual brain bursting Cuban double espresso. They ate every last bite of their desserts, though Carmen did not dilute her shots with coffee. "I still have the company car service, so no need not to savor every drop of this great drunk."

He grinned at her. "Really sorry about this. I think I need to find out whatever this is. Sounds very unlike our ME and I should have been there, anyway. Rain check?"

"It's summer in Miami, that could leave you with a stack of future tequila dates."

"Hope so."

They walked out together, She, towering over him and making that extra effort to stand tall and walk straight, pride wiling the tequila to back off. And Mikey stood beside her, taking the risk of gently putting his arm on her waist, reaching up a bit, but somehow, after what she had told him about himself, he felt taller. He even looked taller.

Edy hated taking the elevator, all that uncomfortable small talk with her fellow SS residents or the snobs who pretended she wasn't even there. She couldn't reach Sunny or Oscar on their phones and in her barely contained maternal anxiety, she decided to go try and find them.

Lousy timing. Rhoda Shmumpkin and one of her twins, were in the middle of some paternal fray when she stepped in. Rhoda, as usual, was attired from head (sun hat to designer sneakers) in her usual Prada fare. Edy only knew this because the brand name was in clear display, not as obvious as Coco's used to be, but clear enough.

Edy realized she'd just plopped a soiled old Mets Cap on her wet hair and hadn't even looked to see if her tee shirt and tights were clean. At least she didn't have, TJ Max or Target written all over them.

Rhoda gave her a finger wave, clearly not wanting to be interrupted or caring (Edy not being on her dance card of people she had any interest in impressing) "Ford, I'm paying that damn tutor a fortune and he says you are still refusing to learn to read! Do you know what that school costs? Do you care how embarrassing this is for your father and I?" Edy fought the urge to correct her grammar, since she was attacking her kid's learning skills and managed not to snort or snicker at the thought of naming a kid Ford. Especially Ford Shmumpkin, that would be enough to screw up his desire to succeed at snooty private school.

"I can't do it. I hate it. They can't make me do it."

"If you flunk first grade, all your friends will go on to second and you'll be left behind!"

"So what! I have lots of friends in Kindergarten, too."

Rhonda stamped her foot and reached back into one of her designer work out pant pockets and pulled out an atomizer bottle and grabbed Ford's resistant shoulder. "Look at me. I'm spraying you. Close your eyes and breathe deeply."

Now Edy had forgotten all about missing kids and dog, was she about to participate in a child drugging. Hmmm.

"This is the Chill Child spray from Goop. Remember what the wellness, Breath Work teacher showed you? What did you just do at Yoga? What did you do at your meditation class? Do you have any clue what this Pediatric energy coach costs us?"

Ford pulled away, leaving whatever was in the atomizer lingering in Edy's nose. One could only hope it really worked, she could use it.

Ford looked so miserable; Edy resisted giving Mom a little face butt and rescuing him.

"My therapist said you're supposed to tell me I'm a special person and say five positive things for every put down. My friend Adam's Mom got him a plate that says, 'You are Special Today' for him to eat off of and he's a lot happier."

"Well, I'll call her. Of course you can have one. You are so special, you just must get over this, this, whatever it is and learn to read! If you promise you'll do it, we'll get you whatever phone you want with all the apps you want. And I'll have Ernesta make the seaweed zucchini bread you love."

"I hate it. It tastes like dirt. I want chocolate cake like normal kids."

"Normal kids who are not as fortunate as you and don't have parents with the education or awareness to instill proper nutrition in their children. Do you want to grow up to be illiterate and fat and sick?"

"Yes."

Thankfully the elevator opened then and Edy followed the Shmumpkin sitcom out, swearing that from now on she would walk up. After all they were only on the third floor, however fancier, it wasn't more of a schlep than she had in Chelsea.

She headed for the front door, punching Sunny's cell again. They were not one of the constant contact mother/daughter teams; she'd just read an article about mother/daughter duos, who lived together, shared bath water, make-up. clothes danced around some co-dependent maypole and spent all their time together.

They all even looked alike, the wonders of modern medicine making it hard for her to even tell which was the daughter. And they called one another all day long.

This had created a vortex of conflicting emotions in her. She knew it was beyond nutso, but, the longing for the kind of closeness she'd never had with her mother, and certainly would not be her desire or Sunny's but still, ugh; sort of like a version of the maternal Collective Unconscious on steroids, all of this in-coming about all of these people, plus elevator encounters not of our choosing, escalating daily. Social Media now made escape impossible. *Well, Miss Edy, you could just stop reading it all! And take the stairs.*

She opened the door to the entrance. The media reporters had vanished for the moment and the humidity had lowered. A breeze from the ocean gently blew against her face, removing the last of poor Ford's Chill Meds and her fear about Sunny and Oscar returned with it.

"Rogers?"

"Yes, Ma'am."

"It's Edy, your anxiety ridden stalker. I'm getting a little frantic. Oscar and Sunny begged me to let them take Lorraine for a walk, and it's getting dark and they aren't answering their phones and I can't find them. I'm trudging all over the grounds and the beach."

"Hmm, first I know your voice, no need to announce yourself and also, your name comes up on my phone, full disclosure and I think maybe I'd really like you to be my stalker, I'd be honored."

Edy laughed. "Well, cowboy, that's because you aren't Jewish.

My long deceased crazy aunt used to say there wasn't room for more than one Jew in any relationship, so I guess that's a plus for us. I mean, not that we're, you know, in a relationship, didn't mean to ...."

"Now, that's gonna hurt my feelings."

"Sorry, I just got out of the elevator with our neighbor Rhoda Shmumpkin and her kid and it's infiltrated my common sense, but, I would definitely rule her out as a suspect of anything but being an idiot.

"Actually it made me feel like a good mother for a change. But then, her husband places ads in the local glam Ad Mags with big pictures of himself sitting in lounge chairs on the beach, with no shoes on, like anyone needs to see his old fat toes and touting his medical practice. Certified in Psychiatry and Dermatology. Sooooo, welcome to Miami."

"You made that up."

"You give me too much credit, even I couldn't make that up. Actually, on dark nights, I've thought about making an appointment sort of a twofer. A little Botox and a session on why I think I need Botox to deal with my low self-esteem."

"Well, if I may offer a moment of stress relief, you can slow down. The kids are here. I needed to talk to Oscar about something and they were walking Lorraine, so I told them to all come down here and turn their phones off. My fault, I thought Sunny called you before they got here."

"Well, I was in the tub, but I didn't have a message. Is something happening? Should I be more nervous?"

"I wish, not your being nervous but something happening. This case is the most frustrating one I've ever been on, including the cold cases. We can't find one damn ulterior motive. Every lead turns out to be a dead end."

"I don't know if this helps, but my shrink in New York once said to me, can't remember the context, that when you can't find an ulterior motive, look for an interior one."

Rogers whistled through his gap. "Well, now, Miz Edy, my stalker of choice, I think you just blew a window in my brain open. Brilliant! Listen I'm waiting for Mikey to get back from seeing Dr. O. Do you want me to send Sunny up?"

"No, let them have the adventure. Just tell her to check in when she can. I was just worried. Ummm, are we still on for a drink, maybe pizza or something later?"

"Highlight of an otherwise brutal day. I'll let you know as soon as I can get out of here. Probably not for a while."

"Whenever. I'll be here contemplating my character and cosmetic flaws."

Rogers smiled and ended the call, just in time for it to ring, only this time it was not pleasant.

"Rogers, I'm coming in. Don't want to talk about this till I get there. Dr. O got the tox screens back on the hair and, um, something else. I'm sort of freaking out. Don't move. It's important."

Rogers clicked off, tension rising in his body and repeating in his brain what Edy said, "No ulterior motive look for an interior one." That thing that was right in front of him, suddenly moved forward.

Rogers switched onto auto pilot after what Edy had said. *No ulterior motive, look for interior motive.* He moved, almost trancelike, out of his office and into the main security pen, which was filled with computers, modems, phones and all manner of camera and high tech equipment, half-finished coffee and soft drink cans, half-eaten remnants of breakfast and lunch, tired, restless or bored security staff, checking for some unknown anything to bring this nightmare to a close. And added to it all, was their unasked questions, their eyes and body language beaming it at him. *Will he be blamed? Will we be fired?* He had no answers, but he did keep trying to keep them motivated and reassure them without misleading them, since he really had no clue what was coming next.

Carmen was their only real connection to management right now, though if Arnold Rothenstein was stabilized and his sons were stepping forward, that might help. He strode across the large open space, not making eye contact or allowing for any attempt to engage him in conversation. He needed to find Oscar Perez and this little whisper in his head, felt compelling and urgent.

Pepe and Oscar were glued to Pepe's computer screen, but Rogers didn't pause to ask why or what they were looking at. Oscar looked up when he saw him registering no surprise on his face. He seemed to be expecting it, or so Rogers thought. Sunny was getting snacks for them and the pups were asleep in that wonderful dog way, not a care in their inner worlds, or, at least, not one available to humans.

"Oscar, I need to talk to you alone if it's okay with your Dad."

Pepe looked up, startled for a moment, and with just a hint of territorial defensiveness. His kid, after all. Oscar, sensing this, looked at his father. "Is it okay?"

"Of course. Though, I hope it isn't secrets you were keeping from me. You know how your Mom and I feel about that."

Oscar looked as if he might cry and his face reddened. "I think it might be, Dad. I screwed up!"

Pepe looked at Rogers. "Okay, boss. But I really would like to know whatever this means as soon as you can tell me. I know it's police stuff, but, well, you understand."

"That, I do. And I apologize for the secrecy, I'm sort of off the grid here, don't worry, he didn't do anything wrong."

Pepe nodded, and Rogers put his hand on Oscar's shoulder and gently led him back across the huge open room to his office and closed the door.

Oscar looked so scared, he had to fight the urge to just hug him and let him go.

"Sit down Oscar, don't be scared. You know I'm your friend and remember, you're my deputy, so consider this a police inquiry.

I just think you may have some information you've not shared because you're trying to protect someone and I need to have full disclosure right now. It may help solve this case before anyone else is murdered."

Oscar nodded, wiping tears from his cheeks. "Yes, sir. I'm here to help."

Rogers leaned forward, looking as straight into Oscar's large, beautiful brown oriental eyes as he could. "Okay, here goes."

CHAPTER 18

Mikey Martinez was driving too fast. He had his police lights and siren on, though that was really overkill, but the urgency he felt was pumping adrenaline from his toes to his solar plexus as if the impending danger he felt was riding right behind him.

He had recorded his conversation with Olivia Perez, just so when he told Rogers, it would sound official and he wouldn't be forgetting or conning himself away from what was now emerging as an almost unbearable possibility.

He pushed his play button to listen again while he drove back to see Rogers.

"Mikey, I've got some really weird tox screen stuff and I have to tell you and it's kind of compromising, so you may need to bring your Captain in, or Rogers, anyway. I'm not sure of what it means, so I'm only going to give you the facts I have."

Mikey could feel the way his heart had started pounding and his fight or flight neurons had taken hold of his muscles, preparing in that primitive Hunter-Gatherer twitching limb way, so much a part of our perennial DNA when danger, real or emotional is about to explode; to burst the bubble of denial about how truly vulnerable we really are, how fragile the line is between chaos and calm, survival and destruction. All myths of control, which can vanish in one split instant of human truth; speeding wrong way driver, bad test result, knife wielding psychopath, lightening on a golf course, sink hole swallowing your bed during a peaceful slumber, anything, at any time. If we were to exist in this heightened state of free-floating fear that reality entails, it would make the living of our lives unbearable.

Mikey thought about a fall he had last year. He was jogging along the ocean boardwalk in South Beach, feeling fit and fine and almost strutting with his good fortune. A Lieutenant in the Miami-Dade Police Dept. Moving up and loving the whole Miami scene. All of it. Lincoln Road Mall and the combo of tourists and residents, all done up to see and be seen, watching one another from outdoor cafes, warm and smug in the middle of winter, full of the Miami vibe, the music, the preening of the human circus; or waltzing around the Biltmore Hotel ballroom in Coral Gables at some relative's show-off wedding, all old Florida glamour and new Florida money; a little bastion of privilege, not as funky as Coconut Grove, though that was changing now, too.

Everything was changing. Money and energy pouring in. Miami was hot, and he was Miami and he was hot and then, bam, his foot hit a loose board on a ramp and down he went. Hard. Flat onto all fours, stunned for a moment, afraid to even move until he knew nothing was broken. Pain seared through his shoulder and his knee and clutched at his hamstring, almost causing him to shout out. People were stopping; coming to his aid, fending off the bicyclists and runners, one of which he had been until a moment ago.

He felt utterly humiliated, diminished by their attention. He was trying very hard not to cry or whimper, but the thought in his head was a child's plea, "I want my momma," He had read something about falling down, that it shredded our illusion of invincibility and we're all three years old, wanting mommy to run to us, sweep us up, kiss our boo boos.

Someone brought him some water. Someone else suggested calling an ambulance. This became so terrifying that he had managed to pull himself up and reassure everyone that he was okay and could make it back to his "friend." There was no such person, but pride made asking for help unthinkable.

His knees were shredded with torn skin and blood dripping down them. And he knew enough from all his police gym time to be pretty sure his left hamstring and right rotator cup were totally fucked. He made it back to his car and home. And then he cried.

It had taken him weeks to feel safe on his own two feet and months for his torn body to heal, but what had lingered was that smack of insight, a ripping away of the illusion that we are ever more than one step away from the fantasy of safety or control over anything to do with being a human being snapped like a too ripe coconut off a too tall palm. Bam. Done.

He shuddered, what Olivia had told him, brought his fall back with an even more active fear, the kind that is always, in lock step with our need to turn the others into who we want or need them to be. Who to trust. How to know. Where to find the courage to see clearly, to accept ourselves and them as they are and face whatever loss and loneliness that entails.

He sucked at it. Rogers was great at it. He envied it, knew it would have made Rogers far better at his job, and moving up to Captain, too.

Now, he didn't even feel the old jealousy and competition with him or the need to one up him or push his buttons. Now he felt they were becoming friends. One thing he didn't doubt he needed to share this with him, fast.

"Mikey, you know that one damn hair I couldn't find any DNA on in the system? This was truly random, one of my techs brought in a little baggie with some gross stuff in it, no offense. They wanted to know if I wanted the results on it, since it was your skin cells, your ichthyosis; remember you were shedding all over my crime scene? Well, the skin cells and the hair sample showed a mega DNA match. Familial."

"So, what the fuck does that mean?"

"It means the hair is Leena's. No one swabbed her, she was lying in that vomit and hysterical, and you were there and she's your niece, so we didn't swab her, but it looks like her hair."

"So, big fucking surprise. She worked for them, she took care of their dogs! I'm sure her hairs are all over the fucking place."

"Yep. We had some, but no DNA so we just assumed they were hers. Lots of hairs from his women, and Coco and Katya, and Rebecca and Irina and Lupe. I could open a wig salon with all this hair shit."

"So? Why is this such a big fucking deal I had to speed over here?"

He could hear Olivia sighing and pausing before she answered his question.

"Well, it isn't whose it is, Mikey, it's where we found it."

By the time Mikey burst into Rogers office, clearly teetering on the verge of panic, Rogers had gently extracted from Oscar one of the missing pieces that was now leading him, intuition and inner beam, to what might become his Poirot moment, which is what flashed in his mind with just a touch of irony, more his style than taking himself or even what lay before him too seriously. He hugged Oscar and released him, reassuring him that he would talk to his parents and not to worry.

Mikey slammed his phone down on Rogers desk. "I recorded this with Olivia. I'm fucking freaking out here, you got any booze left in your drawer? I need to calm down, fast."

Rogers nodded and pulled the bottle of small batch bourbon

out of his desk and poured Mikey a large shot, knowing by the visible signs of his distress and the quantity of caffeine Mikey had probably already consumed today, this would barely do the trick.

Mikey inhaled the bourbon and took several deep, too fast breaths.

"Hey, easy, there. If you hyperventilate and faint, we're in trouble."

"Yeah. I know. Oh man, that helped. Okay, push play."

Rogers obliged and they listened together. Mikey collapsed into the chair recently occupied by Oscar and let the bourbon do what it was created to do, the tequila dinner high – now a distant memory.

Rogers whistled through his gap and shook his head, trying to absorb the way all of these wild puzzle pieces were suddenly forming before them.

"Mikey, I want to make a quick call to Olivia before you tell me the rest."

Mikey nodded, still processing and surrendering the lead to the calmer man, without feeling the old threat to his ego.

"Dr. O, Rogers here. Listen, Mikey just played me the tape, and I need you to do something else. By any chance did someone take a sample from the vomit in the hall. Leena's vomit?"

"Funny you should ask, my man. No one saved it, but one of my guys was smart enough to bag the towel they cleaned it up with and I ran it when I did the last two tests. I didn't even get to that with Mikey, he was too freaked out."

"Please tell."

"It wasn't Leena's. It was Coco Rothenstein's".

"Holy Hades. Thank you, Ma'am; this is mega. One more thing. The gloves. How would she have had gloves?"

"Oh, that did give me some moments, but then I remembered the gloves were cotton and Oscar had some, Leena gave them to him to wear if it was really hot and the dogs' leashes were slippery from their sweat. She always wore them when she walked them. So that fit."

"Wow. We spaced that clue."

"She was off all radar, so easy to miss it. Can't wait to hear it all. Is Oscar okay?"

"Yep. May have a few rough patches, but he's a trooper. We'll talk about it later, gotta jump on this."

Mikey was quiet, his eyes not leaving Rogers face. "What was that about?"

"Played a hunch after listening to the tape. The vomit wasn't Leena's, Mikey. It was Coco Rothenstein's."

"Oh, shit. Oh, fuck, man. This is bad, isn't it."

"It's bad. You didn't tell me why the hair is a big deal, though. I'm just running on my sniffer right now."

"The hair was on Frederick Rothenstein's crotch. FUCK!"

"Whoa, Nelly. Okay. Well, this all comes together with what I found out from Oscar. I just had a feeling he knew more than he was telling me, the way kids, when they're evading, just have this downward tilt, can't make eye contact, sort of shuffle around. So I brought him in to find out if Leena knew more about the codes and security systems than what he'd told me. Poor kid was terrified. I think your niece really played him, Mikey. Turns out, you know, he's lonely, wants her to be his friend, probably has a crush on her, trusts her, is flattered, the whole thing is a perfect set up. She asked lots of questions and he basically showed her how to bypass the codes, how to get in and out of the building without being seen, and even if she was, everyone knew her, knew she worked for the Rothensteins and everyone adored her."

"Because she's adorable. Beautiful and so kind and sweet and hardworking."

"Mikey. You ever hear the saying 'A false self has no enemies', ever notice how people who talk to everyone, never really talk to anyone? I fear your niece may be a brilliant psychopath, who, for whatever reason just snapped. I think we need to find her, pretty quickly. So sorry man. I know how protective you are of her and she's had a pretty rough ride, but no way to not question her. Maybe it's all explainable, no smoking gun, but we need to follow this. Interior motive, Edy said, and Leena might well have one. Actually, she probably has the best one. Rage at all the rich people around her and having to kowtow to them and struggle every day. Pretty good motive."

Mikey sighed and finished off the bourbon. "Yeah. But not one fucking bit of it ever showed, so I'm still giving her the benefit of the doubt. Let's find her and give the kid a chance. I'll call her phone. She may even be here."

Rogers nodded and moved across to Mikey and patted his back. Two childless loners with longings for connection neither of them had ever really explored, but the time had come and they both, for different reasons, knew it.

"No answer. Shit. I'll try her house and maybe Oscar knows, or Sunny. They hang out. Let's go ask them."

"Mikey, don't let on to Oscar what I told you. Not now. He's still too upset. He thinks everything is his fault."

"Yeah. Got it. I can share that with him. Too bad he's too young for bourbon."

"I'm gonna call Edy back. Maybe she knows. Let's do it."

CHAPTER 19

Ooma Lovee took a long deep breath, the call with her lawyer tying up one more loose end of anxiety and slowly walked back inside, leaving the doors open, even if it was summer and nearing dusk and mosquito time.

There was a breeze coming in from the sea, and too intoxicating to shut out.

She needed to find Maria to tell her Sunny and Edy might be coming for dinner, though she hadn't talked to Edy yet. She wasn't in the kitchen, and Lola must still be with Leena, so she made her way, feeling just slightly light-headed. Probably the damn blood pressure medicine causing it and opened her bedroom door.

Her housekeeper was on the floor. Had she had an attack? Gott im Himmel! German emerging in her panic. She crossed the room as fast as she could and kneeled down beside her.

"Maria, Maria!" It was only then, she saw the blood and where it was oozing from her neck. She turned her over, not pausing to think of whether this was wise and quickly realized it no longer mattered. Her throat was cut! The room was spinning now and she crawled on her knees, knowing there was nothing she could do for her, having seen enough death in her life. She was clutching her phone, the instrument she had fought against for so long, loathing what it represented; how it changed people young and old, dehumanizing and hollowing them out, but when she surrendered to its inevitability, the seduction of its power to connect quickly, it had become more and more important the older she got. Now, this was her first time to use it in an emergency. Her hands were shaking, and she could barely push the buttons; feeling a presence, the aura of menace surrounded her. She looked up, afraid even to speak. And the menace moved.

Leena Martinez was standing in the doorway, holding Lola in one arm and Ooma's precious pearl handled pistol in the other.

Ooma had long believed that nothing could still shock or surprise her that had to do with human beings; too many disappointments, heartbreaks, self-deceptions, but she was stunned.

For some reason, in the midst of this unreal situation, she flashed on the moment she discovered the true nature of her second husband. An Austrian of some sort of noble lineage, or so he claimed. Very rich and very Austrian, who liked to dress her up and show her off, but was brutal in bed and cold in heart.

She hid her allowance and her jewels the minute she wasn't wearing them, always knowing at some point, either he would replace her or she would leave. One night after some Opera Gala or one of the endless events their lives were consumed with, any opportunity to strut and hob nob with Vienna society, a need so deep in him, she would never dare say no.

She had gone into his closet, to look for a jacket he wanted to wear and couldn't find. He was furious, because perfection in all attire and in every word, action, gesture and, of course, his trophy bride, was essential to his sense of self, fragile as she knew it was and she had tripped and braced herself against the wall behind his clothes. On the floor, covered by his suits was an oversized, framed photo of Adolph Hitler, personally signed for her husband by the Fuhrer.

And she ran. She ran into her room, grabbed all the money and jewels she had hidden, packed her most expensive furs and small objects, Fabergé eggs, solid silver frames and she left. She never saw or heard from him again. He must have discovered his no longer hidden treasure, and he knew. She didn't stop running until she was on the train to Salzberg. He'd never said an anti-Semitic word, not then, the war still too fresh for a resurgence, even in front of his Aryan wife, his ideal.

This memory steeled her and she got to her feet and looked right into Leena's big almost black eyes, not seeing an innocent beauty now, seeing the monster inside the lie that beauty and its illusion of goodness evokes in us, rendering us blind to what is behind the facades; a new world of photoshopped selfies, permeating our ability to really see anyone for who they are.

But her? Now? She could still be fooled; worse than sleeping with the enemy, the threat now to everything she cared about. Her poor devoted Maria in a pool of blood, probably died trying to keep Leena from taking her gun.

Leena was agitated, as if her control of the situation had been thrown off track and Ooma saw this and moved toward her, no cowering, or pleading she kept moving slowly toward Leena, who backed up into the grand room, keeping the gun pointed at Ooma.

"Alright, young lady. Please put Lola down and tell me what it is you want."

Ooma's quiet, composed power was clearly more than Leena Martinez had expected, and it rattled her resolve. She had not planned on Maria, and Ooma Lovee was so much harder to read than the others. "Don't move any closer to me or I will throw Lola over the balcony."

Ooma's stomach felt as if it could really do what pot boilers said it could do, flip over, but outwardly she grew quieter and stronger. "Miss Martinez, I am an old woman who has lost everything and everyone she loved and I have survived the Gestapo and five husbands, so as much as I love my Lola, I will survive her loss. You can't threaten me so cheaply. But it might be a start if you tell me what this is all about. Confession really is good for the soul and since, I am very sure you plan to kill me, why not, at least let me be your confessor."

"Oh, no, no, not so easy, lady. You have work to do."

"Really? And what kind of work would that be?"

"I heard you. I heard you on the phone with your lawyer, asking him to set up a trust fund for Oscar. Well I want one, too! I want you to sit down and write up a, a..."

"Codicil?"

"Yes! A codicil adding me to your will and sign it and I'll witness it because no one will ever know it was me that did this. Why should Oscar get that!!!I slave for all of you and I have nothing! Nothing! I want $2 million dollars and I want you to say how devoted I have been to all of you and how intelligent and hard-working I am and recommend me for a, an important job at the country club."

"I see. Well, Miss Martinez, this is really truly a tragedy, because, I was just getting to know you. I know Oscar so much better, but I had been thinking about setting something up for you and your family, because you've been so wonderful to Lola and also, I see how smart you are and capable and I happen to be on the Board of the Holocaust Memorial Museum and I was going to call and recommend you for a position there. All you had to do was pretend a bit longer. How truly sad."

"You're lying! And I don't want to work for anymore damn fucking Jews! I liked you because you were rich and elegant, but you weren't one of them, but now I see that necklace, and you are one of them. Why do you think I wrote Kill the Kikes on their feet! I've been surrounded by them and everything that's happened is because of them!"

Ooma fought to keep from fainting, realizing for the first time, that what Leena was doing here was not the impulsive act of a desperate emotionally exhausted, enraged young woman. She wasn't her planned target. This was a monster. She had murdered all of them!

She tried to catch her breath, staying very quiet and not moving too fast was important, all those years on the run, in and out of countries hunting for Jews, without blinking or revealing fear or the dart of an eye, anything they could find, it all came back to her; survival skills, a small but clearly real, personal pogrom.

"But why? Please tell me how this all began to fester so deeply in you. There is always a tipping point, Leena, I know a bit about that. Tell me. If you want me to do what you've asked, I need to know why."

"Fair enough. I want to tell someone. I never thought it would be you. But I will."

"Can you just put Lola down. You have the gun. She's not very big and she won't go far. She protects me. You know that."

Leena leaned down and placed Lola on the floor, with care, gently. The fine line between good and evil never clearer to Ooma.

"My brother is a mental and physical mess and my mother is disabled and has multiple ailments and she's in a wheelchair, so I'm all there is. My father left and never came back or helped, so I had to go to work. No college for Leena, no future. I slaved at that country club. I was the hardest working, smartest person covering the outdoor pool and I covered for everyone, I worked killer hours and events and ran back and forth between there and here, doing all the dog stuff, taking care of my mother and brother. I have no life!!!

"I went to Coco Rothenstein and begged her, begged her, to promote me at the country club, put me in the management training program, which I already could have taught! And offer me some benefits, health insurance, something and she just evaded. She told me to ask her husband, he handled all of that, but I knew it was a lie.

"So, alright, I could play that, and I went to see him. All this #MeToo stuff, I lived it! He was very understanding, and he said he could help me, really help me advance, and that he was in the process of changing his staff, meaning Irina and Lupe for sure. And then, then, he told me to go into his special closet and pick out some shoes and dresses and jewelry.

"I couldn't believe that closet! I just sort of froze. I wanted it all, but I wasn't stupid. Everyone here thinks I'm this sweet, innocent creature and I've been giving blow jobs and hand jobs to so many of the maintenance guys and security guys to get information and access, it's a joke. All disgusting, but that's how I found out about Walter Jenkins. I know you don't know any of this, but I've been stealing jewelry from Coco for a long time and cash. She never even noticed! She'd be in her meditation bull shit room and I'd take stuff at the bottom of her bowl and there was always so much cash, it was so easy, it was a joke.

"So, I started letting Frederick touch my stuff and then, then it got dirty and I did what he wanted, revolting old hebe! But when I asked him to do what he promised, he said 'not yet, but feel free to borrow some things from the closet.'

"My mother needed new medicine and her disability wouldn't cover it and I just snapped. I ran into the closet and got the scarves and the shoes, and I savaged him. I loved it. I always knew I had that violence buried, I knew I didn't feel what people thought I felt, I knew I was a lie, but I didn't know how big a lie until I felt those shoes that cost more than I make in a month smash into his saggy old eyes and ears. I was crazed. I filled the tub and drowned those horrible dogs, but when I came out, Coco was there, she'd heard the screaming or whatever and when she saw me, she freaked and she ran and she fell in the hall and threw up, so perfect as it turned out and I chased her and I killed her and I loved it. Loved it!

"And then I got the idea of writing a hate message, so I took one of her cheapo eyebrow pencils, no one would ever think Coco Rothenstein used CVS make up, but she did, and I wrote on their feet and then I drowned her dogs, too.

"I was totally manic and then I heard the codes being entered and Katya coming so I ran into the hallway and lay down, making it look like I'd just gotten there and was horrified and threw up. Almost too easy! My uncle came, no one even thought it could be me, that I'd been there for hours, had all the codes and knew about the bypass button. Sweet little Leena. Poor little Leena, she works so hard. What a shame."

"You are right. No one ever considered you, but why Rebecca? She would be your boss and you were helping her?"

"Rebecca. I hated her. Hated her! Spoiled creepy bitch. Looked right through me like I wasn't even a person. Sergi was the problem, he was Russian, he was wary, he hated that she left money all around, so I had to be more careful. I followed him a few times and I knew about Irina and I knew if I needed to use it, I could, but I thought, now that her parents were gone, she'd lean on me and she'd help me get what I deserved.

"So, I went to see her and asked her what I'd asked them. And, and that skinny cunt, she told me, 'It saddened her' but she'd decided she had to let me go, that all the media attention had made my face too well known and it was a 'negative vibe' at the club, but even though we all had to sign an agreement that we wouldn't work at a competing hotel or club for two years if we left them, she would waive that!" Can you believe we were all that pathetic!

"No severance, no thank you for all the help I gave her with those pathetic animals or the devotion to her parents and the trauma of finding them. And I flipped out again, and it was wonderful! I loved every horrible minute of it! She was so sickly, so weak, I couldn't even make her suffer enough. She only really resisted when I went for her wig and make up! Sick! Maybe I'm sick, but so were they. All of them! I knew Sergi was fucking Irina. I knew when he came back, he wouldn't go into Rebecca's bedroom, imagine actually having sex with her! And he didn't.

"Poor thug, meathead. I wrote on her feet and I thought I was done. Now I could bat my eyes at him, and I knew how to talk to Carmen Daniels, and I'd get what I wanted, and I had the jewelry from Coco. I didn't know that Rebecca had pictures of everything!

"I had my brother call and pretend to be a seller, no way to trace anything to me! I totally knew how to play Jenkins. That's what blow jobs taught me.

"But, then, then I was walking Lola and Sunny and Oscar were on the beach path and they thought I was who everyone thought I was, and Oscar actually believed I was his friend! What a laugh! Nerdy little misfit. So easy to manipulate. So, they opened up to me and Sunny told us about the adoption. I never could quite understand how you were their grandmother. And I wanted it. I. wanted you to adopt me, too. Or if they died, I would replace them.

"So, I started helping you with Lola and then, then I heard you on the phone and I got mad. You could have told him to add me! Just another lousy, stingy Kike!"

Leena stopped, sweat dripping down her contorted face, morphing her lovely facade into a Halloween mask of hate and fury. She was panting with the force of her purge and Ooma was trying very hard to absorb what she had just heard and not react, Leena still had the gun in a steady hand.

Ooma was using every ounce of her still formidable powers of observation and experience with monsters to decide what to say, knowing every word now, was life or death, her death did not frighten her anymore, but, if she was murdered by an anti-Semitic psychopath she betrayed everything her mother had made her promise. Telling Edy and Sunny was already a breach, but this would be unbearable for her.

And she knew, now, no matter where she lived, her mother had been right. It appeared Leena had, in her impulsive choice from the surprise of Maria's presence, now forgotten that Maria's murder would alter the clean line of her plan and Ooma realized this was her bargaining tool.

"Leena, I will do what you ask. But I will add to it that it is only binding as long as my Edy and Sunny are still alive when I die. I believe that is the only way I can protect them from my fate. Is that acceptable to you?"

"Don't be stupid. If you're gone and no one knows it wasn't a suicide, I get what I want and I don't need to hurt them. In fact they will probably draw me closer and make me part of the family. Now sit down and write and then call your damn lawyer."

Ooma nodded and slowly moved to the dining room table where she always kept one of her silver fountain pens and personal stationary. She liked to work there, looking out at the sea. Leena followed and Lola scampered away and cowered by Ooma's feet. She wrote and then pulled a separate sheet of blank paper out and notated it with the date and time and signed her name and printed it below and then did the same for Leena. "It's done. You can sign."

Leena moved over, the gun never leaving Ooma's fatal triangle. Clearly Leena knew about guns.

"Do you think I'm stupid. I want to read it first."

"Yes. I was afraid of that."

Leena grabbed the paper and read. "Leena Martinez killed the Rothensteins and she is going to kill me if I don't sign a paper leaving her two million dollars."

Leena threw the paper at her, screaming now in frustration. "You want to die! You want your family to die!!! I will kill them both. I won't have anything to lose, you old greedy witch! Write what I said. Now!"

Ooma shuddered, knowing the threat was true. She would do it. She re-wrote the letter and handed it back to Leena, who laughed, almost hysterically and then they both signed Ooma's death sentence.

"Now call your damn lawyer. I want this to be fool proof."

Ooma nodded, trying to calculate if it was possible for her to tackle Leena and wrestle the gun from her. Leena was young and very strong, but she was much bigger and fiercer and had nothing to lose. She went to dial her lawyer and saw that she had never pushed end for the call. Gott! Maybe he had heard this!

"Hello, Raphael, it's Ooma Lovee again, I want to make another addition to my will, I've just written it up and it's been witnessed, but I wanted to have a record of it with you."

"Ooma, is this on speaker?"

"No."

"You never pushed end. I've heard everything and recorded it here, too and called the police. Stall, help is coming."

Ooma almost laughed. So, her lack of techno skills had actually worked in her favor. They continued the sham conversation and when she hung up, Leena was smiling.

"So, now, one more job for you. Write a suicide note, make it emotional and schmaltzy for Edy and Sunny if you like. You won't suffer. I'm very good with guns. Mikey taught me."

Ooma complied, drawing it out as long as possible, waiting for help; her heart was beating so fast she could hardly breathe, now she needed to throw her off. "Leena my dear, maybe you have a plan, but there is the loose end of Maria's body lying there in a pool of blood. No one, no one, will believe I did that and how do you plan on moving her, cleaning it up and getting her out? Edy and Sunny are coming for dinner soon, wouldn't it make more sense to let me help you dispose of her, first. I can cancel dinner, say I'm too tired. There really isn't a rush now that you have what you want."

Ooma could see the skin on Leena's almost lovely again face, turn white. She had forgotten. "Shit! That's what always happens to me! Nothing is just easy. Okay. You bought some time. Move. Where are the cleaning supplies? We can put her in a suit case. She isn't very big. I'll take her out. You fool. You did me a favor. I totally spaced it! Let's go!"

"Yes, Leena. Let's."

Ooma made her every move slow and deliberate which clearly was making Leena agitated again. "I think the supplies are all in the closet in the hall by my bedroom. Maria handles everything, so they could be somewhere else."

"You'd better pray to your Jew God they are close by. You get a suitcase. One of your big ones and I'll check."

Edy Weller here, whoever is reading this. I've tried to stay out of the story even though it was so tempting to tell it all, but until this part, I really didn't know it all. So, I'm going to resume now as your narrator, since this is where we all came back in.

I was getting more and more nervous and I decided to go up to Ooma's and see if she was okay. We usually had dinner there once a week and I'd forgotten to tell her I might be seeing Rogers. She wasn't responding to my texts and she was usually meticulous about that. Call it the old inner gut guide, but I had gotten Ooma's second gun, another almost heirloom, but loaded and operable or so we both thought and mainly because of my general state of hyper vigilance, rather impulsively, I grabbed it from my bedroom drawer and stuck it in the back of my sweatpants and up I went.

I had Ooma's codes and I opened the door. No one was visible and I called out to her. I don't know why I did this. Usually I would tip toe in and peek into her room or talk to Maria to see if she was napping or bathing or dressing. She was very private about these things, I think that's the terrain of beautiful women, of any age, their abultions and "work rooms" as she called her make-up and face care dressing tables, lit perfectly and immaculate and filled with so many exotic concoctions. It was Sunny's favorite play station. But today, I called out for her, picking up the strongest, sense of danger, even the smell of the room reeked of something ugly. Lola ran to me, staring up with her big bug eyes and running in circles, something she hadn't done since the day of the first murders.

Sounds. Strange sounds, not making any sense at all. I called their names.

"Ooma? Maria?" this turned out not to be the best idea. Silence followed. My heart was doing the Salsa and I could hardly breathe. I turned the handle to Ooma's bedroom door and, well, not really any words, even for me, to describe what I saw.

There was Ooma on the floor, bloody and sobbing, holding Maria's clearly no longer living hand, looking frightened in a way I did not believe possible for her. When she saw me, she panicked, crawling on her hands and knees, until she could pull herself up.

"Hide, Edy, hide! She's going to kill both of us if she finds you here. Go! In the bathroom and don't make a sound. Help is coming. We have to stall!"

"Stall? Who did this? Where are they?"

"Leena! Leena did it all and she will kill you and Sunny if you know. Hide!"

This was, as you might have guessed, not exactly a situation anyone can prepare for, but I did know I wasn't going to hide and leave Ooma there. Leena!

Before I could even begin to figure out what to do next, the door swung open and Leena Martinez tossed in all the cleaning supplies Ooma probably had in the condo.

"Oh shit! This isn't supposed to happen! Where's the suitcase! I need the suitcase, now! I need two! You had to put your nose in it. You would have been okay. You stupid bitch!"

I have a thing about rudeness. I really, really hate it. Murder is one thing, but rudeness. Un uh. I had instinctively stepped in front of Ooma and I pulled the gun, not even knowing if it had a safety or how exactly to fire it, but I watched enough movies to make a pretty good show of pointing it and somehow holding myself steady, mainly, I think, because she really pissed me off. Name calling and nasty? I don't think so. "Drop the gun Leena, no way you're going to get away with this. Just run. Go. Maybe you'll get lucky."

Leena was clearly losing her upper hand. "No. I made her sign it. I'm not leaving and if you both have to die, I'll still get away. No one will suspect me. There's still a crazed psycho loose! You drop that gun. I know I'm a better shot. You're Jewish, Jews can't shoot."

"Oh really? Tell the Mossad. Just try me. I spent two years in ROTC, and I won a sharp shooter's medal!" (I wasn't really even sure if that was what you did in ROTC, but I had to think of something fast and I didn't think she'd believe I was Annie Oakley).

Ooma was composed now, clearly her emotion had been expressed in the tiny window she had been alone with Maria, but it was clear, she had far more experience dealing with lunatics than I did.

"Leena, listen to Edy. The police are on their way right now. My lawyer heard your entire confession. This is over. I know about running. You should run, fast and far. Go!"

Leena could not surrender the fantasy, the pot of gold, the way out of her self-sealed trap.

"You're lying! I will kill Edy if you don't come with me. You're going out on the terrace and you're going to jump and Edy is going to fall, trying to save you. Go. Go or I'll shoot Lola!"

Ooma moved in front of me and I grabbed her arm, trying to pull her back. "I told you. You can't threaten me with that."

"I don't believe you."

She pointed the gun at Lola, who, being tiny, but not stupid, ran right at her and bit her ankle hard. Leena lost her balance and fell backward and Ooma and I grabbed Lola and ran into the living room.

"Ooma! We have to get out of here."

"The police should be here any moment."

Before we could get across the room to the front door, Leena came flying out like a banshee in a big release horror movie, shooting wildly. Really shooting. A real gun. I had dropped my gun when we ran out of the bedroom, which shows how truly unprepared I was for this situation; so I dove down and picked it up and fired at her, without my glasses; without one single previous gun use experience and I hit her in her gun arm shoulder and she screamed at the same moment the front door swung open and Rogers, Pepe, Mikey and half the Miami PD came swarming in. Mikey yelled at Leena.

"Leenita, mia preciousa. Por favor. Peinsa de su Madre! I will get you help. It will be okay. Por Dios. I love you. Let us help you."

This was clearly not the ending Leena had in mind. She was still holding the gun, and those huge beautiful eyes were flashing, almost rolling around in her head, trying to change the scene, unable to face this unacceptable reality.

"Fuck you, Uncle. You and all our fucking relatives! You never helped! You could have supported us!"

"Leena, are you crazy! I did. I sent your mother all the money I could and I paid the rent! You never told me you were desperate, you never showed any of this! "

"Well, that was hardly the way you all saw me and it wasn't enough! So, no! I'm not going with you and I'm not going to fucking jail!"

And she moved very quickly, never letting go of the gun, while all the cops and Rogers had guns on her, no one wanting to shoot her, especially in front of Mikey, but before they could take action, she ran out onto the terrace, all of us after her and she jumped. A fallen devil disguised as an angel, leaving a room full of shattered frozen witnesses.

HAPPY ENDINGS, SORT OF.

So, now that I am able to finish the story, I will bring you forward eighteen months, which certainly seems a helluva lot longer. Everything changed out there on Ooma Lovee's terrace.

Ooma lived to see Sunny and Oscar graduate, but the stress of that day and the old wounds it opened for her, just took the fight out of her. I didn't even realize until after she died, peacefully in my arms, how much fear and fight she used every day of her life.

She never went back into her room or out on her terrace after that day, she moved into one of her guest rooms and sealed the other door, but the energy it would have taken for her to actually move, became more than even she could handle. Also, she lived long enough to see me actually have a life!

Rogers and I live together in a funky house off the Hollywood Boardwalk, just one mile outside of Miami, the first house I've ever lived in! Sunny and Oscar are away at college, Oscar at MIT no less and Sunny at Tulane and both are doing well.

The trauma of knowing Oscar could have been killed and alas, their worries about what the events had done to his never robust sense of inner security, brought Pepe and Olivia back together, which probably accounts for Oscar's current happy state. Sunny is overjoyed to see me with a real man (though if it was a real woman that would have been fine with her, too!). Neither of us even know how to really evaluate, what a good love relationship is, but I think we're doing okay here in our new world, a couple with Hildy, Lola and Lorraine, ecstatic to have an actual yard and one another.

When Arnold Rothenstein realized what was at stake, he did snap out of his nervous breakdown pretty fast (though, I'm sure a fair amount of pharmaceuticals are in play) and he and his sons resumed the reigns, which took the onus off of Carmen Daniels.

So, another unlikely couple was created. Carmen and Mikey Martinez moved to St. Augustine, where he started a private security business and she is back as activist/therapist.

Mikey does send monthly support to Leena's mother and brother, who seems to be sober and stabilized. The guilt and shock he suffered after Leena's suicide took a while to heal, but Carmen was most certainly not having it, so he let it go.

And Rogers, really, always a cop at heart, took over from Mikey, but was elevated to Captain pretty shortly after. The positive press following the Day of The Terrace as we started to call it, was a big plus for him and he is smiling a lot now (I do love that gap! Gives me heart flutters).

As for me, well, I've been writing this and mourning our Ooma. She gave her apartment to the Miami Holocaust Museum and I sold mine back to the Rothensteins, in the nick of time before all the in-fighting and hysteria of the remaining residents. They did change the name of the building, which was a big help!

Oh, one more little loose end. The black Taffeta Dress Ooma told me about with the valuables sewn into the hem; it now resides in a special bag on a special hanger in my closet, rather an homage to her and I do sometimes talk to it and open the bag and sniff it in, her smell lingers and it helps me hold onto to her. I plan to save it for Sunny or (this is me inhaling Ooma's fear, of course) if there should be another pogrom, the world being what it now is, I would grab it, the dogs, Rogers, Sunny and run wherever was left to run to! In the meantime, we have never taken off the beautiful little Star of David necklaces she gave us, a daily reminder of what a miracle she was and stroking it is always a source of blessing counting.

So, now for a little woo woo, certainly not my usual style, but, then again, life does send these meteor showers to shake change loose in those of us capable of it.

In all the horror of this, the gifts did abound for the survivors. If it hadn't been for the murders, Rogers and I would never have met, Carmen and Mikey would never have met and Pepe and Olivia would never have re-married. Oscar would not have his education ensured and Goldy Rothenstein would never have escaped a life she hated (she's been in touch, by the way and she and her children are doing fine. I have a picture. She is totally transformed and blond!).

So, those are pretty huge gifts, however horrible the wrapping paper. I think this is really kind of a Shakespearian ending, maybe, All's Well that Ends Well.

I clipped a quote during the aftermath, that seems to fit. "It's not what you go through in life, it's how you emerge." Feels true to me and I think we've emerged pretty damn well.

ABOUT THE AUTHOR

G LORIA NAGY is the internationally best-selling author of twelve books including *The Beauty, Remain Calm, Looking For Leo, SeaSick, Virgin Kisses,* and the *New York Times* best-seller, *A House in the Hamptons.* She Lives with her husband Richard Saul Wurman in the Miami, FL area. They have four children, six grandchildren and Jacob, their yellow lab.

CPSIA information can be obtained
at www.ICGtesting.com
Printed in the USA
LVHW010856130920
665859LV00001B/11